the HEIRESS and the ORC

FINLEY FENN

Visit www.finleyfenn.com for free bonus stories and epilogues, delicious orc artwork, complete content tags and warnings, news about upcoming books, and more!

ALSO BY FINLEY FENN

To Amy,
a bright gift from the gods

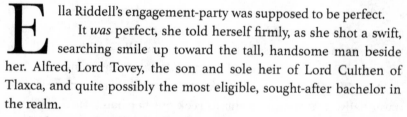

1

Ella Riddell's engagement-party was supposed to be perfect.

It *was* perfect, she told herself firmly, as she shot a swift, searching smile up toward the tall, handsome man beside her. Alfred, Lord Tovey, the son and sole heir of Lord Culthen of Tlaxca, and quite possibly the most eligible, sought-after bachelor in the realm.

And soon to be Ella's *husband*.

"All right, darling?" Alfred asked her, with a meaningful wink. "You're looking a bit peaked."

Ella fought back her wince, and pasted a broad smile to her face. "I'm fine, of course," she said brightly. "How could one not be, on a delightful night such as this?"

Alfred replied with a brief, approving pat to Ella's shoulder, and then turned his attention to their next well-wisher. An unfamiliar, but very beautiful, very stylish young woman, whose laugh seemed to ring through the room, and whose gloved hand had come to rest on Alfred's arm with a light, comfortable ease.

Ella purposely pulled her gaze away, blinking toward the lights and music and chatter of the party all around. It was quite possibly the most extravagant soirée Ashford Manor had ever seen, full of well-heeled, well-dressed guests from across the realm—and objectively, it was a crushing success. It was the moment, finally, when Ella had made it. When she *belonged*.

And she *did* belong, she told herself, as she held the smile to her face. She wasn't just a sheep farmer's daughter anymore. Her skin was perfect and porcelain, even paler than this beautiful woman's. Her auburn hair was shiny and expertly plaited, without a single tendril out of place, unlike this woman's. And she was lovelier than this woman, her bust filled out her own stylish dress far better than this woman's, and the diamonds hanging from her own ears were larger, and far more expensive, than this damned woman's.

But this woman was still chattering to Alfred, still touching Alfred, now leaning up to impishly whisper something in Alfred's ear. Something that made Alfred laugh quite heartily, and then—Ella's throat tightened—he leaned down and whispered something back, his cheek brushing close against hers.

Ella forced her eyes away again, but the party had seemed to blur slightly around her, and she drew in one deep breath, and then another. It was fine. She was fine. Alfred was sure to have many friends, too many to possibly introduce them all—and it was Ella on his arm, Ella who was wearing his ring. *Ella* he was marrying.

And, Ella told herself, it was *her* he wanted. He'd been the one to travel halfway across the realm to seek out her hand. He'd been the only man who hadn't once mentioned her massive inheritance, or the peculiar circumstances surrounding her late father's will. He'd made her laugh, he'd talked cleverly about books and horses and the theatre, he'd whispered reverently of her beauty, his affection, his regard.

And most importantly, late one night when they'd finally escaped Ella's mother's hawkish eye, he'd drawn Ella into the sitting room, and laid her gently down upon the couch. And then he'd knelt before her, lifted her skirts, and used his hands and his mouth to bring stars to her eyes.

And it had been—*fine*. Lovely, even. And in that moment, something in Ella's mind had finally shuddered and slammed shut, locking away certain ancient, unspeakable longings deep inside. She had to face this. Move on. Accept the reality that Alfred was a perfectly handsome, appropriate, and desirable man. And since his father was technically an earl, he was a man of standing, just as her father's will had required. And with this marriage, Ella would keep her home, and fulfill all her father's wishes, and become what her family had always hoped and worked and yearned for.

She would be a real lady, wed to a lord. She would *matter*.

"My deepest felicitations, Little Miss, Lord Tovey," said a deep, familiar voice, and Ella gratefully turned toward the interruption. It was their elderly neighbour Mr. Kemp, one of her father's oldest friends—and he was fixing Alfred with a keen-eyed look which, thankfully, finally sent the lovely woman scuttling away. "When's the wedding-date?"

"In four weeks," Alfred replied promptly, with a quick, rather red-faced smile down toward Ella. "A short turnaround, to be sure, but I simply couldn't stand to wait *months* before my darling could finally join me in Tlaxca."

Left unsaid, of course, was the fact that Ella's father's will had only given a six-month deadline for her marriage—but thankfully, Mr. Kemp didn't comment, and instead turned his beady gaze toward Ella. "So you *are* moving away for good, then, Little Miss?" he asked, his already-furrowed white brows drawing closer together. "I had hoped you might keep a presence here at Ashford Manor. What with these lands being your family's for so long, and you having spent your whole girlhood roaming about them like a wild little beast."

Ella ignored the twisting pang in her gut, and opened her mouth to answer—but Alfred was already speaking, giving her another indulgent smile. "My lady's well beyond such foolishness now, aren't you, love?" he said smoothly. "We'd far rather sell these lands for a tidy profit, and make our home back east in Tlaxca."

Ella flinched at that awful word *sell*, and she fixed her own smile to her face, held her gaze to Mr. Kemp's visibly confused eyes. "I'm afraid you may have forgotten, Alfred, darling," she said, her voice wavering, "that it is a specific term of my late father's will that these lands are not to be sold. They've been in my family for generations, and they're to be kept for me, and my father's grandchildren."

Alfred shot Ella a narrow, sidelong glance, to which she kept desperately smiling, fighting not to betray the sudden, surging rebellion in her thoughts. She would move out east, but she would *not* sell her home. She would not throw away her father's beloved, beautiful house, its sprawling grounds and ancient forest, its breathtaking views of the mountains to the south. Of Orc Mountain, soaring craggy and majestic above them all, puffing out smoke like a rumbling, sleeping dragon.

"Ah, yes, darling, of course," Alfred said, an instant too late, patting Ella's arm with his hand. "We'll rent these lands out to tenants, is what I meant. But we'll most certainly be moving to Tlaxca, as it's much more civilized there, and far safer, too. Well away from this ghastly Orc Mountain."

He gave a practiced little shudder, which was a bit much, considering that it was Alfred's own lord father who, only five months before, had played a critical role in signing an unprecedented *peace-treaty* with said orcs. Halting what had become a near-constant series of raids and thefts and conflicts, in favour of giving the orcs full ownership of their massive mountain, and allowing them to freely wander the lands as they wished.

"Yes, those blasted orcs are a problem, all right," Mr. Kemp agreed. "I can't say I blame your lord father for wanting to put an end to all the raids and fighting, but seeing the big brutes running willy-nilly across the countryside has been quite a nasty jolt to us all."

Thus began a heated discussion about the hideous orcs, and their devious natures, and their barbaric practices, and their horrible habits of stealing away helpless women, in order to sire their massive sons upon them. And while Ella could have participated—of course she properly loathed and feared the orcs, as any proper woman should— she instead found her eyes casting uneasily around the beautiful, bustling room. This was home, and it always would be, no matter where she lived. It would be fine. She would be a *lady*.

"If you'll excuse me, darling," Alfred said to her, once Mr. Kemp had finally tottered away. "I'll be just a moment."

He didn't wait for Ella's reply, and instead just turned and strode off toward the door. Leaving Ella standing there alone, blinking at his back, until several more well-wishers appeared, offering congratulations and good luck. Asking who had made Ella's beautiful dress, and when was she leaving, and her mother had been such a gracious hostess, and wouldn't her dear father be so proud that his beloved only child had made such a spectacular match, so soon after his death?

But Ella's heart had begun skipping oddly, her hands clasping hot and clammy together. And once the well-wishers had finally moved off, she sidled quickly, unobtrusively, toward the room's small side door. Out into the servants' back hallway, where she leaned her trembling body against the wood-panelled wall, and closed her eyes, and breathed.

You'll be fine, my girl, her father had kept insisting, even as he'd had to wheeze for air, and wipe his mouth with his red-stained handkerchief. *I'll not have you lose your home over these fool inheritance laws. I'll see that you're looked after. And I'll even see you made a lady, while I'm at it. Just like you deserve.*

Ella had held his shaky hand, and nodded and smiled, and joined him in enthusiastically disparaging his rightful heir, an awful distant cousin up north she'd never met. And all the while she hadn't truly believed any of it, her wonderful, clever father would surely survive this, and go on to live a long, happy life...

And then, one day, he'd just been—gone. And in his place had been that impossible will, sworn into law by the Sakkin magistrate himself. Six months. Looked after. A *lady*.

Ella pressed her palms against her wet eyes, and dragged in one breath, and another. She was keeping her promise, her end of the bargain. Keeping her *home*. It was fine. It was perfect.

Or was it? Because there, again, was the sound of that distinctive girlish laugh, ringing through the air. Coming from the nearby side drawing-room, which—Ella took a few careful, silent steps down the hallway—currently had its sliding door pulled closed.

That door was almost never left shut, Ella knew very well, and she crept toward it, her heartbeat rising, juddering through her ears. Surely it was nothing. Surely one of the servants had simply been distracted, or some tired guest had wanted a moment's rest—

But there was the laugh again, louder this time, like nails scraping against Ella's skin, and she edged closer to the door. It didn't close all the way, never had, and Ella held her breath as she leaned forward, put her blinking eye to the crack, and looked.

And it was—Alfred. It was *her* Alfred. Ella's betrothed, her saviour, her future *husband*—and with him, caught in his arms, was the woman. *That* woman.

They were both laughing, Alfred's handsome head thrown back, his eyes warm and affectionate. And as Ella stared, struck still and silent, Alfred's hands thrust easily, willingly up under the woman's frothy skirts—and then he did something beneath. Something that transformed the woman's laugh into a low, heated moan, her long stockinged leg lifting up to hook around Alfred's waist, their hips snapping close together.

Oh. *Oh.* Ella staggered backwards, her hands fluttering against her mouth, and suddenly there was no air, no floor beneath her feet. Only the rising weltering urge, flaring bright and all-consuming behind her eyes, to go go go, run, *run, RUN*—

So without thought, without breath, without hope, Ella spun on her slippered heel, and ran.

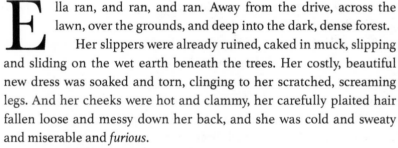

2

Ella ran, and ran, and ran. Away from the drive, across the lawn, over the grounds, and deep into the dark, dense forest.

Her slippers were already ruined, caked in muck, slipping and sliding on the wet earth beneath the trees. Her costly, beautiful new dress was soaked and torn, clinging to her scratched, screaming legs. And her cheeks were hot and clammy, her carefully plaited hair fallen loose and messy down her back, and she was cold and sweaty and miserable and *furious*.

But she didn't stop running. Not until she'd reached the small, stone hunting-cottage, hidden just within the edge of the forest. A place that had gone wholly unused since her father's death, and Ella dodged inside it, and slammed the door shut behind her.

Fuck.

She leaned her sticky, shaky body back against the door, her palms pressed painfully over her eyes, blocking out the moonlight—but even in the blackness, the vision of it kept parading bright and relentless behind her eyelids. Her betrothed husband, *laughing*, in Ella's own *drawing-room*, with his hands up a moaning stranger's *skirts*.

And already Ella was cursing herself, because perhaps she should have stayed. Perhaps she should have thrust open the door, made a disastrous, histrionic scene, and had Alfred thrown out. She should have shown herself jealous, petty, irrational, the kind of simple, class-less woman who didn't understand how these aristocratic marriages worked.

But that would have destroyed all her family's wishes, all her father's carefully laid plans. It would have thrown away Ella's inheritance, and her home, for good.

And gods curse her, but there *had* been hints about Alfred, hadn't there? From neighbours, from friends, even from Alfred himself, that he couldn't often be at home, what with so many important lordly obligations to address. But Ella had wanted to believe his easy smiles, his lovely words, the sweet kisses of his mouth deep between her legs. She'd *wanted* to believe he could be trusted. That she would be *safe*.

She'd been a fool. Men like Alfred couldn't be trusted, not when there was so much money at stake. No one could.

And now what? Now that the moment was past, even Ella's mother would insist that she ignore it, forget it, move on. *You can turn a blind eye to a few indiscretions*, she would say, *as long as his children are with you. You'll still be his wife, a real lady...*

But as the image of it, the new truth of it, kept marching behind Ella's closed eyes, it felt like something had circled around her neck, and was rapidly closing tighter. She'd very publicly accepted Alfred's proposal. She'd stood with him not even an hour ago, in front of all her friends and family, and smiled as he had sworn to take good care of her. The wedding-dress had been commissioned, the paperwork already at the lawyers', the church booked, and hundreds of guests invited.

And worst of all was that damned half-year deadline, which was already down to one measly month. And how in the gods' names would Ella ever find another man of standing—an earl or a baron or a duke, the will had very clearly specified—let alone marry him, within such a short time?

Fuck. Ella's chilled body against the cottage door was shuddering all over, and a ragged, gasping sob escaped out her throat. She would have to walk down an aisle in a wedding-dress toward Alfred, smiling. She would have to go to bed with Alfred. She would have to bear Alfred's *children*.

And would Alfred keep smiling, after that? Would he continue to pretend Ella was his only one, or would he drop the pretence once the wedding was past? And how far did the pretence go, at that? Did he even *like* her? Or had it truly been all about the inheritance, just like all the rest?

The sobs kept rising from Ella's throat, raw and desperate, until she was consumed with them, her face just as soaked as her feet. She was trapped. She was trapped with a man who would lie to her, and disrespect her, trapped having his children, trapped giving up her body and her money and her *life*, and—

And suddenly, in the cottage, she heard a movement. Silent, but not quite, and Ella's head snapped up, her eyes blinking in the moonlight.

And wait, was that—*was that—no—*

She was trapped inside with an *orc*.

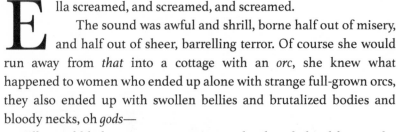

3

Ella screamed, and screamed, and screamed.

The sound was awful and shrill, borne half out of misery, and half out of sheer, barrelling terror. Of course she would run away from *that* into a cottage with an *orc*, she knew what happened to women who ended up alone with strange full-grown orcs, they also ended up with swollen bellies and brutalized bodies and bloody necks, oh *gods*—

Ella scrabbled to escape, grasping at the door behind her as she screamed—but her hands were numb, her entire body caught and frozen. And the *orc*—oh gods oh *gods*—who had been standing there, in the middle of her hunting-cottage—took two loping steps, and put one huge hand against the door, and the other against Ella's still-screaming mouth.

"Stop," he ordered, his voice deep and powerful and authoritative—and without at all meaning to, Ella obeyed it. Just stood there, staring and terrified in the sudden silence, with an orc's heavy, hot hand against her face, his huge body looming over her, a horrifying black shadow in the darkness.

"Good," he said, the single word sending a hard, rippling shudder down Ella's already trembling form. She was trapped, trapped alone with an *orc*, what would he do, what would he say, what fresh hell was going to come next in this complete and utter disaster of an evening.

But then, without warning, the orc stepped backwards. His hand dropping from her face, from the door behind her, and it occurred to Ella that she should make a run for it, now, now, *now*—but instead she just kept standing there, shivering, staring at the orc before her.

Gods, he was huge. A good head taller than she was, with shoulders that were nearly twice as wide, and arms as big around as her thighs. And—Ella shuddered again—he was bare-chested, and wearing only a pair of low-slung trousers, and *no shoes*. And his torso was broad and hard and rippled with muscle, clearly strong enough to bend her double and hold her there, to make her do whatever the hell he wanted...

But he still wasn't moving, only standing there staring back at her, and finally Ella's frantic eyes found his face in the moonlight. Taking in the heavy square jaw, the thick black eyebrows, the crooked nose that had looked like it had been broken multiple times. The pointed ears—supposedly inherited from the orcs' long-lost elf ancestors—with an actual gold *ring* embedded in his left earlobe. And his skin might have been almost *green* in better light, and boasted many prominent scars, one looking like a blade had sliced deep across his cheekbone.

And his *eyes*. They were glittering black coals in his already terrifying face, they were roving up and down Ella's body with shameless frankness—and now they were lingering, holding on her face. Just looking, as though almost *waiting* for something, and why, wait, *wait*—

"*Natt*?!" Ella's voice croaked, and the orc actually—smiled. *Natt* smiled, flashing her a row of sharp white teeth, and what the fuck, what the hell, what had *happened* to Ella's godsforsaken life.

She had to cover her eyes again, try to breathe, try to grasp at the spiralling chaos of her thoughts. She'd been a child, she'd been allowed to run wild all over the grounds, much to her mother's consternation, and her father's satisfaction. *A lady shouldn't be out in the sun and muck*, her mother had complained, so Ella had only done it more. Until it had felt like this forest had become part of her, and her part of it.

And in this forest, one day, Ella had met an orc. A young orc, greenish and gangly, not far from her in age, clearly tracking rabbits.

And rather than running and screaming, guarding her virtue, as Ella had been repeatedly instructed to do, instead she'd thought of her mother, and trotted straight toward the orc, and asked his name.

In hindsight it had been a sickeningly dangerous thing to do—there had no doubt been full-grown orcs nearby, ready to trap her and bite her and infect her with their spawn—but at the time, the gangly greenish orc hadn't seemed dangerous. In fact, he'd seemed just as unsettled by Ella as she'd been by him, but he hadn't run or attacked. And instead, he'd given her his name.

I am Nattfarr, of Clan Grisk, he'd said. *Natt.*

And in the months and years following, Ella and Natt had often met, around the same place. Wary and unsure of each other at first, but once they'd both understood that neither one was about to attack—or worse, involve the grown-ups—they'd become actual, honest-to-gods *friends.*

And Ella had found it utterly fascinating, befriending an orc. Seeing how quickly he could run and climb trees, how easily he could kill and skin game with his slim, sharp black claws. How different his skin and hair were—his skin all that pearly greenish-grey, his hair long and thick and black, tied in a gleaming braid down his back. How he spoke the common-tongue in an old-fashioned, stilted-sounding way, and how his own language—the orcs' ancient black-tongue—was a strange, guttural rumbling, made deep in his throat.

And what Ella remembered most strongly—she swallowed hard, as her eyes darted up and down this orc's huge form—was how oddly *physical* he had been. How his body had been such a part of him, such an immediate and truthful channel to his thoughts. How he'd preferred to touch and smell and taste things, rather than seeing them. How he'd sometimes touched *her*, his hand smoothing easily over her shoulder or against her hair. And even more strongly, how he'd smelled her whenever they met, his grey-green face angling warm and ticklish against her exposed neck.

Ella's entire body shuddered again, but thankfully her heartbeat had slowed somewhat, her breath coming in more manageable gulps. It was Natt. He wouldn't force her, or hurt her. Would he?

"You have not forgotten me," he said finally, his voice so much deeper, more powerful, than Ella remembered. "This pleases me."

That shudder rippled again down Ella's back, but she felt her head moving, much like a nod. "Yes, I mean no, of course I didn't forget you," she heard her shaky voice say. "I mean—not that I expected to find you here, hiding in our *hunting-cottage*, on the night of my *engagement-party*."

The orc—Natt—smiled again, a flash of sharp white teeth in the moonlight. "No," he agreed. "I have vexed you, lass."

Lass. He'd called her that, back then, and until now Ella had entirely forgotten it, and the sound of it was doing something unexpectedly odd in her belly. "No," she said, "I mean, yes, but I was already vexed, it was my engagement-party, and I found my betrothed *husband* with another *woman*, and—"

And gods, why was she telling this to an *orc*, and she clamped her mouth shut, far too late. While the orc—Natt—gave a sudden, ghastly frown, snapping his head to the side. Causing his long black braid to fall over his shoulder, and there was another strange shock of recognition, or perhaps even warmth, at the sight of it.

"This foul man," he spat, with a quick flex of his clawed hand, "ought to die, for such an affront against you. When I am given leave, I shall kill him for you. With joy."

There was another shock down Ella's spine—Natt would *kill* Alfred? Natt had *killed* people? And suddenly, looking at him, Ella realized that of course he had. It had been years since he'd hunted rabbits in the forest, he was a full-grown orc now, and full-grown orcs were raiding raging *murderers*. And before that new peace-treaty, how many men had the orcs killed in Sakkin Province, just this past year? Dozens? Hundreds?

Ella had backed up tight against the door again, her hand grasping desperate for the latch, as the orc—Natt—came an easy, silent step closer. Gods, he was so *big*, who knew orcs could grow so much, and—and—

"Speak, lass," he said, his voice suddenly lower, but still with that thread of command in it. "Tell me how you wish it done. Shall I break his bones? Tear off his head? Carve out his guts with my blade?"

His blade, he had a *blade*? But yes, there, hanging off a loose leather belt at his waist, there was a sharp, gleaming, curved sword. An orc-sword, the kinds the orcs forged and carried and *killed* with, and as Ella watched, Natt's big hand went to touch, natural and easy, against its hilt. And Ella was truly trembling again, staring at his face. So familiar and yet still so foreign, capable of carrying out appalling words like those.

"No," she gasped. "No, please. No killing. *Gods*, no."

Natt's head tilted again, his huge hand still clenched on the sword-hilt, and that—*that*—was the sight of his long black tongue, coming out to *lick* at his *lips*. "Foolish lass," he said. "You should not like to watch, whilst I make this foul man scream?"

"*No!*" Ella countered, almost a wail this time. "And isn't—haven't you orcs just signed that *peace-treaty*? I thought you weren't *supposed* to kill people anymore!"

If she wasn't mistaken, that was an actual grimace on Natt's mouth, a hard shake of his head—and his clawed hand reluctantly dropped from the sword-hilt, back down to his side. "Ach, this is truth. But"—his voice lowered—"I may yet dream of the day when I watch this man's blood pool beneath him, and the life leach from his pale eyes. And I shall *laugh*."

That last bit was said with a harsh, biting satisfaction, sending another wrenching shudder down Ella's spine. Not only did Natt want to torture and *kill* Alfred, but he would take that much pleasure in his death? What in the gods' names had this orc become, in all these years? What else was he capable of?

But Ella's hand on the door behind her hadn't pulled the latch, hadn't even tried. Not even when Natt came a slow step closer, near enough to touch—and suddenly Ella could smell him, the woodsy warm scent almost shockingly familiar in her nostrils. Bringing an inexplicable heat to her face, and even more so when he leaned in, closer and closer, until—Ella's mouth let out a strangled, choked gasp—he'd put his face to her neck, and *smelled* her.

It was just the same as how he'd done it all those years ago, down to the quivery little tickle it left against her skin. His breath warm, the scent of him curling close and familiar, his smooth black hair brushing against her cheek.

And that—Ella gasped again—*that* was a brief, unmistakable touch of his hot mouth, his soft lips, against the curve of her neck. And that was *definitely* new, and what the hell was *happening* to her, because she didn't even push him away. Just stood there and felt it, her eyes fluttering, her head leaning back against the closed door.

Natt seemed to take it for the permission it was, because his face lingered there for far too long, until his deep, steady inhale had filled his chest enough that it brushed against the front of her dress. And that made Ella gasp too, for entirely unaccountable reasons, and when his warmth finally pulled away, there was a strange, irrational twinge of displeasure at the loss of it.

"This man has left his foul scent upon you," Natt said, his eyes shuttered, and was that—was that *reproach* in his voice? "He has touched you, and *tasted* you."

What? Natt *knew* that, just from smelling? Another shiver snaked down Ella's spine, even as the heat surged to her face, sharp and prickling. "That's none of your business, Natt," she managed. "I'm twenty-five years old, I'm the richest heiress in the entire *realm*, and I can do whatever the hell I please. And also, Alfred and I are *engaged*. We're to be *married*. In four *weeks*."

She didn't miss the sudden sneer of Natt's lip in the dim light, the hard narrowing of those black eyes. "Marry *this man*?" he said flatly, the contempt all too clear in his voice. "This faint-hearted fool who breaks his pledge to you, and piddles his weak seed away into another? No. You shall have better."

Ella blinked, and her hand on the door-latch behind her clenched involuntarily, more heat rushing to her cheeks. "Um," she said, high-pitched. "I have no idea what you're talking about."

Or did she, because Natt had stepped even closer, his form looming huge and unnerving above her. "Do you not?" he asked, and Ella blinked again as his big hand came up, and a single finger—complete with a thick gold-and-green ring—stroked slowly, carefully, down her cheek, her jaw. Light, warm, gentle, with no claw out, because orc claws were retractable, and Ella had been fascinated by that back then, had held his hand as she'd watched him do it again and again—

"You do not remember?" he said, as that finger traced lower, down her neck, along the line of her shoulder. "The pledge you made to me?"

The pledge. Ella felt herself swallow, her eyes dropping, following that hand as it trailed its way down her arm. It was so much bigger now, compared to back when she'd touched him so easily. When one day, deep in the forest, these very orc hands had held both of hers, and those orc eyes had looked into her soul.

Will you have me, lass, he had said. *Before any other. When we are grown.*

He had been so serious, so earnest and quiet and—*vulnerable*, almost, in that moment. And Ella had looked at him, at his strange face and his hands and his hair, at his lean, beautifully expressive body. At those bottomless, black orc eyes.

And she'd said, *Yes, Nattfarr of Clan Grisk. I will.*

Natt's other hand had come up under her chin, tilting it back up, making her look at him. And Ella was looking, gods damn her, she was looking. And did he truly still remember that day too, that *pledge*, after all this time, after years and years and *years*. After Ella had finally, *finally* forced herself to forget it.

"That was a long time ago, Natt," Ella heard her voice say, oddly thick. "A *lifetime* ago."

And more than that, he was an *orc*. And Ella knew now that she should never have agreed to such an appalling thing with an *orc*, proper women would never even be possessed of such a thought. Orcs were violent ravaging murderers, they killed men, raided villages, stole goods, drank blood, seduced hapless women and then trapped them in their mountain to bear their sons, he was an *orc*—

"Yes," Natt said, quiet. "It was nine summers past. And you made a pledge."

Ella's mouth had gone dry, her heart fluttering madly in her chest, and that warm hand on her chin slipped up, brushed soft against her mouth. "You did not forget this," he said. "Did you?"

Ella's lips against his finger had parted, as if to speak, but no words came out. Just her breath, far too close and gasping, dragging in that scent of him, filling her lungs and her thoughts.

"You did not forget," he said again, and this time there was a note of satisfaction in his low voice. "Though you foolishly gave this man leave to taste you, you have yet kept your maidenhead for me."

She *what*? That was enough to snap Ella out of this strange stilted stupor, and she felt her body straighten, her eyes fixing narrow on his.

"I have done no such thing," she said, and that was true, wasn't it? "And also, blithely commenting upon a woman's—ahem—*virtue*—is *extremely* discourteous!"

But if Natt registered her tone, or her discomfort, he didn't acknowledge it. Just kept that warm finger against her parted lips, and then—Ella gasped—he nudged it slowly, but purposefully, between them. Sinking his thick orc finger *into her mouth*, brushing against her *tongue*, and he was probably *filthy* and why wasn't she slapping him pushing him away *something*—

"You did not give your maidenhead to this piddling foul man," he said, his voice harder, as if stating an incontrovertible truth. "Or to any other. You kept it for me."

Gods. There was a clenching shudder up Ella's spine, and low in her belly, but she still hadn't moved—and that single orc finger was sliding deeper, deeper into her mouth. Tasting inexplicably sweet, reminiscent of the scent that was swarming the air still further, settling in her lungs.

"And thus," Natt said, his voice full of danger, of heat, of promise. "It shall be *mine*."

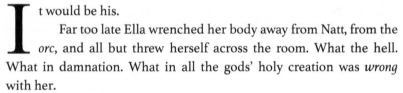

4

It would be his.

Far too late Ella wrenched her body away from Natt, from the *orc*, and all but threw herself across the room. What the hell. What in damnation. What in all the gods' holy creation was *wrong* with her.

"You can't," she gasped, whirling back around to where his form was still standing, still by the door. "You can't just—show up in a hunting-cottage and—and *help yourself* to other people's *maidenheads*, and make them bear your *children!*"

Natt didn't move, but just looked across the room at her, his dark head tilting. "You shall not be with child, should we do this, this night," he said. "I have missed your seed by naught a day. You shall now have more than a week of leave, before your bleeding begins. And it is not until after this that you shall make a new seed, to meet mine."

Ella gaped at him, entirely dumbfounded, while her shouting thoughts distantly calculated that, frantically counting out days in her head. "H-how," she said, her voice audibly wavering, "can you know such things? Or even *speak* of such things, I cannot even countenance—"

She had to press her hot hands to her hot face, wildly shaking her head, but Natt only kept looking at her, his forehead furrowing. "I can smell this upon you," he said. "And why ought I not to speak of this? It is only truth, that your body has spoken to me. And this truth has much weight, should you wish to keep your pledge to me this night, without sparking my son inside you."

His son, *inside* her? Dear gods in heaven, first her shameful monthly courses, and now talk of conceiving his actual *son*?!—and Ella forcibly thrust both those appalling thoughts aside, and clung to the one truth she could speak, in this moment. "That p-pledge," she sputtered, "was *years* ago, Natt. And you can't possibly expect me to keep some ridiculous ancient *pledge* to you when I haven't even set eyes on you in a *decade!*"

Her voice had gone cracked and high-pitched as she spoke, and at the sound of it, Natt's head tilted further. Perhaps reading far too much into her tone, into those words, and it didn't matter, it *didn't*, why the hell was Ella letting on that it ever had...

"You wished for me to return to you," Natt said, slowly, quietly. "You longed for me."

Gods, that was ridiculous, there was no way Ella had missed roaming about the forest with an orc. Climbing trees, catching game, watching him kill and eat. He'd rarely bothered cooking anything, and had always eaten the bones, too, and had grinned at Ella when she'd cringed, and loudly proclaimed orcs the most shocking creatures imaginable.

And they *were*, he *was*, and why wasn't Ella saying that. Why was she standing here, in the middle of her hunting-cottage, on the night of her *engagement-party*, and blinking back an inexplicable prickling wetness behind her eyes.

"I am about to be a *lady*," she said, with as much composure as she could muster. "I am one of the wealthiest women in the realm. I am a busy, beautiful, popular, and highly desired *heiress*, and I have had many other important matters with which to occupy myself these past years."

Like parties. Like petty, empty friendships. Like making the proper impression, pleasing the proper people, moving in the proper circles. Spending less and less time on the grounds, in the forest, because that wasn't something a proper lady would do. *Especially*, dear gods, if she was doing it with an *orc*.

But said orc was here, and coming a step closer, his orc eyes seeing far too much, like they always had. "All this means naught," he said, soft. "I also did not forget you, lass. I have longed for you."

Something seemed to clench tight around Ella's chest, and she drew in a deep, shuddering breath. "Have you really," she heard herself say. "And has that prevented *you* from having other women all this time, Nattfarr? *Forcing* other women?"

There was a low, rumbling growl from Natt's mouth, his shadowed form lurching a sharp step closer. "These are but the tales your men tell," he said. "Orcs do not *force* women. We *give*."

Ella let out a strangled gasp, and she shook her head, took another step backwards. "That's a lie," she said, and thankfully here was the anger, edging out that still-powerful scent of him in the air. "Everyone knows what you orcs really do. You *trap* women, you *make* them lie with you, you make them *pregnant*, and then you make them hand over their *children!*"

Natt's head tilted again, and gave a slow, deliberate shake. "I cannot speak for all my brothers," he said, "but we Grisk do not do this. We do not need to. Women *wish* to lie with us. Just as you wish for me now."

What? That was ridiculous, preposterous, Ella wasn't wishing for anything—and most certainly not *that*, and especially not *tonight*. And had other women wanted that, with *him*, surely it was impossible—but then she made the grave mistake of glancing down at his muscled bare chest, and then lower, to the front of his trousers.

And there was—well. Rather more than she'd expected, jutting out strong and clearly visible against the fabric. Thick and smooth and hard, and was that a stain of pooling *wetness* at the head...

Natt could see her looking, of course he could, and then—Ella almost choked—that big clawed hand actually moved over to grip at it, through the trousers. Brazenly showing her its considerable length and heft, all too obvious through the tight fabric, and suddenly Ella found it impossible to stop staring, or keep herself from letting out a harsh, breathless gasp.

"Do you wish to see?" his voice murmured, his other hand already coming up to unfasten his low-slung belt. "This shall please you, I ken."

Good gods. Ella belatedly squeezed her eyes shut, and took another stumbling step backwards. "No," she gasped. "*Gods*, no."

There was a *thunk* as she spoke, the sound of his sword hitting the floor, but when Ella risked a brief, darting glance toward him the trousers were still safely in place, thank the gods. "Then speak this, lass," his low voice said. "For what do you wish, this night."

Ella had to search for a coherent answer, and found that she didn't seem to have one. What *did* she wish? To run away? To return to her party? To walk back in and smile at Alfred and pretend as though nothing had changed?

And, worse, to bid farewell to this thoroughly shocking orc, to Natt, perhaps *forever*? When he'd finally come back, after so long?

"Do you wish me to leave you?" that low voice asked, almost as if he'd read her thoughts. "I shall, lass. You shall never set eyes upon me again, if that is your wish."

The thought was strangely, surprisingly unsettling, and Ella's head gave a hard, jolting shake. "N-no," she heard herself say, too quickly. "Not yet."

That big body had stilled, and she could feel those eyes studying her, searing far too deep. And when he came a step closer, his head still thoughtfully tilted, she didn't back away this time. Just let him come closer, and closer, until that smell of him was almost overpowering again, hot and musky in her breath.

"You gave this foul man leave to touch you, and taste you," he murmured. "Why should you not grant me leave to do the same."

What? Ella's shocked eyes were trapped on his, gaping at where he was coming another slow, silent step closer. "If you truly do not wish me to kill this man," he continued, even lower, "mayhap you shall instead grant me this vengeance upon him, on your behalf."

This—vengeance? Natt's mouth was smiling again, showing all those sharp teeth, and his hand had gone down to grip, uselessly, at where his sword-hilt had been. "This vengeance," he breathed, "of a hungry orc's tongue, tasting the woman this fool man falsely claims as his own, on the night of this *party*. I shall cover his scent with my own, and bring you the joy he ought to have granted you this night."

Oh. *Oh.* And Ella wasn't actually considering this, she wasn't—but her eyes were caught on Natt's face, his mouth. On where that long black tongue had again come out, and licked slow, sinuous, meaning-ful, against his lips.

Damn. Ella gave a brief, unwilling gasp, and in reply Natt grinned again, even as a low, husky growl hissed from his throat. "I shall bring you deep joy in his stead, lass," he whispered. "I shall give you all that you have longed for."

Ella couldn't move, couldn't think, and now he was near enough to touch again, his gold-ringed finger coming back to brush once more against her cheek. His claw was out this time, sharp and black and deadly, and Ella shivered as she felt it trail lightly, gently, down her skin.

"You shall be safe, with me," he said, the words at strange, thrilling odds with that single claw, now tracing deliberately down her neck. "And I shall never hold you against your will. Should you wish to run, I shall not stop you."

Those black eyes were intent on hers as he spoke, and curse her, but Ella *believed* him. She believed he'd let her go. She believed he wouldn't hurt her. And she even believed—she hauled in another shaky, trembly breath—that he would give her *joy*.

And somewhere, somehow, a stilted, shameful part of her was actually considering it. Actually considering allowing an *orc*—allowing *Natt*—to touch her, and taste her, like that. And what would it *feel* like, to have a tongue like that exploring in one's most secret places, lapping warm and slick against one's skin, while that dark head, that huge muscular orc body, nestled between one's thighs...

"I'm *engaged*," Ella heard her strained voice say, because perhaps that was the last truth left, the last refuge against the heat now pooling hard in her groin. "And I don't approve of infidelity."

Her eyes had darted down toward the diamond engagement-ring on her left hand, and she belatedly shoved it behind her, away. But Natt had seen, Natt *knew*, and his clawed finger hesitated on her collar-bone, while his other hand came up to grip gentle, warm, against her chin, making her look at him.

"You are not this foolish, woman," he said, his voice hard. "You witnessed this man with another. This man who swore fealty to you. Ach?"

Gods, Ella couldn't *think*, and she swallowed, felt her tongue come out brief to her lips. "Well," she managed, "I mean, they weren't in *flagrante*, not really, Alfred just had his hand up her skirts, that's all."

Natt's heavy eyebrows snapped up, and there was a sound almost like a laugh, rumbling from his throat. "That is all, is it? His hand up her skirts?"

And without warning, that clawed hand dropped from Ella's chin, and—oh *gods*—reached down, and grasped a generous handful of her own skirts. Not drawing them up, but just holding them there, waiting.

"Shall we thus begin our vengeance with this, lass?" he purred. "Since this is such a trifle, to you? And after this, should you wish, I shall next show you the many joys to be found upon an orc's tongue?"

That tongue had again come out, licking his lips with slow, purposeful intent, but his body had remained otherwise still, waiting for Ella's answer. And surely there was no answer to this, no conceivable response—but suddenly, somehow, Ella desperately needed to *know*. Needed to know where those words led, what this audacious orc would do next. What it would *feel* like, to take her own secret vengeance against Alfred, for so callously ruining what was supposed to have been a perfect, beautiful night.

And then, afterwards, Ella could still go back to her party. She could still belong. She could hold her head high, and smile at Alfred, and *know*.

"And you promise to keep it secret, Natt?" she whispered, without at all meaning to. "And afterwards, you'll let me go?"

There was another instant's stillness, his gaze gone briefly shuttered—but then his head nodded, slow, purposeful, his eyes on hers steady and sure.

"Ach, my lass," he said. "I shall not speak of whatever joys we take, this night. And once I have wreaked my vengeance upon this man, you shall return to this party, as you wish."

It sounded almost like a promise, another pledge, spoken dark and quiet and true, crackling with hidden, secret power. With justice, with vengeance, with *life*.

And standing here, looking into those solemn orc eyes, Ella could only seem to swallow, and raise her head, and—*nod*.

"Then yes, Natt," she whispered. "I will. Show me."

5

how me.

It almost felt like the words were someone else's, spoken from someone else's lips. But no, it had been Ella, because before her Natt's mouth had broadened into a smile that was equal parts breathtaking and terrifying.

"Good lass," he said, his eyes suddenly brazen, challenging, as his hand still gripping her skirts slowly, finally began to move up. Drawing the damp fabric higher and higher, cool air pooling against Ella's bare legs, until—she gave a choked, desperate gasp—that huge, warm orc hand touched light against her *bare thigh*.

Ella hadn't worn stockings or smallclothes under her dress tonight, for reasons that now seemed abominably foolish—and that meant there was nothing between her and Natt's hand, not even a single scrap of fabric. And his hand had already curved fully against her skin, and was sliding slowly, deliberately, dangerously upwards.

But Ella was doing this, and Natt wasn't stopping, he couldn't dare stop, not now—not even when his hand reached the join of her thigh against her groin. And then—Ella's mouth betrayed a harsh, guttural gasp—there was the desperate, thrilling, impossible feeling of a thick orc *finger*, brushing light but purposeful between her legs. Touching *there*, where Ella's body already felt hot and strangely swollen, and humiliatingly slick against that slow, sliding warmth.

"Speak this, lass," Natt murmured, his glinting eyes held to hers, his white tooth sharp against his lip. "Is it but a small thing for a woman, to have a hungry hand up her skirts?"

Oh gods, Ella was *not* answering that, even as that finger kept exploring, tracing against her. It felt blunt and smooth, no sign of sharpness whatsoever, and she gave another desperate, breathless gasp as it nudged upwards, toward the quivering, dripping core of her.

"Is it, lass?" Natt whispered, and with a silent shift of muscle there was the feel of his huge solid thigh, moving between hers. Giving him better access, spreading her apart for him, but Ella found that she didn't seem to care. Just gasped and shuddered at the feel of it, that strong orc leg between hers, that hot orc finger now delving deeper between her folds, and slipping itself slowly, just slightly, inside.

"Is this a small thing, lass?" he insisted, his other hand come to Ella's chin. Making her look up at him, into those eyes, even as that single finger drove deeper. Exploring her, invading her, while her tight, swollen body clenched hungry and frantic around it. Almost as though she craved it, welcomed it, needed it with a rising, swarming desperation that was trammelling all conscious thought.

"Speak, lass," Natt said, low and commanding. "When last I knew you, you oft could not breathe for your constant words and questions and laughter. Where is your voice."

Ella felt herself twitch against him, around him, as another whirl of memories paraded behind her eyes. She'd indeed been a chatterbox back then, much to her mother's displeasure—but thankfully Natt had never seemed to mind, and had even seemed to welcome her incessant questions. Things like, *Where do you live, who is your mother, how can you eat that, do you ever wear shoes. Why don't orcs like us, why do you always raid like you do, do you really want women for sport.*

Ella hadn't even truly known the meaning of that last one, at the time, but like all the rest, Natt had carefully considered the question, and had given a quiet, measured answer. *My fathers wish for women most of all because they long for kin,* he had said. *They long for sons. And they do not wish for orcs to fade from the land forever.*

"Speak, lass," Natt purred, as that finger slid ever deeper, flaring more sparks behind Ella's eyes, under her skin. "Is this a small thing."

Ella took a shaky, guttural breath, let it out. "No," she heard herself say, her voice choked. "It's not."

There was an approving circle of his finger inside her, and a flash of his white teeth. "No," he agreed. "It is not. And a hungry male does not stop at this. If you saw that piddling man do this to another"—his lip curled, contempt flaring in his eyes—"you may be sure that he has filled her with his prick, and his seed, as well."

His finger slipped a little deeper inside her as he spoke, as if to soften the strength of that claim, and Ella felt her body arch against it, even as her sinking thoughts twisted and churned. Natt was right, about Alfred. Of course he was right. But she still had to go back after this, everything would be fine, she would wear that dress, walk down that aisle, keep her family's home, become a real lady...

There was a low growl from Natt's mouth, almost as if he'd somehow followed her thoughts. "We shall have our vengeance for this betrayal, lass," he hissed. "You shall find deep joy as you scream and writhe upon my tongue."

The words should have been horrifying, but instead Ella had actually moaned aloud. While her dripping wetness convulsed violently against him, telling him very clearly that indeed it would like more, please...

"Good lass," Natt murmured, and suddenly there was the feel of a second blunt finger below, nudging soft and wet against her crease. Pressing, delving alongside the first, feeling very tight and tenuous and full, so full, oh—

"You must breathe," he whispered, his eyes steady on hers. "You must make your womb soft and open for me. You must think of blooming enough to welcome my tongue inside you."

Oh. So *that* was what he was doing, then, he was implying that his tongue was thicker than two entire orc-*fingers*, and Ella felt her whole body shudder and gasp, clenching against that too-tight invasion of him. Bringing another sharp-toothed smile to his mouth, one that looked almost patient, or affectionate.

"I said *open*, lass," he purred. "Were you any other, I should gladly break apart your maidenhead on my tongue. But you"—his smile faded, his voice dropping—"you shall open yours for me. You shall welcome me inside you. I shall not have your blood on my mouth. Not yet."

The words were deeply appalling, in too many ways to count, but Ella had only groaned again as those delicious fingers circled and delved, seeking a way in. But not succeeding, not yet, and despite her harsh breaths, her attempts to relax, it still felt far too tight, too close, what if it couldn't, what if she couldn't—

Natt's head tilted, studying her, and then he slowly, purposely, slid his other hand around, behind her head. Sinking his fingers deep into her hair, almost as if cradling her—and then he drew her forward, and *kissed* her.

It was an explosion of colour and scent and heat, warm lips and slick wetness and a succulent musky sweetness. His mouth soft and open and clever, his tongue brushing light against hers, perhaps in a silent invitation—and to Ella's astonishment, she answered it. Slipping her own tongue into that hot orc-mouth, and feeling the strength of his huge orc-tongue, brushing back. Gentle and soft and open still, perhaps the sweetest, filthiest kiss she'd ever had in her life, and a stilted, distant part of her seemed to understand all at once what Natt was doing, what he was showing her. Using his body to speak, like he always had.

So Ella felt his mouth's openness, revelled in it, drowned in it—and willed herself, somehow, to do the same. To open back to him, to welcome his explorations, to do between her legs what he was doing with his mouth, soft and wet and obscene—and oh gods, it was *working*. That second finger finally slipping up into her, filling her almost shockingly full of him. And while it was tight, there was no pain, just the base wanton thrill of it, an orc with two whole fingers sunk deep inside her.

And now here was that tongue, suddenly slick and sinuous and powerful, pushing back into Ella's mouth. Driving, invading, just like those fingers below, and it *was* huge, it was an unspeakable indecent *monstrosity*. Stretching out her lips, her jaw, around it, curling and tasting inside her, strong and impossibly large—and then, slowly, drawing back again. Even as those two fingers below drew back too, nearly all the way out, leaving her body feeling swollen, strange, empty.

But no, it just meant it was Ella's turn, her turn to kiss and taste back, to explore his mouth with hers. And to do the same below, to embrace the gentle nudge of his fingers, to be open and willing against them, to welcome them as they slowly, purposefully sank back inside, and that huge, glorious tongue did the same.

Gods, it felt good. Felt easy, right, and even more so when Natt kept going deeper, his tongue brushing against her throat, his fingers below sunk to the base. Almost powerful enough to lift her off her feet, but there was no chance of falling, not with his tongue and his fingers locked inside her, holding her firmly in place.

When Natt finally leaned back, ending the kiss, Ella found herself hot and trembly all over, her eyes trapped to that mouth. And her hand, that hadn't been touching him all this time, seemed to lift up on its own, coming to brush against his lips. Touching an orc, *voluntarily*, but that orc's dazed dark eyes had fluttered at the contact, his lips parting, his black tongue slipping out to curl against her fingers.

Damn. There was no way an orc—an *orc*, doing *that*—should be so wildly arousing, but then that orc's fingers between her legs slowly slipped out of her, away from her entirely. Dropping her skirts again, leaving her panting and untouched, while—Ella let out a keening gasp—he brought up those fingers, still glistening with her wetness, and took them deep into his own mouth.

He watched her as he did it, his eyes gone hard and challenging as he sucked with deliberate intent. Tasting her, wanting to taste her, drinking her up—and then he slowly brought those same fingers to Ella's own mouth, sliding them inside. Tasting now of him, and her, a strange blend of salt-sweetness, an even stranger intimacy passing between their locked eyes. Raw and earthy and obscene, sharing kisses juices fingers, peeling away Ella's innocence piece by agonizing piece.

"Are you ready, lass?" Natt whispered. "Shall you now welcome my tongue deep between your legs?"

A hard groan escaped Ella's lips, and her replying nod was immediate, with no trace of doubt. But Natt was still waiting, black eyebrows raised, and Ella gulped for air, made herself speak. "Yes," her voice rasped. "Very well, I will."

She was rewarded with an approving flash of those white teeth, and then the sudden feel of his big hands coming around to her arse. And then he hoisted her bodily up off the floor, light and swift, as though she weighed nothing.

"Brave lass," he murmured, his huge hard bulk suddenly far too close—and it was moving, striding, carrying her, across the room. To where there was an old upholstered couch, set in front of the cottage's largest window, and Natt gently deposited Ella down upon it, and then lowered himself to the floor before her. An orc, kneeling between her legs, looking up at her, his face stark and scarred in the dappled moonlight.

"You shall speak, lass," he said, as she felt both those warm hands against her bare ankles. "You shall speak if I vex you, or bring you pain. You shall pledge me this."

His hands were waiting on her ankles, his eyes glittering. And did Ella dare make any more pledges to this orc, who was clearly wont to remember them for all his days—but his hands weren't moving, why weren't his hands moving, and Ella swallowed, felt her head nodding.

"Yes," she said. "Yes, very good. I shall."

There was another flash of those white teeth, an approving brush of claws against her anklebone. "Good," he said, as both hands began sliding slowly, purposefully, upwards. "I shall hold you to this, lass."

Ella had no doubt of that, and her head gave another jerky nod, her mouth gone bone-dry. Her eyes staring at the unthinkable sight of this orc, kneeling between her legs, dragging up her muddy skirts. Exposing her calves, her knees, her thighs, guiding her legs apart as he went, and Ella trembled against him as he kept going and going, her skirts higher and higher—

And this, Ella now knew from her experience with Alfred, was where Natt would lean forward, nudging his face under the edge of her skirts, concealing the improper proceedings from her innocent eyes. And then there would be the light, teasing touch of tongue, a thrilling perfect jolt to the senses, and Ella wanted to feel that again, desperately needed to feel it again—

But Natt wasn't doing it, yet. Natt was still sliding his hands upwards, curving them smooth and possessive against her bare hips, and over the tight fabric of her corset. And that meant—Ella felt herself gasp, and shudder all over—he was *uncovering* her. Bunching her skirts well up above her waist, leaving her entire lower half—all her most secret, embarrassing parts—exposed to the air, and to his watching, hungry eyes.

And Natt *was* watching. Not moving, not touching, not yet—just looking. His eyes held fast on the sight between Ella's spread legs, and she could feel—could *hear*—her audacious body clenching, twitching, dripping wet, for those watching orc-eyes to see.

Those orc hands were sliding down her legs again, all the way to her ankles, and they nudged her muddy slippers off her feet, and onto the floor. Then he lifted her ankles up, placing her feet on the edge of the couch. And if Ella had thought she'd been exposed before, this was something else entirely, this was every hidden part of her spread open wide, without question the most wanton, humiliating thing she'd ever done in her *life*—

But those orc eyes were on hers again, those eyebrows raised, again willing her to speak. And when she didn't, the orc—*Natt*—leaned in, spreading her thighs even wider, gentle but inexorable—

"Look how open you are, lass," he murmured, low and husky. "Look how soft and wet you are for me. Now, for what do you wish next."

He was looking again at the sight he'd exposed between her legs, his eyes hungry and appallingly brazen, like they truly wanted to see this, Ella's bare, swollen wetness madly convulsing and dripping for his eyes. And while she could admit to herself, perhaps, that she wanted him, making herself say it, out loud, to an *orc*, even if she was spread-eagled on a couch with him kneeling between her legs—

"Speak, lass," Natt said, his voice harder, his gaze once again on her face. "What has taken your voice."

Ella's thoughts floundered, suddenly, darting from her mother to Alfred to her father, lying cold and pale and silent in a casket. And then to the damned lawyer reading that damned will, six months to wed a man of standing, an earl a baron a duke, or the presumptive heir thereto—

But here was Natt's hand, on Ella's cheek. He'd risen up on his knees, his eyes on a level with hers, and gods he was big and *gods* he was close and his eyes, his eyes—

"For what do you wish," he insisted. "From me."

Ella gulped for air, stared at his waiting eyes. What did she wish, from him. His strength, his certainty? His huge, beautiful body? His explanation, his apology, for disappearing with no word for *years*?

"Your—your tongue," she heard her halting voice say, because perhaps that was the only truth that could be relied upon, at this moment. And it was one Natt clearly wanted to hear, because his eyes flared with heat, his big hands gripping against her skin.

"Then this you shall have," he said, promised—and then he bowed his head, took a long, deep inhale, filling his lungs with the scent of her. And as Ella watched, caught and breathless, his huge black tongue slithered out—and *licked* her. Sliding slow, deliberate, utterly maddening, all the way from one end of her exposed crease to the other.

It was sparks and life and ecstasy, shouting all at once in Ella's head, and flailing against a shocked, impossible disbelief. That wasn't what Alfred had done, Alfred hadn't gone anywhere near *there*, and whyever would he want to?

But Natt had let out a harsh, guttural groan of undeniable pleasure, vibrating against Ella's skin, and then—she heard herself groan aloud, too—he licked her *again*. Even harder, deeper this time, lingering against all Ella's most secret, forgotten, shameful places. Laying them bare, and known, and perhaps even *wanted*.

And oh it felt good, it felt like glory itself had descended from on high, to dwell between Ella's spread legs. To lose her in the rapture of a huge, licking orc-tongue, and she felt her thighs dropping slightly further apart, her wet, swollen folds quivering against that sinuous heat as it snaked its way past.

And then he stopped, lingering *there*, right where Ella most craved him—and she felt herself clenching back, hard. Almost as if meeting his lips with her own, kissing him with wanton luridness, but Natt only seemed to settle himself closer, his mouth hot and hungry, his tongue slowly, *finally*, nudging its way inside.

Ella moaned aloud, her legs trembling, her head falling back on the couch, because *damn*, his tongue *was* huge, just as he'd promised. Feeling hot and tight and full as it delved itself further, further inside her, still curling and licking, oh *gods*—and then slipping back out again, back to giving her the same soft, wet, filthy kiss he'd given her mouth.

It was almost unbearable, both the dizzying feel of it, and the outrageous, preposterous sight of it. Natt's big orc head pressed deep between her legs, his long braid tickling her skin, his gold earring glinting, his eyelashes fluttering as he kissed and suckled and licked. Sliding that huge tongue back inside, deeper this time, so full and hot and tight and *alive*, tasting her drinking her eating her whole. And this was nothing like Alfred this was nothing like *anything*, it was impossible that any living being would actually *want* to do this—

"Natt," Ella heard her choked voice say, and in an instant he'd pulled himself away, his eyes narrow and intent on her face. His own face was half-covered in a sheen of wetness—*her* wetness, Ella thought—and she stared at that, and watched as her finger moved to trail against his cheek, almost as if to see if it was real.

But it was, he was, and he was waiting, and Ella swallowed, forced her dazed thoughts to right themselves. "You can't really," her hoarse voice said, "want this, like this. Can you?"

Natt's head again tilted, the way it always had when he'd considered her, evaluated her words. "Why should I not? I have longed to taste you for half my life."

That made no sense, could it, and Ella blinked at him, shook her head. "But it's not—clean," she managed. "Not *proper*. Not like when—"

"When that piddling man tasted you?" Natt finished, as he slowly, lasciviously, licked his lips. "Yes. I can smell how little he had of you. I shall not be so wasteful with my chance, lass. When I am done with you, your womb shall *reek* of my scent, and shall flood itself with juices at the barest *sight* of my tongue."

A desperate, helpless groan escaped out Ella's mouth, and Natt flashed her a sharp, not-so-nice smile. "Even a man shall be able to smell me upon you," he purred. "And his prick shall flag with fear before he can come close to touching what is *mine*."

What is his. Ella likely should have countered that, somehow, but she could only seem to gasp, holding those hard, hungry, triumphant orc eyes. And without at all meaning to, her legs seemed to open even wider, almost as if to brandish herself to him, to say, *Yes, look, this is yours, taste it again—*

It was shameless and humiliating and obscene, but Natt *approved*, he *liked* it. His mouth giving another wicked smile as he slowly, deliberately touched a single finger just *there*, and slipped it slick, smooth, easy, inside.

"Good lass," he whispered, while Ella moaned and whimpered, her body clenching desperately around him. "Look how wide you have opened for me. Do you wish to take all my tongue, now?"

Ella frantically nodded, her entire body aching and screaming for it, and Natt slowly slid his now dripping-wet finger out again, and brought it up to her mouth. Nudging it back between her lips, and she eagerly sucked it inside this time, tasting herself all over him.

"See how wet you are for me, lass," he said. "See how hungry your womb is for me. And"—he pulled the finger out of her mouth with a slippery-sounding *pop*—"as I fill it with my tongue, think on what else you might wish to take inside it."

He meant *that*, that straining bulge in the front of his trousers, and while Ella had pointedly been ignoring it, she hadn't at all forgotten it—and in this moment the very thought of it was almost impossibly arousing. To feel *that* inside her, huge and swollen and hard, making her his, *forever*—

But Natt was kneeling again, licking his lips, and now—Ella nearly shouted—sliding his tongue slow and purposeful against her. Exploring, delving, sinking deeper this time, no longer a wet, filthy kiss but rather a full-on actual invasion. Going where no one else had *ever* gone, deep and hard and powerful, impaling her whole upon it.

It was tight and full and close, more than anything else Ella had ever felt there, and she was whimpering again, writhing against it, even as she spread herself wider, perhaps even pressing back against him. Wanting to be pierced by this, taken by this, and it felt impossible, it *was* impossible, it was bending the lines of truth and reality. Smashing the entire world down to this, to a huge hot orc-tongue filling her, claiming her, drinking her from the inside out, while she gasped and squirmed and pleaded for more.

"Oh gods, oh gods," her mouth was babbling, all of its own accord. "Oh gods Natt, oh please, please, *please*—"

Her voice was rising dangerously, her whole body wide open, filled with orc, stretched to its limit. Teetering on a craving so desperate it couldn't be real, this couldn't be happening, his mouth letting out a dark, satisfied chuckle, vibrating against her as his tongue curled up just there, *there*, again and again and again, oh, *oh*—

The release crashed over Ella with furious force, hurling away her thoughts her senses the world, and swarming her instead with wave after wave of raging, all-consuming pleasure. Her mouth shouting, her body frantically pulsating against the tongue still inside it, her hands scrabbling at his hair and his shoulders and perhaps even dragging him closer, closer, gods he was good, he was *everything*.

When it finally faded, she was left gasping for air, and trembling all over. And Natt was still there, still with his mouth between her legs, but it felt soft again, his tongue back to licking and teasing, rather than invading. And Ella watched, marvelled, as her own hands went down to his face, tilted it up, caressed it with a familiarity that seemed almost to belong to someone else.

"Good gods, Natt," she breathed, trailing her thumb against his warm, wet mouth. "Where have you *been* these past nine years."

His face leaned into her touch, black eyelashes fluttering, but at the last she could see a trace of wariness, flicking across his eyes. "I have been missing you, lass," he said, soft. "I have been dreaming of how you tasted."

But it wasn't an answer, and he knew it, and the beautiful languor that had overtaken Ella's body seemed to ebb slightly, swerving away toward something like desperation. "But you *left*," she said, and there was a raw edge on her voice, her eyes blinking back an inexplicable wetness. "You just disappeared, with no word, no warning, nothing. I thought we were *friends*."

Natt's eyes briefly closed, his head still tilting against her hand. "Ach," he said. "We were friends."

The hurt lurched up again, stronger than before, and Ella heard herself sniff, felt a streak of wetness slip down her cheek. "I searched for you for months," she said. "*Years*. I left you things, made you gifts, you never took them. I thought you must have *died*."

Something moved in Natt's throat, but his eyes were back on hers again, steady, unreadable. "I did not wish to cause you pain. I am sorry, lass."

He was sorry. The misery seemed to sink deeper, crumpling hard in Ella's belly, and she stared at him, at the stark, strange lines of his face. He'd said he wouldn't hurt her, but he already had, hadn't he? He couldn't be trusted. No one could, not anymore. She knew that, how had she forgotten that...

"Then *why*," she said, her voice cracking. "Why did you leave."

Natt's broad shoulders rose and fell, and his eyes dropped down, to where his big hand was still on her pale thigh, fingers spread wide in the moonlight. His ring glittering gold and green, his claws visible and sharp.

"I cared for you, lass," he said finally, quiet. "I longed to bring you to my home, and claim you as my mate before all my kin. But this could not be."

His *mate*. The word seemed to reverberate through Ella's thoughts, deep into her very soul, because she remembered him talking about this. How for an orc a mate was more than a wife, but rather a part of him, *always*.

"You—you would have really taken me away with you, as your *mate*?" she heard herself ask, her voice high-pitched, and while this was entirely the wrong point, she couldn't seem to move away from it. "*Permanently*?"

Natt's eyes angling back to hers looked almost surprised, and his mouth twisted up, into a grim mockery of a smile. "Ach, yes, lass," he said, in a tone that suggested it should be obvious. "Had I been granted this, once you were of age, I should have crawled up your womb at once, and stayed there. I should have whelped so many sons upon you, I would now have a whole *brood* to my name, and your belly would even now be *bursting* with my seed."

The words came out fierce, guttural, almost like a threat—but instead of feeling properly threatened, Ella felt strangely hot and fluttery all over. "*Really*?" she heard herself ask, the disbelief ringing through her voice, because the very thought of it was unreal, ridiculous, *impossible*. "And it never occurred to you—to *mention* that, to me, before you left?"

There was an odd, unfamiliar stillness on Natt's face, something she couldn't ever remember seeing before. "Ach," he said, very slowly, "and had I told you this, should you have been glad to hear it? Had I come to you in the night, once you were of age, and asked this of you, should you have come away with me?"

Ella stared at him, while all the possible responses to that question dipped and soared through her head. *Would you really have done that, would you really have expected that, why do you ask, would I, well—*

But now here were the visions, marching merciless past her eyes, of her father. Her mother. The land, the house, the fortune, her *home*. All the expectations, all on Ella's shoulders. She had to make a good marriage, fulfill her father's final wishes, she was about to become a *lady*, and he was an *orc*...

Natt was still studying her, still seeing far too much, like he always had. "And if I were to ask now, lass," he said, his voice very smooth, "should you stay with me tonight? Shall you come away with me, and show yourself as my mate, before all my kin?"

The questions seemed to hang there, leaving Ella caught, splayed, exposed. Trapped bare and shameful in those damning words, that truth, those eyes—and far too late she snatched for her still-damp, still-bunched skirts, shoving them down with tingling, shaky hands. A movement that Natt only watched in stilted, agonizing silence, his mouth gone tight and thin, his long claws suddenly looking sharp and deadly against the faded upholstery of the couch.

"*Natt*," Ella heard her voice say, sounding reproachful, or perhaps even pleading. "You know I—I can't. I have my mother to think about. My father's legacy. His life's work, our family's lands, our home. He worked so hard to make me a real lady, and keep me our home, it was his final wish, and I—I *promised* him, Natt."

And Natt would know how much Ella had loved her father, how much she loved her home, surely he would understand that, at least— but there was a sudden, bitter twitch on his mouth. "Ach, lass," he said. "You should have had these noble reasons, and these fine excuses. You would have chosen to keep your pampered life, and all your unearned riches. You should never have chosen me, over this."

Ella's mouth opened, but nothing else came out, and Natt's eyes seemed to harden, glinting cold and angry. And then they dropped, looking toward where his hand had found hers, lifting it up. Tilting her fingers with slow, stilted care, making her engagement-ring sparkle in the moonlight.

"And now I know," he said, frowning toward it, "that you have changed. That beyond your own pleasure, mayhap you shall never wish for true justice for a man such as this one. A man who would freely betray his own *betrothed*, before they have yet *wed*."

The bitterness on his voice was stark, painfully thin, and in a jerky movement he dropped Ella's hand and rose to his feet, towering tall over her. "Instead, woman," he continued, his voice deepening, "you yet wish to *wed* this foul man. You yet wish to freely grant him the richest hoard in the *realm*. And have you *once* asked this man, have you *once* used your voice against him, to learn what he seeks to do with all your riches?!"

Ella was scarcely following this now, blinking up at his looming, twitching form. Had she asked. No, no she hadn't, the few times she'd dared to mention it Alfred had laughed it off, waved it away. *That's all to discuss later, darling,* he'd said, *once things are properly settled.*

An odd, shivery chill had coursed down Ella's back, and she stared at Natt's face, at his glittering eyes. "Do *you* know what Alfred plans to do?" she asked, her voice cracking. "Do you, Natt?"

Natt gave another hard, brittle laugh, with no mirth in it. "Ach, yes, I know," he said. "Do you wish me to tell you?"

The words sounded almost taunting, like he was playing a game with her, like Ella was too stupid to be believed. Like what he'd just done, that unfathomable pleasure he'd just given her, had been entirely negligible, when weighed against this, whatever the hell this was.

Ella still hadn't spoken, hadn't moved, and suddenly Natt turned away from her, striding across the small room. Reaching down for his sword-belt, still lying innocuously on the floor, and as he strapped it on with deft fingers, it was almost as though he was arming himself against her. Against this, against *them*.

"Natt," Ella heard her voice say, snapping his eyes back toward her—but then she couldn't seem to find the rest of the words, or the way out of this. And as Natt waited, she could see his lip curling, the contempt rising, he'd never been angry with her like this before, this wasn't at all how it was supposed to be—

"Natt," Ella said again, helpless, lost. "Look, I—I'm sorry. If things were different, I would come with you. I swear. All right?"

But Natt was shaking his head, hard enough to swing his long braid back and forth behind him. "No, lass," he replied, clipped. "You would not. You have changed. You now only care for these riches, and the wishes and regard of others. Other *humans*. Not me. *Never* me."

Never him. Suddenly Ella felt dangerously, desperately close to sobbing, and she lurched to her feet, standing on shaky legs. "No," she shot back. "I loved you, Natt. I *loved* you. And then you *left*, and I never saw you *again*."

There was only stillness from him now, only a caught arrested strangeness in his eyes, and Ella gulped for air, for reason. "You didn't ask," she gasped. "You didn't even give me a chance to speak. You just *left*. Of course I can't trust you. I can't trust *anybody* anymore. I need to be in this for *myself*."

But Natt had only raised a mocking eyebrow, his mouth contorting into a harsh, bitter smile. "And thus," he said, "you shall now leave me, after I have given you such joy, and instead you shall wed a foul piddling *warmonger*, who scorns a true prize like you, and betrays you with another, at your own party. In your own *home*."

Ella could almost *feel* the rage, reverberating from his voice, from his eyes, from every corded muscle in his huge looming body. Looking powerful and suddenly, shockingly terrifying, his clawed hand gripped tight to his sword-hilt. And as Ella blinked up and down his massive armed form, she recalled, far too late, that he was an *orc*. A vicious, brutal, deadly orc, who killed for sport, who'd wanted to kill *Alfred*, and what would he do next, trap her, make her stay—

But—no. He stepped backwards, abruptly, and somehow he had Ella's mud-caked slippers in his hand. And he was—holding them out toward her. Giving them to her.

"Farewell, woman," he said. "I hope that you shall find some joy in this fate you choose. And I hope, beyond hope, that this man shall be kinder to you"—his eyes closed—"than he has been to me."

What? Ella should have stopped him there, asked what in the gods' names he meant—but everything was too tangled, too horrible to be spoken aloud. And instead, she felt herself swallow, her shaky hand reaching out for her slippers.

"Right," her hoarse voice said, through her too-tight throat. "Good-bye, Natt."

And when she grasped for the door-latch, he still only stood there, and didn't stop her. And Ella choked down the rising misery as she turned her back to him, and staggered away into the darkness, and ran.

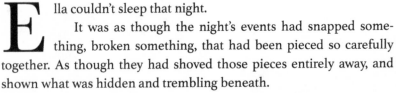

6

Ella couldn't sleep that night.

It was as though the night's events had snapped something, broken something, that had been pieced so carefully together. As though they had shoved those pieces entirely away, and shown what was hidden and trembling beneath.

And beneath had been a fearful, uneasy woman who'd crept back into her house, fastidiously washed herself all over, and sharply ordered her maid to help her re-dress. And when she'd gone back down to the party, she'd smiled and smiled until her face ached, even at Alfred—who, of course, had been the very epitome of gentlemanly manners. As though he were the type of man who would never dream of fondling another woman in his fiancé's front drawing-room, on the night of their engagement-party.

And as Ella and Alfred had danced together, and spoken lightly of this and that, Ella hadn't once asked the questions now screaming in her thoughts. *Why would you disrespect me like that. Do you care about me at all. What do you mean to do with my father's money. What are you doing with the orcs. What have you done to Natt.*

And that, perhaps, was the worst of them all. Natt had been clear that Alfred had done *something*—hadn't he?—and while Ella knew, intellectually, that lords had to direct armies and make difficult decisions and deal with problems like orcs, it somehow hadn't occurred to her that Alfred might do that. Or that her father's money might *help* Alfred do that. And Alfred's own *father* had signed that peace-treaty, along with Sakkin Province's well-respected new ruler Lord Otto—so why would Alfred be doing *anything* against the orcs now?

It all swirled louder and faster through Ella's thoughts as the night plodded endlessly on—until it was finally, finally late enough that she could safely claim exhaustion, and say her farewells, and make her escape.

Or so she'd thought. But before she'd gotten halfway up the staircase, she'd been interrupted by—Alfred. Bounding up the stairs two at a time, and giving her a stunning, sheepish smile.

"Darling, wait," he'd said, all tall handsome warmth. "Should you, perhaps, welcome a bit of company, for a while? Now that we've properly announced, I'm sure your mother will finally look the other way."

He'd said that last part with a meaningful wink, and for the first time in perhaps years, Ella had almost felt grateful for her distant, dragonish mother, with all her fervent enforcement of Ella's propriety. Because even the thought of Alfred touching her, after tonight, after *Natt*, had sent a racing chill to Ella's bones, and an unwilling surge of bile to her throat.

"Perhaps not tonight," she'd replied, as smoothly as she'd been able. "I'm afraid it's *that* time, with my courses."

She couldn't quite believe she'd spoken of such things aloud—*again*—but Alfred's replying look of pure, unadulterated disgust had proven a highly apt closer on the entire disastrous evening. And once Ella had finally, finally been alone, she'd sobbed and sobbed and sobbed, until there'd been nothing left but emptiness.

She stared blankly at the ceiling as the hours slowly passed, as the sounds of gaiety below finally faded into silence. As the visions of Natt, the memories of Natt, kept rising and rising, trampling merciless and desperate through her thoughts.

Will you have me, lass. You have kept your maidenhead. You shall wed a foul piddling warmonger. You only care for these riches.

Never me.

But of *course* it had never been Natt. There had never even been a choice. Not with Ella's father, her mother, the fortune. Ella had always been expected to make a good marriage, to finally confirm her family's good standing. She couldn't love an orc. Especially one who had left her like that, and hadn't even said *goodbye*.

And lying here alone in the bitter silence, Ella could finally, perhaps, face the truth of just how painful that had been. So strong that she'd spent all these years trying and failing to shove Natt away, thrust him out of her mind, pretend he'd never existed. Pretend the orcs didn't exist. Pretend not to pay any attention to talks of battles or threats or peace-treaties. Pretend that she'd never loved an *orc*, who'd hurt her more than any human before or since.

Gods, it was ridiculous, and gods, Ella just needed to get over it. She was engaged to an earl's son. She was on the verge of gaining everything her family had ever wanted. It would be fine. It had to be.

She repeated that to herself as she lay there, enough that she perhaps almost believed it. Until—her eyes snapped open—she heard a sound.

A sound that didn't belong. Close. Scraping just outside her window.

Ella lurched up in bed, the room whirling, her heart suddenly racing in her chest. Surely it was nothing. Just a branch, a bird, a figment of her fevered beleaguered brain—

But as she stared, something sharp and black slid under the sash— and then the sash *moved up*. Slow, inexorable, her window was opening *by itself*, and Ella was losing her damned mind—

And she was, she had to be, because beyond the open window there was now a face, scarred and hideous and utterly terrifying. And as Ella's mouth slowly opened to scream, a massive, hulking dark figure hurled itself through the window, rolled on the floor toward her, and rose up to clamp a huge hand over her mouth.

"Do not shout," a voice hissed, close and hot and appallingly, abjectly horrifying. "Or your whole house shall *die*."

7

Do not shout. Or your whole house shall die.

Ella bit back the scream just in time, choking it desperately down her throat, but her body was already flailing, kicking, drowning her in the pure barrelling panic. She was being attacked, she might be taken, she might *die*, and her attacker was massive and muscled and breathtakingly strong, shoving her down hard into the bed, his black braid falling over his shoulder—

Wait. *Wait.* The clarity was suddenly, shockingly powerful, piercing through Ella's entire being all at once—and she gaped at the huge familiar body above her, and dragged in the telltale musky scent with every thick, gasping breath.

It was—*Natt.*

Her body seemed to lose its fight all at once, sagging heavy into the soft bed beneath her, and she could feel Natt's big body relaxing too, though his clawed hand was still clamped over her mouth.

"Good," his low voice whispered, tickling close against her ear. "Shall you shout, if I release you?"

Ella shook her head under his hand, the movement desperate, compulsive—but he didn't move the hand, and as she blinked up at his face over her, she could just make out the glint of his eyes in the faint moonlight. "If you do, woman," he hissed, "I shall kill every human in this house but you."

Gods. Ella couldn't help a choked whimper against his hand, the fear jolting hard and wide—but her head gave another frantic nod, and after an instant's stillness, that hand slowly, carefully lifted. And Ella could breathe again, and she dragged in deep, heaving gulps of air, her eyes wildly searching the shadowed face above her.

"What the *hell*," she managed, in a whisper, "are you *doing*, Natt?"

But there was only another moment's stillness, the feel of that warm, heavy body shifting above her, settling itself close. And instead of speaking, that dark head lowered itself against her exposed neck, and *smelled* her.

The truth of it, the twisting familiarity of it, seemed to catch at the still-spiralling terror, breaking it off sharp and sideways. And instead, there was only this, Natt's huge muscled body pinning her to the soft bed, his scent filling her lungs, his bare chest hot and damp against her flimsy sleeping-shift.

His breath was still inhaling, filling his chest with the scent of her—and *that*, oh gods, was the feel of his warm mouth, kissing soft against her neck. And then harder, giving way to his sliding tongue, his sharp teeth, scraping close against her skin.

And rather than screaming, shoving, guarding her virtue her very *self*, Ella's wholly traitorous body had seemed to arch up against him, pressing tight. Earning an immediate, replying surge of his weight over her, his hips circling strong and deep, the telltale huge ridge at his groin grinding just *there*, straight between her already parted legs, oh *hell*—

And it was only when those sharp, teasing, desperately thrilling teeth at her neck pressed harder, hinting at actual shearing *pain*, that Ella's awareness seemed to swerve back into place, juddering all at once. Natt had broken into her room, threatened to kill her household, and now he was actually, honestly about to *bite* her—

Ella kicked and shoved and flailed at him, far too late—but thank the gods, he backed away, his big body lurching off the bed with astonishing speed. Leaving Ella lying there spread-eagled on the bed, her sleeping-shift thrust up almost to her hips, her dazed eyes blinking as her shaky hand came up to her neck, feeling the tender, inflamed skin.

"The *hell*, Natt," she gasped, choked, and didn't miss the sight of that long tongue snaking out, licking slow and deliberate at his lips. As if to catch every last taste of her, as if he were still longing for her blood...

Ella could only seem to stare, while the fear once again thudded and soared, and Natt gave a quick, twitchy shake of his head. And then only stood there, looking at her, while she looked at him, and her thundering heartbeat sought to pound its way out her chest.

"Ach," his voice said, finally, almost a whisper, and his hand came up, rubbing hard against his mouth. "You shall rise, lass, and dress."

Rise, and dress. Ella was staring again, caught entirely dumbfounded, and there was a jerky, impatient wave of Natt's clawed hand, toward her adjoining dressing-chamber. "Up," he said. "Dress. Warm clothes. For travel."

What? There was still no possible way to move, or speak, and finally Natt's huge form moved again, now coming over to grasp beneath Ella's arm. Drawing her up, and out of bed, and half-guiding, half-dragging her trembly body toward the dressing-chamber.

"Dress," he insisted. "Now, lass."

Dress. For travel, he'd said. And it was as Ella stood there, alone in her dressing-chamber with an orc, that she finally, finally understood what he meant. Dress. For travel. Natt was—he was—

"You're serious?!" she hissed at him, gaping at his black bulk in the darkness. "You're—*kidnapping* me, Natt?"

There was only silence from his huge shadow, looming in this small room over her, but he was, he would, this couldn't be happening, it couldn't, not now—

"You swore to me tonight," he said finally, his voice hoarse, "that if aught was different, you should come away with me. Ach, so now it is, and now you shall come."

Ella kept staring, open-mouthed, trapped. "You—you can't," she gasped. "You *can't*, Natt. I have a *wedding*."

There was an immediate, guttural growl from Natt's throat, making his view on said wedding far too clear, and Ella's thoughts frantically cast about, grasping for purchase. "And," she breathed, "and the—the *peace-treaty*. You're not *allowed* to kidnap women anymore. They—they'll chase you, and catch you, and *p-punish* you, Natt."

It was appalling, how that thought seemed to dredge up even more fear, more jangling choking misery—but Ella could just make out the hard, reflexive shake of Natt's head in the darkness. "No," he hissed. "They shall not. For you"—and that was the feel of his claw, touching light but purposeful against her chest—"shall leave a letter. And in this letter, you shall say you have gone east with this man, at his sudden demand last eve, to stay with his kin, and ready your new home for this wedding."

Shit. That wouldn't possibly work, or could it—but as Ella's brain circled it, considered it, there was the unnerving, twitching realization that perhaps, *perhaps*, it might. Alfred had in fact planned to ride home again late last night—there had been some urgent council of lords he'd needed to attend—and he wasn't set to return again until just before the wedding.

And while Ella's mother would be furious to learn of such a secret departure, she also wouldn't dare to write Alfred to question him on it, not now. And Alfred was just as unlikely to write to Ella or her mother, and that would give Natt an entire unquestioned *month* with her, to do with her whatever he wished—

"No," Ella gasped. "No, Natt. I *won't*. I refuse. I've been working toward this wedding for months. *Years*. And I only have a month left until the deadline, until I lose *everything*. You can't ruin this for me. You *can't*."

But there was only a close, curdling stillness, and then the feel of Natt stepping silently closer in the darkness. "You mistake me, woman," his voice said, very low, very steady. "You think you have a choice in this, when you do not. You shall dress. You shall write this letter. And *you shall come*."

It was a threat, a promise, sending more jagged bolts of fear down Ella's spine, the panic roaring high in her chest—and without thought, without sense, she was running. Shoving past Natt, darting out into the room, sprinting straight for the door—

But then something huge and hard and hot grasped onto her from behind, dragging her bodily away from the door, and again clamping tight over her mouth. And as Ella's flailing body kicked and swarmed and shouted at him, he only yanked her up closer, his hand pulling back harder, twisting her head sideways—and then, once again, there were *teeth*. On her bared exposed neck, lingering close and sharp and deadly. Waiting to bite, to tear, to *destroy*.

"You shall come," that mouth hissed, soft, cruel, vicious, against her throat. "And you shall either walk hale and upright beside me, or I shall carry your limp body, once I have drunk my fill from you. Which shall it be, woman."

Ella was shuddering all over, the fear screaming wide and bright in her skull, and for an instant there was the twisting, overpowering urge to say, *Bite me, kill me, do as you wish, you horrible wild beast*—but then, slicing strong and strange through her thoughts, was the realization that Natt was—shaking.

And yes, Natt's chest, Natt's hands, Natt's sharp deadly teeth against her skin, were trembling just as badly as she was. And his breath was loud and lurching against her ear, coming in heavy dragging gulps— and suddenly, somehow, the fight seemed to drain away from Ella's body, all at once. Natt didn't *want* to do this. But he would, if he had to.

I have been missing you, lass. I have been dreaming of how you tasted. I longed to make you my mate. I knew this could not be, for us.

Never me.

And somehow, trapped here in this gasping orc's arms, Ella found the strength, or the madness, to nod. Again, and again, scraping her tender neck against those waiting, trembling sharp teeth, until that shaking hand fell from her mouth. Wanting her to speak.

"Yes," she whispered. "Yes, Natt. I'll come."

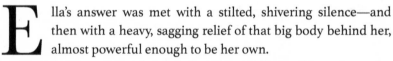

8

Ella's answer was met with a stilted, shivering silence—and then with a heavy, sagging relief of that big body behind her, almost powerful enough to be her own.

There was a moment's harsh breathing, whether his or hers, she wasn't certain—and then a quiet, unbearably soft kiss to her exposed neck, to where his teeth had scraped against it. "Good lass," his voice whispered, wavering in the silence. "Brave lass."

But then he backed abruptly away, his strong warmth vanishing from her all at once. And for an inexplicable, twisting instant, Ella blinked at its loss, almost wanting to follow it—but then she bit her lip, and shook her head, hard. Natt was *kidnapping* her. And he'd just threatened—very viscerally—to *kill* her if she refused.

So she didn't move, didn't speak, and for a moment, neither did Natt—but then his body seemed to twitch, and he strode across the room, toward the table beside her bed. And as Ella blinked, he reached for the half-burned candlestick that had been sitting there, and with a sparking flick of his claws, suddenly it was burning, fluttering with a steady flame.

And at the sight of that, the shock of recognition seemed to flare all at once in Ella's scrambled thoughts. The memories of him doing that in the woods, lighting fire to nearly anything with just a snap of his claws—including, once, accidentally, to his own hair. And Ella had laughed until her sides had ached, until the devious bastard had grasped for her own long braid, and held it up gently, almost reverently, in those beautiful sharp claws.

It had been a threat, enough to make Ella's laughter fade into stillness—but all the same, it hadn't been a true threat at all, because she'd known he would never hurt her. And of course he hadn't, and instead he'd brought the end of her braid to his face, and inhaled it, and given her a slow, rueful smile.

Ella belatedly squeezed her eyes shut, fighting to block the memory away—but somehow, there was enough truth in it, enough strength in it, to propel her shaky legs toward the dressing-chamber. Toward the wardrobe, where she began carding through her many beautiful, frivolous frocks, searching for something warm. For travel.

She could almost feel Natt's astonished stillness, watching her across the room—but then, to her surprise, he was there, *here*, standing close in the dressing-chamber beside her. Starting from the other side, trailing his claw slow and careful along the rows of silk and gauze and lace.

"Are these all you have, lass?" he asked, quiet, tentative, almost an offering in the candlelight. "Where are the kinds of frocks you once wore?"

He meant back when they'd run in the forest—had he been thinking of that too?—and Ella found herself shrugging, her face gone oddly hot as she thought of those old, sensible garments of sturdy cotton and wool. "They're gone. I don't need those kinds of clothes anymore."

There was an instant's silence, a likely fatal clench of Natt's clawed hand against a chemise of delicate lace. "Why do you not?" he demanded. "What keeps you warm when you are out of this house?"

Ella gave another uncomfortable shrug, a grimace at the rows of dresses before her. "I don't go out anymore," she said. "Not really. I mean, the servants do all the gardening and shopping, I travel by heated carriage, and the sun and wind are really quite terrible for one's hair and skin, especially when one wishes to wed a *lord*, like Papa wanted, so—"

Far too late she clamped her mouth shut—why in the gods'

names was she saying such things, to an *orc*, who was currently in the act of *kidnapping* her—but said orc's brows had already snapped together with clear confusion. "It grieved me to hear of your father, lass, and I am sorry you have had to bear this pain. But"—his voice hardened—"did you not oft roam and ride and play together with your father also? Why should he wish you to lose this joy, after his death?"

The memories flared across Ella's thoughts, too bright and vivid, and still painfully bittersweet. *You deserve this*, my girl, he would say, with such warmth and pride on his weathered face. *I know it's hard, but your mother's got the right of it, you'll see. Best to do what she says, so you'll fit right in. Just imagine, my own daughter, a real fine lady.*

Ella fixed her blinking eyes to the row of lovely fabrics and lace, and drew in air. "He wanted this future for me, more than all else," she said, her voice only slightly hitching. "He wanted me to make him proud. To *belong*."

But Natt only growled, a burr of deep disapproval in his throat. "So to *belong*, you must no longer speak?" he snapped. "Or walk? Or run? Or climb? You must no longer meet with your own *forest*? What folly is this, woman?"

And before Ella could think, or react, Natt had grasped for her wrist, shoved up the sleeve of her sleeping-shift, and then turned her arm over, once, twice, almost as if truly seeing it, for the first time. And then he placed it carefully back down by her side, his lip curling with unmistakable distaste. "You have been made weak, to please these foolish men," he said flatly. "This should not be, lass."

Ella couldn't seem to find a response for that—it was utterly absurd that Natt was standing here passing judgement, when he was the one who'd just threatened to *kill* her—but then he yanked something out from behind all her clothes, something her distant great-aunt Maura had sent her as a gift. A hideous, baggy, tweedy suit-dress, entirely practical, and so deeply unfashionable as to be actually offensive to Ella's eyes.

"Absolutely not," Ella snapped. "I will *not* wear that thing in public, I *refuse*—"

But then, without warning, Natt's hand reached out, and grasped for a chunk of her hair. And as Ella's heart seemed to lurch to her throat, his other hand snapped its claws, making them spark in the dim light.

So he *had* been thinking of that, too. And it *was* a threat, but still not quite, trapping Ella whole in this tangled, twisted instant. And if he brought her hair to his face, if he smiled at her like he had back then, even the very thought made her want to weep—

But he only dropped her hair again, and thrust out the ugly dress toward her. And curse her, but Ella silently took it, and pulled it on over her sleeping-shift while he watched. And when he made a turn-around motion with his claw, she even obeyed, twitching at the surreal, ridiculous feeling of an orc, fastening up her *dress*, and when had he learned such things, had he been doing this with other women, all these years?

Once he'd finally finished, and Ella had stiffly turned back around, it was to the discovery that he was now holding out a pair of short, ratty woollen stockings, and—she groaned—a pair of ancient, hideous leather riding-boots. But he only thrust them toward her, the stubbornness all too clear in his eyes, so Ella gave an exasperated sigh, and obediently took them, and knelt to tug them on.

When she rose again, Natt had stepped back to frown at her, his gaze sweeping up and down—and then he stalked away, and went to snatch up the heavy sheepskin from the foot of her bed. And then he came back, swinging it over her shoulders before reaching behind him to yank out a thick silken sash from one of her frocks. And with a hard puncture of his claw, he'd threaded the sash through the sheepskin, and then tied it close around her throat, almost as if it were a cloak.

"Good," he said, with a curt nod. "Now, you shall write this letter."

Ella couldn't help a roll of her eyes at him, but he only stared straight back, and jerked his head toward her writing-desk. So she sighed again, and went to sit at the desk, and pulled out a quill and ink, and a fresh sheet of paper.

But here, again, the reality of this, of what she was doing right now, seemed to rise bright and chaotic in her thoughts—and there was the urge, sudden and compulsive, to simply write the truth. She couldn't remember if Natt had been able to read, back then—she herself had never been much of a scholar, so she'd never brought books around—and likelier than not he couldn't read, and she could therefore say, *I've been stolen away by an orc, I shall leave some kind of trail, please come rescue me at once—*

"Now, woman," interrupted Natt's hard voice. "And should you seek to leave hints in this letter, I shall see this, and make you write it all again. You shall write it just as if you would, if it were truth. In your own hand, and your own voice."

Damn the bastard, but there was no other choice, so while Natt watched over her shoulder, Ella carefully wrote the letter. Telling her mother about Alfred's last-minute offer, his insistence, his unwillingness to be parted from her for another whole month. Even—Ella winced, but wrote it anyway—how Alfred had insisted on her bringing very few clothes and goods, so he could have the pleasure of providing new frocks and trinkets for her, at her new home.

"This is good," Natt said firmly, tapping his claw at that particular line, once the ink had dried. "If this man were in truth a good man, who felt as he should about a prize such as you, this is just what he should do."

The words clenched deep in Ella's belly, but she gave a twitchy nod, and left the letter out on the desk, where she knew it would be found. And when she stood again, looking up at Natt's huge form before her, she felt strangely dizzy, numb. She was being kidnapped by an orc. She was being stolen from her home, against her will, under threat of her own *death*.

But when Natt's hand came down to find hers, his big clawed fingers threading close between her own, there was another odd shock of familiarity, of warmth, of ease. Enough to keep her head held high, her body still, her eyes steady on his.

"My good, brave lass," Natt's voice said, soft, warm, so approving it made something ache, deep inside. "Now come with me."

There was nothing else to do, locked in this moment, in his hand, in his shimmering eyes. So Ella nodded, and took a breath, and went.

9

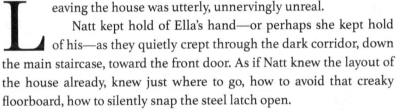

eaving the house was utterly, unnervingly unreal.

Natt kept hold of Ella's hand—or perhaps she kept hold of his—as they quietly crept through the dark corridor, down the main staircase, toward the front door. As if Natt knew the layout of the house already, knew just where to go, how to avoid that creaky floorboard, how to silently snap the steel latch open.

He led her out into the chilly autumn darkness, and then drew her around the side of the house to the shrubbery beneath her window. Where—Ella's breath caught—he'd stashed his sword, and a heavy-looking pack, and a waterskin.

"You didn't even have your *sword* up there?" Ella hissed at him, appalled, because how had she not noticed that fact? "How the *hell* were you planning to kill my whole household?"

There was a twitch of a smile on his mouth in the moonlight, and he took a long, gulping drink from the waterskin. "I ken I might have choked them," he said, holding out the waterskin toward her. "Or mayhap drunk their blood, after I feasted upon yours."

His mouth was still quirking, the fiend, as though threatening to kill Ella's entire household was all an amusing *joke*, and Ella snatched the waterskin from his hand, and took a long, fortifying drink. While her thoughts turned, and turned again, and if he truly *hadn't* meant to kill anyone after all, maybe she could run back, and start screaming—

But as always, Natt seemed to see far too much, and the instant she'd finished drinking, he stuffed the waterskin into his pack, and immediately began striding off toward the forest, dragging Ella by the hand after him. "We shall walk, and run," he said, over his shoulder. "We must build your strength again."

Ella glared at his broad bare back, and she had to jog to catch up, to fall into a trotting step beside him. "And where, exactly," she demanded, "are you taking me?"

Natt's eyes shifted, casting toward the south, and Ella felt her steps falter, her gaze following his. Toward the mountains. Toward—*Orc Mountain.*

Oh. Oh, *gods.* Of course Natt would take her to *Orc Mountain.* And as often as Ella had looked at it over the years, perhaps even admiring its craggy smoking bulk, it was still an impenetrable fortress, teeming with vicious orcs, threatening injury and imprisonment to any humans who ventured near. And to women, more than all else, because even as Ella had fought to ignore the tales, she'd still heard of how the orcs would share women, pass them around, use them again and again until their bellies swelled full and their huge sons broke free—

No. *No.* Suddenly Ella's feet were scrabbling, kicking up earth, fighting to run. Needing to escape this horrible fate, to get away, back home, somewhere, anywhere, *please*—but Natt's hand was still clamped firmly to hers, their fingers intertwined. And that big body spun very close, too close, radiating warmth against her, while his other clawed hand came around to her back, snapping her flailing form tight against him.

"Hear this, lass," he said, his voice firm. "This mountain is not what you humans think. Have you forgotten what I once told you, of this?"

Had she forgotten. And blinking up at his intent watching eyes, it was far too easy to dredge up the memories, the words, the way his mouth had twisted as he'd spoken. *I know what you humans say of this mountain,* he'd said. *But it is not just this. It is a place made for those like me. It speaks its tales of ages and heroes past. It is the only place I am truly safe.*

Ella swallowed hard, but her heart was still racing, the fear churning deep. "It might be safe for *you*," her shaky voice countered. "But I'm a *woman*, Natt."

Natt's arm against her back suddenly felt very large, his body huge and hot and close above her. And as Ella blinked up at his scarred face, there was a twitch on his mouth, and—she gasped—also at his groin, that telltale hardness flaring thick and powerful against her belly.

"Ach," he said, "you are, lass. But you are *my* woman. I shall keep you safe."

His woman. The sheer, brazen audacity of that statement was enough to catch Ella up short, her body gone stiff and breathless against him—and when she shoved hard at his solid chest, thankfully he backed away, though his eyes had shuttered, his hand still clamped tight to hers.

"I am *not*," she managed, "your *property*, Nattfarr. I *never have been*, especially since you disappeared for nine whole *years*. And if you think that me coming with you tonight somehow *changes* that, you'd do well to remember that you threatened to *kill* me if I refused!"

Those eyes narrowed, gone to glittering slits in the moonlight, and Ella could feel the slight flex of his claws against her hand. "I did not," he said, "threaten your death. I would never do this."

Ella heard herself laugh, hoarse and high-pitched. "You did," she said, her voice rising. "You said you would bite me, and feast upon my *blood*, and carry my body away!"

"Ach," Natt growled back, his lip curling. "And you would yet live, and soon regain your strength. I should never kill you. We swore a *pledge*."

Oh, so they were back to *that* again, and Ella scoffed at him, and gave a hard shake of her head. "No," she snapped, "we were young, and stupid, and you asked me what I thought was a stupid, meaningless question, so I gave you a stupid, meaningless answer!"

The snarl from his throat was steady, simmering, and he shook his head too, whipping his braid behind him. "No," he said. "You knew. You are not a fool, lass, as much as you might now wish to act the part. I asked for your fealty, and you gave it!"

Ella felt briefly struck still, staring at this appalling orc's appalling face. And instead of arguing that last point, like she perhaps should have, she jabbed a finger into his bare chest, and gulped at the too-thin air. "And then you *left*! You *left*, and you never even bothered to say *goodbye*!"

Natt's eyes were still narrow, still angry, and he shook his head again, jerkier this time. "I had reasons for this, woman."

"Yes, you said," Ella shot back. "You thought I would choose my cushy pampered life and my money over you, so you didn't bother asking! How the hell was I supposed to choose *you*, when you weren't even an *option*?!"

Natt's eyes blinked, once—but then his gaze flicked away, toward the nearby forest over her shoulder. Avoiding her, shutting her out, and the replying anger sparked bright and explosive in Ella's thoughts. "And then," she gasped, "you have the utter *audacity* to show up almost ten years later, and break into my house, and kidnap me against my will, and take me to *Orc Mountain*! I am *not yours*, Nattfarr!"

Natt's eyes snapped back toward her, something jumping in his hard jaw. "We swore a pledge," he hissed. "You bear my scent. You gave me leave to kiss you, and taste you, and *drink* you. *You kept your maidenhead for me.*"

There was a grim triumph on his voice, as though this were a convincing closing argument, rather than utter *rubbish*, and Ella gave a frantic, furious shake of her head. "No," she countered. "I did no such thing. I was trying to wed a *lord*. And if my maidenhead were not a valuable currency in such a transaction, I should have eagerly given it to Alfred *months* ago!"

The sound from Natt's mouth was deep and guttural and dangerous, almost like a bark. "No," he growled back. "You would not, and you did not, and now you *never shall*!"

Ella's entire body was vibrating with rage, like the fury was a breathing living thing, and she fought and failed to yank her hand away from his crushing grip. "You *swine*," she breathed. "Of course I shall. You shall safely return me home, before this wedding, so you don't break that peace-treaty, and singlehandedly start another *war*. And then, I will marry Alfred, as planned, and finally become a *real* lady, and he will take me to bed as often as he damn well pleases!"

Her voice had cracked at the last, perhaps betraying more than she meant—but there was another one of those guttural barks from Natt's throat, deep and raw and broken. "No. You shall not. You shall not betray me thus. You shall not betray your own *self* thus. You care not for this man, this man cares not for you, he shall take you and use you and *destroy* you, lass!"

Ella's head was wildly shaking, so hard she nearly stumbled sideways. "I don't care," she heard her wavering voice say. "I don't. I'm in this for my family, and for *me*. I'll keep my home, and I'll be a *lady*. I will *matter*. I'll *belong*."

The look in Natt's eyes was something Ella had never seen before, the clutch of his clawed hand almost painful on hers. "You shall not belong," his voice croaked. "You shall *never* belong with them. You belong here, in these trees, under the sun. You belong with *me*."

It was like the words were scraping deep inside Ella, clawing ragged at her very soul, and the shake of her head was compulsive, desperate, panicked. "No," she choked out. "I don't. I won't. I can't, Natt. I can't, I can't, I *can't*!"

She was very near to sobbing, for reasons she couldn't even begin to follow, and she felt her free hand grasp for Natt's muscled arm, gripping with all her strength. Almost as if needing him to see her, to know, to understand—he *had* to understand—and his unreadable eyes had followed her hand, blinking hard down toward it. Her thin pale fingers digging into his grey-green skin, her taut trembling body leaning close and desperate into him, the cursed wetness streaking down her cheek—

"I can't, Natt," she whispered. "I *can't*."

And when those eyes came back to hers, their blackness almost seemed to widen, to twine deep into her soul. While she kept pleading with them, begging them, he had to, he *had* to—

There was the sound of Natt's breath, heaving in and out of his chest—and then movement, *life*. His big body whirling strong against her, around her, dragging her up whole and safe into his arms.

And before Ella could think or speak or even breathe, Natt turned, kicked off, and *ran*. Not toward Orc Mountain, but toward—Ella gasped, close into his hot sweaty chest—the *hunting-cottage*.

He thrust the door open with his foot, striding easy and familiar inside, and then he slammed the door shut behind them, just as easy, without even looking. And suddenly it was like time had reversed, the world spun wholly back again, as Natt dropped his sword, stalked across the small room, and all but hurled Ella's shaky, pliant form down onto the couch beneath the window.

Ella stared, aghast and whimpering, and there was another flurry of movement, his huge muscled body coming up tall and close over her. Straddling her on the couch, as those hands went to the waist of his trousers, and thrust them downwards.

And there, before Ella's maiden eyes, was a massive, raging orc-prick. Long and thick and swollen, and already dripping with copious white.

"You can do this, woman," he said, his voice an oath, a deep new pledge, rumbling rich and powerful between them. "And you *will*."

10

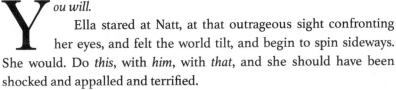

You will.

Ella stared at Natt, at that outrageous sight confronting her eyes, and felt the world tilt, and begin to spin sideways. She would. Do *this*, with *him*, with *that*, and she should have been shocked and appalled and terrified.

But instead, she just kept staring at him. At *that*. Hovering so near to her face, dripping that sticky-looking white from a deep slit at the tapered tip. And just as thrilling, further down, was the thick veined length of it, the mass of black hair at the base, the taut ridges of his abdomen above, the swollen heavy bollocks hanging below. And Ella had never seen such a sight, had never once properly imagined what it would look like, or smell like, all musky woodsy maleness, heady and delicious enough to bring water to her mouth.

A brief glance up at Natt's eyes showed them gone to hard, glittering slits as he looked down at her, and something seemed to stutter in Ella's thoughts, breaking off stilted and breathless. Snatching, suddenly, at the visions of just hours ago—had it only been hours ago?—when his wicked tongue had spread her apart, opened her up, drunk her from the inside out...

But Natt was breathing hard now, his eyes squeezed shut tight, and Ella's dazed, streaming thoughts still recognized that look, from so long ago. It was the same as how he'd looked when he'd smelled her, or touched her, and then pulled himself away. And he was *not* doing it again, the bastard, so Ella drew a breath, drew in courage, hunger, *madness*—and then leaned forward, and took his hard, dripping cock-head into her mouth.

Natt's gasp was hoarse and unfeigned, his entire body gone taut and arrested over her—but Ella scarcely noticed, suddenly, because he was in her mouth, and he felt strange, and utterly new, and *glorious*. Vibrating thick and hard and *alive* between her lips, pumping out more of that viscous liquid onto her tongue, and oh that was good too, a smooth musky sweetness. The essence of him, of Ella's orc, slipping down her throat, *hers*.

She heard herself moan around him, and he was moaning too, his huge hands abruptly coming to her hair, her face. Tilting her chin upwards so he could look at her, she could look at him, his eyes already glazing with hunger as she sucked harder, took him deeper into her mouth.

"Oh, my lass," he murmured, his voice rough and raw, sending sharp shudders down Ella's spine. "Look at you, with my prick in your sweet little mouth. Suck me, yes, drink me, taste me, *ach*—"

The words broke off into moans, his eyes on hers as that huge heft slid slightly in, and then out again. Vibrating against Ella's tongue, dripping more of that sweet liquid down her throat, and she sucked harder, sought to relax, to welcome him inside. Just the way she'd welcomed his invasions before, his thorough trampling of her inno-cence underfoot, and if only she'd known it would be this good, she'd missed out on this for years and years and *years*—

She felt herself sucking harder, taking less care to keep her teeth out of the way, and she heard him hiss, his sharp claws now touching light against her hairline, perhaps in a silent warning. And he was such an utter *bastard* and he'd denied her this for *years*, so in return Ella *did* let her teeth scrape, not hard, but enough to make him rear back, a deep growl rumbling from his throat.

But Ella didn't even blink, not at that, or his narrow-eyed frown down at her, or the way he was holding her head still, sliding himself back inside, bearing down deeper into her throat. Nearly making her gag on him, but Ella didn't care about that either, because it only brought out more of his sweetness, swarming succulent in her mouth.

She couldn't stop a helpless moan as she swallowed, and damn Natt but he saw it, he *knew*, and now he was speeding up, driving in and out and in again. Slicker and sloppier, bringing out noises that should have been humiliating, but were equal parts arousing and enraging, how *dare* this orc take his pleasure with her after what he'd done, after everything else he'd taken from her—

She shoved him away, hard, his cock bobbing out of her lips, stretching a string of gleaming white from her mouth—and in an instant his big body had gone utterly still, but for those claws, flexing sharp against her cheekbone. Stopping again, and Ella stared back, blinking, breathing hard—wait, he couldn't actually *stop*—and she grasped at his immobile hips, dragged at them, needed more, *please*—

"Don't stop," she gasped toward him. "*Please*, Natt. I want this from you. I've been waiting for so *long*."

His eyes blinked, astonishment warring with something not unlike rage—and suddenly there was a breathtaking flurry of movement, Ella's whole body spinning around, Natt's hands tight against her waist. And when the world came right side up again, it was with Ella kneeling on the couch, facing toward the window, with a furious orc standing behind her, and yanking her hideous dress off over her head, and then doing the same with the shift, and even her stockings and her boots, hurling it all to the floor beneath them.

It left Ella entirely bare to the room, she was naked with an *orc*— but he was touching her, caressing her, running his big hands down her sides like he owned her. And *gods* Ella craved this, craved more, even as she glared over her shoulder at him, and he glared back, shoved her down, bending her double, oh—

"You lie, woman," Natt said, his voice hard, accusing, as those strong hands went to her arse, tilted her up, opened her wide. "You have not waited for this. You did not *wish* for me to stay, and whelp my sons upon you."

Oh gods, oh please, because that—*that*—was his cock. Slick and smooth and powerful, touching just *there*, against Ella's quivering, swollen wetness. Feeling like honesty long lost, like deliverance, and

Ella let herself feel it, touch it, accept it. Let the truth flare up, and finally force its way free.

"I wanted it," she gasped. "*Gods*, yes, I wanted *you*. And you never even *asked*. Never gave me a chance to say yes. You just *disappeared*."

There was another hard growl, burning from his throat, and she could feel that tapered head nudging deeper, delving itself further inside. "You said, just this night, that you should not have wanted me," he hissed back. "You did not care for me, as I cared for you."

Gods, he was huge, and he felt so damn *good*, and Ella squeezed her eyes shut, willed herself to open, to breathe. "You really think I didn't *care* about you?" she heard herself say, her voice coming out far too high-pitched. "Did you never *notice* that I spent nearly every free moment traipsing about the forest with you, for years on end? Do you think my life has been *better*, these past nine years, without you?!"

The head of him had to be almost all the way inside now, breaching Ella, splitting her wide open upon it. And her own body was clenching and gripping against it, both resisting and welcoming it, and she could hear his breath, coming out harsh as he bore down deeper, cleaving her wider...

"It is what you wished for," his hard voice said behind her. "You *just* spoke this to me, woman. You wish to wed this man. You wish to be a fine lady. You wish to *matter*. Orcs like me do not matter, to selfish little humans like you."

There was a funny tilt to his voice at the end, a very slight thrust of that invading hardness further inside her. Enough to bring a gasp of shock to Ella's mouth, and more chaos to her already-screaming thoughts. He was speaking truth, but he wasn't, he was missing it, losing it, forgetting—

"You mattered, Natt," she heard her choked voice say. "And I would have come with you. I'd have given up *everything*. If you'd just—*asked*."

There was only silence behind her, stilted and empty, and somehow, without at all meaning to, Ella was weeping. Sobbing into the back of this ancient couch, her shoulders shaking, her whole body trembling, its only remaining strength the pulsing heft of that invading orc-prick, still speaking its own truth inside her.

But then that was gone too, drawn swiftly out and away, leaving her abandoned and empty. And *why* would he do that, after everything else he had done, and Ella whirled around toward him, to where his face was stricken and staring and shadowed in the stark moonlight.

"Ach," he said, his hand rubbing at his mouth, and his eyes squeezed shut, his head giving a hard shake. "I have—I ought—I ought not—"

He didn't finish, his head still shaking, and as Ella stared, his big body took a swift, purposeful step backward. Toward the door, away, and he wouldn't, he couldn't, no, not now, not when he'd finally come back, and she needed him so desperately—

Ella leapt up and yanked at him again, grasping at his broad shoulders, dragging him back toward the couch. And he didn't resist, thank the gods, just sank his big body heavily down onto it, blinking up at her with dazed, regretful eyes.

And now it was Ella's turn to straddle him, to spread her naked body over his hips, to hold his face in her hands. And there were no words, suddenly, and perhaps no need of them, as she reached downwards, found that thick hardness, and guided its smooth head back up toward her, settling it deep against her swollen, hungry heat.

Natt let out a harsh, guttural growl at the contact, his hands coming to slide against her hips, her waist. And now up to her bare breasts, smoothing soft and reverent against them, brushing a peaked nipple with a careful trace of his claw.

Ella was gasping too, lowering her weight just slightly down against that waiting heft, feeling it once again delving inside her. But it was still so huge, impossibly so, there was no way she could actually manage to do this, and she felt the sobs lurking up again, too close. He was here now, she had him now, but she didn't, what if she couldn't, what if he still just gave up and *left*—

But now those warm hands were back on her face, tilting it up. Making her look at him again, at his own strangely bright eyes, his trembling bottom lip. "Ach, lass," he whispered, his voice wavering. "You must breathe, and be soft, for me. We shall have this, now."

Now. Ella gulped for air, for the truth of that in his eyes, and felt herself nodding, her body sagging against him. Earning her the barest glimpse of white teeth, and then—oh gods—he leaned in, and pressed one of those soft, filthy kisses to her open, gasping mouth.

Ella's hands had fluttered down to his broad shoulders, her mouth suddenly desperate and craving against his, but he kept it easy, warm, succulent. His tongue twining gentle into her mouth, teasing her lips apart, coaxing her to reciprocate, to welcome his sweet, inexorable invasion.

"Yes," he whispered, once he'd pulled away, and given a slow, sensuous lick of his lips. "This is how it shall be. You shall again be soft and open, and welcome me inside you."

The warmth raced down Ella's spine, deep to the core of her, which was still being invaded by just the head of him. And just like before, when he'd done this with his mouth, with his fingers his tongue, she thought of softness, of openness, of welcoming him, Natt, where he should have been all this time. Where he belonged.

"Yes, lass," he murmured, his eyes dropping to the sight of his swollen cock, jutted just slightly up between Ella's spread legs. "Kiss me with your lips. Taste my seed. Feel how I long to fill you."

Ella felt herself moan at the words, at the feel of it, the truth of it. Her body kissing this driving hardness, tasting it, clenching and flaring against it. Feeling how it longed to be inside, how it was swelling and vibrating back against her, whispering its pleasure, its heat, its hunger.

"Yes," Natt said again, one hand still on her face, one now spreading wide against her bare hip. "Kiss it. Taste it. See how easy it is. How it is made to fill you."

And Ella could see that, could feel that. How it was so slick and smooth and tapered, made to spread her apart, and seek its way inside. How even now it was sinking further, breath by breath, her body still open, still kissing, welcoming its strange powerful fullness, deeper and deeper inside her.

"Good lass," Natt gasped, his eyes still intent on the sight, on his ramrod cock, halfway buried between Ella's legs. "Feel me inside you. Feel how my prick longs to surge my seed deep within you. Learn what it is"—his chest heaved, his eyes fluttering—"to offer your maiden-head to one who could have taken it, but did not."

Who could have taken it. Either now, perhaps, or previously, before Ella had been of age, and fully capable of understanding what it meant. And that was something too, that had been intended as a kindness, from an orc who was brutal, wicked, deadly, who had *kidnapped* her...

But the thought vanished as swiftly as it came, as he sank deeper inside her, tight and hot and close, but still bringing no pain. Working with her body, rather than against it, and this too was a gift from this orc, from *her* orc, and Ella dragged in a breath, settled herself deeper, felt him shudder and gasp in return.

"Ach, you shall do this," Natt said, husky and breathless, his eyes flicking back up to hers again, holding them intent and powerful. "You will take me, you will welcome me, you will seat your untouched womb full upon me without a single drop of blood. You kept your maidenhead for me, now I keep it for you, now I will feed you and fill you and *flood* you with my seed—"

And that was it, yes that was it, this orc's filthy words with the filthy driving kiss of his cock, and Ella could feel him finally sinking all the way home, her groin pressed flat and flush against his. And it was so tight, so full and raw and strange, and when her stretched-out body clenched, it was against a solid silken heat that—she gasped aloud—actually flared back against her, speaking silent and true and wonderful, inside her very *skin*.

"Oh," she choked, as her body reflexively clenched again, seemingly on its own—and again Natt's body spoke back, vibrating hard and full inside her. Bringing a helpless moan to Ella's mouth this time, and a hint of a sharp-toothed smile to his.

"Learn me, lass," he breathed. "Taste me. Milk the seed from me, and make it your own."

Gods, this orc, because Ella was already doing it, her hungry wet heat was doing it, twitching and throbbing against him, all around him. Feeling him speaking back, feeling the size and power of him buried so deep inside her, and if she were to settle just a bit closer, tilt the angle of her hips—

"Oh," she gasped again, even as he groaned too, eyelashes fluttering. Meaning he liked that, and she liked that, so she did it again. And this time he met her in it, his hips tilting against hers, angling himself slightly deeper inside. And fuck that was good, so good, so she did it again, again, again—

Natt met her every movement, gentle but purposeful, and there was the realization that he was letting her take the lead, feel her way. Not pushing, only meeting, using his body to guide to show to give, and that was so like him, speaking with his touch, his hands, his eyes.

And his eyes on her now were intent, watchful, worshipful. Like there was nothing in the world but her, but this moment, Ella firmly impaled on his lap, riding him, skewering her maidenhead upon him. Giving this, taking this, her back arching her mouth gasping, her body grinding harder deeper closer. A huge orc-prick inside her, Natt inside her, flaring and swelling and stretching her around him, he would give her his seed, he would give her life, she would have this she would have *him*, now—

His answering shout felt like it shook the room, his hips driving up, his big hands holding Ella down—and that strength deep inside her gave one final sinking gouge, and then fired. Spraying out with such force that she could feel it, spurting in pulse after pulse, drenching her all through with the proof of his promise.

It was a power unlike anything Ella had ever felt before, it was life and colour and madness. It was actual orc-seed within her, already spilling out between her legs, bathing them both in its truth.

And the orc who'd put it there, Natt, *hers*, had sagged back hard against the couch. Every taut corded muscle seeming to relax all at once, even the one still trapped deep and secret inside her.

"*Ach*," he breathed, his hands come to press against his eyes, and for an instant there was a surge of unease, spiking under Ella's skin—but then those hands were here, sliding back against her, dragging her down to lie flush against his sweaty, heaving chest.

"Are you all right?" Ella heard herself ask into his neck, her voice oddly tentative—but in reply his arms only circled tighter around her, his fingers spreading wide.

"Ach, lass," he said, warm and perhaps almost amused. "How could I not be all right. I have finally had my own fair, sweet, lovely woman. I have claimed your maidenhead for my own. I have honoured your pledge, and struck great vengeance upon my enemies. I have made you fully *mine*."

There was an unmistakable triumph in the words, rising as he spoke, and Ella pulled back to blink at him, to find those eyes looking at her. Looking warm, tolerant, undeniably affectionate, as his mouth tugged up into a slow, breathtaking smile.

"I am most pleased with you, lass," he murmured. "It is not always so easy to learn to ride an orc. I shall take great joy in showing you all the pleasure you may have upon me."

But those words were dragging at her, suddenly, pulling taut in the wrong directions, and Ella felt the warmth slowly ebbing away, pooling into darkness. *It is not always so easy. I have claimed your maidenhead. I have struck great vengeance upon my enemies...*

His enemy. Alfred. Ella's *betrothed*.

The panic screeched and soared all at once, driving deep into Ella's bones, and she gaped at Natt—at the orc—beneath her. The orc inside her, she'd just given her maidenhead to an *orc*, who'd kidnapped her, she was supposed to marry a *lord*—

She scrabbled backwards, kicking and shoving at him, but she was still trapped on him, he was still *inside her*—until those big hands carefully came to her waist, and lifted her off. Easing his huge heft out of her with a humiliating squelching noise, and Ella fought to ignore the sudden chilly emptiness as she lurched away, and onto her shaky feet—

But then, something seemed to catch and heave, deep and secret inside her. And before Ella could follow, think, hide—there was a *flood*. A flood of hot white orc-seed, surging out from deep between her legs. Spraying down her thighs in thick rivulets, spattering onto the floor and the couch, and even onto *Natt*. Natt, who was still sitting sprawled on the couch, his eyes dazed and blinking, his huge wet orc-prick still jutting out straight toward her—

The entire scene was shocking, utterly *outrageous*, but Ella's thudding, twisting thoughts were somehow caught on Natt, on his pliant muscled body, on that stunned, debauched look in his eyes. And there was a sudden, almost overpowering urge to move closer toward him, to let him look his fill at what he'd done. Perhaps, even, to put her hand to her thigh, and slide that sticky white heat all over her skin, while he watched like this, with those blinking, dazed eyes—

No. *No.* He was an *orc*, Ella was *betrothed*, she was supposed to make a good marriage, honour her family, and do this with Alfred, Alfred, *Alfred*—

Ella's sticky, messy body stumbled backwards, her hands fluttering up to press hard and painful against her eyes. What had she done. Gods, what the hell had she done.

Far too late she groped at the floor, for clothes, for covering. But there was only her shift, and the hideous dress—and after an instant's blinking she grasped for the dress, and frantically wiped it at her skin. Mopping up the mess, there was so much of it, how was that even *possible*—

But she managed to wipe off the worst of it, desperately scrubbing with shaky hands, and fighting to ignore the feel of Natt's eyes, watching her. He hadn't yet moved, he was still sitting there with his legs spread, spattered with white. And it wasn't until Ella had hurled the ruined dress to the floor, and yanked on her shift over her head, that she finally risked a glance up again, at his blinking eyes.

And in this moment, instead of the dazed warmth they'd held before, those eyes just looked—pained. Almost—hurt, or maybe even reproachful. As if this were somehow Ella's fault, as if Ella were in the least responsible for this complete and utter *disaster*, rather than *him*.

"Are you happy now?" she heard her thin voice say. "Now that you've had me, and used me, and *ruined* me, for your petty *revenge*?!"

There was another moment's stillness, broken only by the heavy sound of his breath. "I have not ruined you," he said, oddly strained. "I drew no blood. You bore no seed. This vengeance was not against you."

The words caught Ella up short, staring at him from where she was yanking on her boots with her shuddery, sparking fingers. "Good gods, Natt," she choked out. "Do you really think this won't affect me? I was supposed to do that with Alfred, I'm supposed to marry *Alfred*, and become a real *lady*, and what the hell will he do if he *ever* finds out I gave my maidenhead to an actual *orc*?!"

Her voice had gone high-pitched and panicked, her shaky body backing toward the door, and suddenly Natt was on his feet, towering huge over her, dragging up his trousers with tight clawed fists. "You wished for this, lass," he hissed. "You asked me for this. You took *joy* in this."

No, no, she hadn't, she couldn't, and Ella desperately shook her head, and fumbled behind her for the door-latch. "I can't," she breathed. "I'm to be a real *lady*, Natt. I *can't*."

And here was the need, lurching and desperate, for Natt to understand again, to agree, to *know*—but his big body had only gone stiffer above her, his eyes flaring, his head shaking. "You shall not be a lady," he growled, his voice slow, deliberate, vibrating with power and purpose. "You shall be what you are. And you are a woman who chose to give your maidenhead to *me!*"

There was no answering him, no justifying that, no thought no sense no safety—and Ella grasped for the door, yanked it open, and ran.

11

Ella had *given* her *maidenhood* to an *orc*.

The reality of that, the utter impossibility of that, thundered again and again as she ran, sprinting and ducking around trees and brambles and ponds and ditches. Following her own ancient well-trodden paths, from years ago, a lifetime ago—and though the paths were thick and grown over now, they were still there, here, part of her, utterly unchanged, deep inside.

Just like the appalling, incomprehensible part of her that had *given her maidenhood to an orc.*

It didn't make sense, none of this made sense, not least the fact that Ella was running *away*. Away from her lands, from her house, from the memories of that awful engagement-party, from every tedious, painful, endlessly banal day she'd lived these past years. Making the proper impression, pleasing the proper people, moving in the proper circles, putting on the proper face. Everything the realm's richest, most desirable heiress was supposed to do.

She leapt over one last stream, and scrambled up the rocky familiar hill, toward the old familiar copse of trees. So much taller than they'd once been, their branches thicker and closer together, but they were still there, still *safe*—and Ella dashed into the midst of them, and finally stopped. Pressing her hands to her sweaty face, and dragging in heaving, gasping gulps of the cool night air.

What in all the gods' holy creation had she just *done*.

She kept hauling in air, almost choking on it as the memories dipped and swirled. *Don't stop. Please, Natt. I want this from you. I've been waiting so long.*

I'd have given up everything. If you'd just—asked.

And yes, Ella had said those things. She'd said those things, and perhaps she'd even meant them—to an *orc*. A *beast*, who'd left her without a single word of farewell, and who'd then *kidnapped* her, and threatened to kill her household. And who'd just freely admitted to doing that—taking that heated, filthy, *indescribable* pleasure together— as *vengeance*. Against Ella's betrothed *husband*.

Ella sagged back against the nearest tree-trunk, and let her hands fall from her wet, blinking eyes. Natt couldn't be trusted. Alfred couldn't be trusted. No one could. She had to be in this for her family, for her father's legacy, for *her*.

She had to go back home.

It was the only possible solution, of course—but Ella couldn't seem to make her legs work, couldn't risk going out beyond the protection of the trees. The sun was just beginning to rise, she was wearing only a sleeping-shift, and even if she did manage to sneak back into the house without a full interrogation from her mother, next there would be thank-you cards to write to the party guests, invitations to tea from well-wishers, dress fittings and gossip sessions and dinner plans—all the while thinking of *this*. Of *Natt*.

There was a faint, telltale crack from the tree above her, and Ella's heart skipped, awareness prickling down her back—and when her head snapped up to look, there he was. *Natt*. Balanced silent and graceful on a trembling branch, his long claws digging deep into the thick tree-trunk, holding him aright. As though he'd always been there, watching over her, waiting.

He leapt down with a swift, fluid ease, landing lightly on the balls of his bare feet, his braid flaring up behind him. Standing here in front of her, tall and broad and bare-chested, with his sword strapped back to his side, the pack slung over his shoulder, the waterskin in his clawed hand. And looking at him, something seemed to slam all the breath out of Ella's lungs at once, clamping tight and close around her chest.

"Still that good at stalking your prey, are you?" her voice croaked, for want of anything else to say, and Natt's shoulders sagged, his hand holding out the half-full waterskin toward her.

"Ach," he said, quiet. "And you are yet the easiest of all, lass."

The memory flared up without warning, their wild games of hide and seek, tromping and laughing through the forest. Almost always with Ella hiding, because Natt had been way too good at it—but he'd always been too good at seeking her out, too, following her scent through fields and marshes and streams and even, once, across a *lake.*

I should find you anywhere, lass, he would say, warm and smug, flashing her his sharp-toothed grin. *I know your scent better than any other.*

And it was odd, Ella thought disjointedly, as she belatedly grasped the waterskin and brought it to her mouth, that he *hadn't* found her at any point, after he'd left. It had been so easy for him, second nature, and why could he not have just taken a moment, come to her, and said *something—*

I had reasons for this, he'd said, and Ella hadn't actually heard any legitimate ones, had she? And as she handed the waterskin back, wiping at her mouth with her sleeve, she drew in breath, about to ask—

When there was a—bark. Yes, a bark, surely from a dog, and then another over it, closer this time.

Ella didn't own a kennel, or lapdogs—dogs were dirty, her mother always said, and entirely unsuitable for an heiress of Ella's standing— and while this little copse of trees was a good distance into the forest, it was still technically on Ella's land. So what the hell were *dogs* doing here, at this hour of the morning?

But in front of her, Natt had gone unnervingly stiff, his previously easy form crouched and corded, his hand clamped tight to his sword-hilt. His eyes had squeezed shut, his head shaking, his grimacing mouth spitting out a quiet steady stream of harsh, guttural words Ella couldn't begin to comprehend.

"What?" she said, without at all meaning to. "What is it, Natt?"

Natt's head jerked toward her, and he visibly winced, almost as if he were in pain. "Up the tree, lass," he hissed. "Now."

Ella blinked at him, and shrank backwards—she hadn't climbed a tree in nearly a decade, and she was currently wearing a *sleeping-shift*—but Natt's strong hand suddenly grasped at hers, and dragged her toward the tree he'd just jumped out of.

"Up," he breathed again, as the sound of the barking dogs came closer, and closer. "Else you shall *never* have this life you wish for. You shall never marry this lord. Up, *now!*"

Ella could never remember seeing Natt look like this before, with such panic and urgency all over his form, and it was that, more than the bizarre Alfred threat, that finally set her climbing. Grasping at the tree's lowest branches, flinching at the hard scrape of bark on her pristine skin—and then, with Natt's strong hands half-shoving, half-lifting her, she somehow swung a foot up onto the branch.

She'd torn her sleeping-shift in the process, but she was standing in the tree now, and she carefully crept to the next branch, and then the next. Up and up and up, as the bark of dogs came nearer, and with it—Ella froze—the distinctive sounds of horses, stamping and whinnying nearby. And then—voices. Men's voices. Coming closer.

"There he is!" one called. "We've got him, boys!"

Ella couldn't seem to breathe, or follow that, and she craned to look downward through the branches, her heart lurching in her chest—and here, already dashing into her copse, were three lean little hunting-dogs, barking and growling at Natt's stiff, unmoving form. And close behind the dogs were *men*, five armed men, all with black cloth masks tied over their mouths and noses. They were scrambling up Ella's hill, straight toward Natt, and Natt *still* wasn't moving, why the *hell* wasn't Natt moving—

The first man charged into the copse with his sword drawn, his voice shouting—but when he caught sight of Natt he reeled back, his steps faltering, his sword bobbing in his gloved hand. But he seemed to regain his composure as two more masked men rushed into the copse, and then two more. Every single one wearing stiff leather armour and helmets, and every one with a gleaming, straight-edged sword in hand.

But Natt still hadn't moved. Not even to draw his own sword, and not to run, or climb, or escape. And he could have so easily escaped, it should have cost him *nothing*, and Ella couldn't stop staring, her hands grasping painfully at the rough tree-trunk, while her heart sought to thunder its way out of her chest.

The masked men had formed a loose circle around Natt, near enough that they could have reached their sword-points and touched his bare chest. But Natt still hadn't drawn his sword, why hadn't he drawn his sword, and instead he just kept standing there, every muscle locked tight, as though he might explode at any moment...

"Trespassing on private property," one of the men said, his cool, mocking voice muffled under his mask. "Breaking the *law*. And thus, violating section three of our recently ratified and *extremely* generous *treaty*, right boys?"

Several of the men nodded—one of them laughed behind his mask—and the first man, perhaps the leader, stepped even closer to Natt, his sword nearly nudging Natt's stiff bare chest. "We've got you, you ugly beast," he said. "Will you come quietly, and face your punishment? Or are you going to put up a fuss, and make us show you who's still in charge around here? Who'll *always* be in charge around here?"

Natt didn't move, didn't speak, and another one of the men snorted under his mask. "He probably can't even understand you, Byrne. They've got about as much brains as one of these dogs."

The man gave a callous kick at the nearest dog as he spoke, making it give a high-pitched yelp before darting away, and Ella's scraped, shaking hands gripped harder at the tree. They were here to take Natt, to *hurt* Natt, they couldn't, they *couldn't*—

But Natt still wasn't moving. Wasn't speaking. Was just standing there, tall and tense, like a spring wound too tight, coiled and cramped and waiting—

"He's had his warning, boys," the first man said, every word a sickening thud in Ella's gut. "Now, *get him*."

12

It was like the world swerved and screamed, all at once. Filled with shouting masked men and flashing steel swords, all swarming at Natt in a flood.

Surely Natt had been caught in it, drowned, his beautiful warmth already seeping away, bleeding out on the earth—but somehow, thank the gods, he'd ducked, and *rolled*. Out of the copse entirely, to where there was a little clearing, more space.

He didn't seem hurt, rising gracefully again to the balls of his feet—but he still hadn't drawn his sword, and Ella's distant, shouting thoughts noted that he'd somehow lost the pack and waterskin, leaving both his bare arms free. But his claws weren't even out, and the men had already chased after him, coming to circle him again—

"Get him!" the first man yelled, and all five seemed to charge at once—but again Natt ducked and rolled. In the process grasping for one of the men's swords, wrenching it out of his hands. And then hurling it against another nearby tree, where the pointed blade sank deep into the thick tree-trunk, the exposed hilt wildly vibrating at the impact.

It meant the man had to rush after his sword, struggling to yank it out of the tree, but there were still four more men, advancing back toward Natt. The leader signalling at the other three, in some kind of silent command—and then he lunged at Natt again, his blade flashing in the brightening morning light.

Natt knocked the man's arm away, ducking sideways beneath—but when he came up to standing again, shifting on the balls of his feet, Ella could see the cut on his bare shoulder, the red blood already trickling bright against the grey-green skin. And what in the gods' names was he doing, why didn't he draw his sword, use his claws, *something*—

But the men were only circling again, clearly now taking more care, silently speaking to one another. Spreading out a little wider, two of them angling behind Natt's back, while the others charged from the front—

Natt still managed to roll away, but now there was another deep, ugly cut in his skin, dripping liberally from the back of his forearm. He must have used his bare arm to stop a blade, and surely he knew how to fight, surely he could run, what was this, this was *madness*—

But the hell before Ella's eyes only kept unfolding, the men surging at Natt again and again, the sounds of shouts and clangs rising through the trees. And somehow Natt had wrested away another sword, this time hurling it high up into the distance, but he was bleeding liberally from multiple cuts, even on his *face*, and Ella could see the pain in his eyes, could feel it in her bones.

"Give *up*, you *beast*," one of the now-swordless men gasped, as he flailed for Natt, his fists flying. Natt again blocked him, hurling him bodily away, but here was another man, blade whirling wild. Natt knocked him sideways, and rolled out of the way of the next, but that meant he'd come up in front of the leader. And the swine didn't aim for Natt's torso or his face, like he had every time until now—but instead, he swung his sword straight toward Natt's *leg*.

Natt's howl filled the air, exploding in Ella's thoughts, and the blood exploded too, spraying wide from the deep, vicious gash in Natt's thigh. While the men shouted with triumph, one of them laughing—and in a breath they swarmed Natt's crumpling form, arms swinging and steel flashing and no no NO—

Suddenly, Ella was moving. Scrambling wild and desperate out of the tree, jumping and sliding against its rough trunk, not caring if her shift was tearing or her hands were bleeding. Natt was hurt, Natt could *die*. And the rage and the horror at that thought was enough to hurl her onto the earth, her feet pelting panicked and powerful toward them. Toward Natt, who she couldn't even *see*, under the mass of horrible, vicious men.

"Stop!" she screamed, her voice piercing shrill through the air. "Now! At *once!*"

Thank the gods, the men stopped. Clearly more out of surprise than anything, every one of their masked faces whipping sharp toward her, and Ella ran straight into the midst of them, straight to Natt. He was crouched on the ground between them, his bloody arms curled protectively over his head, and he was liberally bleeding from cuts all over, his audible breaths gasping with pain. The sight shocking and almost devastating to Ella's staring eyes, how could these men do such things, to one who hadn't even raised a *weapon* toward them.

"He's got a *woman*?!" the leader's voice said, and when Ella jerked her head to glare at him, the bastard actually *laughed*. "You had a *woman*, orc," he said again, with a sudden, hard kick of his booted foot into Natt's crouching side. "You were *kidnapping* too, you beast?"

Natt's breath had wheezed at the impact, and the fury and misery flared again, deep and agonizing in Ella's gut. "You will not touch him *again*," she ordered, with all the strength she could muster. "You will leave at *once*."

The man only laughed again, and then he reached out, and gave a mocking tug at Ella's torn sleeping-shift. "Look, she's already been caught in the foul orc-spell," he said. "She's probably chock-full of his spunk, too. Go take her and check, Colley, will you? And don't do anything I wouldn't do."

He'd laughed again, actually *winking* toward the man closest to Ella—and in reply that man gave a hearty guffaw, and reached to grasp painfully at Ella's upper arm. "Come along, wench. We'll sort you out."

Ella's shocked, staring horror was broken by a guttural hiss from Natt's throat beneath her, and she belatedly, forcefully yanked away from the foul man's grip. "You shall not *dare* to touch me again," she barked. "And you shall leave these lands *at once!*"

The man only guffawed again and came a step closer, the scent of his nauseating breath swarming the air. "A stubborn little miss, aren't you?" he said. "I'll enjoy putting you in your place, wench."

Ella could again only gape at him—did he truly mean to do what that sounded like?!—but again, Natt's choked, desperate growl beneath her said that yes, perhaps he did. And when the man grasped for her arm again, this time Ella didn't fight it, and let him pull her close—and then she scraped wildly at his face with her fingernails, yanking down his mask.

And he was—handsome. Clean-shaven. Young-ish, maybe thirty. Not at all the filthy bearded ruffian Ella had expected, and she blinked at him, while the shock swarmed again, and the recognition slowly crept across her thoughts. She was good at faces and names, one had to be in her line of life, and—

"Mr. Colin Galliford?" she said, her voice blank. "But—you were at my *party* last night."

It would have been satisfying to see the horror flare across his blue eyes, if not for the fact that Ella was perhaps more disgusted, and more nauseated, than she'd ever felt in her life. Mr. Colin Galliford had been a particular friend of Alfred's, Alfred had introduced him last night with genuine warmth, and he'd bent over Ella's proffered hand with all courtesy, in every aspect the perfect wealthy gentleman.

"And Mr. Byrne, was it?" Ella said now, turning toward the man who seemed to be their leader, and watching the alarm flare across his eyes, as well. "Mr. Jack Byrne, if I recall?"

He didn't move, or reply, but curse him, he was another close friend of Alfred's, another one who'd come all the way from Tlaxca for Ella's engagement-party. Or for *this*?!

"It's the *lord's* new wench?" one of the other men whispered, far too loudly. "The *heiress*?"

The rage surged behind Ella's eyes, and she whirled toward the man, no doubt another shameful coward who'd freely partaken of her hospitality last night. "The heiress, indeed," she snapped, with as much chilly haughtiness as she could muster. "I am Miss Ella Riddell, currently one of the wealthiest women in the realm, and the betrothed of your *friend*, Lord Tovey of Tlaxca. And here you are *trespassing* on my land, and threatening to *defile* me!"

The words were greeted by utter silence, but for Natt's still-gasping breath beneath her, and Ella winced at the sound, and shot him a furtive, fearful look. Gods, he looked utterly *broken*, but he'd still managed to somehow sit up on the ground behind her, his black head bowed, his hand clenched tight to his thigh, the blood streaming red between his fingers.

"We beg your forgiveness, miss," came a smooth voice, Byrne's voice. "But you're in the forest, alone, wearing a torn *sleeping-dress,* and looking, ah—*quite* unlike the dignified woman we met last night. And, you're with an *orc.*"

Ella's eyes had still been fastened to Natt, and that awful sight of his streaming red blood, and she belatedly spun back toward Byrne. "I *own* this land," she said, through gritted teeth, "and therefore I can walk upon it at whatever hour I wish, wearing whatever I wish. I could not have *conceived* that I might find my party-guests trespassing at this hour, seeking to force hapless women to their will, and trying to *kill* innocent unarmed people!"

Her words rang against the trees, against the men's staring eyes— but then one of them laughed, the sound harsh and mocking. "This one's not *people*. He's an *orc*. And you're *fraternizing* with him."

The rage bloomed again, almost too powerful to be borne, and Ella clenched her hands to fists, and very nearly spat at the coward's still-masked face. "My betrothed husband's lord *father* signed this treaty with the orcs," she growled. "And thus, I have eagerly sought to support it, with all the means at my command. And therefore"—she shot another furtive look at Natt, her thoughts searching, churning—"I have recently hired this orc to patrol my lands on my behalf, and alert me of any trespassers. And this morning, I was enjoying an early leisurely stroll, when he came to warn me that there were unfamiliar armed *cowards* barging through *my* forest!"

The men didn't speak—there was a satisfactorily stunned look in Byrne's eyes—and Ella stalked toward him, and glared at his masked face. "And then, you almost *killed* my *employee*," she hissed. "Before my maiden eyes. Do you know how much this shall cost me in surgeons' bills? And how deeply and irrevocably scarred I shall be, thanks to this cowardly, crude, *unthinkably* violent behaviour on your part?!"

Byrne finally backed a step away, thank the gods, and his eyes darted uneasily between Ella and Natt. "Our apologies, Miss Riddell," he said, his voice smooth and ingratiating. "We were truly unaware of your unusual, uh, arrangement. We only sought to protect you, and defend your honour against what we believed to be a true threat."

Ella gave an unladylike snort, and crossed her arms tightly over her chest, feeling her heart hammering against it. "You shall leave my lands at *once*," she said thinly. "And you shall *never* again return, without my express permission. Or else I shall have my betrothed— and the Sakkin magistrate, and perhaps even Lord Otto himself—haul you up on charges of trespassing, and attempted murder, and *defilement!*"

There was a flare of something Ella couldn't read behind Byrne's eyes—particularly at her mention of Lord Otto—but he took a step backward, and bowed his head. "Very well, Miss Riddell. We shall depart, and you shall have no need to speak of this unfortunate misunderstanding again. And once again, our deepest apologies."

Ella gave a stiff, imperious nod, and watched as Byrne signalled to the men, and they finally retreated, with the dogs at their heels. Several of the men still giving Ella uneasy glances over their shoulders, but she kept standing there, glaring, until they'd vanished from view, and she could hear the distinctive sounds of horses' hooves, moving into the distance.

It was only then that Ella whirled around, and rushed back to Natt. He was still sitting there on the ground, his bloody hand pressed against his dripping-red thigh, but his head lifted to look at her—and at the sight of his bruised, battered face, streaked with blood and cuts and dirt, Ella felt something lurch in her throat that might have been a sob.

"Dear gods, Natt," she choked, reaching out a hand toward him— and then yanking away again, because there was scarcely anywhere left to touch that wasn't marked by cuts or blood. "Are you all right? What can I *do*?"

She could hear the panic rising in her voice, her eyes darting desperately at the trees, the forest. The house was a good distance away now, perhaps a half-hour's walk, perhaps she could run back home, find a physician, bring help here—

"Ach, I shall heal," came Natt's hoarse voice, though he winced as he spoke. "I only must—wrap this."

He gave a shaky wave toward his still-bleeding thigh, still with his other hand clamped onto it, and Ella blanched at the sight of the sticky, pooling blood, the smell of it sharp and pungent in her nostrils. And what in the gods' names could they wrap it with, and she frantically glanced all about them, and then down at her own shift—but even as she grasped at the ragged hem, about to tear it, Natt gave another jerky wave, this time toward the tree Ella had been hiding in. Or rather, toward his pack and waterskin, which were both on the ground beneath it, propped neatly against the trunk.

Ella accordingly hurried over to grab for them, and then ran back, yanking the pack open. And there, sitting innocuously folded on top, was the old hideous dress she'd been wearing earlier. Still bearing a highly distinctive, musky scent, and—Ella couldn't help a twitch—still very wet.

But there were yards of fabric, some of it still clean and dry, and Ella made quick work of it, tearing it into long strips. And then, as Natt silently gestured, his breaths coming harsh and short, she wrapped a makeshift bandage around his bloody thigh over his trousers, and tied it as tightly as she possibly could. Even so, the blood was already pooling through it, staining thick and red, and at his trembly wave she tied on another strip, and another.

Her hands were numb and chilly by this point, horribly stained with Natt's sticky red blood, and once she had finished, and leaned back to look at him, she felt the panic start to rise again. What the hell was she supposed to do with him, he needed help, he couldn't possibly function like this—

But then, as she stared, Natt shoved himself onto his good knee—and from there he somehow leapt up onto that foot, in a quick, agile movement that must have taken an astonishing amount of strength. And one that had clearly caused him pain, his breath wheezing, and Ella again rushed toward him, barely making it in time for him to lean his weight, hard, against her shoulder.

"Ach," he said, his voice thick. "Should you help me to the old c-cave, lass, I sh-should be g-grateful."

His teeth were actually chattering, the pain again spasming across his face, and Ella frantically nodded. The cave. Of course. It was another old haunt of theirs, a deep, low-ceilinged cleft in a cliff of jagged rock, and it was close by, near a brook, and not easily detectable from outside. So Ella slung Natt's pack over her shoulder, and then gingerly slid an arm around his sticky, sweaty waist, so he could better lean against her.

"All right?" she asked, and in reply he grimaced, and grasped his arm around her shoulder. The sudden weight was almost enough to buckle Ella's knees, but she remained upright, and once Natt seemed stable, she started moving in the direction of the cave.

It was slow, tedious going—Natt could scarcely put any weight on his bad leg, and while Ella chose the easiest possible paths, the terrain was still tricky and uneven, and his body against her felt heavier and heavier with every plodding step. But there was no thought of stopping or complaining, only the desperate, surging need to get him somewhere hidden, somewhere safe.

After what felt like hours, they finally reached the cave, still tucked away where it had always been, close against what they'd always called Chilly Brook. And once Ella had eased Natt down toward the low entrance, he very slowly knelt and crawled his way inside, dragging his injured leg behind him.

Ella only had to duck under the edge—the ceiling was perhaps up to her shoulders—and she helped guide Natt's trembly, sweaty bulk down onto the cave's stone floor. And as he lay back upon it, his big bloody body flinching at the impact, it was like something had finally broken in Ella's thoughts, the wetness prickling hot and close behind her eyes.

"What the *hell* was that, Natt," she choked out, without at all meaning to. "*Why* didn't you leave me in the tree, and run away. Or kill them!"

It should have been shocking, to hear those murderous words roll so easily from her lips—but she could only seem to blink at Natt's bloody, pained face. Watching his mouth grimace, his tongue coming out to lick at his split lip.

"I could not kill them," he said finally, his glazed eyes briefly closing, his voice rasping. "We have all sworn never to raise a blade against a man, and thus risk this new peace, and start another war."

What? "Not even as *defense*?" Ella demanded, and Natt gave another grimace that clearly meant, *No.* And gods curse him, he'd all but sacrificed himself to keep the peace-treaty, while those swine had nearly *murdered* him in violation of it, and Ella gave a bracing shake of her head, tried to think. "Then why didn't you run," she snapped. "You could have escaped so *easily*, Natt!"

But there was a jerky movement of his head that was, again, saying no. "The dogs," he croaked. "If I had run, they should have next found my scent all over *you*."

All over her. Ella stared at him, fully about to demand what the hell that had to do with anything—but then she followed that truth where it led. If the dogs *had* found Natt's scent on her, and Natt himself gone, what would the men have done? Would they have insisted upon—*checking* her, like Byrne had said? *Sorting her out?*

And then, surely—Ella gave a convulsive shudder—they would have reported their findings to her mother, and to *Alfred. Your daughter was found full of orc-seed in the woods. Your betrothed was compromised by an orc.*

And even if Ella had claimed it wasn't by her choice, it would without question still have been the sudden, certain end of her betrothal. It would have been the end of her and Alfred, forever. The end of her inheritance, and her home. All her dreams, dashed, irrevocably, in one single fatal blow.

And Natt had *known*. He'd sought to protect her. Even going so far as—Ella blanched, the vision of it flashing bright behind her eyes—to place his own things at the base of the tree he'd put her in, to better hide her smell.

Ella's breath felt locked in her throat, her already-painful hands scraping at the stone beneath her knees. "They might have *killed* you, Natt," she said. "You didn't have to do that. Not for *me*."

Natt didn't reply, but for the thick heaviness of his breaths, and looking down at him, Ella suddenly found that she was very close to weeping. He'd clearly thought he'd had to do that—and did that mean he had truly been going to let her go, too? Would he have let her run back home, after all? To *Alfred*?

"I thought you wanted vengeance," she heard her wavering voice say. "Against Alfred."

"I do wish for this," Natt said, almost a whisper. "But against him. Not—*you*, lass."

Ella could only blink and stare at him, at how every heaving breath looked like pain. "I did not follow," his hoarse voice continued, "how deeply you wished for this. For—him. For this life, away from me, where you think you are real. I did not wish to leave you, and destroy this for you, for always."

Oh. The words seemed to slice deep and powerful in Ella's chest, breaking her wide, baring her whole. Away from Natt, where she was *real*, and he'd been willing to *die* for that. For *her*. And Ella's head was wildly shaking, the misery rising, the panic swerving, he couldn't, she couldn't, no, no *no*—

But before she could turn, escape, run away, there was a low, heavy sigh from Natt's mouth, emptying his chest. And then—Ella stared, choked, fought not to scream—his eyes fluttered closed, and he was still.

13

For a moment, there was only sheer, bellowing panic in Ella's ears, shattering all else with the strength of it. Natt was dead. Natt might be dead. Was Natt *dead*?!

But as Ella's fluttering, badly trembling fingers went to Natt's neck, desperately feeling for a pulse, his broad chest abruptly rose—and then fell. He was breathing. Good gods, he was breathing.

Ella's body was suddenly shaking all over, the cave spinning in her vision, and she sank down onto the stone, and ducked her head between her knees, sucking back slow, dragging breaths. Natt was alive. He was here, he was breathing, he was *alive*.

But he was out cold, that much was clear, and once Ella's vision had settled again, she gritted her teeth, and raised her head. He was alive. He'd saved her. And—she took a deep breath—the least she could do was repay that debt.

She began by washing his many wounds, making trip after trip to the creek with the waterskin, and pouring the cool water out over him. His sleeping form didn't even twitch, not even when she washed his face, and not even—Ella winced, but made herself do it—as she peeled off the blood-soaked bandages from his thigh.

The wound beneath still looked ghastly, but it had at least seemed to stop bleeding. So Ella carefully ripped his trousers open around it, and then cleaned it too, pouring the fresh water over it again and again.

She mentally catalogued the wounds as she went, marking which ones were the most severe, and which were more superficial. The gash on his right leg was by far the worst, followed by the vicious gouge where he'd blocked the sword with his left forearm, and then, a deep slice across his left shoulder. There was also considerable bruising all over him, turning his grey-green skin a mottled blackish colour, including a thick ring around his right eye.

But even in the time Ella had been doing this, she could see how some of the shallower cuts were already beginning to knit themselves back together. Calling back a warm sunny day, half a lifetime ago, when a recently acquired scrape on Natt's hand had suddenly and mysteriously vanished, and Ella had flat-out refused to believe that orcs could possibly heal so quickly.

Try me and see, Natt had said, with a wicked grin, handing Ella his sword, pommel first. *Just a scratch.*

Of course Ella had refused—*I could never do such a vile thing*, she'd protested—and as she'd watched, Natt had done it himself, sliding the cold steel across his forearm, bringing up a startling line of red blood.

Foolish lass, he'd said, with another sharp-toothed grin. *You could never hurt me.*

And then he'd *licked* the blood off his *arm*, and Ella had been caught in the throes of loud revolted disgust—but she'd gingerly held his arm afterwards, and watched the cut knit back together. Almost like watching a flower bloom, like it hadn't changed at all—until it was there, entirely new, before one's eyes.

She swallowed hard, her gaze lingering again on Natt's massive frame, on the height and breadth of it beneath the wounds. It was still so odd to see how different he was, all hard rippling muscle, every line corded and visible. And so many of those older scars, as well, and it belatedly occurred to Ella that those must have all been serious wounds too, otherwise they'd have also healed quickly, wouldn't they?

And truly, what *had* Natt been doing, all these years? Fighting off random bands of men in forests? Or had that been random at all, because Natt hadn't seemed *surprised*, had he? And what had those awful men been *doing* on her property in the first place? With masks, and dogs, and *weapons*?

The questions only swirled louder as the day passed, and Ella sought to distract herself, as best she could. First exploring about the little cave—it had fallen in a bit, at the back, but was otherwise unchanged—and then, after considerable hesitation, she dug deeper into Natt's pack. Finding it mostly filled with the remnants of her clothes—the rest of the dress, and the makeshift sheepskin shawl he'd given her, which she now eased under his head—and also with a large quantity of dried meat. And suddenly Ella was ravenous, and she tucked into the meat with gusto, even if it was quite possibly the toughest, least palatable thing she'd tasted in years.

She studied Natt's sleeping form again as she ate, this time lingering on the other things on his huge body, the things he'd clearly chosen. The thick, bright gold earring, embedded in the lobe of his pointed left ear. The sword still strapped to his belt, its blade curved gleaming steel, the hilt studded with costly-looking black gems. And finally, on the middle finger of Natt's right hand, that gold-and-green ring. Large and heavy and powerful, the gold beautifully bound around what looked to be three large, perfectly cut *emeralds*.

The ring was orc-forged, Ella knew very well, and she dropped a finger to trace lightly against it. She had always been irrationally intrigued by orc-forged jewels, and though she'd never seemed able to bring herself to purchase any, she knew that this ring would have cost a fortune in a human market, and likely the sword as well. So why did Natt wear them now, when he never had before? How had such precious items become *his*?

It was only more questions, with no answers in sight, and Ella finally forced herself away from Natt's sleeping form, and outside the cave altogether. Where she explored a little around it, relearning all the stones and paths and crannies, and finding a patch of berries to snack on, as well. All the while watching and listening for any signs of activity in the forest around her, and almost feeling herself relax—until she heard a telltale, ringing bark, off in the distance.

Ella froze in place, straining to hear—and there it was again. The same bark. *That* bark. The *men*.

Wait. Those awful men were *still here?* Still following them? *Waiting* for them?!

Ella scurried back into the cave, her heartbeat jolting in her chest—and found her frantic eyes blinking straight at Natt's. Natt, who instead of sleeping, was bemusedly blinking back at her in the dim light.

"Oh, thank the gods you're awake!" Ella gasped, as she rushed over to kneel beside him. "Because the men, Natt, those horrid men are still *here*, Byrne *lied* to me, they haven't left at *all!*"

Natt only kept blinking at her, his eyelashes thick and dark against his mottled cheekbone. "No, they would not," he said, his voice hoarse. "But I ken they shall not yet attack again, not if you are here."

That wasn't even slightly reassuring, but Ella shoved the thought away for the moment, and belatedly cast her eyes up and down Natt's blood-stained form. "How are you feeling? How's your leg?"

Natt carefully shifted his thigh against the stone, flaring a sudden, pained wince across his face. "Ach," he said. "Better."

It didn't look better, to Ella's eyes, but she attempted a nod, and abruptly handed over the sloshing waterskin. Watching as Natt grasped it and drank, his hand seeming somewhat steadier, before he glanced downwards, to the folded sheepskin beneath his head. And then to his leg, which Ella had left open to the air, now that it had stopped bleeding.

"Ach," he said again. "You are—still here."

There was confusion in his blinking eyes, in his rasping voice, and Ella realized that he'd expected her to run. To leave him alone, suffering, in a state like this, while those awful men were apparently still lurking about. And the fact that Natt thought that, that he truly thought Ella had changed that much, seemed to clamp in her chest, squeezing out her breath.

"You *kidnapped* me," she heard herself reply, because that was perhaps the only safe thing to say, in this moment. "Remember?"

Something moved in Natt's eyes, and there was an unmistakable, beautiful twitch at the corner of his mouth. "Ach," he said. "So I did. And thus"—his body shifted on the stone, the pain again flashing across his face—"you must obey all that I command. Or else."

There was a flare of warmth, low in Ella's belly, and she couldn't quite hide her smile. "Or else what?"

Those eyes narrowed at her, all mock imperious disapproval. "Or else," he said, his voice deepening, "I shall make you wear this frock you hate. All the way to my mountain."

His hand had reached down to weakly rattle at his sword, and Ella couldn't seem to stop the sudden, lurking bubble of laughter from escaping her throat. "A dire threat indeed, Nattfarr of Clan Grisk," she said, with as much solemnity as she could muster. "I shall sacrifice much to avoid such a cruel fate."

His replying grin was life itself, shuddering deep into Ella's bones, and bringing enough heat to her face that she had to look away. "In all seriousness, Natt," she said, "what hurts? What do you need? What can I do?"

Her voice sounded panicky again, and she twitched at the unexpected feel of Natt's warm hand, curling against her knee. "You have done much," he said, quiet. "I shall heal enough to walk, with mayhap one night's further rest here. And thus, I expect"—he took a breath—"naught else from you."

Ella blinked back toward him, at that sudden intent seriousness in his eyes. He was—letting her go. Giving her permission. Even though he *knew* those horrible men were still waiting for him. To *kill* him.

The tightness was back in Ella's chest, and she managed a shrug. "You *kidnapped* me," she said again, and there was an unmistakable relief in those eyes, in his big body sagging against the stone. And his hand on her knee had only spread wider, silently speaking of his approval, or perhaps even his gratefulness.

"*Is* there anything else you need?" Ella asked, her voice oddly thick. "Food? More water? Anything to ease the pain? At all?"

Natt's warm hand had begun sliding slightly upwards, sending a cascade of goosebumps up Ella's thigh. "In truth?" he asked, his voice low, and at Ella's replying nod, there was a wry twitch on his mouth, a clench of those fingers. "Then mayhap, lass," he continued, even quieter, "might you suck my prick, for a spell?"

Wait, what? Ella's mouth had fallen open, her wide eyes searching his scarred, battered face. "What, *now*?" she demanded, her voice shrill. "You're *serious*, Natt?"

But his eyes were blinking again, his mouth grimacing, and his gaze flicked away, up to the low stone ceiling above. "Ach," he said, "and you are not. Forgive me, lass, I am"—he grimaced again—"fogged, I ken."

But Ella was biting her lip, her eyes darting up and down his form—and then catching, too easily, on *that*. The sight at the front of his torn trousers, previously a large but indistinguishable bulge, and now—her breath choked—a shockingly long, tapered ridge. And as she stared, it seemed to swell even larger, pressing up against the trousers. Almost as if silently speaking to her, whispering of when she'd already done this, tasted this, just last night...

"Y-you really," Ella managed, through her suddenly dry mouth, "think that will *help*?"

There was a low rumble from Natt's throat, another swell of that hardness against the rapidly tightening trousers. "Ach. Pleasure is always good, for edging away pain."

Always good. As if he'd done this innumerable times before, had his cock sucked to distract from possibly deadly wounds—and the sudden replying ache in Ella's gut might have been sympathy, or raging jealousy, or both.

But her gaze had reflexively darted toward the cave's small opening, and the threat of whatever was waiting beyond it. "But—the *men*," she breathed. "What if they come? Or attack?"

"Then I shall speak this to you," came Natt's firm reply, his eyes glittering on hers. "I can smell where they wait. It is yet more than a half league away."

Well. The truth was there in his eyes, in his voice, and another glance toward the exit showed indeed no sign of movement beyond. And that dog's bark *had* sounded a fair ways away, hadn't it?

"Right," Ella said, her voice almost a whisper. "Um. Well. Where should I begin, then?"

Because there was no question of doing it, suddenly—of *course* she was doing it again, if this would possibly help—and she was rewarded with a hoarse, guttural gasp from deep in Natt's throat. And as she stared, his clawed hand dropped to his trousers, shoved them downwards, and drew himself out.

And the *sight* of that—Natt's black claws holding that swollen veined grey hardness, with such casual, familiar ease—seemed to catch something in Ella's throat, and strike her entirely still. Watching, bated and breathless, as those fingers slowly, smoothly slid up, all the way to that deep slit, where they—Ella choked again—squeezed out a thick, viscous bead of white.

"Mayhap," Natt's voice murmured, as his hand did that again, oh *gods*, "you shall first only touch me. You must feel me, and learn me."

Oh. Ella swallowed hard, but her head somehow nodded, her eyes utterly trapped on the sight of his audacious hand, doing that again. Sliding up, milking out even more of that mesmerizing white—and this time, slipping a finger into that slit, smearing it with wetness before sliding back down again.

He'd let out a low gasp as he did it, slicking himself in his own seed, leaving that shaft wet and glistening, the distant light catching on every ridge and vein of it. And that clawed hand now slid down to the thick, hairy base of it, nudging its suddenly massive-looking length toward Ella. Almost as if to say, *Here, touch it, it's yours.*

And somehow, without at all meaning to, Ella obeyed. Her fingers moving up, shaky and uncertain, to only brush against it—but even that faint, furtive touch made it twitch purposefully toward her, while Natt's mouth gave another low, heated moan. He'd liked that—*it* had liked that—so Ella touched it again, longer this time. Feeling the astonishingly smooth velvet of him, both hard and soft at once, vibrating raw and powerful against her.

A harsh gasp escaped Ella's throat, but she scarcely heard it as she slowly, hesitantly explored him. Tracing over all those ridges and veins, up toward the strangely compelling head of it. And when she cautiously mimicked what Natt had done, delving a finger into that deep, impossibly smooth slit, it was almost like it was—alive. Like it clenched against her, or perhaps even *kissed* her—and then it spluttered out more of that white seed. Coating her finger in it, and then dribbling down the glistening, twitching length of him in thick, hungry rivulets.

Gods. The water flooded in Ella's mouth, her groin clenching as the visions of last night—had it just been last night?—swarmed her in a rush. That huge, tapered hardness, dripping with his wet, filthy seed, sliding up between her legs, spreading her apart—

"Taste it," Natt's voice whispered, soft, as his hand again stroked up and down, showing himself off for her. And oh, it looked good, that long, veined, vibrating cock glazed all over with a viscous, glossy sheen. Even as more seed drizzled down onto it, like a rich honeyed frosting on a delectable, irresistible treat—

Ella was leaning closer over him, looking, wanting, needing—but not quite daring to, not yet. And there was a heavy huff from Natt's chest, and then the thrilling feeling of his other hand, brushing gentle but purposeful against the back of her head.

"It is yours," he whispered, in an oddly apt summary of his silent words from before. "Kiss it. Taste it. Drink."

The relief felt like a palpable thing, like a long-awaited deliverance—and Ella desperately, gratefully obeyed. Moving down over him, closer and closer, until her lips had met that smooth head, and lightly, carefully kissed it.

The pleasure surged in a torrent, in a flood. In the impossible, inexplicable feeling of his deep, filthy cleft actually *kissing back*, clenching slightly on her delving tongue—and then swarming her with that delectable rich sweetness. While Natt's entire body kicked and flailed beneath her, the moan a rising howl in his throat.

It was utterly glorious, utterly irresistible, shoving away the rest of the world in one easy, devastatingly powerful thrust. In the swerving, stunning sensation of Natt's hips bucking up, that cleft spurting hard against her tongue. Saying, *Kiss me, drink me, more, deeper, more*—

Ella did, frantically sucking that length deeper inside, thrusting her tongue harder into its clenching, spurting depths. Almost as if drinking him from the inside out, lapping and flicking and twisting, drawing her delving tongue's reward deep down her hungry throat...

Beneath her Natt's groans were steadily rising, his claws sunk firm and demanding into her hair. Begging her, *Don't stop, keep kissing me, deeper, more, MORE*—

And it was when Ella's tongue was almost somehow *inside* him, and the dark cleft still kissing and clenching against her had seemed to open up, sucking her in—that it suddenly, shockingly exploded. Blasting Ella's maiden tongue with surging streams of pure pleasure, firing out again and again and again with so much force that she had to yank back, away from him, desperately fighting to swallow—

But there was too much, so much, and Ella moaned as she watched that slit spray the rest of its seed wide across the cave. While the thick whiteness bubbled its way out between her swollen lips, running messy and hot down her chin.

There was an instant's breathless stillness, as Ella blinked up at Natt's dazed, wide-eyed face—and then, oh hell, the feel of his big hand thrusting up under her torn sleeping-shift. And then there was glorious warmth, pressure, as his palm slid hard and flat against the very core of her, pressing just *there*, his delving fingers spreading her apart—

Ella actually screamed as the ecstasy rocked and roiled, her swollen, dripping-wet heat desperately pulsing and kissing against his hand. Soaking him, craving him, while the sparks shot wild and white across her eyes, her heart, her very *soul*.

She finally sagged against the strength of his hand, against the hard stone floor beneath her—and after giving a brief, reassuring pat against her still-shivery wetness, his hand gently drew away. And then—Ella stared—Natt brought that wet hand to his mouth, and then *licked* it. Swift, sinuous, hungry, with the flat of his tongue, making sure to catch every drop.

Good *gods*. Ella gave a deep, shuddery sigh, and next Natt's hand came up to her own face, fingers sliding deft and easy against her messy chin. And then slipping themselves between her parted lips, inviting her to lick, to kiss, to drink.

Ella did, eagerly, without thinking, though she winced at the new sting in her tongue, where the blast of his seed had struck her. And Natt's intently watching eyes had perhaps winced too, but those fingers didn't stop, only kept wiping, feeding, sliding smooth and familiar between her hungry lips.

"Ach," he murmured, so soft Ella could scarcely hear it. "It was cruel of me, to kiss your tongue so deeply, and then sting you unawares with my seed. Next time, I shall speak first."

Next time. Ella should have argued that, but she was instead caught on the rest of those words, on how they again seemed to speak so aptly what his body had already silently whispered. *Kiss me*, he'd said, *deeper, more.*

"Oh, but you *liked* doing that, and you know it," Ella heard her voice say, husky and low. "You are the filthiest creature *imaginable*, Nattfarr of Clan Grisk."

Natt actually laughed, the sound ringing warm and lovely through the cave, and his hand came to cup gentle and approving against her sticky, heated cheek. "Ach, I did like this," he confessed, his eyes sheepish, twinkling, affectionate. "It is not every day one has a mouth so sweet as yours. Or one so quick to learn a true orc's kiss."

Oh. The warmth flared again at the praise, almost as if compelled—but beneath it there was a sudden, disconcerting chill. *It is not every day.* Suggesting that there had been other days, perhaps many of them, with many other women, and Ella belatedly twitched herself away from him, while the reality of this moment seemed to swarm all at once. She had just sucked off an orc in a filthy cold cave, while men waited outside to *attack* him, and she was wearing only a tattered sleeping-shift, and she still had an orc's actual *spunk*, smeared across her face—

She jerked further away, fully about to jump to her feet, when there was a hard clasp of Natt's hand against hers, holding her there. "Do not run, lass," he said, his voice choked. "Not now, for this. I ought to better think, before I speak."

The words sounded sincere, his hand hot and sweaty against hers, and Ella held herself stiffly in place, her eyes held to the cave's opening, to the dimming sunlight beyond it. "For someone who seemed to care so much about being my first," she said, her voice thin, "it might have been nice if you'd thought to grant me the same courtesy."

There was a moment's stillness, a heavy exhale of his breath. "I am sorry, lass," he said, quiet. "It has not been—easy, these past years. I learnt to take what pleasure I could, when I could find it."

"And you couldn't have found it with me?" Ella shot back. "You couldn't have stopped by *one single time*, to perhaps say, *Ach, hello lass, I am not in fact dead, as you feared, and instead I have been amusing myself gallivanting about the realm, and seducing any woman who would have me*?!"

She turned to glare at Natt as she spoke, and he visibly grimaced—

and then, with effort, struggled to shove himself up onto his elbow. "No," he said, the single word snapping out flat, grim. "I could not."

"Why," Ella said, almost pleading, almost a sob. "*Why.* You came yesterday, didn't you? So why in all the gods' holy names did it take you *nine whole years*?! We swore a *pledge*, Natt!"

And gods, what had come over her, why was she saying such things. She was an heiress, she was one of the richest women in the realm, she was about to become a lady, to *belong.* So what the hell did it matter what this damned orc had done, or hadn't done, half a *lifetime* ago?

But all the same, Ella was dangerously close to sobbing, and her body lurched again toward the exit—but Natt's hand was still on hers, gripping tight, his claws scraping against her skin. And his breath was coming out in rough, strangled gasps, and each one sounded, looked, felt like pain.

"I know," he said, the words choked in his throat. "I *know*, lass. But *this* is why. I could not risk *this*, upon you."

This. Ella frowned at him, blinking through appallingly wet eyelashes, watching as his other hand jerked up, and waved at—himself. *This*, meaning—his leg. The injuries. The *attack.*

"I don't understand," Ella said helplessly, shaking her head. "Why, what do you mean, what does that have to do with *anything.*"

Natt's eyes briefly closed, his hand clamping even tighter on hers. His chest rising and falling, his jaw set, his throat convulsing deep in his neck.

"I am—*hunted*," he said finally, his voice blank, bleak. "I have been hunted, all these past nine years."

Hunted. Ella blinked at him, fighting to follow that, to turn it in a way that made sense. Hunted. For nine years.

"Hunted," she repeated, the word strange, awful on her tongue. "By—men? For nine whole *years*?"

There was a twitchy nod of Natt's head, his hand again clenching on hers, tight enough to be almost painful. As if to say, *Now that you know this of me, don't run, please don't run—*

But Ella couldn't even move. Could only stare at him, and fight to pull the pieces together. *Hunted.* No, it was impossible for any man to be so cruel, surely, and yet she'd seen it with her own eyes today, and...

"Who, Natt?" she whispered, through the sudden, menacing thunder of her heartbeat. "Who is hunting you? *Tell me*."

But his eyes, the look in his eyes, she knew, she *knew*. Before he even spoke.

"I am sorry, lass," he said, every quiet word a deafening thud. "The man who hunts me is Alfred, of Tlaxca. The man you are to wed."

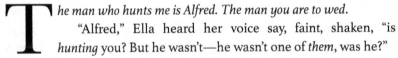

14

The man who hunts me is Alfred. The man you are to wed.

"Alfred," Ella heard her voice say, faint, shaken, "is *hunting* you? But he wasn't—he wasn't one of *them*, was he?"

And dear gods, maybe Alfred truly *had* been one of those horrible men earlier today, and somehow Ella had entirely missed him—but Natt gave a curt shake of his head. "No," he said. "He rode east last night, for this council. But these men hunt at his command, and he oft rides with them. If they had defeated me, they should have bound me, and taken me back for him to kill."

Ella's hand had clamped over her mouth, while the appalling visions of that marched across her thoughts. "But *why*," she pleaded, through her fingers. "Why would anyone *do* such a thing?"

Natt's eyes shuttered, and something jumped in his jaw. "For men like this," he said slowly, "with these high titles and lands, hunting an orc has long been a—feat. A proof of strength. It is akin to"—his eyes closed—"killing the largest mountain-lion. Or the buck with the greatest antlers."

Ella was about to protest, to argue, to say that she'd never heard Alfred *hint* at such a thing—but then, far too strong, there were the sudden memories of Alfred's disparate, offhand comments of hunting-parties, tracking prey, using bloodhounds. Of his kennel, which he'd spoken of with pride, claiming it to be one of the finest in the realm.

And Ella had just assumed, of course, that he was hunting deer. Foxes. Boars. Not orcs. Not—*Natt*.

"But there are *thousands* of orcs out there," she said, almost desperate. "Why is he hunting *you*?!"

Natt took another heavy breath, his eyes fluttering open to fix on something beyond her. "They found—things, of mine. Clothes. An orc's scent does not soon fade from such things. And thus, these men can teach these dogs an orc's scent, and then seek until it is found."

"For nine whole *years*?!" Ella demanded, her voice shrill. "But *why*?"

Natt's chest heaved again, his breath coming out thick. "It is better—*sport*, to chase worthy prey," he said. "And it seems, for this man, I am now a—thorn. A sign of weakness. A thing that must be conquered, for his pride."

Ella could only keep gaping at him, the revulsion rising in her throat. "But—the new *treaty*, Natt. Isn't that breaking the *law*?!"

His mouth grimaced, and he made a sound that might have been a laugh. "He is a lord," he said, bitter. "The law means naught, for him. He shall do all that he wishes."

The vision of Alfred and that woman in her drawing-room swarmed across Ella's thoughts, and she squeezed her eyes shut, shook her head. "So how have you *survived* all these years?" her choked voice whispered. "What did you *do*?!"

"I hid, at first," came Natt's answer, slow and deliberate. "I sought refuge in our mountain, and in the tunnels deep beneath it. My brothers hoped that mayhap, with time, the men should forget my scent. But the first day I went out into the forest, these dogs again found me, one new dog among them, and I was almost killed."

Ella flinched, her gaze darting back to Natt's scarred, battered body, to the way his eyes glittered in the faint light. "After this I went far to the south," he continued. "To the badlands, where these men would not follow. I lived with my Clan Bautul brothers there for many moons. But I did not belong there with them, and as such, there was much to pay, for the safety they granted me."

Ella could only stare at Natt, trying and failing to grasp the implications of that, and he took another breath, gave a harsh exhale. "When I could no longer bear this," he said, "I came back, and spent many moons only running over the land, giving these men the sport they wished for. But I yet had to rest, and thus I was caught four times, and almost killed each time."

"And you couldn't have fought back?" Ella countered. "You couldn't have killed them? Attacked them in the dark, or something? I *know* how fast and strong you are, Natt!"

It came out sounding accusing, somehow, but Natt only took another thick breath, his head slowly shaking, saying no. "Even before this peace," he said, "killing a lord's sole heir should have brought down great wrath upon my head. Not only from the men, but from my own kin. I could not risk losing what safety I did have, from them."

Ella's heart was lurching, and she belatedly realized that she was clasping Natt's hand with both of hers, gripping it as tightly as she could. "So what now?" she demanded. "What are you doing now?"

And suddenly Natt just looked tired, worn, his eyes staring blank at the stone behind her. "Now, I stay in the mountain," he said dully. "I come out, for a time, once I can no longer bear this. Then I am almost caught, and I run back, and stay again, until the next time."

Good gods in heaven. It sounded like pure and utter *hell*, especially for someone who'd always loved being outdoors as he had, running and roaming and exploring. He'd been so—playful, back then, so wild and carefree, and to think of him cornered, imprisoned, trapped underground for years on end, it was cruel, appalling, utterly unconscionable.

"I longed to come to you," Natt continued, even quieter. "I longed to speak of this to you. But I knew the men had followed my scent to these lands, and searched for me here, and sought to find what had drawn me here. I could not risk leading them to you, and thus teaching them that they could lure me, through you. I feared that they might use you, or hurt you. Or worse."

Oh. It all made sense, suddenly, horrible, *horrible* sense, and Ella's eyes were blinking hard, her fingers sweaty and clammy on his. "But you came last night," she whispered. "Why?"

There was an instant's stillness on his form, Natt's eyes still shuttered, distant, far away. "I heard," he said slowly, "of this party. I heard you were to be wed. And"—he drew in another long, heavy breath— "it seems I am not at all as noble as I had wished, for I could not face this. I could not bear to see you taken by a man—*this* man—when you should yet by rights be mine. When I yet had the right to take this vengeance upon my enemies."

The vengeance again. Ella couldn't seem to find an answer to that, and she swallowed hard, her eyes trapped to his distant, blank eyes. Waiting.

"I knew there should be time for me to do this," he continued, "whilst they were all at this party, but I did not know how to draw you from it. It was the gods' own gift that you ran, and came to me."

Ella's head was nodding, of its own accord, and a betraying sniff had escaped from her nose. Natt had risked his own *life* to come to her, to speak to her, and she'd said—she'd told him—

"Why didn't you tell me the truth," she pleaded. "In the hunting-cottage. Why didn't you *say* any of this, Natt."

But there was only bleakness in those eyes, pained and distant. "You spoke your wishes to me," he said. "You chose this man, over me, even after I sought to show you the joy I could bring you in his stead. I could not"—his chest hollowed—"dare to tell you this man hunted me, when you might have rushed back to tell him this, and sent him after me at once."

"But," Ella said, helpless, lost, "but Natt, I never would have done that. *Never.*"

There was a hoarse sound from Natt's mouth, perhaps almost a laugh. "But you have changed," he said, bitterly now. "You wished for your riches, and this new life away from me, where you think you are *real.* When I asked you to leave this, and come with me, I tasted your *fear.*"

Ella couldn't follow, couldn't face this, couldn't even argue it—and when Natt's flat eyes finally flicked back toward her, it was like he *knew.* Like he saw through her, into her, all the way to her soul.

"It was nine *years*," she heard herself say. "I thought you were *dead.*"

Natt didn't even argue this time, didn't push back. Just gave a small, tired-looking nod, and sagged onto the sheepskin, his mouth letting out an undeniable hiss of pain.

"Ach," he said, to the cave's ceiling. "Many days, I thought I was dead also."

And before Ella could speak, or even think, he closed his eyes, turned his head, and slept.

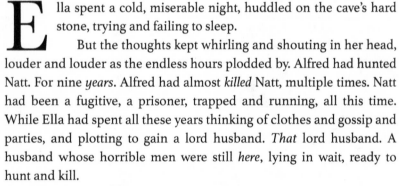

15

Ella spent a cold, miserable night, huddled on the cave's hard stone, trying and failing to sleep.

But the thoughts kept whirling and shouting in her head, louder and louder as the endless hours plodded by. Alfred had hunted Natt. For nine *years*. Alfred had almost *killed* Natt, multiple times. Natt had been a fugitive, a prisoner, trapped and running, all this time. While Ella had spent all these years thinking of clothes and gossip and parties, and plotting to gain a lord husband. *That* lord husband. A husband whose horrible men were still *here*, lying in wait, ready to hunt and kill.

The cold finally got the best of Ella, perhaps halfway through the night, enough to make her tentatively nudge her numb body up against Natt's heated one in the darkness. And when Natt's big arm shifted to curl around her, yanking her close without censure or blame, she very nearly sobbed as she rested her head on his warm shoulder, her body tucked tight against his.

She finally slept, then, but only lightly, flitting in and out of dreams. And the instant Natt's warmth shifted beneath her, her eyes snapped open, and she jerked up, off him, away.

But not *away* away, and she could see Natt's eyes blinking in the faint morning light, the confusion creasing his brow. He looked better this morning, not nearly as worn and broken as he had yesterday, and as he gingerly eased himself up to seated, his eyes on hers were wary, watchful, alert.

"Lass," he said, slow, careful. "You are still here."

Ella swallowed hard, and lifted her chin. "Yes," she said, more haughtily than she meant. "I am indeed still here. I have decided"— she drew in a breath—"that I am escorting you back to your mountain."

Those eyes blinked, once, and then flicked to the cave's exit. "Why."

Ella's cheeks felt suddenly warm, and she pulled her knees up to her chest, hugged her arms tight around them. "Because you—you *kidnapped* me."

But that excuse was beyond flimsy now, and Natt only arched an eyebrow, and looked at her, and waited. And Ella looked back at him, and drew up breath, and strength, and courage.

"We can't risk you being attacked like that again," she heard herself say, too quickly. "And you said they shouldn't, as long as I'm still with you. Which makes sense, because they clearly didn't know what to do with me, right? They surely don't want to risk escalating the situation with me, or have me get Lord Otto or the authorities involved. Not when Otto is allied to the orcs, and I'm supposed to marry Alfred in a month."

Natt just kept watching her, those careful eyes not betraying anything, and Ella drew in another oddly shaky breath. "So as long as I'm in the way, you'll be safe," she continued. "And I should have time to be in the way, right? My mother still thinks I'm with Alfred, and Alfred's men are still here, waiting for you. No one really knows I'm gone. And they won't, for at least another few days. Right?"

The words were tumbling over each other by the end, but Natt had seemed to follow easily enough, his head giving a slow, cautious nod. "Yes," he said, "there ought to be time for you to do this. But"—his eyes sharpened on her—"these five men are yet close, lass, and they shall not stop tracking me, now that they have caught my scent. And they may yet go to your mother at any moment. Or ride off after your betrothed."

"Indeed," Ella said, voice crisp. "And I shall be exceedingly glad to tell anyone else who asks—including all the proper authorities—that due to the unwarranted bloodthirstiness of Alfred's *friends*, I found myself with a badly injured employee, in an entirely untenable position. Only, my mother shall hear that this occurred on our journey to Tlaxca, and Alfred shall hear it was while I remained here. But"—Ella hauled in a breath—"from either angle, my only available option, at that point, was to escort you home at once. Before you *died* on my property, and exposed me to the *excessively* dangerous liability of violating this tenuous new peace-treaty, by means of having a dead orc's *blood* on my hands!"

For a moment, Natt only blinked at her, his eyes entirely unreadable—but then there was a twitch of unmistakable amusement on his mouth. "Even if these people swallow all these fancy words, lass," he said, "your betrothed shall not be pleased with this. And his dogs shall yet smell me all over you."

"Yes, because you *bled* on me," Ella snapped back. "Copiously, and repeatedly. Orcs are *extremely* uncouth, you know, and wont to start spurting blood at precisely the most inconvenient moments, all over anyone unfortunate enough to be nearby."

The twitch on Natt's mouth had slowly broadened into a smile, warm and sharp and wicked. "Ach, this is true," he murmured. "And who is to say I could not manage to spurt this—blood—down your throat, or up deep between your legs."

Ella's face had gone very hot, but she managed a jerky, imperious little nod toward him. "Indeed," she snapped. "*Extremely* uncouth, as I said. And also arrogant, and ungrateful, as well."

Natt laughed out loud at that, the sound low and oddly reassuring, and then he carefully crouched, and leaned over to grasp his pack, and the sheepskin. And after beckoning Ella to come closer, he again furled the sheepskin over her shoulders, tying it warm and tight against her.

"Thank you, my lass," he said, quieter. "You have shown me great kindness."

Ella could only seem to shrug, her face still decidedly hot, and she watched with strangely greedy eyes as Natt turned away and crept toward the entrance, his pack in hand. Exposing the round, high muscles of his arse, shifting against his trousers, his bulky form still favouring his right leg over the left.

"Can you still tell where the men are?" Ella asked, once he'd hesitated just inside the opening, with her crouched close behind him. He was sniffing the air, inhaling slow and deep, and he gave a thoughtful nod.

"South," he said, "but yet mayhap a half league away. This is luck, lass. We shall have a good start. And, time for a bath."

With that, he shot her a jaunty little smile, and eased himself out the cave's small entrance. And then, without any warning whatsoever, he turned and dropped his entire body sideways, full into the creek below.

Ella yelped and lurched over to look, but the creek was only waist-deep, and Natt was already rearing up again. His black hair arcing up long and loose behind him, while the water streamed from his grey-green skin, and his hands came up to splash more water over his face, again tilting his fluttering eyes up to the light.

"Ach," he breathed, an undeniable sigh of pleasure—and as Ella watched, her mouth gone entirely dry, he did it again. Dunking himself whole before arching up again, this time shaking himself off in a shivery rush, just as a dog might, sending water-droplets spattering all around.

"Should you like to join me?" asked his shocking voice, as Ella belatedly wiped the water off her face—and there was a hitching, jolting instant where she blinked at him, at this *orc*, standing there streaming water, with his hair long and unbound, almost to his waist, plastered messy against his gleaming wet skin.

And somehow, there was the inexplicable, unnerving realization that Ella *should* like to join him. Really very much so, and she hadn't splashed in water like that, let alone gone swimming, for *years*—

"No, thank you," she made herself say, too late. "I'm sure it's filthy. And probably freezing."

"Ach, I shall keep you warm," came his audacious reply, complete with a devious grin, and a beckon of his sharp claw. Almost—almost—enough to draw Ella forward, but she barely managed to hold herself in place, and fixed her eyes away, safe, on a huge old oak-tree behind him.

"No, we really should get going, shouldn't we?" she said, as firmly as she could. "If you're certain you're well enough. Which"—she risked a look at where he was now leaping back onto the bank, only slightly favouring his injured leg—"you seem to be, clearly."

He did look much improved, many of his wounds fainter than before, or entirely vanished. The worst was still his leg, by far, and Natt visibly limped on it as he came back toward her, his clawed hands combing through his long wet hair.

"Ach," he said, with a wince, and a dark glance at the still-obvious wound on his left shoulder. "I am better, lass. But I ought to take more care, instead of showing off thus, for you."

He'd dropped his left arm to his side, grimacing at the movement, while he kept jerking his other hand impatiently through his wet hair, clearly wishing it out of the way. And against all her better judgement, Ella sighed, and then stepped around behind him, and drew his hair back. Tucking it behind his pointed ears, and away from his earring, as she combed her hands through the long wet strands, and then began to braid.

It wasn't the first time she'd done this—Natt had always had beautiful hair, thick and black and glossy, and Ella had always longed to touch it, and plait it, and play with it. A desire that Natt had been all too willing to accommodate, and just like this, he would tilt his head back, allowing her to do all that she wished, while he purred low and contented out his throat.

Ella braided all the way to the end, fighting valiantly to ignore the rather heated tone his breath had taken. And when Natt slowly turned around again, she couldn't quite look at him—but she shivered all over as he stepped closer, closer. And then leaned in, his head angling, so he could lower his face to her neck, and—*smell* her.

There was no moving, no resisting it. Only standing there, her eyes fluttering closed, while she felt him slowly inhale, filling his chest with the scent of her. And just like last time he'd done this, back in the hunting-cottage, there was the slightest brush of those warm lips to her skin, sending a hard shudder down her spine. And then again, and again, and a dripping-wet *orc* was *kissing* her *neck*, but Ella could only seem to stand there, and feel it, and breathe.

"Ach," he murmured, as he finally drew away, his irises looking even blacker than usual in the brightening sun. "Your scent is already so much sweeter, lass."

Ella blinked at him, not quite sure whether to take that as an insult, or not. "Why," she managed, through her thick-feeling throat. "Because now I smell like *you*?"

He gave a rueful, twitching smile, his thumb coming up brief to brush against her lips. "Yes," he whispered, almost too quiet to be heard. "Only of me. *Mine*."

Ella's breath had vanished, the world had vanished, everything—and all that was left was this. Natt slowly leaning forward, sliding his clawed hand to her cheek, and bringing his mouth to hers.

His kiss was soft, slick, sensuous, even with his still-split lip. His long tongue delving deep inside, spreading her mouth apart, sparking heat bright and powerful within. And speaking, all too clearly, of what else he wished to do to her, slippery filthy warmth stretching her, filling her, making her its own—

Ella jerked back, much too late, her breath catching, her face hot. While her eyes cast wildly about them, searching the trees, because he'd said the men were coming closer, what if they'd seen her doing this, willingly *kissing* an *orc*?!

There were still no men within immediate view, but that helped very little, and neither did the shuttered look on Natt's face. Hiding something, something new, something that might have almost been—*hurt*.

"Listen, Natt," Ella said, with an unwilling grimace. "I need to be clear with you about this, all right? Me escorting you safely to your mountain is still *not* me volunteering to be—*yours*. All right? I still need to go home, after this, once you're safe. I still have commitments. Obligations. Important ones."

"Ach, like this man?" came Natt's voice, suddenly chilly, brittle. "And your *hoard*?"

Ella flinched, and shot a glare at his still-distant eyes. "No, like the rest of my *life*," she countered. "The life I've lived for the past nine years, without you, before you *kidnapped* me. The life my father wanted me to have. And perhaps you're not as familiar with Sakkin's inheritance laws as I now am, but my father's wealth should, by rights, now belong to my distant cousin, up north. And the only reason I still have it, or my house and my forest, my *home*, is because my father spent appalling amounts of time and research and money to buy me six months, after his death. Six months to marry a man of standing—now only one month—and then my *home* stays with me."

"With this *man*," Natt's smooth voice corrected. "To do with as he wishes."

Right. He was referring to *that* again, to what he'd said at the hunting-cottage, before Ella had left. *Have you once asked this man? Have you once used your voice against him, to learn what he seeks to do with all your riches?*

Ella's throat felt very tight, her eyes darting back to Natt's stiff face, to his glittering eyes. And surely, by saying that, he'd meant—surely he'd meant—that Alfred would use her money to keep hunting Natt. To *kill* him.

"Look, Natt," Ella said, over the sound of her suddenly hammering heartbeat. "Once we have you safely home, I—I'll talk to Alfred, all right? I'll tell him I *did* hire you, and you were kind to me, and not cruel or vicious in the least. And I'll say"—she took a breath—"that as a condition of our marriage, he needs to let you go. *Forever*."

She couldn't quite read the look in Natt's eyes, but her resolve was tightening, condensing, becoming truth. "And if you like, after that," she said, more quickly now, "I really *would* hire you—at *very* generous wages—to patrol my lands, and stay nearby. So we could still—see one another."

The words came out almost triumphant, because in truth, it really was the perfect, neat solution, wasn't it? Well, except for the fact that Alfred had wanted to leave and live out east in Tlaxca, but perhaps Ella could argue that as well. Perhaps—perhaps she could even suggest that they live apart, due to her many responsibilities here, and Alfred's seeming proclivity toward blatantly fucking other women. And that truly *was* the perfect solution, for everyone involved, wasn't it?

But Natt's face hadn't changed, his eyes still glittering watching blackness. "So you shall finally use your voice against this man," he said thinly, "so you may keep me near you, to use me as you wish. As a *pet*."

What? Ella blinked at him, and made herself shove down the rising, twitching unease. "Of course you wouldn't be a pet," she snapped. "We're still *friends*, Natt, aren't we? You're my oldest friend in the *world*, I've missed you so *much*, and after all this, I"—she drew in a heavy breath—"I don't ever want to be parted from you like that again. I couldn't bear it."

It was an admission, a true confession, and there was a replying shift in those eyes, something changed. "Foolish lass," he said, quieter than before. "After this, we shall never again be only—*friends*. If you yet wish to see me, after you have wed, you shall betray this man with me. Again, and again, and *again*."

There was an odd, bitter-sounding triumph in his voice, like he knew he had her, and this would be the end of it. But Ella felt herself swallow hard, take a breath—and nod.

Saying—*yes. I know. I will.*

Natt's face was a blank mask again, his big body before her gone almost dangerously still. But Ella knew him, she *did*, and suddenly there was the hurtling, shuddering awareness that he wanted that. Of course he wanted that. He wanted vengeance, he'd kept saying. And what better vengeance was there than to thoroughly and repeatedly cuckold the man he hated? The man who'd hunted him, for nine whole years?

But Natt still wasn't moving, wasn't speaking, and the unease flared again, close and uncomfortable in Ella's gut. Waiting, and waiting, until finally his throat convulsed, his eyes sliding away. "Ach, lass," he said, the words a heavy sigh. "You know not what you ask for. What you wish for."

But Ella *did*, and she squared her shoulders, gathered her courage. "I do," she whispered. "I want you safe, Natt. And I don't want to lose you again. And I have the resources to accomplish this, I should have the influence with Alfred. So why shouldn't we at least try, if it's what we both want?"

There was another heavy sigh from Natt, a hard clench in his jaw. "Foolish lass," he said, and it sounded almost pleading this time. "You know not what I shall want from you. Or what vengeance we shall take."

Vengeance again. But even so, the sudden shiver down Ella's back wasn't dread, or fear, or unease. Just pure, rippling, bright-hearted excitement, unspooling under her skin. Natt was saying yes. He was. Wasn't he?

"But you *do* want vengeance," Ella whispered, as her brazen hand reached out to brush, careful and tentative, against his bare chest. "Don't you?"

His eyes dropped to follow her hand, watching her touch him, and when his gaze finally came back up, it was dangerous, warm, alive. "Ach," he said, so quiet. "I do."

He did. And that was all that mattered, in this moment, and Ella's relieved smile was so sudden, so broad, it felt like it might split her face.

"Then that's our plan," she said firmly. "I escort you back to your mountain, I return home in time to deal with Alfred, I make him stop hunting you, *forever*, and afterwards, we stay—friends."

Natt's mouth twisted, his eyes again looking intently away—but he'd taken a deep breath, and he was nodding. Saying yes. *Yes.*

"Ach, my foolish lass," he said. "Friends."

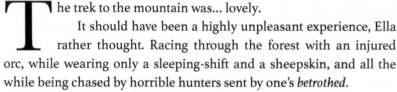

16

T he trek to the mountain was... lovely.

It should have been a highly unpleasant experience, Ella rather thought. Racing through the forest with an injured orc, while wearing only a sleeping-shift and a sheepskin, and all the while being chased by horrible hunters sent by one's *betrothed*.

There was no question of them not being followed, now, between the regular barks off in the distance, and the punishing pace Natt had set, alternately striding and running along invisible paths through the trees. But the sky above was bright and clear, Ella's boots were sturdy and dry—and, most of all, she was with Natt.

And despite his injuries, Natt was still, after all these years, utterly at home in the forest, and therefore, a highly amusing travelling-partner. Swinging on tree-branches, darting off to look at this or that, coming back with handfuls of seeds and berries for Ella to snack on while they walked.

"Ach," he said brightly, once he'd dumped another batch of bright red berries into Ella's cupped hands, and popped one into her mouth with easy familiarity. "Look at this, lass."

With that, he leapt up onto yet another tree, swinging himself bodily up over the branch with his good arm, and landing on it with his good leg. And then he strode down the branch, scarcely seeming to notice its narrow width, and plucked something off the tree-trunk before swinging back down to stand before her.

"See?" he said, thrusting it out toward her—and Ella did see, what seemed to be an unremarkable little seed-pod. But then Natt's other hand came up to stroke gently at the pod—and suddenly it exploded into bloom, into a spray of yellow and white.

Ella first yelped, and then laughed, and then stared, fascinated, as she reached a careful finger to touch at the bright flowers. And then she watched, oddly trapped, as Natt brought the sprig of flowers up, and tucked it into her hair.

"Fair, lovely lass," he said, with a twitch of a smile, and a light flick of his claw to her cheek. "You have bloomed, like these flowers, whilst we were parted."

Ella felt her face warming, her eyes glancing down to her current ensemble. "No, I've become thoroughly ridiculous," she corrected him. "I'm wearing bedclothes, and a *sheepskin*, and my face is probably sprouting freckles as we speak. And my hair"—she winced, and reached a hand up to feel the haphazard mess of loose waves—"is a total *nightmare*, Nattfarr."

But Natt only leaned in, grasping for a handful of Ella's hair, and then he brought it to his nose, inhaling deep. "Your hair," he said, husky, "is a bright crown from the forest-gods, lass. And were this mine to choose"—he stepped back a little, his assessing eyes darting up and down—"you should only wear furs thus. And jewels. And naught else."

He'd reached a purposeful claw to tug at the neckline of Ella's sleeping-shift, almost as if to tear it. And while she should have jerked away, and began walking again—they were being *followed*—she only stood there as that hand slid down, and came to cup slow, intent, over her breast through the thin fabric.

"These ought to be seen," Natt murmured, every word a low thudding thrill to Ella's groin. "They ought to be bared and flaunted, where they can be plucked, and suckled, and kissed, whenever I should wish."

Ella's breath choked in her throat, her nipple already jutting hard and aching against his palm, and Natt stepped closer, and cupped his other hand over the other side, heated and shocking and close. "I ken this should please you, lass," he purred. "You should like to be dressed by your orc, and walk tall and proud by his side."

The vision of that fired at once through Ella's thoughts, alarmingly vivid, and alarmingly intriguing. Walking tall and shameless at Natt's side, wearing only orc-jewels and furs. Her nipples bared and peaked and reddened, loudly proclaiming whatever he'd just done to them...

"Of course not," Ella managed, lurching back and away from his too-tempting touch, while her eyes darted uneasily around them. "A lady would never permit such a scandalous thing."

But Natt's head only tilted, his braid falling over his shoulder, and there was a brush of that black tongue against his slightly split lip. "Ach, but you are not yet a lady," he said. "And we now have only this one day together, before we are again parted. Should you not grant me this great gift, only for today? And then, mayhap, after you have teased me thus for a spell, we shall find a secret place, and share our joy under the sky?"

Ella was again struck speechless, because Natt really, really *meant* that. He wanted her to walk beside him, now, like *that*, and then take their *pleasure*, right out in the open—and it was almost impossible to find words, to make herself speak.

"No, Natt," Ella choked out, over her suddenly racing heartbeat. "That's ridiculous. I *can't*. I *will* be a lady soon, and, Alfred's men are *chasing* us, and *spying* on us."

Her eyes were again darting furtively around them, searching for any hint of shadows and faces, hiding in the trees. But Natt didn't even spare a glance, and those glittering eyes held to hers, looked into her.

"They are not yet near enough to see aught that we do," he said flatly. "They shall learn naught of what vengeance we take today."

Vengeance, *again*. But as Natt drew Ella back to walking, and then darted off after some other thing he'd noticed, Ella's thoughts kept circling at that, lingering, feeling almost... guilty. Natt was right, they only had this one day together before they were parted again. But surely that didn't require *public copulation*, did it?

Natt stayed away for longer this time, long enough that Ella began to feel an unmistakable unease—what if his injuries had gotten the better of him, what if he'd changed his mind, what if he'd been *caught*?—and when he finally bounded back to her side, she shot a relieved grin up toward him, and even put an eager hand to his bare arm. At least, until she caught sight of the distinctive red smear on his mouth, and—her eyes dropped downward—the *dead rabbit* in his claws.

"Oh, *gross*, Natt," she said, with a revolted little shudder, but Natt only gave her a slow smile back, showing off all his red-rimmed white teeth.

"Ach, you are now too fine even for good fresh meat?" he said. "Foolish lass. We shall alter this."

With that, he turned and knelt before a nearby large rock, and started skinning the rabbit *right in front of her*. Sending drops of blood flying onto himself, and onto Ella's sleeping-shift, while also—she grimaced—popping the occasional raw bloody morsel into his mouth.

It was utterly disgusting, but all the same, Ella couldn't seem to look away. His claws were so sharp and deft and deadly, his movements purposeful and easy, the born predator, making quick work of his prey. And when he grasped behind him for some moss, tearing it off a nearby tree without even looking, and then set it aflame with a single snap of his claws, there was a sound much like a gasp, escaping from Ella's throat.

Natt shot her a brief, amused glance, but kept working. Adding a few twigs and bits of brush to his makeshift fire, while his other hand began cutting off thin, curling chunks of meat with his claws. And then holding several slices close over his little flame, not even twitching as the fire licked at his fingers, and the delicious smell of roasting rabbit furled through the air.

"Come," he said to Ella, with a jerk of his head, and she obeyed, almost as if compelled. Coming to kneel before his fire, watching as he brought the meat up to blow on it, cooling it off—and then he raised his fingers to Ella's lips.

"Eat," he said, the word a clear order—but Ella's mouth was watering too much to refuse. And when she leaned forward, and took a careful, delicate bite of the meat from his claws, Natt gave a smug, approving smile—and even more so at her unwilling moan of pleasure as she chewed, because *gods* it was delicious, tender and savoury and hot.

"Good," Natt said, as he tucked another slice between her lips, and his other hand reached back, getting more. "I knew this one should be an easy lesson."

There didn't seem the space to argue that, not when one was being so gently, generously fed by a brutal, bloody orc. Whose other hand had continued slicing, cooking, adding to his fire, supported by only the occasional brief glance from his eyes.

Ella ate until she couldn't any longer, giving Natt a rueful shake of her head. And as she watched, he next snapped those long claws back deep into his fingers, and then gave her his fingers to suck off, one by one.

They tasted of blood and smoke and meat, with just a twinge of his musky sweetness. And for a bizarre, hanging instant, there was only this, only suckling on Natt's fingers, and perhaps wishing they were something else. Something just as alive, something that could kiss back, and feed her just as sweetly...

Natt's last finger was lingering in her mouth, his eyelashes fluttering as Ella's tongue nudged at his fingertip, as if to search for something inside. Flaring a telltale hardness across his eyes, while a rather satisfying growl hissed from his throat.

"Good lass," Natt murmured. "Mayhap now you shall also welcome some sweetness, with your meat?"

His other hand had dropped to clutch brazenly to the front of his trousers, showing off that far too visible—and far too tempting—ridge beneath. And even as Ella's betraying mouth watered, again, she couldn't help a swift glance around, toward whatever danger might be watching from the trees.

"I *can't*, Natt," she whispered helplessly. "What if Alfred's men *see*?!"

"I told you, they shall not," Natt countered, his voice flat. "I shall smell when they come close."

But that wasn't helpful, not in the slightest—Ella could *not* risk such a thing, not with so much at stake. Not even with that strange, almost angry look in Natt's dark eyes.

"You do not trust that I speak truth to you?" he asked. "Or you only no longer wish for me, until you are safe as this high lady, and I am fully your *pet*?"

Ella felt a sudden, jerking rebellion at the question—he was really caught on that pet thing, wasn't he?—and she belatedly leapt to her feet and turned away from him, pulling the sheepskin tight around her shoulders.

"We really ought to get going," she said, holding her eyes to the sight of the tall, craggy mountain up ahead, now looming much closer than it had been. "I need to make sure I get back in time. How much longer, do you think? Will we reach the mountain before nightfall?"

Natt didn't reply, but only began walking again, limping ahead of her, his shoulders stiff and square. Leaving Ella to hurry along behind on her increasingly tired legs, while her thoughts twisted and churned. She'd said nothing wrong. She was perfectly justified, in all of this. No true lady would ever take her pleasure out in the open like that, where anyone could see. Especially with an *orc*, who only really wanted it for vengeance anyway. Right?

But the silence only seemed to deepen between them, Natt's previous playfulness replaced with a stillness that felt inexplicably heavy. His limp became more pronounced as they walked, moving faster and faster, and he only used his right arm to clear the path for Ella, holding branches out of her way until she'd passed.

"So, what's your mountain like, these days?" Ella finally made herself ask, into the taut silence. "Do all five orc clans live there now?"

Natt shot her a narrow sidelong look, but gave a curt nod, and Ella cast her thoughts back, to the tales he'd used to tell her of his people, his home. Of how the mountain had first been discovered by an ancient elf named Edom, who together with his mate, had birthed five sons, who'd then become the five clans of orcs. And even after all these years, Ella could still remember all the clans' names: Ash-Kai, the strongest, then Bautul, the bravest, and Skai, the swiftest. Then came Ka-esh, the wisest, and last, the Grisk. The kindest. The ones who cared most for safety, and family, and home.

"Is your father at the mountain, too?" Ella heard herself ask, with another glance at Natt's inscrutable face. "Or does he still spend most of his time outside it, in your second home, with the other Grisk?"

Because Natt's father—Rakfarr, Ella remembered—had been some kind of leader among the Grisk, and had therefore split his time between the mountain, and a large Grisk camp to the west. Well over a day's journey away from Ella's home in Ashford, but the forest between them had been wild and unbroken, which was why Natt had been able to meet her there in secret so often.

"No, my father is not there," Natt said, his eyes straight ahead. "My father is dead. For many years now."

Oh. Ella felt herself flinch, her hands pulling her sheepskin tighter around her shoulders. The sun was close to setting, there was a marked chill in the air, her trotting legs were exhausted—and Natt's father was *dead*. And Ella knew that Natt had never met his mother— she'd died giving birth to him—but he had always adored his father, and thought him wise and strong and fearless.

My father's calling is to speak for our Grisk brothers without fear or shame, Natt had told Ella, more than once. *When I am grown, this shall be my calling, also.*

"I'm so sorry, Natt," Ella said, quiet. "I know how much you loved him."

Natt gave a jerky shrug, his head still straight ahead, and Ella kept eyeing him, dropping her gaze down to his clawed hand. To that distinctive, beautiful green-and-gold ring.

"So is that," she said, with a grimace, "your father's ring?"

"Ach," Natt replied, without inflection. "My sword was his, also."

Oh. Ella could almost taste his grief, she *knew* that grief, and she swallowed hard, her eyes studying his face. "So are you the Speaker of the Grisk now? Like you were supposed to be?"

But she already knew the answer before Natt spoke, could see it in the blankness of his eyes. "No," he said. "I am not."

He didn't elaborate, but Ella could understand easily enough, and felt a pang of misery flare deep in her chest. Natt was hunted, and one couldn't very well be a leader, or speak for one's brothers, if one was chased and in hiding all the time, right? And it was just more that Alfred had taken away from him, more bitterness and cruelty and suffering.

"If I can—deal with Alfred, and make him stop hunting you," Ella said, tentative, "could you still become Speaker of the Grisk, after that?"

"Mayhap," Natt replied, his voice and eyes still distant, but he didn't say anything more. And looking at him like this, there was the compulsive, almost irresistible urge to step closer, to touch him. To circle an arm around his stiff shoulders, perhaps, to bring the warmth back to his eyes, the smile to his mouth.

But Ella didn't, couldn't, and instead just kept trudging on, over ever-rougher terrain, moving faster and faster, feeling the tiredness dragging heavier and heavier as she climbed over rocks and boulders. The mountain was abominably close now, soaring high and dangerous overhead, and its smoke was streaming out to the sky, near enough to fill the air with the scent of it.

And suddenly it occurred to Ella that perhaps this—this was it. She'd escorted Natt safely home. She'd done what she'd meant to do. They'd had their day together, and now it was already over. And now what?

They came to a halt before a jagged-looking wall of stone, and finally Natt turned to look at Ella in the twilight. His eyes tired, wary, lingering on her face, and then flicking toward the trees behind them.

"I shall not ask you again to touch me," he said, his voice weary. "But is there aught else you might wish for this night, from me, before we part?"

Ella felt frozen, suddenly, caught in place, held in the strength of his eyes. Was there anything she wished for, from him. Before they parted.

And here, rising with shocking truth, were all the shocking words she somehow wanted to say. *I don't want to part. I don't want this to be over. Not yet.*

Her mouth had opened, about to speak—but then, behind them, there was the sudden, familiar sound of a dog's bark. The *men*. Coming closer.

Ella's heart was hammering, her eyes again catching, holding, on Natt's. And somehow there were more words, clamouring to escape her lips, the compulsion so strong she almost felt faint.

I want you to take me, Natt. I want you to be a proper orc predator and kidnap me again, so I don't have to choose. So I can still be a real lady afterwards.

Ella was truly going to say it, *I want you to force me, Natt*—and she clamped both hands against her mouth, squeezed her eyes shut, and wildly shook her head. She couldn't say such appalling things, to an orc. She *couldn't*—

"Then I thank you for bringing me here, lass," came Natt's voice, smooth, quiet. "I thank you for the joy you have brought me. I hope you shall find the life you wish for, with this man."

Wait. It sounded like goodbye, it wasn't goodbye, he couldn't, not yet—but when Ella's eyes snapped open, it was to the sight of Natt slowly, carefully leaning toward her, and bending his head to her neck. Inhaling her, slow, deep, as the dogs' barking rose louder and louder, and Ella's heart understood, thudded, broke.

He was *leaving*. Natt was saying *goodbye*.

"Safe journey home, my fair lass," he whispered. "Farewell."

17

In another world, another day, Ella might have turned, and ran.

But instead she only stood there, gaping at Natt, as he limped away from her toward the wall of stone, and those barks grew ever louder. Natt was saying goodbye. And he was—leaving? Already? Here? *Now*?

"You're just—leaving?" Ella demanded, her voice shrill. "And leaving me out here *alone*? In the dark? With these men? Next to *Orc Mountain*?!"

Natt's broad shoulders sagged, and he turned to face her again, his eyes blank. "These men are allied to your betrothed," he said. "And thus, they shall surely not harm you now. They shall grant you safety in their camp this night, and take you back to your lands, and your betrothed, come sunrise. Is this not what you wished and planned for, lass, all this day?"

What she'd wished for, all this day. And there was the sudden, lowering realization that Ella hadn't properly considered this at *all*. Not the fact that she would be stranded outside Orc Mountain in the dark, or that Alfred's awful men would be waiting. Waiting for Natt... or for *her*?

Ella's entire body flinched, her arms crossing over her chest, her head frantically shaking back and forth. "I shall never *speak* to those horrid men again," she snapped. "Let alone camp with them, or travel *anywhere* with them! I shall—"

But there was nothing, only the tense waiting watching in Natt's eyes, the barks coming ever closer. And then more comprehension, even more sickening than before, that Natt fully expected her to go, because—that's what Ella had told him she was doing. *I have obligations*, she'd said, more than once. *We really ought to get going. I need to make sure I'm back in time. I am to be a lady.*

"You shall what," came Natt's voice, steady, maddening enough to make Ella flinch again, her eyes darting up to the huge, smoking mountain behind him. Orc Mountain. His home. *I want you to take me. I want you to kidnap me...*

She choked the appalling words back, and desperately searched for other words, other truths. "Well, I'm just—quite tired," she heard herself say. "I'm not—accustomed to this kind of sustained activity, any longer. And it's increasingly dark. And I shall *not* travel *anywhere* with those men."

Natt's eyes were still watching her, flat, unreadable. "If you wish," he said, "I shall go and bring you more food, and mayhap a lamp. Or a warm fur, if you wish to climb a tree, and sleep until sunrise."

And here, vivid and almost entirely forgotten, were Ella's memories of doing that, with him. Sneaking out of her bedroom, under cover of darkness, and flitting through the trees with Natt in the moonlight. And then the joy of finding a good tree to climb, the struggle of finding a comfortable spot, while Natt would watch, amused, from the branches above. And then the peace of falling asleep, easy and pure and safe, hung between the moon and the earth.

The sheer, sweeping longing was so strong Ella had to close her eyes, tighten her arms over her shivery body. And she had to speak, she had to answer this, but how, how to say it...

"I don't want to," she blurted out, to her feet. "Go back. Not yet."

The world had gone very still all around, but for the barking dogs, and now the sound of distant crashing in the trees. But Natt's eyes didn't spare it a glance, and instead held dark and demanding to her face. "Then for what, woman," he said, quiet, deadly, "do you wish."

Ella couldn't *think* through her hammering heartbeat, and she gave a rough shake of her head, blinking downwards. She couldn't speak, she couldn't say it—until there was the feel of a single claw, nudging up under her chin. Making her look at him, trapping her eyes on his— and here were words, finally, impossible words, spilling from her lips. Not *those* words, thank the gods, but still shameful, still *wrong*.

"I should have a few more days," her voice said, too quickly. "Before I really need to go back. And we've come all this way, and I'm here now, and I'd really rather make sure you're fully healed before I return. And I'm tired, and cold, and I don't *want* to sleep in a tree, without you."

There was a bitter twist on Natt's mouth, and those glinting eyes stared, demanded, spoke. "Truth, lass," he hissed. "You shall speak truth, to me."

Ella was gulping, nodding, fighting for breath, trapped. "I want to stay," she heard her voice whisper. "And—and visit. For a while. With you."

Stay, visiting Orc Mountain. It was laughable, it was completely ludicrous, but neither of them was laughing, and Natt's face was a mask, betraying nothing.

"And what," he ground out, "do you think to do, lass, whilst you *visit*. Speak of your betrothed, and your duties, and your dreams of *real* life as a lady, before all my brothers? Shall you spurn my touch, as you have done all this day, and treat me as only your *friend*? Shall you talk of your plans to take the rightful Speaker of the Grisk as your *pet*, once you have wed the man *hunting* him?"

Ella's gut twisted—did Natt really think she'd do such things?— and her head was shaking, hard, desperate. "N-no, Natt," she said. "I'd wish to be a good guest. To—learn more of your home, and your ways. To—honour you, before your people."

There was a brief stillness in those eyes, holding onto hers—and then a purposeful glance away, his gaze flicking beyond Ella's shoulder. Toward the sounds of distant crunching feet, coming closer, closer.

"Ach," he said, slow. "Then tonight, once we are in my mountain, you shall seek to please me, and welcome my touch, and my taking? You shall swear never to speak of this man, or this betrothal, before my brothers? And"—those eyes snapped back to hers, suddenly brazen, challenging—"you shall give me leave to dress you just as I should wish, so that you may honour me, as I show you to all my kin?"

Good gods, he wasn't back on that again—but the look in his

eyes said that he damn well was. And that this was perhaps even some kind of test, some kind of proof to him, something to show that he truly did matter to Ella, after all. He wasn't just a friend. A *pet*.

Natt was waiting, his eyes glittering on Ella's, almost mocking. Almost as if daring her to say yes, knowing she wouldn't say yes, being utterly sure that she wouldn't. Not with these men so close, and with them respectability, and safety...

Ella's eyes darted desperately over her shoulder, but the men weren't in sight, yet—and this would only be for a week, at most. A small, measly fraction of her life. And would it truly be so terrible, to embrace a week's worth of secret wild wantonness, before the lifelong public constriction of her marriage? Surely Ella could give Natt this, even if only as part of his vengeance, after everything Alfred had done to him, for *years*?

She gulped down the fear, the unease, the shame—and felt herself nodding, *nodding*. "Very well, Nattfarr of Clan Grisk," she whispered. "I will."

But Natt's eyes on hers were still hard, mocking, inexplicably angry. "Do not speak false to me, foolish woman," he hissed. "You do *not* wish to be at my mercy. You do not wish to be bared and marked by me, before my brothers. You do not wish to belong to an *orc*, who has no wealth or standing, and has lost all that matters!"

He was nearly shouting at the end, *Natt* was shouting at her, his eyes flashing with anguish and rage. And Ella couldn't *think*, couldn't breathe, could only seem to stare at his huge menacing bulk, and shiver at the ever-rising sounds of men approaching.

"B-but," she heard her thin voice say, "you're my *friend*, Natt."

It was the wrong thing to say, clearly, because the rage only seemed to kindle higher in Natt's eyes. "Ach, your *friend*," he spat at her. "Your *pet*. I do not *matter*. I am not *real*. I longed for you all these empty years, I *dreamed* of you in the dark, and when finally I come to you again, you reek of *him*!"

Ella was barely following, her eyes darting again and again behind her, caught in the sudden clawing, miserable fear. "I—I didn't know," she stammered. "I thought you were *dead*."

"And now that you know I am not, you wish to make me your *pet*, and hand all you pledged me to *him*?" Natt shot back, his voice bitter and furious. "To *this man*? Of all men?"

To Alfred. To Alfred, who had hunted Natt, and destroyed his life for nine whole *years*, and Ella fought for air, for thought. "I—I didn't," she managed. "I kept my pledge. I gave you my *maidenhood*. I stayed with you, when you were hurt, even after you *kidnapped* me. I'm *here*, Natt. I want this, and I—I'll prove it to you. *Please*, Natt."

She shot another fearful glance over her shoulder, her heart pounding so loud she could hear it, the men's crashing feet even louder—

When suddenly, there was—*Byrne*. Coming over the ledge toward them, with his sword drawn and gleaming, and a dog leashed to his belt. And as Ella stared, his hand snapped to the belt, and yanked the leash off, and the dog was running straight for them, so fast it was a little brown blur—

"Halt!" Byrne's voice shouted, carrying over the trees. "*At once!*"

Ella flinched and froze, caught—but then Natt's hot, powerful hand clasped hers, and dragged her toward the rock. Toward a tall, jagged crack around the side of it, scarcely large enough to fit through—

But Natt yanked her through it, and suddenly Ella was plunged into pure darkness. So black there was nothing, only the feel of solid flat stone beneath her boots, cool air tickling against her skin, the clench of Natt's powerful hand against hers—and then the sound of the dog's furious barking behind them, echoing shrilly through the air.

Natt didn't even hesitate, but just kept moving. Dragging Ella behind him in the total darkness, turning one way, and then another. Dragging her into *Orc Mountain*, deeper and deeper, twisting and turning, pitch-dark and dangerous, she would never escape, not from this—

But the dog's barks had faded, gradually slipping into silence—and then, with a sharp turn sideways, it was like the cool drafty air had changed, become warmer, stiller. And Natt's warm hands grasped for Ella's tired body, yanking her close—and then he shoved her down, onto something flat and soft. A bed.

"You wish to prove this, woman," Natt's voice hissed, "then do so."

Do so. Ella's breath was gulping, her heart still hammering, her frantic thoughts fighting to catch up—she was inside Orc Mountain, prove this, *prove this*—and at least it was dark, they seemed to be alone, the men wouldn't dare follow them here. And Natt was here, prove it, he deserved it, Alfred, kidnapped, vengeance...

Ella's hands seemed to search for Natt on their own, finding his warm body still standing massive and stiff beside the bed. But when she yanked, and yanked again, he finally came, his big bulk sinking hard onto the bed in the darkness. But not touching her, not moving, not speaking.

He had to, he *had* to—and with a hurtling lurch of bravery, Ella kicked off her boots, and then reached to fumble for Natt's hand in the blackness. And before she quite caught what she'd done, she'd yanked up her shift, and parted her legs—and then shoved his big warm hand up against her bare thigh.

There was a choked, halting quiet, broken only by Ella's desperately dragging breaths, while Natt's huge bulk stayed entirely still against her—but then, oh thank the gods, his hand moved. Curling tight against Ella's bare thigh, and then sliding upwards with slow, deliberate intentness.

It was glorious, it was truth in the chaos, it was Natt saying he was here, Ella was here, they could do this. And even as that hand kept sliding up—an orc was disrobing her in a strange dark room in a terrifying *Orc Mountain*—there was only feeling it, gasping for it, Ella's traitorous body arching closer into his touch. Willing for more, begging for more, while that strong, torturous hand slid not between her thighs, as she might have wished—but rather over the curve of her hip, her waist, easing her filthy sleeping-shift up, and up, and up.

"Once this is gone from you, lass," Natt hissed, as his hand slid to her bared breast, gripping brief and proprietary against it, "you shall never be clothed thus again, as a *lady*, in my mountain. You shall only dress as I wish."

He hesitated there, waiting, perhaps again giving Ella room to refuse, to run—but she felt herself nod, and thrust her arms up over her head. Again granting him permission to take this, to do this, please—and he did, giving a low, husky growl as he yanked the shift off, leaving her entirely naked and exposed in the foreign darkness.

But Ella was proving this to him, and his big hand was already stroking down her front again, sliding smooth and wide and hungry. Almost as if he were discovering this again, learning her again, and her frantic, exhausted body could only seem to welcome that, to perhaps even revel in it. Gasping and twitching on its own accord, leaning into every tantalizing touch of that warm hand, feeling her skin flare and prickle as it passed.

And when that hand finally nudged between her already-trembling thighs, Ella took a shaky breath, and spread her legs wide. Welcoming him between them, perhaps even begging him to seek between them—and she moaned aloud as he did, as his hand slid slow and purposeful over the curve of her, cupping close and hungry and hot.

"In my mountain," he said, husky in her ear, "this shall be *mine*, to do with as I wish. To open and use as I wish."

And oh, he was already doing it. Those strong fingers gliding against her swollen lips, and then carefully, gently pulling them apart. Just enough that he could nudge a finger between them, sinking slightly inside—and Ella bucked and moaned, oh it felt good, as he slipped in deeper, harder, fuller.

"See how you are yet wet with my seed," he whispered. "Feel how your womb longs to drink yet more. Feel this, lass, and know"—he gave a low growl, and Ella felt a second finger slip inside, stretching her around it—"that in my mountain, this womb shall never run dry. It shall be filled to dripping each day with my fresh strong seed, and it shall coat your pretty thighs with my scent as you walk before my brothers."

Ella should have been repulsed, appalled, afraid—but instead she was gasping and writhing beneath him, her hands clutching at his hot, smooth skin. Dragging him sideways over her, desperately needing him nearer, and he gave a deep, rolling groan as he obliged, his body heavy and powerful, his fingers still playing with astonishing familiarity between her spread legs.

"And you shall speak to me," he breathed, his breath hot, his braid tickling against her cheek. "You shall use your words, to tell me what you wish for. *Now*."

And perhaps it was the tiredness, or the darkness, or the mouthwatering musky scent of him, so close. Or, perhaps, even the surprising, unnerving relief of being half-pinned, *safe*, beneath a huge orc's warm weight. But whatever it was, Ella drew in breath, turned toward where she knew his face to be, and just—spoke.

"I want you, Natt," she whispered. "I want you to kiss me, and—and—*take* me. Like you did before."

The words were sheer humiliation, burning at her cheeks, but she didn't take them back, and instead gulped in air, and waited. And waited, until there was the feel of Natt's hand on her cheek, clawed fingers spreading wide—and then, in a breath, he kissed her.

It was a firing cascading stream of heat, of hunger and power and pleasure. Natt's mouth on hers, his long tongue twining inside, and he tasted divine, felt *glorious*, his big body heavy and safe and everywhere, all over her, filling her thoughts her mouth her breath. And now—Ella arched and gasped against his lips—that slick hot heft was *there*, nudging between her spread legs, delving smooth, strong, inexorable against her raging clenching heat.

Natt abruptly broke the kiss, and there was again the feel of his big hand, skittering on her face. "Are you sure of this, lass," he said, hoarse. "You are yet new to my prick, I do not yet wish to draw your blood—"

But Ella only dragged his head back down, and her other hand reached down to clasp at his round muscled arse, drawing it closer. And there was a fierce, guttural groan from his lips, crushing against hers, while between her legs that hot, swollen cock began to press forward, plunging slow and strong into her open, inflamed wetness.

It felt easier than last time, smoother, with less resistance—but it was still a full-scale invasion, a splitting apart at the core of Ella's body, of her entire being. Taking her, filling her, breath by agonizing breath, his tapered hardness so warm and solid and alive, twitching and flaring inside her skin...

Natt again broke their kiss, this time to haul in huge, choking breaths, his chest heaving against hers. "*Mine*," he gasped, and in reply Ella felt her whole body arch and flare against him, around him, her legs spread as wide as they could go. Willing him deeper, and he was, he *did*, his hips bearing down stronger, his cock slowly but surely sinking its way inside—

"Ach," he breathed, "ach, lass, yes, kiss me, learn me, suck me in, drink me up. I shall give you my seed, I shall flood you to bursting with me, until you are dripping with me, and *begging* me for more—"

Gods, he was truly saying these things, but Ella only nodded in reply, dragging him yet deeper, craving and writhing and moaning beneath him. And here was his mouth again, his tongue swirling strong and demanding against hers, his cock just as powerful deep below.

And with one final, thrilling drive of his hips, he was there. Buried to the hilt, with Ella helpless and spread-eagled and trembling, impaled on the huge hungry heft of him.

"Oh," she gasped, rocking up against it, feeling it, tight and close and utterly *magnificent*. "Oh gods Natt, don't stop, oh gods, please please please—"

He didn't stop, he was rocking back against her, meeting her hips, pinning her to the softness beneath her with his full weight. His throat letting out a heated, sustained growl, his face buried into the curve of her neck, his warm mouth suckling against her skin, his teeth nipping sharp. His big body suddenly almost overwhelmingly strong and deadly, covering her trapping her blocking out everything, until there was nothing left. Only an orc taking her, his muscled form moving desperate and fluid and beautiful above her, it was too much, too close, the smell the world swarming exploding fire and light in her blood, in her heart—

Ella's release shot to life with a scream, a dazzling dazed relief, blaring out from her groin, lighting up every nerve in its path. Making her entire body soar up against his driving weight, and in reply that weight met her, caught her—and then exploded out deep inside. Pumping hard and full and *wonderful*, flooding her filling her to the edge of her breath, her being, almost too powerful to be borne.

But then that big body stilled, that hardness slowly softening inside her, and somehow, there was air again. Air, and quiet, and now freedom, as Natt's heavy bulk lifted, his warmth carefully drawing out of her—

But then—Ella couldn't help a gasp—was the sudden, shocking surge of his seed. Spewing out with stunning force between her spread legs, spurting thick and hot all over her thighs, the furs beneath, and even Natt's *hand*, which had snapped down to cup between her legs, to witness this, to coat itself in the mess.

Ella's face was burning, suddenly, and she could feel the shame rising, whispering, mocking. She was supposed to become a *lady*. And real ladies would never have thrown themselves at an orc thus. Real ladies would never find themselves lying debauched and spread-eagled beneath an orc, their betraying bodies gushing out hot orc-seed all over whatever might happen to be beneath.

But Natt's groan was low and steady against Ella's ear, his sharp teeth giving a painful little nip at her earlobe, while his hand purposely slid against her, smearing itself in the proof of what he'd done. And then—the heat flooded Ella's cheeks again—he slid that dripping-wet hand up, over her belly, painting her with his hot, sticky seed.

A lady would have protested, perhaps said, *No, you should be cleaning me of your foul leavings*—but Ella could only seem to lie there, red-faced and wondering, as Natt's warm hand again went down to linger between her spread legs. And then sliding back up, this time curving that hot, sticky hand over her still-heaving breast.

"W-what are you doing," Ella managed, and in response that hand only went down again, lingering, getting more.

"I am covering you with my scent," he murmured. "I am readying you to meet my kin."

Oh. Ella felt her body stiffen, while the impossible visions of that marched past her eyes. Natt had kept saying this was what he wanted. And she'd agreed to it, she'd sworn to prove it, she'd escaped her betrothed's men so she could have *this*—

"This is what it shall be, lass," came Natt's voice, close and menacing against her ear. "Should you yet wish to stay. You shall be used, taken, marked, lain bare. You shall reek all over of my scent. You shall please me, and obey me, and seek to honour me before my brothers. You shall be *mine*."

A reflexive shiver chased down Ella's spine, and she could feel Natt's watching eyes, prickling against her skin in the dark. Not forcing, not kidnapping, but making her choose. Wanting her voice.

"In *private*, for—a week," Ella said, finally, shakily. "And then I'll go back. I'll tell everyone I was only here for a visit, to make sure you healed properly. And no one outside the mountain will ever know the truth. *Especially* Alfred and his men. Right?"

There was an unmistakable tension in that body against her, its weight gone hard and still. "Ach," he said, his voice distant, careful. "You shall speak as you wish, and I shall not seek to stop you."

Well. And lying here in the quiet darkness, with an orc's hand gripping at her breast, Ella only seemed able to breathe, and nod. It really *was* the best solution, wasn't it? They could take vengeance on Alfred together, with this. Ella would please Natt, enjoy Natt, have the surreal, scandalous experience of knowing what it was truly *like*, to be fully caught in an orc's thrall, bent to his will.

And when she went back to Alfred, surely it would be easier to face him, after this. Easier to smile at him, and even take him to bed, and think of how appalled he would be, to know what his innocent new wife truly was. To know she'd been used and exposed and ravaged by an orc. To know that she'd done far worse, far more to Alfred, than he could ever do to her.

It would be true vengeance, and it would be devastatingly sweet. Especially if Ella could keep meeting Natt in secret, afterward, and taking this for her own. A little like a pet, perhaps, but Natt would soon understand that it wouldn't be the worst thing, would it?

"And you wouldn't hurt me, or betray me, in this," Ella said, tentative, into the darkness. "Would you, Natt?"

There was another instant's stillness, and then his exhale, harsh against her ear. "I should never wish," he whispered, "to harm one such as you, lass."

It was all Ella needed, in that moment, and she felt herself sink closer into him, into this warm quiet safety. They would have their vengeance. And it would be *wonderful*.

"Then I want to stay, Nattfarr of Clan Grisk," Ella whispered. "For these next days, I'm yours. Do with me as you will."

18

Ella slept deep and content that night, held close in Natt's strong arms, her face buried against his chest. Inhaling his delicious, musky scent with every breath, and knowing, with an odd, fundamental certainty, that she was safe.

At least, until her eyes snapped open, blinking at darkness—and behind them was a vision of *Byrne*. Byrne's face, as he'd watched Natt drag Ella into the mountain, and his dog had charged straight toward them.

Ella winced into the pitch-darkness, and rubbed hard at her eyes. Good gods, how that must have looked. Almost as though Natt had *forced* her to go into the mountain. And Ella should have thought to at least tell Byrne what she was doing, she should have done *something*, right?

Natt had still been lying close beside Ella, their legs intertwined, his arm slung heavy around her. But as her panic kept rising, she could feel him shifting, his hand coming up to slide gentle against her face.

"You are vexed, lass," he said, gravelly, in her ear. "What is it?"

"The *men*," Ella replied, without hesitation. "They *saw* us, Natt. They *knew* you brought me inside, and I didn't tell them why. And what if they go back, and say you—you *kidnapped* me? That's grounds for *war*, Natt!"

And gods, the more Ella considered it, the more she realized just how foolish she'd been. It had been pure madness, last night, stupidity beyond belief. What in the gods' names had brought on the delusion that one could just decide on a whim to visit *Orc Mountain*, while one's betrothed's men were *watching*?

"Do not fear," Natt's rumbling voice said. "I have had news of this, whilst you slept. Our captain has already met with these men this night, and addressed this, for now."

Oh. The relief shuddered Ella all over, even as she opened her mouth to ask how such a blatant provocation could possibly be *addressed*, and what *for now* meant—but Natt's big hand suddenly pressed over her mouth, while his other hand stroked down her front. To where—Ella winced—her naked body was now covered with a dried, hard-feeling film. Of his *orc-seed*.

"You swore to please me, and be *mine*, whilst you stay," he murmured, sliding his brazen hand against it. "And thus, you shall no more speak of this, until it must needs be spoken of. I shall not yet have this day's joy tainted by this man. Do you understand?"

Ella's urge to ask more questions was almost overpowering, and she took a breath to speak—until she felt the shocking, blaring truth of Natt's *teeth*. Hovering close against her neck, about to sink deep. *Threatening* her.

But the chill down Ella's back wasn't all fear—not even close—and she found herself nodding, quick and forceful, against the scrape of his teeth. Earning a grunt of satisfaction from Natt's mouth, a soft kiss to her skin.

"Good," he said. "Now, feel all this seed upon you, my filthy little lass. You are in much need of a bath."

Ella blinked, reorienting herself around that, and then tried for an elbow to his stomach. "You devious orc," she heard herself say. "That was *your* doing, Nattfarr. Not mine."

"No?" he asked, the challenge too clear in his voice, as his warm hand went straight for her groin, nudging gentle between her still-parted legs. Spreading her wider open, from where she had somehow seemed to be *stuck together*, and—Ella gave a low, humiliated gasp—releasing yet another bubbling surge of thick, hot orc-seed from deep inside her, spurting out strong against his hand.

"You again speak false to me, lass," he murmured, as he again stroked his wet hand up, coating her even more with his mess. "Your hungry womb seeks to spew my seed all over, for all who wish to see."

Ella gave a hard, betraying shudder against him, and Natt only chuckled, close and satisfied in her ear—and then he eased himself up, drawing her with him. And then—there was light.

He'd lit a lamp, Ella realized, through her squinting eyes. An actual, human-made oil lamp, now burning with a steady flame, lighting up the room around them.

And it was—surprising. Not at all like the cave they'd hunkered in, drippy and craggy and full of loose rocks. Instead, this was an actual *room*, with four slightly curving walls of smooth grey stone, and a flat, high stone ceiling. The floor was smooth stone too, and set upon it were several furnishings, including a small wooden table and chair. And Ella was currently—she glanced downwards—sitting on a *bed*, a simple one, but covered over with layers of soft, silken furs.

When she blinked back at Natt, he looked almost—uneasy, as if waiting for her to run off screaming for the men, after all. But Ella felt herself give him a rueful smile, drinking in the sight of his messy braid, his flushed cheeks, and—her head tilted—his wounds that now looked nearly negligible, but for the still-ugly gash on his leg.

"Oh, you're looking *so* much better, Natt," she said, with an impulsive brush of her hand to his arm. "Do you feel better, too?"

He gave a slow nod, still looking oddly wary, and Ella shot another quick, curious glance around the room. "Is this room yours?" she asked. "It's lovely. Very cozy."

Natt's eyes blinked, once, but then he shook his head. "It is for any Grisk, who wishes for a night of peace. My own rooms are deeper in the Grisk wing."

"Your *rooms*?" Ella echoed, with another impulsive smile. "How very extravagant of you, Nattfarr."

He twitched a smile back, but gave a rolling shrug of his shoulder. "They are my father's rooms," he said. "For the Speaker, so that he may meet with other Grisk in safety, and hear their words. And so he may offer refuge to any who need it, and house his guard and his mate close."

His guard. His *mate*. That word sent a strange twist through Ella's belly, but she fought to ignore it, shove it back. "Your guard?" she made herself say instead. "As in, another orc? To protect you?"

"Ach," Natt replied, his eyes settling on the wall beyond her. "But more than one. My father had eight orcs in his guard. I shall soon have four, should the captain allow this."

Ella studied him, considering that, her hand tightening against his arm. "Why only soon, and not now? And why does your—captain— get to decide? Is this still the same horrible captain you used to talk about?"

Because she could remember, a bit foggy now, how Natt had spoken of the orcs' powerful, brutal captain. Of how this captain and Natt's father had often been at one another's throats, and how there had been grudges, and thefts, and vicious battles between them. How Natt's father had held the Grisk orcs' loyalty in his sway, and how this awful captain had needed that, and hated it.

"No, this captain is not the same," Natt said, his voice clipped. "He is Kaugir's son, and a far wiser orc than his father. But he yet does not wish to have one with power standing between him and the Grisk. He does not wish to hear our true voices, or be forced to heed them."

Ella's hand reflexively stroked at Natt's arm, her eyes still caught on his face, the bitterness in his voice. "But maybe that will change soon?" she asked. "If he's willing to grant you your guard? That would help against Al—I mean, your hunters—too, wouldn't it?"

And gods curse her, because the displeasure flared across Natt's form, his eyes shuttering, his jaw taut and tense. "Mayhap," he said, the word purposely vague. "Do you hunger, lass? We ought to eat."

With that, he lurched to his feet, and strode over toward the small table. He was entirely unclothed, Ella belatedly noticed, his high arse-muscles smoothly rolling as he walked. And as he turned to drop his naked body into the chair, he gave her a full, unbroken view of—everything.

Ella swallowed hard, blinking at the sight, because despite all that they'd done so far, she still hadn't seen—*this*. His body so tall and lean and powerful, every scar and ridge and muscle lined stark and shad-owed in the lamplight. The broad shoulders, the rippled abdomen, the hollows at his hips, the capable thickness of his thighs and calves, and—most compelling of all—the half-hard heft of his tapered grey cock, jutting out from that mass of black hair, with a pair of obscenely large bollocks bulging below.

Natt knew Ella was looking, the bastard, and as she watched, he settled his body on the chair, sprawling his legs wider. And then—she nearly choked—his clawed hand dropped to that cock, circling around it, and stroking up.

Damn. Ella's breath was already heaving, her eyes caught on this audacious, impossibly fascinating sight. On how he was growing thicker and longer with every sure stroke of his hand, and how that viscous white seed was already pooling at the tip.

"It pleases you, to feast your eyes upon me thus," came Natt's voice, thudding straight to Ella's groin. "Does it not, lass?"

A furtive glance at his eyes showed them looking hard and intent toward her, and he gave a casual, imperious wave of his other hand. Meaning, *Get up*—so Ella did, standing shaky to her bare feet beside the bed.

"Speak this," he said, his voice cool, commanding. "And come. Stand here before me."

Ella immediately obeyed, even as she winced at the surprising soreness in her legs, and deep up between them. But Natt's eyes only watched, glittering, unrepentant, as that insolent hand kept sliding slow and deliberate up his length, again and again.

"Speak," he said again, harder this time. "This is a lesson you must learn, lass. You wished for this."

And had Ella wished for this—*that*? Truly? But looking at his imperious, half-lidded eyes, at his still-stroking hand, she realized that yes, good gods, she had. She'd said, *Do with me as you will*. And Natt, of course, would want any number of shocking things. And Ella had known that, and *wanted* that.

"Very well," she heard her wavering voice say. "Um. It, um, pleases me. To see you thus."

Natt's free hand gave another commanding little wave, so Ella drew in air, drew herself tall. "You're, um, very—fit," she said. "Very, um, virile. Good at this. Like you are with everything, really. And your—*seed*, I—"

It was stringing down from the tip of him, now, in a long unbroken strand of mouthwatering white, and as Ella stared, his hand pumped out more, bubbling it out thick and lewd and utterly enthralling. "You what, lass," Natt's low voice hissed. "You long for this? You long for me to coat you with it, yet again? To spew it all over your bared, filthy little form?"

Gods in heaven, Ella *did*, and she gave a swift, heated glance downwards, to the streaks of white already smeared over her naked belly, and her breasts. Which looked *debauched*, suddenly, her peaked, painted nipples jutting out flushed and humiliating toward him.

"Yes, Natt," Ella choked out. "I long for this. I long for you to—to cover me with you. To make me as—as *filthy* as you might wish."

Her face was burning, and there was the almost overwhelming urge to cover herself, to hide from her own outrageous words—but Natt was groaning, deep and guttural, his eyelashes fluttering, his hand jerking up his swollen length with sudden, desperate force.

And as Ella's trapped, trembling body stood there, exposed and staring and wanting, Natt curled over, crying out harsh and hoarse—and that huge, grey orc-prick in his hand sprayed out his pleasure. Spurting hot and sticky onto Ella's bare skin in pulse after pulse, catching on her, marking her, coating her breasts and her belly and her thighs all over with more of him, leaving her drenched and dripping and thoroughly, unspeakably obscene.

Natt's eyes were held fast to the sight, almost as though he were dazed with it, drowning in it. And when his shaky hand beckoned Ella closer, she immediately went, standing between his parted legs—and then she choked out a low, betraying moan as his hand came up, and deliberately spread his mess wide.

"Good lass," he whispered, as he watched his hand do it again, again. "Look how filthy you are, dripping thus with my fresh seed. Does this please you?"

It was appalling, surely it was frightful and unladylike and *wrong*, but Ella's head gave an ashamed little nod, all the same. And the sudden, sharp-toothed approval on Natt's mouth made it almost entirely worth it—and even more so when he drew her sticky body close, and down onto his lap.

"You must hunger, lass," he purred, and as Ella blinked, he pulled over a large bowl that had been sitting on the table. And inside it was what looked to be a good quantity of dried meat and seeds, as well as a few actual *apples*.

"Eat," Natt ordered, with a wave of his hand toward it. "We must rebuild your strength."

Ella meekly nodded, reaching for an apple, and taking a tentative bite. It tasted surprisingly delicious, crisp and juicy and sweet, and her next bite was far larger, earning another approving smile from Natt's mouth. He'd grasped for an apple too, sinking his claws deep into the shiny red skin, and as Ella watched, he bit off the entire top half, stem and all, with a single crunch of his sharp white teeth.

"Orcs," Ella said, with a roll of her eyes, and in reply Natt tossed the rest of his apple in the air, and caught it in his teeth. And with two sharp snaps of his head it was gone, too, leaving only a drop of juice running down his chin.

"This pleases you," he said, as he wiped his chin, and then reached for another apple, and took another deadly bite of it. "You are such a filthy lass, I ken you should not even balk if I were to take down a whole moose before you with only my claws, and have myself a feast."

Ella made a face at him, but he only looked amused, and tossed the rest of his apple into his mouth. "Ach, you should whine and gripe," he said, "but then, you should watch me do this, with your eager blue eyes. And should I then come to you covered with blood, and tell you to suck me, or bend over for me, you should not refuse. Should you?"

The hitch in Ella's breath was a highly unfair betrayal of all her so-called decency, and she ducked her head away from him, her face flushing hot and mortified—but Natt only laughed, and nudged her half-eaten apple back to her mouth. "Eat," he said. "There is much we must do today."

He seemed quite chipper at the prospect, and Ella obediently ate the apple, and then the dried meat he handed over, and some seeds. It was all simple, bland food, especially when compared to the output of Ella's pricey kitchen-staff, but it still tasted surprisingly good, and she again ate more than she'd eaten in one sitting in months, or perhaps years.

"Good," Natt said, with an approving pat to her sticky, slightly rounded belly, once she was too full to possibly eat any more. "Now come. Next we shall bathe."

The thought was a truly wonderful one, if rather unnerving, due to the fact that surely the baths were elsewhere, and liable to be filled with other orcs, and Ella was still *naked*. But thankfully, once Natt had risen to his feet, he bent to grasp for their clothes, which had been strewn haphazardly on the floor.

"I shall grant you leave to wear these to the baths," he said, as he tossed Ella's shift and boots toward her. "But after that, you shall walk my mountain barefoot. And I shall have this foolish frock *burnt*."

He spoke with a rather vindictive satisfaction, and instead of arguing, as she surely should have, Ella only pulled her shift on, and then made a face down toward it. It was probably unsalvageable anyway, and it *smelled*, and also, it was *sticking* to her.

"Come," Natt said, once he was dressed again, with his sword at his side, and the lantern and pack in hand. "I shall take you around back, so you shall not yet meet my brothers."

That was a blessing, Ella supposed, and she willingly followed Natt out of the room, and into a corridor. It was surprisingly broad and high, with the same flat grey stone on all sides, and it seemed to smoothly twist and curve up ahead, snaking off into pure, empty blackness.

But Natt's steps were assured and unafraid, his hand tight on Ella's, and he shot her a quick, assessing look over his shoulder. "Do not fear, lass," he said firmly. "You are safe here with me."

Ella nodded, though she leaned a little closer into him, all the same. "Can you tell me about it?" she asked, glancing uneasily ahead, toward the darkness. "As we go?"

Natt's nod was decisive, immediate. And as he led Ella down the twisty corridor, turning off this way and that, he told her how the mountain was separated into five wings, one for each of the clans. The Ash-Kai held the uppermost part, and a section to the west, with the Skai and Bautul next beneath, with areas to the south and east. And the Ka-esh were furthest below, tunnelled deep under the earth, because they preferred the dark, and often wished to be left alone.

"And all this," Natt said, as he drew Ella around yet another corner, waving at the occasional black opening in the stone wall, "is for the Grisk. We are between Ka-esh and Bautul, on the north side, with some rooms above ground, and some below. We are the largest of the five clans, and thus have the largest wing, also."

"Is it all in use?" Ella asked, peering into another dark opening in the wall. "This area seems fairly deserted, doesn't it?"

"Ach, for now," Natt said, flatter than before. "But with this new peace, we seek to fill it again, with our mates and sons. It is my dream, before my death"—his voice hesitated—"to see my sons, and those of my brothers, once again filling these empty rooms. And to see the sons of our sons running free and wild through these halls, and filling this mountain with joy."

Oh. Something clenched at the words, deep in Ella's belly, and she cast a sidelong glance at Natt's sharp profile in the dim lamplight. "And do you think this new peace-treaty will accomplish this, by then?"

"Mayhap," came his answer. "But we are yet hunted and attacked under this peace, and powerful men yet plot to destroy us. Women yet run from us, and they fear, with cause"—he grimaced—"to mate with us, and bear our sons. Many orcs, and many Grisk, refuse to yet live in this mountain, or bring their women here, fearing what has befallen them and their mates before."

Ella's thoughts had flicked back to Natt's father, to that awful, ongoing feud with the orcs' previous captain. "Then what do you think will help?" she asked, quiet. "What do you plan to do?"

Natt did plan to do something, that much was clear, and his jaw flexed, his mouth gone tight and grim. "When I am Speaker," he said, "I shall defend the safety of every orc, whether in or out of this mountain. I shall never allow a lone orc to be hunted, as I have been. And I shall work with my brothers across all five clans to make this mountain a better place for all women, and their sons."

"How so?" Ella asked, genuinely curious, and Natt gave a jerky wave of his lantern toward the grey corridor all around. "We need light, and food humans will eat, and easy means for women to reach sun and open air," he said. "We need our own rules and laws to protect women and our young, and we must enforce these with all speed and strength, even if we must cast a brother out. And we must offer women safety in bearing our sons. We must use our wisest orcs not only for drafting and mining and forging, but also in *science*"—the word sounded careful on his tongue—"and medicine."

Ella felt herself nodding, her eyes held to his face. "That seems like a worthy plan to me, Natt," she said. "Have you spoken to your captain of all this? Surely any wise leader would wish for such things?"

"Ach, Grimarr says he wishes for this," Natt replied flatly. "But he is still too caught in these wars and plans against men, and his own dream of five orc clans as one, all held under his thumb. But I say, if the Ka-esh do not wish for lamps, or the Skai and Bautul do not wish for laws to foil their deeds, then we Grisk should not suffer, for this. We ought to stride forward alone, and hope that the rest of our brothers will see our wisdom, and seek to follow."

Ella was still nodding, and eyeing Natt with an odd, rising admiration. "So you need your captain to grant you the authority to proceed, on these things," she said slowly. "And the resources."

Natt gave a curt nod, and Ella felt her head tilting, considering that. "What kind of resources?" she asked. "Your guard? Money?"

Natt's jaw twitched again, but he didn't answer, and drew her toward another opening in the rock. Into a room that smelled starkly of sulphur, and which—Ella blinked—held several large, square, stone-carved baths, heavily steaming with what looked to be hot water.

"You have heated baths, just sitting here to use whenever you wish?!" Ella asked faintly, because even with her wealth, this would be an unthinkable extravagance—but Natt only shot her a smug grin, and kicked off his trousers. And here, again, confronting Ella's formerly maiden eyes, was the sight of a tall, naked, muscular orc, showing off his spectacular backside as he strode to the nearest bath, and leapt in.

He sent water spraying everywhere, and more steam billowing through the room, and Ella watched with increasing amusement as he stood, streaming hot water, and then hurled himself in again. Twisting and splashing like a child, or perhaps an exuberant puppy, and then coming up and shaking all over, his wet hair whirling out like a fan behind him.

But then he turned to look at Ella, and she was looking at him. And when his finger beckoned, saying, *come here*, she nodded, and lowered her eyes as she pulled off her smelly, filthy shift, revealing her painted, sticky body beneath. And feeling Natt's intent gaze prickling on her bare skin as she dropped the shift to the floor, and took a careful step closer to the bath's smooth edge.

It really was remarkable workmanship, she thought disjointedly, blinking at the straight, clean cut of the stone—but then all thoughts had vanished at once, because warm wet hands had grasped for her, and dragged her bodily down into the hot, steaming water. And even as Ella shouted and flailed, she felt herself sink into the utterly glorious feel of it, and into the strong arms already wrapped around her, pressing her up against his silken skin.

"Do you remember how to swim?" Natt murmured, soft, into Ella's ear. And at her tentative replying nod, he gave a triumphant growl, and then—*threw her in.*

The shock and the rage and the laughter seemed to swarm all at once, as Ella's sore muscles revelled in the lovely heat, and her legs kicked her straight toward where her stinging eyes could see Natt's blurry form through the water. And when she surged up, and tackled him back into the pool, he only laughed, allowing her to shove him deep under the rippling splashing warmth.

When they both came up again, Ella was facing Natt in the water, her legs spreading apart around his waist, his big hands curving familiar and protective against her bare arse. Encouraging her to settle closer against him, until—Ella froze all over—there was the distinctive feel of that smooth, tapered hardness. Jabbing not against her still-tender heat, which had somehow spread rather gratuitously against his abdomen—but instead further back, to a shameful place it was surely not supposed to be.

But the sudden flutter of Natt's eyelashes suggested otherwise, as did the long, sustained shudder of that hardness against her. And his warm wet hand had come up to pluck gently against Ella's suddenly peaked nipple, while his mouth gave her a slow, devilish smile.

"I shall not take this maidenhood from you yet," he murmured. "But mark me, I *shall.* And you shall enjoy this, my filthy little lass."

Ella's traitorous breath gasped, her chest heaving, arching her bare breast into his hand—and curse her for it, because Natt only laughed, and settled her closer against him. Closer against *that,* still nudging foreign and oddly, thrillingly powerful against her.

"Stay," he ordered, as he reached for what looked to be an actual bar of *soap.* "Feel me, and kiss me, whilst I wash you."

And then, gods damn the audacious bastard, he did it. Rubbing his big hands with soap, and then running them all over Ella's wet, shivery form. Starting at her neck, her shoulders, and then slipping down her arms, to her hands, sliding between her fingers—and then, under the water, over her hips and thighs, and even reaching around to her legs and feet behind him.

And all the while, that twitching, tantalizing hardness just kept nudging against her, against *that*. And Ella's equally traitorous body felt it, and trembled all over, and perhaps even—*kissed* at it, just like he'd wished.

"Good lass," Natt whispered, husky, as his soapy hands came up her front, rubbing against the white, hardened mess he'd painted on her belly. "Can you feel how you might wish to kiss me deeper? How you might wish to flood your very innards, too, with my scent and my seed?"

It was a truly abominable statement, made only more atrocious by the replying gasp from Ella's mouth. Enough to make Natt laugh again, all warm approving eyes and sharp teeth, as his slippery hands finally, *finally* came up to curve close around Ella's peaked, juddering breasts.

"I ken you shall take great joy in this," he breathed, and he leaned forward, and pressed one of those slick, succulent kisses to her mouth. "I ken you shall writhe and scream as you are pierced deep upon me, like the filthy little beast you are."

The hunger lurched higher, sharper, while Ella's breaths came shorter, shallower. Her eyes darting between the sight of those huge, soapy hands, curving over her hungry breasts, and his glittering eyes, his crooked smile, his long tongue coming out to lick slow, merciless, devastating against his lips—

The pleasure flashed, and flared out bright and wide. Escaping in the furious, desperate clenching of Ella's open groin against Natt's belly, in the strangled, wild shout from her mouth. In the way her traitorous, scandalous, most secret place had gripped and pulsed and opened against that impossible invading strength, almost as if to say, *Yes, please, take it, Natt, now.*

But Natt was already easing away, his smile rueful, his hands sliding softer against her soapy skin. "I knew this lesson should please you, lass," he purred. "Now shall I wash your hair, also?"

He should, of course, and when those big hands spun her around under the water, Ella's pliant, sated body willingly went. Leaning into his solid strength, and into—she moaned aloud—the feel of his claws, sliding gentle against her scalp, and carding through her hair.

Good gods, it was lovely, and Ella tilted her head back, and breathed. Feeling those claws slide careful and slow, tugging her hair out long behind her, and then slicking it with soap, rubbing it in, combing it out again.

When he was finished, Ella felt fresh and clean and new all over, and perhaps more relaxed than she'd been in *years*. And when Natt leapt out of the bath—a surprisingly impressive feat for someone who was still supposed to be injured—and stretched a hand toward her, she eagerly took it, and let him drag her out, streaming water all over the smooth stone floor.

Natt gave one of his massive full-body shakes, and then reached for what appeared to be an actual towel—large enough to be a small blanket—and began wiping Ella down with it. Starting at her face, moving carefully over her eyes and nose, and then down over her still-peaked breasts and her belly, and even kneeling to wipe her legs and feet. While Ella only stood there and watched, fighting to swallow the rising, inexplicable tightness in her throat.

"Next, I shall clothe you," Natt said, as he stood back up, and slung the damp towel around Ella's bare shoulders like a cloak. "Come."

He hadn't bothered dressing again, but had only grasped for their clothes, and his pack and lamp, as he led Ella out of the room. And thus began another trek through the twisty deserted corridors, with Natt fully naked this time, until he drew her into another room. A room fronted by a long counter, with rows of shelves and racks behind, and—Ella's feet halted in place—another *orc*.

It was the first orc she'd seen in the mountain, beyond Natt himself, and he was huge and frowning, and—Ella felt herself edge sideways, closer behind Natt's naked bulk—utterly, astonishingly *hideous*. His face harsh and scarred, his hair lank and dull, his black claws on the counter before him almost resembling curved, deadly *bird-talons*.

Natt, of course, seemed entirely unaffected, and he dropped his supplies and their clothes onto the counter with a loud *thunk*. "Brother," he said, with an incline of his still-wet head. "I shall need free run of this room, for a spell. And, I wish to have what remains of the Grisk hoard."

The orc's narrow eyes were firmly fixed to Ella, flicking up and down her towel-cloaked form, and she felt her cheeks flush hot—but finally the orc bent down, and pulled out a large steel box from under the counter.

It was covered in strange carvings, and Ella watched with fascination as the orc's talons plucked at them, following some kind of pattern, until the top of the box popped open. Inside it was another box, smaller and made of wood, which the orc reverently lifted out with both hands, and placed on the counter between them.

"You shall take great care how you wield these, Nattfarr," he said, his voice deep and gravelly. "You are not Speaker yet."

"Soon, Ymir," Natt shot back, with a jaunty smile. "Ach, and when we are done, I wish you to burn my woman's clothes. But keep her boots safe."

The orc nodded, as though this were a perfectly unremarkable request, and then shuffled around toward the door. While Natt tucked the wooden box under his arm, and snatched for his lamp before leading Ella behind the counter, and deeper into the room.

It was truly a fascinating place, filled with row after row of long shelves, each of those shelves holding incongruous piles of—things. Cooking-pots and pans, and bags of flour and oats, and baskets of dried meat and vegetables. And now barrels, and tools, and weapons, and packs and waterskins like the ones Natt had carried, followed by rows of boots and shoes. And then—Natt pulled Ella to a stop behind him—stacks of furs and textiles.

"Here," he said, flashing a grin toward her as he carefully placed his lamp and his box on the nearest shelf. "Stay."

With that, he whipped the huge towel off Ella's shoulders, leaving her standing there stark naked, while he began darting around her, digging through the piles. Pulling out first one item, and then another, sniffing it, shaking his head. And then throwing it back again, and reaching for yet something else, some kind of skirt, holding it up before Ella's increasingly bemused eyes.

"Does wool itch you?" he demanded, keenly eyeing her over the top of it, and when Ella nodded, he threw it back again. Making a remarkable mess, one that the grumpy Ymir orc would surely be displeased about, but Natt seemed wholly unconcerned, and only grasped for another item, from the very bottom of the stack nearest.

"Ach," he said, with satisfaction. "This, lass, shall suit."

This, apparently, was some kind of man's kilt, made of sturdy brown leather. It was short enough that it wouldn't even reach Ella's knees—and as Natt slung it low around her hips, and buckled the leather strap, there was the equally distressing realization that there would be a deep slit up the side, showing absolutely indecent views of her bare hip and thigh with every step she took.

"I can't—*wear* this, Natt," Ella managed, but he only finished fastening it, and then stepped back, frowning, as if to survey his handiwork. And then he gave a decisive nod, and began rummaging again through the piles, making another unholy mess as he went.

"*Natt*," Ella said again, helplessly, as he grasped for something else, and then unfurled it around her shoulders. It was soft grey fur, it looked almost like a *wolf-skin*, and it fit her like a cape, covering her back and shoulders. But in front, it only scarcely concealed her bare breasts, even once Natt had produced a long leather strap to tie it with, and fastened it tight.

"Good," he said, again stepping back to look, and then—Ella gasped—reaching a hand under the bottom edge of the fur to cup close and proprietary at her breast. "This hides you, so you shall be at ease among my brothers—but I shall yet be able to touch you, whenever I should wish."

He seemed deeply satisfied with this, leaving Ella thoroughly dumbfounded as he finally went for that wooden box the orc had given him. Snapping it open to reveal contents that glittered bright in the lamplight, and Ella realized that they were—*jewels*. The Grisk hoard, he'd said.

Natt combed through them with visible care, and then drew out what looked to be a large, dangling earring. It was beautifully forged, glittering with gold and green—or rather, with actual inlaid *emeralds*, very like the ring that glinted on his finger.

Natt held the earring up to Ella's face, his lips pursing, almost as if he were considering it against her skin. While Ella held herself very still, her eyes fluttering, her pulse rising. Natt surely wouldn't loan her such a beautiful thing. Would he?

But Natt was nodding, he *was*, and his fingers were careful as he finally brought the lovely earring closer, and fastened it to Ella's ear. "Our Grisk jewels have not oft been worn, through this war," he said, and she could feel him flick a claw at it, sending a hard shiver down her back. "But now, it is time to bear them again. I wish you to have this one, for this side, and"—he reached over, and then dangled another smaller, simpler gold hoop from his opposite hand—"this, for the other."

Ella might well have shuddered, because she hadn't worn mismatched earrings in her *life*—but she only held herself still, her heart jerky and skipping, while Natt hooked the second earring on, and then stepped back to look at her again. His eyes sweeping thoughtfully up and down, his claw tapping absently against his chin.

"Should you allow me to pierce your nose, lass, so you may wear more of my jewels?" he asked. "Or mayhap, here?"

By *here*, he meant Ella's *nipple*, because his hand had again reached under her fur, and tweaked lightly against it. Leaving Ella staring slack-jawed toward him, *envisioning* that, and feeling the heat pool in far too many inappropriate places at once.

"Of course I shouldn't allow you to do that, Natt," she said, through her oddly tangled tongue. "I've never *heard* of such a scandalous thing."

And what should Alfred say if his future wife did such a scandalous thing, was the unspoken question—and one that Natt perhaps followed, judging by the sudden distance in his eyes. And Ella remembered, too late, about the men, and the *war*, and the matters yet to be addressed. And yes, she'd agreed to do this with Natt, but surely it wouldn't extend *there*...

"Then mayhap this," Natt said, his voice very smooth, as he reached back into the wooden box, and pulled out two thick, matching, intricately woven gold chains. Much more innocuous than actual nipple-piercings, at least, and Ella willingly ducked her head as he settled their cold weight around her neck, slipping them under her cape.

But then—Ella's body snapped still again—Natt lifted one of her breasts, and eased one of the chains close and taut beneath it. Then he did the same on the other side, so that each chain was now slightly propping up each breast, almost as if obscenely displaying them for his eyes.

And Natt was looking, holding up her fur, and again tweaking at Ella's jutting, reddened nipple with his claw. "Better," he said. "Do you not think so, lass?"

There was an undeniable challenge in his voice, and as Ella glanced down at her frankly appalling ensemble, she found her face again very hot, her eyes not quite able to meet his. Of course this wasn't better, even if he'd loaned her such breathtaking jewels. It was lewd and indecent and uncouth, she was barely clothed, utterly on display, she looked like a—

"Come," Natt said, his hand grasping at hers, and Ella allowed him to draw her further into the room, toward the very back. Toward where there was, to Ella's surprise, a large silver looking-glass, propped against the wall.

It appeared to be human-made, and looked as though it had seen better days. But as Natt drew Ella to stand before it, and held up his lamp, she could see the reflection as clearly as it if had been another person, standing there before her.

And perhaps—it *was* another person. A person with *freckles*, and with long, tousled reddish hair, already brightened by the sun. A person dressed in leather and fur, with gold and a bright flash of green hanging from her ears. A person with more gold chains crossed over her chest, glinting where the fur didn't quite cover, hinting at something beneath.

There was so much bare skin—bare legs, bare arms, a midriff fully exposed from chest to hips—but perhaps it almost suited a wild, bright-eyed woman such as this. A woman who was glancing toward the huge, still-naked orc beside her, and reaching a hand, to draw him in close.

And when the orc came to stand behind the wild woman in the frame, his big hands coming to rest on either side of her bared waist, the woman's reddened lips parted, her half-naked body leaning back against him. Gasping as the orc's hands slowly slid upwards, cupping hot and familiar against each breast, his claws purposely tracing against braided gold, vibrating it deep into her skin.

The woman gave a helpless, choked-sounding moan, and dropped her head back onto the orc's shoulder. A movement that revealed a mess of faint red scrapes on her neck, where the orc's teeth had nipped and teased. Not full-on bites, at least not yet—but still a sure, startling proof of his ownership, and their pleasure together.

"You see," the orc murmured, heated and close into the woman's ear, "how my jewels in your teats might please you?"

The words were impossibly audacious, complete with a hard, thrilling snap of the orc's sharp teeth against the gold ring in her ear. But the wild woman only moaned again, her eyelashes fluttering, her hand reaching around to grip behind her at the orc's hot, muscled bare thigh. And when the orc's deadly hand moved up to the woman's heart, she didn't even flinch, but only watched as he unstrapped the fur over her shoulders, and let it fall open to the light.

The sight beneath was downright obscene, the woman's full, pale breasts chained in gold, and entirely bared to the orc's huge hands. And their rounded weights were jiggling and heaving under his touch, jutting out flushed nipples into his hungry clawed fingers, and the woman in the glass only moaned again, and bit her red lip with a sharp white tooth as she watched.

"Does this please you?" the orc purred, his voice a husky silken embrace all its own. "Speak, lass."

Lass. And suddenly there was the jarring, twitching truth that this wanton, shameless woman in the glass was—*her.* It was Ella Riddell, the heiress, betrothed to a *lord*, and she was not supposed to look like this, she was not *allowed* to be this, she *couldn't*—

Ella whirled around, away, her body reflexively aiming toward the door—but Natt was here, close, safe. And when he tucked her trembly form tight into his powerful strength, she felt herself clinging to him, and fighting him, she had to go, she was supposed to be a *lady*—

"Shhh, lass," Natt's voice said, low into her ear. "There is naught to run from. Naught to fear. I shall keep you safe."

Ella's body seemed to wilt against him, but she shook her head, squeezed her eyes shut. "What if they find out, Natt," she whispered. "What if they *see.*"

And the visions marching behind her eyes weren't only of Alfred and his men, but her mother. Her neighbours. Her many associates and acquaintances, all the people who knew Ella Riddell to be proper, poised, respectable. An heiress, soon to be a real lady.

"They shall not," Natt replied, harder than before. "You shall be safe here with me, to be as you are. This truth is ours, and *yours*. This has naught to do with them."

It was inexplicably comforting, his fierce words, his fierce arms around her. His hands, now coming up to her face, tilting it to look at his glittering eyes. "You are the fairest gift ever to greet my eyes," he said, quiet, intent. "You are a bright jewel, a flame in winter, a blade new from the forge. It shall be pure joy to walk my home by your side, and flaunt such a rare prize."

Oh. The rest of the tension snaked away from Ella's form all at once, and she felt her face heating, her eyes dropping from the intensity of his gaze. "You orcs," she said, a little choked, "are utterly *depraved*, Nattfarr."

He gave a wry chuckle, his hand sliding with obvious approval against her bare back, because he knew he had her, the bastard. And Ella couldn't even seem to argue, but only took a fortifying breath, and raised her eyes back to his face. "So what next?"

Natt's smile was slow, sharp, gloriously wicked. "Next you shall come," he said, "and meet my kin."

19

When Ella left the dressing-room with Natt, it was with her head held high, her hair tossed back, her steps as sure as she could make them. She could do this. She could embrace a week of exposure, of secret debauchery, if it meant so much to Natt. No one would know. The men had been *addressed*, he'd said. It would be *fine*.

It helped, oddly, that Natt hadn't fully dressed either, only yanking on a knee-length leather kilt of his own, and, to Ella's vague surprise, snapping another thick gold ring into his left ear. Making him look even more dangerous, somehow, especially when he strapped on his sword-belt again, hanging the gleaming, gem-studded scimitar back in its place at his side.

And as they strode down the corridor, hand in hand, Ella could almost see how she might—*fit*, like this. How a half-naked, shameless orc like Natt perhaps *should* have a wild, brazen, scantily clad woman by his side, wearing his furs and jewels.

It was enough to keep Ella moving, her bare feet padding silently on the smooth stone floor, as Natt led her down the slowly widening corridor—at least, until there was someone else. Another *orc*. Huge and hulking and deadly, and walking directly toward them.

Ella's steps faltered, her body instinctively angling itself behind the safety of Natt's form—but Natt was slowing down, he was *stopping*, he was talking to this strange orc in their incomprehensible black-tongue. While Ella's panic kept steadily surging, straight down to her feet— and she might have run, if not for the way the strange orc suddenly turned and smiled at her, and even gave a flourishing little bow.

"Greetings, woman," he said, in a warm, melodious voice. "Welcome to our mountain. I am Baldr, of Clan Grisk."

Ella was still caught in the orc's scarred, greenish face, the big muscled form that seemed far too large for his tight-fitting tunic—but thankfully her many years of social training seemed to take over, and she felt herself curtsey, her own head bowing. "It's lovely to meet you, Baldr of Clan Grisk," she said, her voice only slightly wavering. "I'm Ella Riddell, of Ashford."

When she looked up the orc was still smiling, and if he'd noticed Ella's shocking ensemble, he gave no sign of it, his twinkling black eyes remaining safely on her face. "We've all been most eager to meet you, woman," he replied. "Especially the captain and his mate. Will you bring her up to us, Nattfarr, at your first opportunity?"

"Ach," Natt said, both his voice and his eyes betraying an unmistakable stubbornness, but Baldr only gave another bright smile toward Ella, and then turned and walked away. Leaving Ella to blink bemusedly after him—until she was confronted by the appalling sight of four more orcs, striding up the corridor toward them.

These ones were even more alarming than Baldr had been, not least because they were all bare-chested, like Natt, and boasted scars all over their huge, muscular grey forms. And their glittering eyes on Ella were far more familiar than Baldr's had been, more openly assessing, and the nearest one—who had a perfectly straight nose, and long black hair that hung loose down his back, and a thick gold ring through his *nipple*—was looking Ella up and down with frank shamelessness, his black eyes lingering particularly on her chest, and then her bare midriff, and her groin.

But Natt was grinning at these orcs, with far more warmth than he'd shown Baldr, and his clawed hand had come to clap at the frowning one's shoulder. "Lass, these are my most faithful brothers," he said to her. "They are to be my guard, when I take the name of Speaker. And brothers, here is my sweet little lass. Ella."

His voice was careful on her name, but proud, too, and his other hand slid close around her bare waist, drawing her forward. Wanting these terrifying orcs to see her, and though Ella slightly trembled, she managed to hold her head up, and even tried for a smile.

"Hello," she said, with a little curtsey. "It's so lovely to meet you all."

Natt's hand gave an approving squeeze to her waist, and then he began the introductions, while Ella fought to embed the names and faces into her memory. The tallest two orcs, both spiky-haired and similar-looking, were named Thrain and Thrak, and they were apparently blood brothers, born to the same mother. Next was Varinn, slightly shorter and broader, wearing a long braid, and flashing Ella a sharp-toothed smile that felt wary, but genuine. And last was Dammarr, the loose-haired, nipple-pierced orc who was still looking Ella up and down, and sneering as though she were somehow offensive by her very presence.

"You did not say, brother," he said, his eyes finally flicking to Natt's face, "that she was scent-bound to you."

It sounded almost—accusing, somehow, and Ella could feel Natt shift beside her, the muscles tensing under his skin. "Ach," he said, "for now."

Dammarr's eyes snapped back to Ella, narrowing with clear disapproval. "Are you not betrothed to a man, woman?" he demanded. "Do you not seek to wed this man? The one who hunts our brother, and seeks to *kill* him?"

Ella felt herself wince, her eyes casting a furtive, uncertain glance toward Natt. "Um," she said, under her breath, "I'm not certain we should speak of such things, here?"

"Ach, we know all his secrets," cut in one of the tall, spiky-haired brothers—Thrak—with a smirk toward Natt's forbidding face. "But these are not spoken of among the rest of our kin. *Ach*, Dammarr?"

He'd reached around Varinn to yank at a handful of Dammarr's loose hair, but Dammarr ignored him, and kept frowning at Ella. "So you yet mean to wed this man," he said, the contempt all too clear in his voice. "So why has this man not claimed you for his own? Why has he not touched you? Why are you yet scent-bound to an *orc*?"

Ella was feeling entirely lost, and she shrank backwards, darting another helpless glance up at Natt—only to find that he was already glowering at this Dammarr, his face thunderous, his jaw set. "Ignore my brother, lass," he hissed. "And you shall *leave* this, Dammarr."

But Ella was oddly caught on that unfamiliar word *scent-bound*, and she heard her traitorous voice speaking, before she could stop it. "I—I don't understand. What do you mean, I'm scent-bound to him?"

Dammarr's lip curled, but he didn't reply, and beside him Varinn cleared his throat. "He means," he said, with an elbow into Dammarr's side, "that you smell only of Nattfarr, and no one else. We call this scent-bound. It is"—he shot a glance at Natt's face—"a rare prize, among orcs. And most of all amongst the Grisk."

Oh. Ella's cheeks felt very hot, and Dammarr pointed a clawed finger at her, again almost accusing. "Why have you not touched this man, or another? You are not a new woman. Is there aught amiss with you?"

Natt twitched beside her, and Ella felt her own body reflexively stiffening in response. "I—I don't think so," she said, her voice thin. "I mean—my mother didn't approve, and virtue is a valuable currency for women like me, and I, well"—she drew in breath, and just said it, in a rush—"I swore a pledge. To Natt."

And she couldn't explain why, but standing here beside Natt, dressed like this, facing four strange orcs, in Orc Mountain—that last part felt real. Felt the most true. And surely, that pledge hadn't been why Ella had waited, all that time? Or had it?

All four orcs were looking at Natt now, Dammarr with raised eyebrows, Varinn with something not unlike sympathy, and the other two with surprised, identical faces. To which Natt gave a jerky shrug of his shoulder, and said something in black-tongue that made Varinn grimace, and had Dammarr angling another sullen, sneering look toward Ella.

"You smell as though you have *bathed* in our brother's seed, woman," he snapped. "You ought not to tease him thus. The Speaker of the Grisk ought to have better than one who should dangle such a gift, and next steal it away, and grant it to the man *hunting* him."

Oh. Ella flinched, her eyes held to the floor, her exposed body drawing backwards. And suddenly the need to leave, to run, was almost overpowering, and she tugged against Natt's grip, as surreptitiously as she could, needing to go—

But Natt was too strong, his hand clutching her close against his side. "I told you to leave this, Dammarr," he growled. "If you wish to keep your place in my guard, you shall obey my commands, and treat my woman with kindness. I shall not warn you again."

There was an instant's quiet, in which Thrak gave another surreptitious yank at Dammarr's hair, and Natt took a swift, threatening step closer to Dammarr, while keeping his arm firm around Ella's back. And Ella could see the moment when Dammarr relented, his eyes angling uneasily away, his head bowing.

"Forgive me, Speaker, woman," he said. "I ought not to have spoken thus. I only wished to ensure my *lifelong* brother's honour, and his *peace*, when he has too oft been robbed of these. When he"—his eyes flicked back to Natt's, an obvious challenge in them—"too oft robs *himself* of these."

There was meaning behind those words Ella couldn't identify, but Natt surely did, judging by the replying hiss in his throat. "You shall pay no heed to my brother, lass," he said loudly, as he roughly shoved forward past Dammarr, dragging Ella close behind him. "Should he speak thus again to you, I shall gladly break his pretty nose whilst you watch. You shall find joy in this, I ken. I know I shall."

There was a muffled laugh behind them—Thrak, perhaps—but Natt didn't look back, and only pulled Ella down the corridor beside him. Walking past even more huge, unfamiliar orcs now, every single one giving them curious or uneasy looks, but Natt only nodded as they passed, and didn't stop to speak.

"Where are we going?" Ella asked, tentatively, once the most recent of these unnerving orcs was out of view, and Natt's steps slowed, his narrow eyes blinking at her. He was still angry, she realized, at whatever Dammarr had said, and she could see his shoulders rise, and fall.

"We have been summoned by the captain," he replied smoothly. "I take you there now. We shall pass through the Bautul wing next, to reach the Ash-Kai."

"And your captain is Ash-Kai?" Ella asked. "The last one was too, right?"

Natt nodded, his gaze back on the corridor ahead. "All our captains have been Ash-Kai, back to the oldest tales. And to match this, our Speaker is always Grisk. There ought also to be a Priest, from Ka-esh, to guide our zeal and learning. I am told that Skai and Bautul once had these leaders also, though the truth of them has been lost. For now."

Ella considered that as they walked, the corridor gradually tilting upwards. There were more openings at steady intervals in the walls, most of which she couldn't see into, but there were the distinct sounds of movement and voices beyond, and more occasional orcs passing by in the corridor.

And these orcs, Ella noticed, seemed even larger and more alarming than before. Their faces craggy and harsh, their hair wild and thick, their bodies marked and heavily scarred. Their eyes on Ella and Natt had almost seemed to become more dangerous as well, some guarded, some disdainful, some scornful. And some, oddly enough, perhaps even *fearful*.

Natt had continued nodding as he passed, but more curtly now, and when one gigantic orc muttered something in black-tongue, Natt snapped back in kind, the growl burning deep in his throat. Setting the orc scurrying against the opposite wall, his eyes gone wide and blank, and Ella only had a moment to digest that before Natt's hand tightened around her waist, and pulled her closer against his side.

"Next," he said, "we shall need to pass through the Bautul common-room, as it is open to this path. So I must warn you, lass, that you may see sights that shall vex you."

Ella shot him an uneasy look, and felt her steps slowing against the stone. "Like what?" she asked. "Like—orcs? Together?"

And looking at Natt's unreadable face, she could still remember his very careful answers to all her incessant questions, from years ago. *What do orcs do, without any women. What happens when an orc can't find a mate. What do you mean, orcs often mate with each other?*

"Ach, that," Natt said, slowly. "But also, my Bautul brother Silfast has of late found a mate. A woman. They oft take their joy here also."

Ella couldn't deny the spark of interest at that—there was truly another *woman* here, among all these highly terrifying orcs? And when Natt guided her forward again, toward the distinct sounds of noise and voices up ahead, Ella went willingly beside him, her eyes searching in the slowly brightening light.

Abruptly the stone corridor opened wide all around, curving into a large, circular room. There were low stone benches cut into the walls, and wooden tables and chairs scattered about, and in the middle of the room there was a tall, cylindrical chimney of some sort, going straight up into the stone ceiling. At the base of this there burned a crackling fire, dancing orange light on the surrounding stone walls.

And upon closer inspection, Ella could see that there were *carvings* cut into the walls. Clear, unmistakable depictions of armed orcs and men, fighting viciously against each other. And also—Ella's face heated—images of naked orcs and women, and even *men*, all cavorting together, with the orcs' enormous appendages jutting into every orifice imaginable.

But Ella's shock at the sight was short-lived, because her eyes had darted back to the room itself, and the dozen-odd living orcs filling it. And while much of their activity was entirely innocuous—some of them were eating, some were talking together, a few were playing some kind of war-game at a table—some of the orcs were—*doing things*, to one another.

One orc was using his hand on another's long, dripping cock, sliding up with sure, steady strokes while the first orc gasped and moaned. Another one had his trousers down to his knees, showing his bare arse, while his hands pinned another orc face-first to the wall before him, his hips snapping powerfully against the orc's equally bare backside.

And there, on the opposite side of the room, a massive, particularly hideous orc sat sprawled on the stone bench, his trousers pulled low, with a *naked woman* kneeling between his legs. And the woman's head was bobbing up and down over the orc's groin, her mouth sucking his huge, glistening length deep down her throat.

The woman was plump and dark-haired, her face partially hidden by the fall of her hair, but the orc had raised his eyes toward Natt and Ella, and actually lifted a sharp claw, and *beckoned* them over toward this unspeakable sight. And more astonishing still, Natt actually *went*, still holding Ella against him, while Ella's traitorous eyes held fast to the rapidly nearing reality of this woman, with this hideous orc's huge cock sliding steadily in and out of her stretched, sucking mouth.

The woman didn't even look at them as they approached, and instead kept her fluttering eyes fully on the orc's ugly face, while one of her hands gripped tight around the base of him, the other curled over his heavy hanging bollocks. The orc had a clawed hand carded deep into her hair, but he wasn't even looking at her, and had instead nodded his shaggy head toward Natt, and then Ella.

"Speaker," he said, his voice gravelly. "Our women ought to meet one another."

"Ach," Natt replied, his eyes flicking with astonishing casualness to the still-sucking woman, who hadn't yet spared them a single glance. "Shall we return, when she is done?"

"No, she has almost earned her seed," the ugly orc said, with an unmistakably affectionate look down toward her dark bobbing head. "Now, woman, you shall show them how this ought to be done. You shall take me as hard as you can, and you shall not spill a *drop*."

The woman gave a jerky little nod, as much as she likely could under such circumstances, with this orc still bearing into her desperately swallowing throat. And then, as Ella watched in stunned, staring fascination, the woman seemed to double her efforts, taking the orc deeper, harder, faster. Her eyes madly fluttering, her hands clutching against him, her mouth moaning with audible, undeniable pleasure as her gaze darted, brief, up toward Ella.

But the ugly orc's hand had actually *slapped* against the woman's *face*, gentle but purposeful, and her eyes immediately snapped back to him again, her throat giving another low, heated groan. And Ella could see the orc's body tensing, his black eyes glazing, his claws clenching in the woman's hair—

His growl of pleasure was hoarse and rasping, his hips thrusting up deeper into the woman's throat, until he was buried almost all the way—and Ella could actually *see* the base of that cock shuddering as it surged its seed into the woman's mouth. And the woman was moaning too, her eyes squeezing shut, her mouth making shocking slurping noises as she swallowed again and again, eagerly taking this hideous orc's leavings deep down her throat.

Once he'd finally seemed to finish, the woman kept him there, his seemingly softened length now fully concealed inside her reddened mouth, until he gave another light slap to her cheek. Only then did she draw away from him, that slick, glistening grey heft sliding slow, smooth, and astonishingly long from her still-sucking lips.

"Good," the orc said, as his clawed hand tilted the woman's face up toward him, his other hand come to brush a finger against her swollen mouth, which indeed betrayed no trace of his seed. "Good woman. This pleased me."

The woman gave another sigh of palpable pleasure, sagging against his parted legs, and the orc abruptly reached down, and drew her up onto his lap. Revealing her plump, naked body entirely to Ella's blinking eyes, and even—Ella couldn't help a gasp—reaching one hand around to squeeze her heavy breast, while the other hand deftly spread her voluptuous thighs apart, and began to delve up between.

"Now you may greet our new guest," he said to the woman, with rather wicked satisfaction, and Ella felt a surprising twist of solidarity as the woman's dazed, blinking eyes finally darted up toward them, her face gone a deep, betraying red.

"Hello," she said, her voice soft, almost a whisper. "I'm Stella. Of Clan Bautul. And this is my mate Silfast."

The orc gave an approving squeeze to her breast, making the woman—Stella—gasp, her eyes dropping to where his other audacious hand was still playing between her spread thighs, his fingers sliding deeper, while his mouth came close to her ear, and murmured a deep, guttural stream of filthy-sounding black-tongue into it. To which the woman moaned again, and then turned to sweetly kiss the orc's scarred cheek, whispering something back into his ear.

The entire scene was so utterly distracting that it took Ella a full moment to find her voice again, her strangely tingly body belatedly gripping to Natt's solid, reassuring bulk beside her. "Um, and I'm Ella," she said faintly. "It's very lovely to meet you."

Stella flashed her a genuine, if flustered smile—but it swiftly faded into another heated gasp, her red lips parting, as Silfast's fingers vanished deeper between her thighs. And when Natt nudged Ella toward the corridor opposite, she willingly went, though her legs felt dangerously wobbly, her breath coming in short, desperate gulps.

"Um," she said to Natt, once they seemed a safe distance away, "is that, um, *normal*, around here?"

"Ach, I ken," Natt replied, his voice steady, but when Ella looked at him, his eyes on her were wary, searching. "Has this vexed you, lass? Or made you afraid?"

Vexed. *Afraid.* Ella couldn't seem to find an answer to that, currently, her eyes only blinking blankly at Natt's watching face. And when he hesitated, and then pulled her sideways into what appeared to be an empty room, there was no resisting that either, no coherent thoughts left in her head.

"Speak, lass," Natt said, as he dropped his lamp beside them, and then pressed Ella up against the stone wall, his warmth close and safe before her. "I know not this scent, that is upon you. It is"—he leaned in, and Ella willingly tilted her head as his face ducked into her neck, and inhaled deep—"hunger, and awe, and *what else.*"

Ella still couldn't speak, but there was something in this, in Natt's warm, familiar face tickling against her skin. And when her trembling hand came to brush against his bare chest, there was something in that too, and again when he pulled back to look at her, his eyes dark and intent and demanding in the flickering lamplight.

"You shall speak this to me, lass," he said, hard, an order. "What is in you."

And between his voice, his familiar warm scent, the intensity in his eyes, he seemed to almost draw out the words, reeling them jumbling and desperate from Ella's choked throat. "I don't kn-know, Natt," she stammered. "I just—I'm shocked, obviously, and utterly scandalized, of course, I've never seen such things in my *life*—but then she *wanted* that, and he wanted *her*, and he was *proud* of her and he"—her hands flailed—"they weren't *ashamed* of that, and is that what you want to do to *me*, Natt?!"

The last came out sounding shrill, almost panicked, because Ella *had* promised him a week of secret debauchery, hadn't she?! But Natt's warm hands were cupping her face now, quiet, safe, and his eyes studied her, searched deep and knowing inside.

"Do you wish me to do such things to you, lass?" he asked, very steady. "Shall this bring forth your hunger, if I make you walk fully bare before my brothers, and strike you when you displease me?"

"No!" Ella nearly wailed. "No, *gods* no! I don't want *that*, I want—"

And for some ridiculous, inexplicable reason, her thoughts had snapped back to Alfred. Smiling, well-mannered, entirely appropriate Alfred, who had been so courteous to Ella's face, and then turned around and lied to her, and betrayed her. He was a man who couldn't be trusted, no male could be trusted—

But the way Stella had *looked* at that orc. The way she'd willingly submitted herself to his command. He'd been using her, dominating her, but it had somehow felt—*safe.*

"You want *what,* lass," Natt's voice demanded, deep, powerful, almost compulsively commanding. "Speak."

Again it was like there was no other recourse, only words spilling from Ella's throat. "I want—how she *felt,*" she said. "She *trusted* him, Natt. Enough to *be* that, for him. For *her.* To be what she wanted to be, who she was, no matter how shameful it was. And to know she'd still be—*safe.*"

There was only silence for an instant, Natt's watching eyes held deep inside, searching for more—but there was nothing else. Nothing but his breath, coming short and shallow from his mouth.

"And you cannot," he said, very quiet now, "trust *me.*"

It was a question, Ella knew, those eyes still caught, waiting, impossibly compelling—and suddenly there was more truth, truth she hadn't even known, until perhaps this moment.

"No," she breathed. "No, Natt, I *can't.* You *kidnapped* me, you didn't tell me about Alfred *hunting* you, you disappeared for almost ten *years.* You took pleasure with other women, repeatedly, maybe even like *that*"—her hand frantically waved down the corridor—"while some mad, miserable part of me *waited* for you, and *kept waiting,* for *years.* And then my father died, and it was *horrible,* and I loved him so much but he gave me this awful deadline or else I'll lose *everything,* and you don't understand, you don't even *want* to understand!"

Natt didn't move, those eyes still burning on hers, and Ella gulped for air, again, again. "And you only want me for *vengeance,*" she gasped, "and you've never *once* recognized that I *did* keep my pledge to you! And you haven't told me what happened to *your* father, or why you're not Speaker of the Grisk now, or even what happened last night with Alfred's horrid men—or, what Alfred wants to do with my money! Because he *surely* doesn't need a fortune to keep chasing you through the forest with a few dogs, and we both know he doesn't even *like* me enough to keep his hands to himself at our *engagement-party,* so what the *hell* is the truth, and *why* haven't you told it to me!"

The words seemed to echo against the stone all around them, laying Ella bare, betraying *everything*—and far too late she snapped her mouth shut, and for good measure, clapped her hands against it. She truly hadn't said all that, had she? And had she even *meant* it?

But she couldn't seem to take any of it back, either, could only stare at the glittering power in Natt's watching, demanding eyes. A power that would have had her speak even more, if there'd been more to say. And Ella's hands had begun to tremble over her mouth, her head shaking, her eyes blinking at Natt with a sudden, sickening comprehension. Vexed. *Afraid.*

"And do you—do you have some kind of—*magic*, Natt?" she whispered. "Did you—did you just—*make* me say all that to you?"

Natt's eyes immediately snapped shut, his head abruptly turning away from her—and just like that, it was though a spell had broken. As though Ella could think again, and form her own words again. And dear gods in heaven, had Natt been doing that to her, all this time?! *Forcing* her to speak to him?

"Th-the *Speaker*," Ella said, her voice badly wavering, her shaky body pressing to the cold stone behind her. "N-not just you speaking for your brothers, but—*making* them speak, to you. It's why they're all"—her thoughts cast back to the orcs in the corridor, their guarded faces and wary eyes—"they're *afraid* of you."

There was no denying it, suddenly, looking at Natt's sharp profile, the tightness on his mouth. And when his eyes finally blinked back at her, bleak and empty, Ella knew, before he even spoke.

"Yes," he said. "I am Nattfarr of Clan Grisk, the twelfth orc of my line to Speak for my brothers. Should you not grant me your truth, I shall draw it from you, and speak it for all to hear."

It sounded almost like a vow, like a—a *pledge*. A pledge he'd sworn, to force others to speak truth. And surely he'd known this for *years*, even all those years ago when they'd run together in the forest, and he'd never *once* spoken of it.

Natt had *lied*. He'd used his magic on Ella, making her speak truth to him, while he himself had *lied*. Again, and again, and *again*.

And before Ella could speak, and again betray herself to whatever dark sorcery this was, she whirled around, and fled.

20

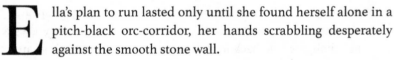

Ella's plan to run lasted only until she found herself alone in a pitch-black orc-corridor, her hands scrabbling desperately against the smooth stone wall.

"Gods help me," she heard her voice say, high-pitched and on the verge of panic, as her shaky legs edged back in the direction they'd come, back toward that unsettling room with the fire. And while even the thought of going in there alone was sparking more terror behind Ella's blinking eyes, it seemed the only answer, perhaps Stella would help her, perhaps if she begged—

When suddenly, of course, there was a warm, familiar-smelling body in the darkness, the heated grip of a hand against her arm. And even as the relief unfurled down Ella's back, there was still anger, and fear, enough to make her shove away from him, her teeth actually chattering in her mouth.

"Stop this, lass," Natt said, ordered, his voice harsh. And for some appalling reason, Ella's shivering somehow did stop, and she heard herself laugh, the sound grating and foreign to her ears.

"Oh, was that your twisted magic too, Speaker?" she choked. "Does it work when throwing out orders, as well?"

The fear rippled stronger, deeper, because what if Natt *could* make people obey him, what if he'd been doing that, too, all this time?! But his clenching hand had twitched on Ella's arm, his breath heavy in the stillness.

"I cannot command obedience," he said thinly. "I can only seek truth. And only if I look at another, and they at me."

Ella gave another one of those grating laughs, enough to make her wince. "Oh, *only*," she snapped. "And has it not occurred to you, Natt-farr, that other people might like to *know* you could do such a thing? And that you've been doing this to them? To *me*?!"

And as her panicked thoughts flipped backwards, there was the understanding, sudden and staggering, of all the times Natt had done it these past days. All the questions he had asked. *You do not remember the pledge you made? For what do you wish. Is this a small thing. You shall speak.*

And then, further back, years back—*Will you have me, lass. Before any other. When we are grown.*

"You—you even did it with our *pledge*," Ella said, her voice hitching. "Didn't you?

She was trembling again, blinking at where she knew him to be in the dark, and there was an odd catch in his breath, the sudden feel of his other hand, coming to grip to her other arm. "Ach, I did," he said. "Why should I not seek truth in such a pledge. This was for your sake, lass, as much as mine. I sought to keep you *safe*."

Keep her safe. The weight of that stopped Ella short for an instant, and she had to search for a response, her eyes darting about in the darkness. "But you didn't *say*," she countered. "Why didn't you tell me any of this. Now, or then!"

There was another instant's stillness, a shift of those fingers against her skin. Natt was hesitating, again, he was going to *lie* to her, again, and Ella jabbed a shaky finger against his hot chest, and shook her head in the blackness. "And I want the truth, Nattfarr of Clan Grisk. *You* speak truth to *me*."

She could feel his chest rising and falling against her finger, the faint pulse of his heartbeat deep inside. "I did not speak of this to you," he said, slowly, "because you did not fear me. I have been feared by most of my kin for most of my days, and it was—relief, with you, and peace. It was *joy*, to look at you, and run with you, and speak as I wished, and not have the bitter taste of fear on my tongue."

Something twisted in Ella's gut, alarmingly close to sympathy, and she jabbed her finger against him again. "So why haven't you told me now. Until today."

She could feel his replying sigh, the exhale harsh against her skin. "Now," he said, quiet, "you *do* fear me, lass. Even without this."

Oh. And he hadn't wanted to make it worse, he meant. And the sympathy was surging again, but Ella thrust it down, gave another bracing shake of her head. Natt had lied to her. Again and again. And not just about this.

"And what about the rest of it?" she demanded. "Everything else you're not telling me? About Alfred, about your father, about *you*?!"

There was still more silence, broken only by the sound of his heavy breath. "It is not," he said, "easy to speak of these truths."

"Well, you're supposed to be the Speaker, aren't you?" Ella shot back. "So maybe it's time to start speaking about the difficult things, Nattfarr. Especially to someone who's supposed to be your *friend,* and who's made you a *very* generous offer of future friendship this week, apparently under an *entirely* false set of pretenses!"

The silence felt very heavy, suddenly, perhaps even pained, and Ella could almost feel Natt's eyes shuttering, blocking her away. And maybe she should have apologized, taken some of it back, but no, no, he deserved this. Didn't he?

"Our captain wishes to meet with us," he said finally, his voice blank and smooth. "I shall ask him to speak these truths to you. They are as much his to tell as mine."

He had already pulled away from Ella, setting her panic lurching high and wide—but no, he'd only gone back for that room, for his lamp. And the lamp must have gone out at some point, but a snap of his claws easily lit it again, casting a much-welcomed glow on the stone walls all around.

But Natt didn't look at her, didn't speak further. Just turned and started walking again, leaving Ella to rush along behind him, to catch up to the steady bobbing light.

"So why," she made herself say, "should I believe anything your captain says, when *you* don't even trust him."

The silence seemed to settle heavier around them, Natt's big body gone even stiffer by her side. "I should not expect you to believe aught that Grimarr says," he replied. "But his mate is a woman, and a true lady among the humans, just the kind you so long to be. Mayhap you shall thus hear *her* words, if naught else."

There was surely an insult in there, but Ella was fatally caught on the rest of it. There was a true lady? Here? Mated to the orcs' *captain*?

"Who is she?" Ella demanded. "What's her name? A lady of where?"

"She is the daughter of the late Lord Edgell of Salven," came his flat reply. "And cousin to Lord Otto. And she was wed to Lord Norr, before his death."

Ella's mouth had fallen open, her eyes darting to Natt's clenched-looking profile in the lamplight. She'd heard of Lord and Lady Norr, of course—Lord Norr had ruled over Sakkin Province for many years, as well as the neighbouring provinces of Yarwood and Salven. And while Ella had never met either Lord or Lady Norr, there had certainly been some scandalous whispers about them of late, especially given Lord Norr's recent and sudden death.

His wife had him killed, the worst of those whispers had gone. *His wife didn't even come to his funeral.*

But Lord Norr had been a particularly nasty man, disliked by his friends and his enemies alike—so his death had been largely a relief for all involved, and it was universally agreed that his successor Otto was a far superior lord. Otto had also been instrumental in signing that peace-treaty with the orcs—and unlike Alfred's father Lord Culthen, Otto had continued to publicly defend it to its many detractors, including his fellow lords.

And perhaps—Ella gave Natt another uneasy glance—there *had* been some talk of Lady Norr and the orcs, entangled in all that. And perhaps she should have actually listened, rather than so desperately blocking out any mention of orcs, and the last gossip she could recall had suggested that Lady Norr had run off with Lord Norr's money, and set up a new life elsewhere—that, or she was dead.

"Lady Norr is here?" Ella said finally, the disbelief thinning out her voice. "Mated to your *captain*?!"

"Ach, for many months now," Natt replied stiffly. "She carries his son. And she has put away the name Lady Norr, so do not call her thus."

Good gods. It was impossible, unthinkable, that a true lady would actually give up her title, her *life*, for a life with an *orc*, carrying an orc's *son*—but suddenly Ella's shock had become reality, because Natt had drawn her into another room, this one with a large, low square table in the midst of it, and a fire crackling in the opposite wall.

And sitting on the floor around the table were five huge orcs—one of them was the Baldr orc they'd met in the corridor—and, there, at the far end, a woman.

The woman was already rising to her feet, a touch unsteady, gripping for balance to the shoulder of the huge orc beside her—and that was because her belly was indeed very full and round. And more than that, it was partially *exposed*, displaying an expanse of taut skin, because the woman's short tunic only just covered her full breasts, and she was wearing actual *trousers*, tied low beneath the swell of her waist.

The sight was so suddenly, inexplicably alarming that Ella couldn't seem to move, or speak—but the woman was now striding toward her, and giving her a warm, delighted smile. Forcing Ella to finally take in the rest of her—she was tall and capable-looking, with strong, symmetrical features, a long dark braid, and broad shoulders—and Ella smiled back, even as her eyes gave another betraying glance down to the woman's unusual ensemble.

"Oh, how lovely to have another human among us!" the woman was saying, and when she reached out her hands to grasp Ella's, they were warm, strong, surprisingly reassuring. "I'm Jule, of Clan Ash-Kai. Welcome to our home."

Her smile was truly contagious, setting her dark eyes sparkling, and Ella felt herself relax slightly, even as her brain distantly registered the woman's cultured accent, the low, well-trained timbre of her voice. It was the kind of speech Ella had long sought to attain, firmly stamping away any remnants of her father's working-class twang—and finding it here, in Orc Mountain, was still so stunning that Ella could scarcely seem to speak.

"Um, hello, I'm—Ella Riddell," she managed. "You've perhaps heard of my father, John Riddell? From Ashford, in Sakkin Province."

"Oh, yes," Lady Norr—Jule—replied. "We met several times, he was an absolute *dear*, and I remember him speaking about his wonderful daughter, and all the fun you had together. I was so sorry to hear of his passing. You must have been devastated."

Her genuine-seeming sympathy seemed to strike deep in Ella's chest, and she made herself nod, her eyes blinking hard. "Yes," she said. "I was. I still am, I think."

The understanding flared across the woman's eyes, and she gave another smile, almost sad this time. "But here you are," she said firmly, "and I hope you've been made to feel welcome. How long have you and Nattfarr been mated?"

Her eyes had darted down toward Ella's neck as she spoke—good gods, to Natt's *teeth-marks*—and Ella was still feeling thoroughly confounded, enough that her mouth seemed to open on its own, and say things she didn't mean in the least. "Oh, for *years*, ever since we were—"

She bit off the words far too late, her eyes casting a truly chagrined glance up at Natt's blank, unreadable face beside her. No, it hadn't been years, he'd been with other *women* all that time, and Ella was *betrothed*, to Alfred—and she swallowed hard, took a bracing breath. "I mean," she said, "we're not—*mated*, like that. We're—friends. For a long time, I meant."

It came out sounding pathetically foolish, but the woman—Jule—only nodded and smiled, as though this were the most natural thing in the world. "Of course," she said. "How rude of me to presume. And I haven't even done any proper introductions! Won't you come, and meet my kin?"

Her *kin*? But she'd already drawn Ella away from Natt, toward the table of strange, staring orcs. She didn't seem alarmed in the least, however, and was particularly smiling at the huge, heavily scarred, barrel-chested orc she'd been sitting next to, who was now giving Ella a slow nod.

"This is my mate, Grimarr, of Clan Ash-Kai," Jule said, with unmistakable warmth in her voice. "The father of our son, Tengil, who we'll fully meet in the spring. And this"—she nodded more formally toward the next orc, seated to Grimarr's right—"is Drafli, of Clan Skai. My mate's Right Hand. He is fierce and strong, and sees much that others do not."

This orc was just as big as Grimarr, sporting just as many scars all over his bare chest and shoulders, but he was also perhaps more wiry-looking, his face harsh and angular. His eyes were narrow and glittering, and they were currently assessing Ella with a frank, chilly gaze that surely would have been frightening, had they been alone.

"And I believe you've already met Baldr," Jule continued, with a nod toward his huge greenish form, seated across the table from this unnerving-looking Drafli. "Grimarr's Left Hand, also of Clan Grisk, like your Nattfarr. The gods have gifted Baldr in many ways, but perhaps most of all with kindness."

Baldr's greenish cheeks had gone rather pink, but he smiled again at Ella, inclining his head toward her. And Ella again found herself smiling back, more genuine this time—until Jule directed her attention to the orc beside Baldr. This one was also alarmingly large, with heavy, craggy features and massive shoulders, and his eyes on Ella were watchful, wary, assessing.

"And this is Olarr, of Clan Bautul," Jule said, with a quick smile toward him. "One of the most fearsome warriors in our mountain. He serves as one of our two battle-captains, along with his brother Silfast."

This Olarr did bear a strong resemblance to the shameless Silfast orc from the Bautul common-room, Ella noted, as she gave him a careful nod, and earned a curt nod in return. And finally Ella followed Jule's gaze toward the last orc, seated across the table from Olarr.

And this orc—Ella blinked, and looked again—bore a smooth grey face that was utterly unmarked, with no scars or bruises whatsoever. His features also seemed softer than the other orcs', the lines of his face not etched quite so deep. And combined, the effect was almost as though he might have better been a man, or an elf.

"And this is John," Jule said warmly, ignoring Ella's twitch of surprise at that too-familiar human name *John*. "Of Clan Ka-esh. He likely knows more than the rest of us combined, and after the recent passing of our wise elder Fror, now serves as our chief advisor on many important matters."

John seemed entirely unimpressed by the praise, only eyeing Ella with a steady gaze, his head slightly tilting. To which Ella managed a nod back, and then attempted a smile at Jule, and then the table at large. "Thank you for welcoming me to your home," she said, with a little curtsey. "It's so lovely to meet you all."

Jule beamed toward her, visibly pleased, and when she gestured for Ella to sit at the empty side of the table, there seemed no other option but to obey. And after a moment's stillness Natt thankfully sat too, close beside Ella, his knee brushing against hers.

But Natt wasn't looking at her, and was instead staring straight across the table. Toward Jule's mate, the orcs' captain. Grimarr.

This Grimarr was staring steadily back at Natt, one thick black eyebrow slightly raised—and even at this distance, Ella could perhaps understand how this orc had become captain, and perhaps even gained a real lady's hand. There was a—weight about him, a kind of latent, settled power, as though he could be either supremely generous, or extremely dangerous.

But Natt seemed entirely unaffected, only gazing back toward him with flat, unreadable eyes, and finally it was Grimarr who spoke first. "I heard you were again attacked, brother," he said, his voice rumbling from deep in his chest. "Did you gain any wounds?"

"Ach," Natt said, curt. "There were five men, and I did not draw my blade. As you wished."

There was no change on Grimarr's harsh face, but he nodded. "We thank you, brother. You must go see Efterar, after this."

Natt gave a stiff nod, but didn't reply, almost as though he were waiting—and Grimarr spoke again, his voice slow, deliberate. "I wish you to account to me, Nattfarr," he said, "for why we have a band of Lord Tovey's men camped outside our mountain. Men who claim you have *stolen* Lord Tovey's betrothed."

Shit. The *men*. And hadn't Natt said, earlier, that the men had been *addressed*?! Surely that meant they weren't still *here*?

"After you entered the mountain last night, these men called for a hearing with us," continued Grimarr's deep voice, his eyes steady on Natt. "They asked that we return their master's betrothed to them. When we refused this, they swore to ride after Lord Tovey at once. To proclaim to him, and his allies, of how we have broken our treaty, and given them just cause for war."

Ella winced, and beside her Natt had briefly closed his eyes, and opened them again. "Ach," he said. "But Varinn told me, last night, that you countered this."

"We did," Grimarr replied flatly, his gaze angling toward Jule beside him. "My mate wisely spoke, and swore to these men that she had asked your woman to stay with us for a spell, to help build our new peace. She also bade them wait while she went and wrote letters to Lord Tovey and his kin, Lord and Lady Culthen, asking them to join us here also, and visit as our guests. She also invited the lords of Preia and Dunburg, who have of late allied themselves with Lord Culthen against us."

Ella winced again—she could not imagine a world in which Alfred, or his father, or their titled allies, would welcome such an invitation to Orc Mountain, let alone accept it—and across the table she caught Jule wincing, too. "It was the best we could come up with, in the moment," Jule said. "But it seemed to set Alfred's men back a little, at least. It becomes far more difficult to accuse us of kidnapping a lord's betrothed, when the lord himself—and his parents and allies—have also been officially invited to visit."

She flashed a rueful smile toward Ella across the table, and for a moment Ella could only seem to blink back. Dear gods, they truly had courted another full-on *war* last night, and how could she have possibly been so foolish?!

"And what did the men do, after that?" Ella heard her strained voice ask. "Are they all still here?"

"Three of them yet camp here, but two of them rode out with this letter, last eve," came the reply, from Grimarr this time. "Last I have heard from my Chief Scout Joarr, they are sure to catch Lord Tovey tomorrow in Baryn. Mayhap even tonight."

Something was shouting in Ella's head, so loud she had to put her hands to her temples, squeeze her eyes shut. They would catch Lord Tovey tomorrow in Baryn. Only three days' ride away. And then what?

"Do you expect Alfred will turn around and come for me at once?" Ella heard her choked voice ask, through the noise still blaring in her skull. "Or do you think he'll go on to Tlaxca, and Preia and Dunburg, and then come back with—"

With more men, she'd been about to say, *with an army*—but surely Alfred wouldn't go that far, would he? Between Ella's tale of her injured employee, and then this official invitation to visit? Surely Alfred wouldn't throw all that away, and immediately launch straight into war, without at least coming to investigate first?

"We cannot know this man's path until he chooses it," Grimarr replied, slow. "But I ken he shall soon return, most of all if he knows Nattfarr is tangled in this. But"—Grimarr's gaze on Ella's seemed to sharpen—"it shall help us, woman, to learn how you mean to face your betrothed, upon his return to you. What shall you tell him about your time here? Do you yet wish to wed him, after this?"

Ella's thoughts were again screeching wild through her head, and she cast another furtive glance toward Natt's blank, distant face. "I *have* to marry Alfred, to keep my inheritance, and my *home*," she said, though she felt her mouth twisting as she spoke, her eyes darting uneasily at Jule, a real lady, who'd perhaps given up all those things, for her life in Orc Mountain. "But I shall tell Alfred just what you've written. Natt was grievously injured, and I wanted to escort him here safely—and once I arrived, you invited me to stay. Which was most kind of you, indeed. The invitation, and also your generosity, in so cleverly helping us."

There was a waiting, hanging stillness, in which Jule's mouth twitched into another one of those understanding, reassuring smiles. "It's our pleasure, of course," she said. "And just to be clear, Ella—you *will* publicly make it known, again and again, to anyone who asks— including any number of lords and magistrates, and *especially* my cousin Otto—that Nattfarr has *not* kidnapped you, or brought you here against your will, in clear violation of our peace-treaty? Will you pledge this to us?"

Another pledge. And beside Ella, Natt's face was still an entirely unreadable mask, staring straight ahead—but Ella was fervently nodding, for reasons she didn't want to examine too closely. "Of course I promise this," she said firmly. "And of course Natt didn't kidnap me, or force me to come here. I wanted to see his home. We're *friends*."

The relief in the room was almost palpable, except for Natt, who beside Ella felt even stiffer than before. "Does this answer you, *Captain*?" he said, his voice brittle. "Do you have yet more to ask of me, or my *friend*?"

Grimarr's gaze hadn't faltered, but a visible furrow deepened on his brow. "You have answered naught that I have asked today, Nattfarr," he said finally, his voice deceptively mild. "Nor have you thanked me, nor my mate, for all we have done to help you. It is only your woman's brave voice, and her thanks, that I have heard."

Ella felt herself grimace, her eyes casting a chagrined glance toward Natt, but he only gave a mocking snort, a hard shake of his head. "Do you *wish* to hear my voice on this, Grimarr of Clan Ash-Kai?" he said, just as cool. "All my truth, spoken here, for all to learn? Now?"

Grimarr's eyes were unflinching on Natt's, but Ella could see something passing between them, some kind of shared understanding. "I am content," Grimarr said finally. "You may go."

But Natt actually laughed, the sound harsh, almost angry. "Ach, rid yourself of me, before I risk this upon you," he said. "Mayhap I do not wish to go. Mayhap"—he raised his eyebrows, and crossed his arms over his chest—"if you wish me to keep my silence, you shall look me in the eyes, and break yours."

It was undoubtedly some kind of challenge, thrown out with purpose before all these watching orcs, and while Ella still wasn't following, she didn't miss how again something had changed, how every eye in the room was looking at Grimarr, and waiting. At how Grimarr wasn't speaking, and how something convulsed in his scarred throat.

"And of what," Grimarr finally said, very slowly, "should you wish me to speak."

Ella blinked at him, and then at Natt—and there was the sudden, surprising understanding that even the orcs' powerful *captain* was afraid of Natt. Because as Speaker, Natt could make him speak truth, publicly, before all the other orcs. And even if Grimarr were to refuse, that would be its own kind of truth, a mark against his bravery or his leadership.

And—wait. Was *this*, perhaps, why Natt had been left to be hunted alone, all these years? Because that was *easier*, for the orcs in charge, with no one to hold them to account?

"My lass wishes to know the tale of my father's death, and how I came to be hunted," Natt said, clipped. "She wishes to know why you have done naught to help me, nor heard my voice, nor made me Speaker. She also wishes to know more of this foul man who seeks to take both my life, and her hand, and why he seeks these things."

The room had gone very silent, every eye still fixed upon Grimarr, and Ella could almost see him weighing it, weighing Natt, weighing her. And then Jule leaned toward his big body, her hand spreading close and familiar against his arm, to whisper something in his ear. Something Grimarr intently listened to, his head tilting, and when he drew back, Jule's eyes had settled on Ella's with a warm, firm determination. As if to say, *Don't worry. I'm with you.*

Beside her, Grimarr's huge form had shifted, his gaze intent on Natt across the table. "As you wish, brother," he said. "I shall speak."

For a moment, the entire room went still. Natt's body beside Ella had frozen, Baldr's mouth had fallen open, John looked mildly confused, and Drafli's clawed hand had dropped to grip at his sword-hilt. Only Jule appeared unperturbed, beaming first up toward Grimarr, and then across the table at Ella.

It was Drafli who moved first, his hands gesturing wildly in the air before him, and then Baldr began speaking, murmuring in soft black-tongue. And though Ella couldn't comprehend his words, Natt surely did, and spat something under his breath that made Baldr flinch, and glance at Natt with an almost hurt look—but he didn't stop speaking, his eyes darting between Drafli and Grimarr.

Grimarr listened until Baldr had fallen silent again, and then replied in kind, again in the incomprehensible black-tongue. But when Grimarr looked back at Natt again, he nodded, and his eyes spoke of a grim, settled determination.

"I await your questions, brother," he said, and again, Ella could almost feel the shock reverberating through Natt's form. Making it quite clear that this had never happened before, this had *never* been granted to him by this captain before, and Ella couldn't seem to stop her hand from reaching toward Natt's, her fingers curling tight against his hot, sweaty skin.

His hand suddenly gripped back, so hard it was almost painful. And she could see his throat bobbing as his body leaned forward, his eyes fixing firm to his captain's face.

"I wish you to speak your truth," Natt said, "of my father."

The captain's big shoulders rose and fell, but he didn't look away, his eyes held steady to Natt's. "Your father was Rakfarr, of Clan Grisk," he said. "He served as Speaker of the Grisk, and oft raised his voice against my own father, Kaugir of Clan Ash-Kai, who was then captain of Ash-Kai, Grisk, and Ka-esh."

"And your father hated mine, for speaking this truth," Natt said, his voice curt. "And for the power he wielded through this."

Grimarr nodded, slow. "Your father sought not only the truth of the Grisk, but that of all five clans. He gained the trust of many orcs, and began to move the Grisk away from the mountain, to this camp at Meinolf, where you were whelped. There, he sought to keep his orcs and their mates and sons safe from men, and from my father."

Natt only kept watching Grimarr's eyes, staring at him across the table, and Grimarr sighed again. "As Rakfarr's power grew, he began to call for my father's truth, spoken aloud before all five clans. This my father could not risk, not with Rakfarr so powerful, and all the Grisk at his back. My father feared that Rakfarr sought to defeat him, and take his place as captain."

"And what did your father do to mine," Natt hissed, his clawed fingers again gripping painfully against Ella's hand. "And to *me*."

Grimarr's harsh face looked almost weary, but he still didn't look away. "My father wished to be rid of yours, without drawing blame upon himself," he said slowly. "Thus, he first spread word among the humans of a fearsome orc—and his son—who wielded powerful black magic, and who sought to use it against the men. Once my father had sparked this fear, he then spread your belongings to the men, so that you could be hunted."

What? Ella was staring between Natt and Grimarr, caught in the tension of their eyes, in the raw fury all over Natt's face. *This* was why Natt had been hunted all these years? Because the orcs' own *captain* had sold him to their enemies?!

"In doing this," Grimarr's slow voice continued, "my father also gave up the Grisk camp to the men, since this was where your scents were held most strongly. And thus, when the men attacked, it meant not only Rakfarr's death, but also the deaths of many Grisk orcs. Many Grisk women, and sons. Near to one hundred deaths, this one day."

The room felt even stiller than before, the air gone thick and heavy all around, and Ella could hear Natt's choked breathing beside her. But he hadn't spoken again, and to Ella's vague surprise, it was Baldr who spoke next, his voice hushed, perhaps even pained.

"It was truly *Kaugir* who did that?" he asked, his blinking eyes held to Grimarr's. "I know Nattfarr has spoken of this, but many of our brothers have dismissed him and denied this, and you have never—"

He bit his lip with a sharp tooth, clearly not about to openly accuse his own captain of intentionally keeping such a horrible secret—but beside Ella Natt laughed, the sound hard, bitter, broken.

"Ach, our *captain* has never spoken of this," he snapped. "He cannot risk losing the Grisk to his father's betrayal. He cannot risk losing them to *me*. And thus, he has left me to be hunted, so that I shall stay out of his way, and not hold him to account for his sins and his *lies!*"

Ella could feel Natt's body vibrating under her hand, and his eyes on Grimarr were glittering, merciless. "This is truth, *Captain*," he demanded. "Is it not?"

There was silence all around, the room's full attention on Grimarr's stony face, on the slight spasm on his mouth. "I did not know what my father had done until it was too late," he said. "But I ought to have seen this. For what Rakfarr did, with the Grisk—it was not *safe*. It only courted danger, to set up this camp so far away from the mountain. It put an entire clan at risk. I cannot have you do this again, Nattfarr."

But his voice sounded oddly laboured, his breathing heavy, and Natt abruptly thrust Ella's hand away, and instead gripped at the table, leaning over it, his eyes cold, blazing, on fire. "You shall speak truth to me," he growled. "It shall only be to your gain when I am dead, with no son to my name. And it was *your* father who killed the Grisk. *Not* mine. Is this truth, *Captain*?!"

The power seemed to snap through the room, drawing Grimarr's big form closer over the table, his eyes wide and unblinking. "Ach," he said, his voice very quiet. "This is truth."

The stillness swarmed again, broken only by a gasp from Jule beside Grimarr, and a sound like a moan from Baldr's mouth. And Natt had recoiled as if he'd been struck, and he shoved himself up and away from the table, onto his feet, claws out, ready to strike.

"And even now," he rasped, "you do *naught* to help me. You do naught to avenge your father's wrong, or make right the wrongs of this mountain. Instead, you seek to force me to do your bidding, and betray my own *soul*, so that I may be trapped always in your web. It is only now that I have—"

His voice broke off sharply, but his eyes had shot a brief, betraying glance downward, toward—Ella. And Ella wasn't even slightly following now, only blinking up at his face, uncertain, lost.

"It's only now that you have—what?" she heard herself say, very thin. "What, Natt?"

But Natt's head only jerked away, his glittering gaze back on Grimarr. "You have not yet told her," he hissed, "why this man seeks her hand."

Grimarr's eyes had closed, but when they opened again, they flicked back to Natt's, looking tired, resigned. "Lord Tovey and his father, Lord Culthen, regret this peace-treaty they have sworn with us," he said. "They have made allies of their neighbouring lords in Preia and Dunburg, and together they seek to sway more lords to again spark this war against us. But they are greatly hindered by all they have lost on their last battles against us, and so they seek for yet more wealth, to aid this goal."

It was like the air had been sucked out of Ella's lungs all at once, and her eyes gaped at this awful orc, at the awful truth written all over his awful face.

"You mean," she said, between the rising gulps in her throat, "that not only is Alfred hunting Natt, for money, but he's also plotting to start another *war*? And he's marrying me so that he can—he can use *my* money to *pay* for that war? Against *you*?!"

Grimarr's black head nodded, his eyes still held to Natt's glittering, flaring ones. "Yes, woman, this is truth," he said, with a sigh. "These men wish to take your hoard, and use it to break our peace, and destroy us all."

21

Alfred wanted to use Ella's money, to destroy the orcs.

Ella was trapped in those words, in that truth, blinking at Grimarr, at this sudden shouting misery. Of course Alfred hadn't really cared about her in the slightest. Of course he wanted to use her money—and defile her father's memory—for a *war*. Of course he couldn't be trusted.

When Natt's hand clutched at Ella's, and dragged her toward the door, there was no opposing him, no way to silence the mayhem charging through her head. Alfred had lied. Natt had lied. Grimarr had lied. And Natt's father had been *killed*, with a hundred other people, because he'd been betrayed by his own.

And Natt was *still* being betrayed, by his damned *captain*, and his rage seemed to seep into Ella as he hauled her back through the corridors. Everything was pitch-black now—he must have left the lamp behind—and it was thoroughly, heart-poundingly disorienting, Ella's body fighting to keep up, feeling walls slide close, hearing voices and bodies she couldn't see, while the world tilted up and down and sideways.

"*Why*, Natt," Ella choked out, once he'd finally drawn her to a halt in a place that felt more enclosed, where the sound and air didn't seem to carry. "Why didn't you tell me about Alfred. About *you*. About any of this!"

Natt's movement hitched in the blackness, and she could feel his eyes on her, could taste the heat of his fury. "Foolish, selfish little woman," he hissed, his voice cracking. "You did not *wish* to know these things. You wish to live in your darkness, with your unearned hoard, and your silly pampered life. You wish to give *naught* to an orc, and most of all to an orc who stands between you and all this, and has naught but *death* to his name!"

Dear gods, he was on this again, and Ella frowned at where she knew him to be, and gave a hard shake of her head. "That's not true, Natt," she shot back. "I kept my pledge to you. I gave you my maidenhood. I stayed with you, when you were hurt. I'm wearing your *clothes*. I even *lied* to your captain about you *kidnapping* me! I'm *here*, Natt, I'm doing whatever you wish, what more do you want from me!"

But Natt's replying laugh was hard, mocking, entirely unfamiliar. "Ach, you are here," he said, "for mayhap three more days, until this foul man comes for you. And then you shall return to him, and take him into your bed, and hand him your hoard. And then, you shall watch as he *kills* me, and then turns his swords upon my brothers!"

Ella's head was pounding, her hands gone clammy, her throat tight. "I wouldn't," she began, but Natt only laughed again, and suddenly here was the feel of his clawed fingers, tapping warm and deadly against her cheek.

"You would, my sweet little lass," he said, in almost a parody of a caress. "And you shall. Shall you not? You shall do all that must be done, to become a fine lady. To be *real*."

Ella swallowed hard, felt her head shake against his hand—but Natt only laughed again, the sound unbearable in her ears. "Ach, you shall," he murmured, and that was the feel of his other hand, coming to rest against her bare waist. "You shall go back to this man when he comes, even with my seed still hidden inside you. And you shall smile at him, and speak false to him, and tell him I have not touched you. You shall tell him you are yet a maid."

That hand was sliding downwards now, over the too-short length of her leather kilt, until it found her bare thigh. "You shall take him to your bed," Natt whispered, that hand now slipping up under the kilt, "and spread your legs for him. You shall take him *here*, where I have opened you."

Ella's mouth gasped, her entire body twitching, because Natt's clawless fingers were indeed there, delving against her, spreading her apart. "You shall take his foul little prick within you," he breathed, as he slid a single finger halfway inside, gave it a mocking wriggle. "You shall take him into what is *mine*, and moan and gasp for him, and all this time you shall be coating him with my seed, and thinking of *me*."

This was wrong, this was so wrong, *Natt* was wrong—but Ella couldn't seem to break it, couldn't find any words to speak. And her hands suddenly grasping against his hot bare chest only made it worse, made his upper body flinch away from her, sharp and purposeful, even as that finger slipped deeper, stronger inside her. "Speak this, lass," he ordered. "Speak your truth to me."

That was wrong too, Ella couldn't even see him, couldn't at all feel that compulsive draw upon her thoughts. But maybe he was mocking her in this too, and when her mouth gave a helpless moan he indeed laughed again, hard, sardonic, vicious.

"Ach, my sweet little lass," he breathed, as more fingers pressed against her, plunging deep and almost painful inside. "You yet wish for my power and my taking, do you not? Even as you fear me, you yet wish to fill your womb with my seed, so you may have yet more to give your foul little man."

There was no answering this, only gasping for air, only feeling those invading fingers seeking, stretching, pushing. Sparking impossible pleasure, her swollen, betraying body clenching greedily against him. And when Natt abruptly spun Ella around into him, so that her back was flush to his bare chest, that was even more whirling pleasure, his fingers still driving deep, his breath hot against the nape of her neck.

"Speak truth, lass," Natt hissed, as that huge heft at his groin pressed hard and demanding against her bare, exposed crease. "You long for me, as you shall *never* long for him. You shall think of my prick inside you, each time he fucks you. Even now, you long for me to take you, and fill you, and thrust even the *thought* of him away from you. Ach?"

Ella's head was violently nodding, *yes, please, do that, please*—and

behind her Natt laughed again, and shoved her forward. So that she
was bent over something—something soft, at least—but then Natt's
fingers yanked out of her, and suddenly it was—*him*. That huge,
tapered cock. Strong, commanding, unyielding.

"You shall think of me," Natt growled, promised, pledged, as that
slick hardness began to spread her apart, opening her wet heat around
it. "You shall think of me, and *scream* for him!"

And before Ella could move or speak or even think, he slammed
inside. Filling her with thunderous, astonishing force, impaling her
whole upon him—and gods curse her but Ella did scream, the sound
helpless and shrill, shredding at the darkness.

"Ach, you wish for this," Natt snarled, as that invading heft yanked
out—and then punched back deep. Making Ella scream again, her
entire body flailing and trapped, but he only gave that scornful,
painful laugh as he did it again, setting sparks flaring behind her eyes,
her heated groin frantically grasping for him, fighting to keep him still,
for a moment, a moment—

"Foolish little lass," he breathed, cold and taunting, as that hot
hardness filled her again, and wrenched away. "You know not what
you have done, what you have asked for. You shall *never* forget me, and
even if you have taught yourself not to speak, you shall speak this truth
to me!"

But Ella couldn't, she couldn't even think, the pleasure and the
misery all hurled too close together, fierce and dark and terrible. And
the only truth was Natt, this, his powerful force inside her, but he kept
taking it away with every thrust, pummelling her with it, punishing
her. And it felt so good and it was far too much and why couldn't she
speak, only moans and gasps and screams—

"Speak to me!" Natt shouted behind her, the words burning at
Ella's ears, her groin, her heart. "You shall never forget me, you shall
never stop feeling me inside you, you shall *never* stop grieving me
when I and all my brothers are *dead* at your husband's hand!"

And it was like something broke deep within her, screeching out
white and hot and utterly unbearable—and it was him, it was *them*, his
invading strength finally holding fast. Surging out its truth inside her,
while Ella's own body writhed and clamped around him, soaring stuttering ecstasy, raw and wretched and aching.

It didn't stop, Ella couldn't stop it, escaping now out her mouth in bleak, broken gasps. But Natt was there, still there, trapped deep inside, his claws sunk into her skin—and it was enough, finally, enough. Ella could speak truth, to this. She could.

"You can't die, Natt," her voice choked. "You can't, you *can't*. And of course I'll never forget you, or stop feeling you, but I can't grieve you, because you can't die, because I *love* you."

And was this his magic, or something entirely new, because Ella couldn't see his eyes, it was dark, there'd been no compulsion to say it—but she still needed to say it, needed him to know, needed him to understand, *please*.

"You're right," she gasped. "I don't know what I've gotten into, or what I've done. I'll try to do better, I'm sorry I've hurt you, I'm so sorry that any of this ever happened to you. You should be the Speaker, you should always have been, you're brilliant and you deserve it and I wish I could have *helped* you. I wish I could have been there for you. I love you, Natt. I *love* you."

There was no reply behind her, only the harsh sounds of Natt's ragged breaths. And then, oh, the feeling of his huge, hot, sticky body, sinking its weight down against her, pressing her close into the softness below.

"Ach," Natt's voice whispered, finally, and there was the sound of his throat swallowing, another breath coming out thick against her ear. "Ach, my lass. I have drawn your blood, this time."

His voice was choked, flat, bitter—but he was here, he was himself again, he was Natt. And the relief was almost alive, something Ella could taste under her skin, and she blinked back the wetness in her eyes, and nudged her head against his.

"Well, it's not like I'm surprised," she said, the words coming out hoarse, but true. "You've been threatening to do so for days now. You dreadful orcs."

It was like she'd plucked at a taut string, and deflated his hard, brittle body all at once—and he made a sound that might have been a laugh, or something else. "I am sorry," he whispered, so quiet. "Are you in pain."

Perhaps it was just this relief, having Natt's warm body sunk against her, his warm voice in her ear—but Ella shook her head, and wriggled herself a bit further beneath his protective weight. "Not—like that," she heard herself say. "But—I'm sorry too, Natt. I should have asked you all this, and sought your truth, from the start."

She could feel his chest fill and empty against her, and she drew in her own breath, her courage. "Will you tell me, then?" she whispered. "The rest of it? What happened to you? Please?"

Natt gave a low, heavy-sounding groan, but she could feel him nodding, his silken hair rubbing against her cheek. "The day it began," he said, hoarse, "I was with you. We laughed and ran, and I caught you a rat to eat. But you would not eat this, so I did instead. And you groused at me for this, but you yet smiled at me, and teased me with your eyes. And when I went to leave, you kissed my cheek, and I wished to kiss you, but I did not."

The images were swirling through Ella's memories too, almost staggering in their vividness. He'd been so absurdly compelling that day, even as he'd eaten an actual *rat*, and his eyes on hers had been so dark, watchful, glinting with a meaning that Ella had so desperately wanted to follow. And she could still see the regret in those eyes, could still almost taste it, when he'd said he was late for his father, and had to go.

Afterwards, she'd wondered if it had been on purpose, that farewell. The way he'd drawn away after she'd kissed his warm cheek, his eyes held intently elsewhere, his usually easy body gone tight and tense. All hinting that perhaps he'd meant to leave, that day, and never come back.

But the familiar, twisting pain of that memory had shifted, some-how, and Ella swallowed, and reached to find his hand in the darkness, curling her fingers over the taut fist of it. "And then?"

She could feel the slow exhale of his body over her, his head ducking against her shoulder. "And then I went home," he said, without inflection. "And found all my kin either dying, or dead. My brothers, their mates, their babes, both small and half-grown. And then, my father, with his sword yet in his hand, and his head gone."

There was a choked noise in Ella's throat, another heavy sigh from Natt above her. "One orc lived long enough to warn me," he said. "This saved my life. I took my father's sword and ring, and I ran. It took me five days and nights to escape them, and find a way back to the mountain."

Ella's eyes squeezed shut, her trembly hand finding the ring on his fist, and covering it with her fingers. "And then what?" she made herself say. "Surely that awful captain wasn't pleased to see you?"

"He was not," Natt said, "but he could not yet kill me, and betray himself, not with the whole mountain grieving this loss, and seeking vengeance. For some weeks I sought to escape his eyes, hiding in the tunnels beneath the mountain, and running into the forest when the risk became too great—but this only called more death upon my head, from all sides. And it was"—he sighed—"Grimarr, who saw my doom, and sent me away to the Bautul deep in the south, where his father and the men could not follow. The southern Bautul were not allied to the mountain then, but enemies."

"And they—made you pay," Ella whispered, remembering his words from before, the horrible hints behind them. "For your safety."

"Ach," Natt said, with a laugh that wasn't a laugh at all. "I was young, I was Grisk, I was foolish and untouched and unguarded. They did all that they wished with me."

The smooth, easy casualness of those words made their truth all the more sickening, and Ella pressed her face into the softness beneath her, felt her hand gripping tighter at his fist. "But there are Bautul still here in the mountain, aren't there?" she said. "Like—Olarr. And Silfast. All of them in that room. How can you—"

The tension was back in Natt's body above hers, and she felt his fist flex under her fingers. "There are many who were not there, or who did naught to me," he said. "And there were some among them who protected me also. But"—his body twitched, or perhaps shuddered—"there are indeed some upon whom I yet owe vengeance. Once I am Speaker, I shall make them shout aloud the truth of their sins, for all their kin to hear."

Oh. So that was part of this too, then, part of why Natt needed to be Speaker, why he carried such bitterness. Because those who'd hurt him still walked free, while he still suffered. Hunted, wounded, alone, betrayed by both orcs and men.

Betrayed by *her*.

And even as Ella's twisting thoughts rebelled at the idea, it seemed to embed itself deeper, wrapping itself in bitter, unassailable truth. She hadn't known about any of this, when she'd agreed to marry Alfred, and for that, she could be forgiven—but now? Now that she knew all these horrible truths, all that Natt had gone through, she still wore Alfred's ring? She would return to Alfred, and give him all he needed to kill Natt, and his people?

But no, *no*, she'd told Natt she would demand Alfred give up hunting him, and she'd meant that—but then again, that would mean very little if Alfred was still planning to use her money to wage war against the orcs en masse. And—Ella winced—she had wanted to keep seeing Natt, through it all. Keeping him around. Like a—*pet*. Like what those awful orcs had done to him. Wielding their power, their advantage, to *use* him.

You shall go back to this man. You shall smile at him, and speak false to him. You shall take him into what is mine.

Suddenly it seemed abominably cruel, that Ella had proposed Natt do such a thing—and worse still, that Natt had agreed to it. He'd wanted vengeance, he'd said, and maybe cuckolding Alfred would be vengeance—but it would also be more betrayal. More injustice. More grief.

And where did this leave Ella, after this? She had to return to Alfred, and even if that didn't happen, Alfred's awful men were already *here*. And she still wore Alfred's ring, she still had to marry in less than a month, and if she didn't she would lose everything. Her wealth, her home, her beloved lands, her dreams of being a lady. Everything gone, lost, forever.

And above that, beyond all that—Ella *still* couldn't trust Natt. He'd lied to her, about too many things. And—she drew in breath, bravery—perhaps he'd lied about that, too. Perhaps...

"You didn't mean it, did you," she whispered. "When you said we could still be—friends. After I married Alfred."

There was more stillness above her, and then another sigh, rasping against her ear. "No," he said, very quiet. "I could not, lass. I could not bear to smell his foul scent upon you, warring against mine, shouting at me of each time, each place, he has touched you. And I"—she could hear his swallow, too loud in the quiet—"I shall never again be a pet, to be held and used at the whims of another. I shall *die* first."

He said the last with a ferocious, shuddering certainty, and Ella felt herself shudder too, something seeming to shrink and wither, deep inside. "So you lied about that too, then," she said, her voice hollow. "And these next few days together—they're maybe just—*goodbye*."

The word seemed to hang between them, so small but so breathtakingly fatal, and made only worse when Natt's face in her neck tilted, and inhaled, deep. Like it *was* goodbye, like every breath, every time he did this, was one closer to the last.

"Ach," he said, so quiet. "I am sorry, lass."

He was sorry. Again. And it was true, he'd lied to her again, she too was betrayed and lost and alone. And what happened now, what came next, what was left in the wake of such emptiness?

There was nothing, *nothing*, and finally Ella relented to the darkness, and wept.

22

Ella's sobbing was loud, shameful, and impossible to stop. Complete with leaking eyes, a running nose, and desperate, high-pitched gasps that seemed to wrench into her bones.

But in it, somehow, Natt had maneuvered her into his strong arms, and tucked her face close into his warm chest, against the steady pounding of his heart. And his gentle, clawless fingers wiped at her wet eyes, and smoothed back her hair, and silently said, *It's all right, you'll be all right, I'm still here.*

When the sniffling finally faded to silence, Natt *was* still there, still petting and stroking Ella with an intent, fierce gentleness. Speaking with every touch of those hands, whispering of his regret, his care, his affection.

But not love, Ella knew. Because she'd spoken that painful word, earlier in this, and betrayed that dangerous truth—and Natt had seemed to entirely disregard it. Because did one lie like he had, to someone one loved? Did one deceive, and mock, and yell, and make demands, and—Ella swallowed—draw *blood*?

"So is there anything else I should know?" she made herself ask, her voice coming out croaky, cracked. "Anything else you're not telling me the truth about, *Speaker*?"

Natt's big body twitched against her, and his hands still stroking her had briefly hesitated. Saying yes, in fact, there was, and suddenly Ella wanted to shake him, to scream at him, to run away and never come back—

"I have not," Natt said, his voice halting, "yet told you of the other side of my gift. As Speaker."

Ella's heart was pounding, her face jerking up to look at him, and finding only this damned darkness, hiding him from her eyes. "And?" she demanded. "What is it?"

His hands had begun stroking her again, smoothing at her cheeks, her hair. "It seeks truth," he said, "from both speakers. From not only the one I speak to, but from—me. Whether I wish for this, or not."

From him. Ella blinked, her thoughts twisting away after that, and finding—more memories. Natt looking into her eyes, into her soul, and speaking. *Will you have me. You shall be safe. This truth is ours. You belong with me. Mine.*

Ella sighed, slow, and gave a little bump of her head against Natt's solid chest. "You orcs," she said, with another bump, "are *abominable.*"

There was a rumble from Natt that might have been a laugh, and then the distinct feel of warm lips, kissing soft against her forehead. "Ach," he said. "Mayhap now I shall catch you a fresh rat to eat?"

Ella's replying shudder felt like sheer relief, somehow, especially when Natt chuckled again, and pressed another kiss against her skin. "Or should you like a pigeon?" he asked. "Or mayhap a snake? I could give you the rattle to wear, as a gift."

Ella elbowed at him this time, but she was smiling too, and when Natt drew her up, she willingly went. But still folded into his arms, and she could feel his chest rise and fall, his hands gripping her strong and close.

"I ought not to have shouted at you, or mocked you as I did," he said, soft. "I must learn to hold better sway over this. My anger is not"—he swallowed—"only toward you. You are a bright gift to me, lass. You have brought me great joy, these past days."

Oh. But that didn't mean he *wasn't* angry with her, either. Angry because Ella hadn't asked the real questions. Hadn't wanted to know. And instead, she'd wanted to use him. To keep him, just where she wished. As a *pet.*

And why, truly, would Ella have thought she had a right to such a thing? Because of her wealth, her standing? Because she would be a lady? Or because Natt was—an orc? Not human? Not—*real*?

Ella's face had gone uncomfortably hot, and she drew in breath, felt the warmth of him, the strength of him. "You've brought me joy too, Natt," she whispered. "And I should have thought. I should have asked. I need to—*think*, more, about all this. It's been—a lot."

There was a squeeze of those claws against her, a brush of warm lips to her temple. "Ach, I ken," he whispered. "I ought to seek to bring you only peace, and ease, these next days."

Ella's chest tightened, but she heard herself snort, a rueful smile curling at her mouth. "And yet, Nattfarr of Clan Grisk, we both know you shall do no such thing. You shall only continue being devious, and obnoxious, and—utterly *indecorous*."

Natt's laugh sent a shiver of warmth down her spine—and so did the sudden, purposeful slide of his hand under her fur cape, his claws plucking lightly at her nipple. "I know not of what you speak," he murmured, as his fingers tweaked, squeezed, staked their claim—but then he pulled away, and suddenly, there was light.

It was from a candle, Ella noted, as she squinted through her fingers—and wait, he'd had a candle there, within reach, this whole time?! But her accusing glance up at his face met a wry half-smile, a brief pat of his hand against her cheek.

"I did not wish you to wonder if I was using my Speaking against you," he said. "I wish to give you room to—*think*, upon these things."

There was a curious clench in Ella's belly, but she managed a nod, an attempt at a smile. And when Natt drew her up after him, his hand strong and warm against hers, it was easy to go, to cling close against his warmth—at least, until she felt even more of his mess, slipping down her bare thighs.

"Might you have a rag?" she asked, glancing around. "Or my old dress?"

There was an odd glint in Natt's watching eyes, and then a deliberate, unhurried glance downwards. "No," he said coolly, "I do not. I had your frocks burnt, remember?"

Right. Ella's mouth opened, and closed, and Natt gave a smug little pat to her cheek. "If you are a good lass," he said, "I shall clean you later. With my tongue."

Ella's gasp was loud and shameful and utterly betraying, but Natt only grinned back, and made a show of licking his lips with his long, lascivious tongue. "This shall please you," he said. "Yes?"

The heat in his eyes was asking, seeking, speak truth—and Ella swallowed her instinctive rebuff, and took a deep, fortifying breath. Truth. She could do this.

"Yes," she whispered, humiliating, true. "That would surely please me, Natt."

His broad, wicked grin was reward all its own, as was the approving grip of his clawed hand at her breast beneath her cape. "Good," he said. "Now come. Do you wish to see my rooms?"

His rooms? The sudden spark of interest was genuine, easy to speak, and Ella eagerly nodded, and belatedly glanced around the room. "Yes, of course. Is this one of them?"

Natt nodded too, suddenly looking almost—shy, and Ella blinked at that, and then at the room around them. It was a bedroom, surely—they'd been lying on a large, square bed, covered all over with furs, and boasting tall steel poles at each corner—and there were shelves along one wall, piled with a haphazard array of what looked like clothing and tools and trinkets. And on the other walls—Ella's head tilted, and she stepped closer to look, keeping Natt's hand in hers—there were carvings. Beautiful, impossibly detailed stone carvings, of orcs, and women, and *babies*.

Ella could see where they started, on the far right of this wall, and how they seemed to follow a path, from one group, to the next. The first depicted a huge naked orc with hair that beamed out like a sun, and in one clawed hand he held what looked like a pickaxe, wielded against the wall's corner. And in his other arm he grasped an equally bared woman, small but smiling, and the woman's hand—Ella flushed—was clenched around his huge, dripping cock.

And from there, a gorgeous spray of delicate carved lines led over to five more orcs, each one markedly different than the others. The first was huge and fierce-looking, his muscled arms crossed over his broad chest. The next wasn't quite so tall, but broader, with a sword gripped in both hands. The third was tall and slim, with wild hair and oddly arresting eyes, and the fourth was shorter, and held a book and a quill in his clawed hands. And last in the line—Ella's eyes studied it in the flickering candlelight—gently cradled a pointy-eared, black-haired babe in his powerful arms, while lines of beautiful, curling, unreadable script soared from his open mouth.

It was Grisk. The Speaker.

"What does he say?" Ella whispered to Natt's silent body beside her. "Can you read it?"

Natt's replying nod was quick, immediate. "It reads, *I am Grisk*," he said. "*I Speak for my kin. Should you not grant me your truth, I shall draw it from you, and speak it for all to hear.*"

They were the same words Natt had spoken earlier, the same vow, and Ella's hand on his had gripped tighter, pulling him closer. And then she moved to the next grouping, connected by more of the delicate carved lines, drawing from the Speaking orc's groin.

"His son, right?" she asked, with a smile up at Natt's face. "You orcs are not subtle, at least."

Natt grinned back, and then began to lead Ella down the row of carvings, following the lines from one orc to the next. These orcs all had women by their sides, some tall, some short, and they were almost all scantily clad, like Ella was, with short capes and skirts. And in their arms there were always children, usually one, but sometimes two or three, and from one of the children would come the next grouping, and then the next, and the next.

"This orc," Natt said with pride, gesturing at a tall, dangerous-looking orc, with an equally tall, topless woman by his side, "was my father's father. Thrakfarr. He and his mate Joya bore two sons. One of these was my father"—he tapped at the taller of the two children, standing beneath them—"and the other fathered Thrain and Thrak, who you have met. And thus..."

Natt's voice trailed off as he led her to the next carving, the last one in the row. "My father," he said, quiet. "And my mother. And me."

Ella stepped closer to the wall, studying it, searching first the depiction of Natt's tiny face, the adorable pointed ears and snubbed nose, the already-sharp teeth. And then, Natt's father, big and scarred and powerful-looking, with Natt cradled in the crook of his arm—and beside him, a lovely, smiling woman with long, curling hair.

"Her name was Sonja," Natt said, quiet. "My father said this is a good likeness of her."

His clawless hand had reached out, stroking reverent and gentle at the woman's stone face. And blinking at her, at him, Ella realized, again, that the clothes this woman was wearing were almost identical to her own. A short skirt. A fur cape. And mismatched jewels hanging from her ears, and her *nose*, and—Ella twitched—even a long chain dangling out from under her cape, just where a nipple piercing might be.

Ella was still blinking, digesting that, when Natt followed the curving lines from Rakfarr, to—nothing. A blank wall. Emptiness.

It was startling enough that Ella flinched, her eyes darting up to Natt's beside her, and he gave a grim smile, flattening his hand against the smooth stone. "They are not yet carved," he said. "Not until I have lived long enough to gain a mate, and a son, to carry on this gift for my kin. If I fail in this"—his mouth tightened, his gaze sliding away—"it shall be Thrain or Thrak, if the gods see fit to bless one of their sons as Speaker."

Oh. *Oh.* Ella's eyes were fixed to the blank wall, suddenly, because once again, she hadn't even *thought*. Natt wanted a mate. Natt wanted a *son*. Not an illicit, secret liaison as an already-wedded lady's *pet*.

And he'd spoken to her of that truth, that first night, hadn't he? *I longed to claim you as my mate*, he'd said. *I should have whelped so many sons upon you, I would now have a whole brood to my name.*

But this could not be.

Ella had to rub at her eyes, at the sudden heat prickling at her face. Dear gods, she'd been foolish, and so superior, so presumptuous. Twelve generations of Natt's lineage carved into a gods-damned *wall*, just waiting for him to pass on his rare, impossible magic to his own son—and she'd wanted him for a *pet*.

"Your portrait will be lovely, Natt," she said, through the tightness in her throat. "And you'll have an entire brood, I know it. You'll set a new record, and all your descendants will admire you, and wonder at your shocking virility."

Natt was still for a moment, but then smiled again, if rather half-hearted this time. "They shall give me the largest prick of them all," he said lightly. "And mayhap they shall carve it spewing seed, all over the floor at my feet."

"Indeed," Ella replied, twitching a smile back toward him. "And all over anyone with the misfortune to be nearby, as well."

Natt turned to face her at that, his eyes still shadowed, but he brought his finger up, and flicked at her cheek with his claw. "Only if they are sweet, lovely lasses like you," he murmured. "And only if they are dressed just as an orc's mate should be."

And oh, he'd *said* it, he'd said it and his eyes had glanced toward the wall, toward his own mother, who looked just the same. And something in Ella's chest had wrenched so tight she couldn't breathe, and her swallow was audible, echoing against the damning stone walls of this ancient, beautiful, devastating room.

"I—I *like* dressing this way," she whispered, to his chest, because there wasn't the courage to meet his eyes. "I like pleasing you, Natt. I— I'd like to do it more."

And curse him, but here was the feel of his warm hand, tilting her chin up, making her look at him. Those eyes crackling with power, with meaning, with truth. "Say this again," he whispered, soft, and Ella gulped, nodded, breathed.

"I like pleasing you, Natt," she said, easier this time, and that was his magic, but in this moment, she didn't care. "I want to please you more. I want to be truly yours, these next days. I want to trust you. I want to be—*her*."

She didn't need to say, because Natt knew, he *knew*. "You wish to be not only my willing guest, here to honour me," he breathed, "but you wish to play a deeper game with me, my filthy, foolish lass. You wish for me to treat you as my *mate*."

Gods, Ella wanted that, and she nodded, fervent, exposed, longing. "Yes," she whispered. "I wish to be—Ella, of Clan Grisk."

It was madness, pure and indefensible, those scandalous words escaping from her mouth—but Natt gave a hoarse, shuddering groan, his eyelashes fluttering, his sharp tooth biting against his lip.

"Again, my lass," he breathed, "you know not what you wish for. To play a game such as this, you must show me that you are a worthy mate for a Speaker. You must show yourself not only a willing guest in my home, but a willing *partner* to me. You shall freely speak truth without my prodding, you shall aid me in my calling, you shall uphold my work with my brothers, and help my cause with our captain. And, you shall not only welcome my touch, but you shall eagerly seek it, without shame or regret. And from henceforth"—those eyes darkened, held to hers, and he was speaking truth too, he was—"this man shall be dead, to you. His name shall mean naught to you. His *jewels* mean naught."

Oh. The words flashed behind Ella's eyes, heated, powerful, dangerous—but the raw, desperate craving was even stronger, winding tight, circling close. And when Natt's hand moved against her own, scraping against the hard gold of her engagement-ring, it was as strong as a shout, a slap, a blast of wind to the face.

Again, she hadn't even *thought*. Natt had bathed her and dressed her all over, but throughout it all, still she'd worn *this*. Probably even smelling of Alfred, still, taunting Natt with it every time she moved.

So Ella gave a quick, twitchy little nod—and then purposely held out her hand, that hand, trembling, waiting. And with those black, all-seeing eyes intent upon her, Natt's claws slowly, purposefully, drew off the ring—and then he casually, viciously tossed it over his shoulder, toward the shelves opposite, where it bounced on a pile of clothing, and then stilled, its large diamond glinting innocuously in the candlelight.

"You know not what you wish for," Natt said again, with an almost regretful stroke of his hand against Ella's now-bare finger—but in this moment, with all these new truths warring in her head, the strongest of all was this one. Here. Whispering quiet, a promise, between them.

"But I want to learn, Natt," Ella whispered. "These next few days. With you."

Natt's smile was wry, resigned, still whispering of promise, or perhaps regret. "Ach, you shall, my foolish little lass," he said. "You shall."

23

The next day passed in a whirlwind of shocking, utterly surreal encounters, each one more outrageous than the last.

First was Ella's awakening to find herself sleepy, sore, and sprawled over Natt, his hardness already nudging between her legs—and feeling her audacious body slip down to pierce itself upon it, seemingly on its own accord. And then taking him in a dreamlike, wondering silence, Natt's hands on her hips the only sign that he wasn't asleep—at least, until he sprayed himself out inside her, while a stream of groaning black-tongue growled from his throat.

Ella was truly a dripping mess when Natt stood her to her feet, and this time he did produce a rag from somewhere, and partially wiped her up, without being asked. But not entirely, and when he finally lit a candle, and escorted her out of the room, it was to the discovery that his guard—all four of those unnerving orcs—were right there, lurking about outside the open door, witnessing absolutely everything that had gone on inside.

The humiliation seemed to swallow Ella alive, and was made only worse by Dammarr's thunderous frown, Varinn's delicately furrowed brow, and the curious, sweeping glances of Thrak and Thrain up and down her form. Lingering particularly below her too-short skirt, and when Ella shot a brief, furtive glance downward she found her bare thighs still marked with white, and red, and—she nearly groaned—the distinctive streaks of someone's clawed *fingers*. A sight that Dammarr was studying too, his hand clenched to a fist, his jaw jumping in his cheek.

"Are you well, woman?" cut in Varinn, in a genuinely worried tone, his nose giving a careful little sniff. "Do you need healing?"

Ella truly could not speak, or move, and thank the gods Natt was here, slinging a heavy arm over her shoulder—but cursed orc that he was, he then flashed her a cool smile, eyebrows raised. "Ach, we go to Efterar now," he said lightly. "My lass' sweet maiden womb has not yet learnt to take a full fucking."

The coarse, filthy words sent a staggering chill down Ella's spine, her eyes held huge and alarmed to his—but this was it, this was fully what he'd meant, by saying she needed to prove this. And surely she couldn't fail his test already, not yet, not with all his brothers watching.

"Indeed," she made herself say, as steadily as she could. "Especially with a prick so large as yours, Natt."

Her face immediately flushed scarlet—had she truly just *said* that?—but Natt's wicked replying grin made it almost worth it, as did the approving grasp of his hand to her arse. "Ach, you shall learn, lass," he said cheerfully. "Now, come see the rest of my rooms, before we go."

Ella nodded, with true gratefulness, and allowed Natt to guide her further out into this room. It appeared to be an antechamber of some sort, with a variety of benches and tables scattered about, many covered with the requisite furs.

"This is our meeting-room," Natt said, with a wave toward it. "And this"—he drew her to another door, showing a large room hung with an impressive quantity of deadly-looking weapons—"is where we train, and duel. And here is where my guard sleeps, and oft me also."

This last one was a small, cozy room, with thick furs scattered all about the floor, and Ella felt an odd twinge at the thought of Natt sleeping here, in this room, with *them*. With this—*Dammarr*.

"And here," Natt continued, waving at an inset of doors at the back of this room, curved around a little circle, "is where any orcs may come who need safety, or peace. They stay beyond the Speaker's guard, where they may not be reached."

It was a thoughtful layout, to be sure, and when Ella said as much, she earned another approving pat from Natt, another glare from Dammarr. And next, Natt thankfully drew her away from his brothers, into a small room hung with fabric, and smelling strongly of incense. There was a long, narrow table at one end, featuring a row of carved figures, and when Ella stepped forward to look, she realized that this was a shrine. A place to worship one's ancestors, perhaps, or one's gods.

"Who are they?" she asked, eyeing the row of figures, and Natt accordingly went over, and told her their names as he touched each one with a careful, quiet reverence. Lingering particularly on one that looked vaguely familiar—"This is Grisk, the first of my people," he said, while Ella's thoughts flicked to the wall, and the image of the first Speaker upon it. And next Natt hesitated on a figure that was carved, oddly enough, in the shape of a woman, but with a large, rounded belly, and a pair of disproportionately swollen breasts.

"I wish you to come, and pay honour to our goddess Akva," Natt said, with a wave over his shoulder toward Ella. "She is the mother of all five clans."

Ella nodded and stepped closer, eyeing the fantastical figure—it was beautifully carved, and really quite vivid—and she glanced uncertainly up at Natt. "What should please her? Should I kneel?"

There was more amusement on Natt's mouth, another flash of a challenge in those eyes. "A woman does not honour Akva with kneeling," he said. "You must freely share with her proof of your joy, with an orc. Only then shall she count you among her daughters."

He truly meant that too, and Ella was really doing this, she *was*—but even so, she felt herself swallow hard, her eyes darting furtively between Natt, and the figure. "Is it enough if I stand here before her," she said, "and show her this?"

She twitched a fluttery wave down at her messy, sticky thighs, sure proof of their pleasure together—but of course that would be far too easy, and Natt gave a slow, purposeful shake of his head, his eyes glimmering with amusement. "Not enough," he said. "Here, I shall help you learn this lesson."

With that, he came closer, and spun her bodily around, so her back was to the carving—and then, as Ella gasped, he bent her double, and yanked her too-short skirt up. Displaying *everything*, wanton and humiliating, to a damned *goddess*, and then—Ella moaned—sliding his clawed finger gentle, tantalizing, into her dripping-wet crease.

And then, as his fingers carefully opened her wide, and Ella could feel more of that betraying wetness slipping down her thigh, Natt spoke. Not in words that she understood, but instead in slow, rolling, reverent-sounding black-tongue. Asking the goddess' favour, clearly, on Ella's behalf, and it was all she could do to hold herself there, bared and exposed and leaking before a *goddess*, fighting to follow, to breathe, to *be*.

When Natt finally drew Ella up again, his eyes were both dark and oddly bright, as his wet fingers came up to her mouth, sliding their salty-sweet mess between her lips. "Good lass," he said, soft. "Akva sees you, and knows you. She is pleased with you. She is sure to bless you."

Well. An inexplicable relief unfurled under Ella's skin, and she gave Natt a shy, shaky little smile. "Thank you," she murmured. "I'm sure I shall need some blessing, in all this."

Natt's grin was warm, approving, all sharp white teeth. "Ach," he said. "Now come. The sooner we go to Efterar, the less he shall scold us."

But, Ella soon discovered, after another blessedly uneventful trek through the black corridors, that this big, bare-chested, scar-faced Efterar orc was indeed a scolder, and particularly when it came to Natt. "How long have you been walking around on this leg, Grisk?" he demanded at Natt, in flawless common-tongue, once he'd ordered him to sit on a lone wooden table, in what appeared to be an examination-room. "This bone has a stress fracture, your muscles are held together by *threads*, and"—he peered down at Natt's arm—"what the *hell* has happened to your rotator?"

Natt gave a meaningful roll of his eyes toward Ella over Efterar's shoulder, prompting this Efterar orc to stand up tall, and glare at Natt's face. "I felt that, you fool Grisk," he said flatly. "One of these days, you'll lose a damned limb, and you'll deserve it."

"Ach, Ash-Kai, and some day you shall show some worry that your Speaker is *hunted*," Natt shot back, though there was little true heat in it, and Ella couldn't help feeling that they'd done this many times before. "And that your swollen-headed captain has forbidden me from even lifting a blade. Let alone drawing the blood that is *mine*."

"Yes, and he also forbade you from going out at all," Efterar countered, now holding his big hand carefully against Natt's wounded thigh. "And look how that worked."

"Ach, well, he did not forbid it this time," Natt snapped back, his eyelids fluttering closed, as he drew in a hiss through his teeth. "This time, he—"

But he abruptly broke off there, his eyes darting a furtive glance toward Ella. And there was something in that, something Natt still didn't want her to know, and Ella fought to swallow down the surprising hurt, to hold her head high. She would prove this to him. She would.

"Will Natt be all right?" she asked, toward Efterar's scarred back. "He really was quite grievously wounded."

The look Efterar shot her over his shoulder was wry, and far more mild than the look he'd just given Natt. "Yes, he'll be fine," he said, as he moved his hand to Natt's shoulder, and gently rested it over the wound. "You, on the other hand..."

He dropped his hand from Natt's shoulder, fully turning toward Ella, and behind him Natt gave an experimental roll of the shoulder, his expression undeniably pleased. No doubt because—Ella's mouth fell open, shocked, again—there was no sign of where Natt's wound had been, not even a scar, or a scratch. More impossible magic, from these impossible orcs.

"Ach, I ought to have taken more care with her," Natt said now, leaping down from the table with ease, and coming to frown down toward Ella. "She is a hearty lass, but shall you look, brother? Please?"

Ella twitched, both at the odd referral to herself as *hearty*, and then, at the surprising politeness, because surely she'd never heard Natt say *please* before? But the Efterar orc was already nodding, stepping closer, and looking—down *there*. Almost as if he could *see* Ella's most secret places, through the leather of her skirt, and she fought the urge to cover herself, to hide away. Assuredly, if Efterar was some kind of physician, he'd have seen such things before, wouldn't he?

"She'll heal, Grisk," he said finally, "but I can help it along, if you like."

Natt immediately nodded, and patted the counter where he'd just been sitting. "Come, lass," he said. "And no touching, brother."

That last bit was said quite sharply, and Efterar sighed, and rolled his eyes. "You Grisk and your delicate noses," he replied. "Over your hand, then?"

Natt gave another curt nod, and thus began another surreal, thoroughly humiliating incident, in which after a moment's explanation, Natt thrust up Ella's skirt, spread her legs wide apart, and once again pressed his hand flat against the dripping, messy core of her. While this Efterar then rested his own hand over Natt's, ostensibly using his astonishing magic to heal her, even through Natt's warm, cupping fingers.

"That should do it," Efterar said, once he'd pulled away, and Natt pulled away too. And then—Ella's shock felt closer to an amused resignation, this time—Natt began licking his fingers clean, slowly and deliberately, as though Efterar weren't even there.

But Efterar didn't seem to notice, either, his eyes intent on Ella's groin again, even after she belatedly yanked down her too-short skirt. "Is that better, Grisk?" he asked her. "Do you feel any pain?"

Grisk. There was another moment's shock, more deafening this time, because this orc thought—he thought Ella was *Grisk*. He thought she and Natt were *mated*.

Natt's eyes looked mutinous, suddenly, glinting at her from behind Efterar's shoulder, and Ella felt herself give a slow, careful shake of her head. "No pain," she said, with an attempt at a smile. "Thank you so much, sir. We're very grateful to you."

That earned Efterar's approval, and Natt's as well, and as Natt led her back out of the room, his grin on hers was jaunty, his big body stretching up high to trail his fingers against the stone ceiling. "Ach, this is much improved," he said, with a sideways skidding leap on his previously injured leg. "What shall you say to a run?"

And thus began the day's next shocking incident, in which Natt barrelled through Orc Mountain, with Ella racing at his heels, while alternately laughing uncontrollably, and desperately gulping for air. She hadn't freely run like this in months, or likely years, and the bright, unfettered joy of her body flying through space, cool air flowing over her skin, was something she'd perhaps entirely forgotten.

"Sorry!" she called behind her, as she nearly careened into what seemed, inexplicably, like a smaller orc, even shorter than she was—

but then she skidded to a halt, panting heavily, because there had been something, in that orc's face, that was different than the rest. And in an instant Natt had halted too, sliding his lamp into Ella's hands, and giving her shoulder a brief squeeze as he passed by.

"Timo," he said, "what is it? What vexes you?"

His voice was suddenly quiet, wary, and he crouched down before the small orc, and tilted his face up with gentle hands. And here was Ella's next shock of the day, because this little orc was just—young. His grey face symmetrical and unmarked, his ears perfectly pointed, his body smooth and slim and gangly. And Ella was strongly, unnervingly reminded of how Natt had looked, around that age, all those years ago.

But the reason Ella had stopped, and the reason Natt had stopped, was because this young orc was—*weeping*. Trying to fight it, to be sure, his long-lashed eyes blinking hard, his sharp tooth biting his lip. But even as Ella watched, another streak of wetness escaped from his eye, and he dashed it away with an impatient clawed hand.

"It is naught," the young orc said, darting a swift, uneasy look toward Ella—but Natt's hands on his shoulders gave him a gentle shake, drawing the young orc's gaze back to his face.

"You shall have no fear of my lass," he said. "She has known grief and distress such as this also, and has long ago proven that she shall keep our truths safe. Now, brother"—his voice softened—"shall you grant me leave to Speak with you?"

The young orc again hesitated, but his eyes remained on Natt, and he gave a short, twitchy nod. To which Natt nodded too, and this time, watching it, Ella could almost feel the flare of his magic, the mesmeric, glittering hold of his eyes.

"Brave Grisk," he said, quiet, once the young orc's eyes were held, wide and unblinking, to his. "Now, I wish to hear what has vexed you."

"It is Skaap," the orc said, immediate, choked. "He has been sparring with me these past weeks, he has taught me many good Skai tricks, but now"—his face twisted, his lip trembling—"he says I must pay him, for what he has given me. And I must now give him this each time we spar together."

There was a low, sustained growl, rumbling from Natt's throat, but his body stayed very still, his eyes held to the smaller orc's. "Skaap is wrong, to demand this of you," he said. "You are not yet of age, and you have not yet been touched by one of your own choosing. And thus, brother, I must forbid you from sparring with Skaap again, until both these terms are met."

The young orc made a whine of protest, but Natt shook his head, his eyes glinting, unyielding. "I must also Speak with Skaap of this," he said. "But he shall know it is me who has sparked this, and drawn this truth from you. And once I have done this, I shall find another Skai to spar with you. One who shall not make such demands of you."

The young orc nodded, quick and fervent, and Natt smiled at him, and gave an approving pat to his cheek. "You are a good, brave Grisk, Timo," he said. "Once you are grown, should you wish, you shall be one of the most fearsome fighters among us. Even Skaap shall quake with fear of you."

That was also spoken under the truth-spell, Ella could feel it, and it was clear that the young orc knew it too, his mouth curving up, his eyes warm, relieved, almost hopeful on Natt's. "You really think so, Speaker?"

"Ach, I know this," Natt said firmly. "Now, mayhap you shall go find Trygve, and tell him I have given you two leave to spar in my rooms. Dammarr has a new spear that shall please you, and mayhap he shall let you try it, if you ask kindly."

The young orc's sudden grin was broad and delighted, and he gave another fervent little nod. "Yes, Speaker, I shall," he said. "I thank you."

With that, he scampered off down the corridor, and Ella felt herself smiling after him, and then up at Natt—but then her smile faded, all at once. Because rather than the patient warmth he'd borne a moment before, Natt's face was dark, and thunderous with rage.

"I must now address this," he said, voice flat. "It shall not be pleasant. Do you wish me to return you to my rooms, whilst I do this?"

Ella blinked, but her head was already instinctively shaking, saying no. No, Natt couldn't leave her now, not when he looked like that—and he gave a curt nod, and grasped for her hand and his lamp, and all but dragged her down the black corridor.

Ella had always had a decent head for directions, at least, and despite the twisty maze that this mountain was, she could tell that he was taking her somewhere new, somewhere she hadn't yet been. The corridors narrower than before, and perhaps even darker, without a single sign of light behind any of the doors they passed.

Natt finally veered off into one of those doors, one with the distinct sounds of noise beyond it. Noise that seemed to quiet slightly as Natt stalked inside, and then raised the lantern, and surveyed the room with glittering eyes.

And here was Ella's next shock of the day, because the room's dozen-odd occupants were almost universally in a state of undress, and almost all—touching one another. Not only touching, but writhing and stroking and—*fucking*, openly using mouths and hands and—other places. And Ella found herself staring slack-jawed at the alarming, outrageous sight of the massive, muscled orc nearest her— perhaps the biggest orc she'd yet seen in this mountain—who currently had another naked orc bent over before him, and was sliding his slick, impossibly large heft deep between the orc's spread arse- cheeks.

Good gods. Ella couldn't seem to move, or stop staring, not even when the huge orc's head turned to look at her, his long-lashed eyes dark, challenging, perhaps even contemptuous. And he was moving even slower, drawing his thick hardness out nearly all the way as she watched—and then holding Ella's gaze as he easily slid it back in. Slow, taunting, utterly insolent, while the orc bent under his hands gasped and choked and moaned—

Thankfully Natt tugged Ella away, striding across the room with sure steps, and his narrow eyes had fixed on one particular orc, who was currently thrusting his groin into a kneeling orc's mouth. "Skaap," Natt snapped. "I call you to Speak with me."

The orc's movements had briefly stilled, his eyes shifting—and he roughly shoved the kneeling orc away from him, and yanked up the trousers he'd thankfully been wearing. "And I call you to go fuck your- self, *Nattfarr*," he said, in a deep, heavily accented voice. "You have naught to Speak with me about."

"Ach, I do," Natt snapped back. "I shall gain your word today that you shall never again touch a brother, or demand or offer to do so, until he is fully of age. And until he *asks* you."

The room had quieted all around, the orcs slowing their cavorting to watch, to listen. "Ach, little Timo has run to tattle upon me, has he?"

the orc said, with a sneer. "I broke no law and no vow. I only made an offer that brings gain to both sides."

"Do not mock me with your lies, Skaap," Natt shot back. "I made our brother speak this truth to me. You gave what he thought was a gift, a gift he wished for very much, and then you stole it from him, and set these terms upon its return. This is wrong. This is beneath you. This betrays your own *kin*."

"I broke no law, and no vow," the orc repeated, his voice mocking. "And you are not even truly Speaker. And thus I have no more to say to you. I shall do with your pretty little brother as I wish."

With that, he actually yanked his trousers back down, and turned back to the orc who'd been sucking him, and thrust his half-hard cock into his mouth. Giving Natt a very blatant, and very public, *fuck-you*.

Ella's shock was tempered with a snapping, furious rage, one that she could see mirrored in Natt's glittering eyes before her. And when Natt again pressed the lantern toward her, she took it, and then even took an instinctive step backwards, toward the nearest wall.

Natt's sudden, surging swing at the orc's face was a blur of sharp black claws and coiled shifting muscle—and though the orc swiftly dodged out of the way, it wasn't quite quick enough, and Natt's claw had caught his cheek, the long stripe already pooling with red blood.

The room had gone abruptly, wholly still, as the orc's head slowly turned, his eyes fixing on Natt with a bare, bitter hatred—and then, with astonishing speed, he leapt around, and tackled Natt bodily to the floor. Their combined weight slamming against stone with a sickening thud, their fists punching and swinging and driving into muscle and bone.

Ella clapped her hand to her mouth, and she backed up further against the wall, her eyes darting at the orcs all around, who were surely this orc's friends. But none of them had made any move to participate, though they were all watching with undeniable interest, and many of them had moved away, as if to give Natt and the orc more room, as if this startling scene actually had their *blessing*.

And while Ella knew nothing about brawling, and her heart was currently seeking to escape out her throat, even she could see that Natt was good at this, quick and forceful and determined. And while the other orc was good at it too, just as fast and aggressive, he was fighting to defeat Natt, while Natt was only fighting to grasp at the orc's neck, at his thick spiked hair—

It was when the orc had slammed Natt down onto his back, his fist upraised to punch straight down, that Natt's hands gripped for the orc's head, and wrenched it toward him. And again, Ella could feel the familiar snapping flare of his magic—and suddenly everything was still. The two orcs' bodies held in place, their eyes locked, the only movement their harsh, shuddering breaths.

"Now, Skaap," Natt said, with astonishing coolness, "we shall Speak, before our brothers' eyes. And since I am a patient Speaker, I shall give you leave to choose. Do you wish to vow to me that you shall never again touch one who is not of age? Or do you wish to tell us of the youngest orc you have taken? The youngest Skai, mayhap? Mayhap even a brother, or a son, to one who hears us now?"

The tension seemed to crackle through the room, and a darting glance around showed the watching orcs now looking shifty, suspicious, perhaps even angry. Their eyes held thankfully not on Natt, but on their still-silent brother, and Ella couldn't deny a distant, shaky relief at the sight. So even if these orcs *were* all blatantly debauched exhibitionists, at least there were *some* rules around all this, some things that were still sacred, after all.

"As if *you* have a right to judge this, Speaker," the orc panted at Natt, though his face was slick with sweat, his eyes held wide to Natt's below him. "We all know how you gained the Bautul to your side, when you were yet young and fair. How many of them had you? Twenty? Thirty?"

The fear and the disgust surged in Ella's gut, because she now knew that Natt was caught in this, he had to speak truth too—but his eyes on the orc above him didn't even flinch. "Ach," he said coolly, "and those who have not yet tasted my vengeance for their sins shall soon do so, when our captain makes me Speaker of this mountain. Now, you shall speak this vow, Skaap. Or else tell us this orc's name."

His voice had deepened as he spoke, unfurling steady and powerful through the room, and Skaap's big body was visibly trembling, his eyes bulging wide as he stared at Natt below him. As if he was fighting to escape, but there was no escaping, and Ella could see his mouth opening, his breath dragging deep—

"I shall not touch one who is not of age again," he said, in a rush. "This I vow, before all my brothers."

There was a brief, hanging stillness, the orc's eyes finally squeezing shut, his head jerking back and forth—and Natt easily shoved him off to the side, and leapt back to his feet, his claws out, his body giving a rippling shake. Looking suddenly huge, powerful, dangerous, deadly.

"I seek a strong Skai who will train with Timo, and teach him your ways with naught in return," he said, to the room at large. "Who shall grant me this kindness, in the face of your brother's sins?"

There was an instant's silence, dark eyes darting all around. And then, across the room, the first orc Ella had seen—the huge one who'd so insolently watched her as he'd taken his brother's arse, and who, she realized with a shock, was slowly and silently *still doing so*—raised his head from what he was doing, and nodded.

"I shall," he said, in a heavily accented voice. "Start in morning."

Natt gave a curt nod toward the orc, and finally reached toward Ella, grasping her hand in his. "I thank you, Simon," he said, as he led her back toward the door. "I shall remember this, and seek the Skai's lost truths on your behalf, when I am Speaker."

The orc solemnly nodded back, his eyes briefly holding to Natt's, more truth flaring between them—and then Natt turned and stalked out of the room, dragging Ella after him into the blessed emptiness of the corridor. While Ella blinked blankly at his stiff back, his square shoulders, had that awful Skaap orc said *thirty*, he had, he *had*—

And without at all meaning to, Ella darted up behind Natt, and slid her arms around his waist. Drawing him to a halt, in the midst of the corridor, so that she could hug him as tightly as she could, pressing her still-blinking eyes into the hot strength of his back.

"I'm so, so sorry, Natt," she whispered, choked, into his skin. "Are you all right? I didn't know that you were—that must have been—"

She couldn't even say it over the bile rising in her throat, but Natt twitched, jerked a rigid, not-quite-dismissive shrug. "Ach, this was many summers past," he said thickly. "I now wish to look ahead, to how I shall henceforth keep my own kin safe, when I am Speaker."

Ella swallowed and nodded into his back, squeezed him tighter. "You're such a wise, generous orc, Nattfarr of Clan Grisk," she croaked. "Your kin should be so grateful, to have you as their Speaker."

Natt made a sound that might have been a scoff, but she could feel the tension seeping away from him, his big body sagging into the touch of her arms. "Most of them shall be glad when I am killed," he said, with a sigh. "Just as the captain shall be. I am indeed but a thorn, to them all."

But Ella's thoughts had flicked to that young orc in the corridor, to the true gratefulness in his eyes. "Yes, but they still *need* you," she said firmly. "Whether they know it or not. You cannot die, Nattfarr of Clan Grisk. I utterly forbid it."

And thank the gods, that was the sound of a chuckle, rumbling from his throat. "Ach, well, if *you* forbid this, lass," he said, finally turning his body around, settling his arms warm against her back, "I shall have no choice but to heed it."

And blinking up at him, at the sudden dangerous warmth in those eyes, it occurred to Ella, far too strong, that this, too, was why Natt needed a mate so much. Why that room had shown those twelve generations of families, with those barely clothed women standing so staunchly and brazenly by their orcs.

The Speaker bore deep grief. The Speaker made enemies. The Speaker stood for truth and justice, against his own kin. And the Speaker needed someone always on his side. Someone, like he'd said, who he could trust. Someone who would support him in his goals. Someone who wouldn't even *think* to wear his enemy's ring, after he had so carefully dressed her as his own.

He needed someone like Ella, of Clan Grisk.

Ella couldn't seem to stop considering that as the rest of the day passed, as Natt kept guiding her around the mountain, introducing her to his countless brothers, and showing her his home's many disparate, curious, stone-walled rooms. More shrines, more sparring-rooms, and also trading-rooms and meeting-rooms and brightly lit forges. And, most plentiful of all, more rooms with beds and tables and orcs cavorting, more shocking sights that had, in their ubiquity, almost ceased to be shocking, to Ella's blinking eyes.

Natt, of course, seemed to be shocked by nothing at all—but again, watching him with his brothers, Ella could feel that it still wasn't easy, on either side. That even as most of these orcs did seem to respect him, and acknowledge his role as Speaker, they also regarded him with a consistent, unmistakable fear. The Grisk were clearly the most comfortable with him, generally speaking and meeting his eyes with ease—but across the other four clans, no matter how lightly or kindly Natt spoke, no matter how often he laughed, most orcs still looked at him with shifty, askance glances, avoiding his touch and his eyes. So much that Ella could almost taste Natt's tension, and his increasing tiredness, or perhaps even loneliness, as the day passed.

And, though it almost hurt to see, Ella couldn't miss how that tension also extended toward her. How Natt would smile as he introduced her, and run his warm, familiar hand against her back or her bare waist—but how he carefully avoided the word *mate*, and also that loaded word *friend*. And instead he only called Ella his *lass*, again and again, while his brothers looked at her ensemble and the still-present mess below it, and drew whatever conclusions they wished.

And when some of them again referred to Ella as Grisk, or praised her as scent-bound—and one old, white-haired orc named Sken even congratulated her on snaring the Speaker as her mate—Natt didn't correct them. And neither did Ella, though she could feel the ever-increasing tightness in Natt's smile, the clench of his hand on her back.

There was thankfully no mention of Alfred throughout, no acknowledgement of his existence from Natt or any of the other orcs. And though the urge to ask rose in Ella's thoughts more than once—have you had news of Alfred, or the men—she fiercely quashed it down, and instead focused on smiling, and remembering the strange orcs' names, and showing herself a worthy mate to Natt. A worthy partner, to the Speaker of the Grisk.

They ate a hearty, much-needed meal in the mountain's kitchen—but it was only after waiting in line for what felt like an age, with perhaps a hundred other orcs, that Ella discovered that the proffered roots and deer-meat were entirely uncooked, and thus impossible for her to eat. And after Natt threw a casual, but slightly irritated, order at the two orcs working in the kitchen, they hurriedly cooked a plate of food for Ella, handing it over with bowed heads, and furtive, fearful glances toward Natt.

Natt's polite but curt reply led to open whispers, and even more uneasy glances as they ate. And it wasn't until they'd returned to Natt's rooms that Ella could finally feel him relaxing, his form sinking heavily down onto one of the fur-covered benches. And then, much to her inexplicable relief, he drew her down after him, and curled her close into the warm, comforting safety of his lap.

"Your mountain," Ella said, muffled, into his chest, "is hugely fascinating, and completely shocking, and also thoroughly *exhausting*, Nattfarr."

"Ach, is it not?" Natt said, with a faint sigh into her hair. "This is why I must yet escape it some days, even at this risk of my death. I ken I shall go mad, if I am trapped in here for too long a spell."

Oh. So that was part of all this, too. And suddenly there was a rising, jolting urge to drag Natt up and away with her, out of this dark, twisty mountain altogether, and back to their forest. Where they would run, and laugh, and no one would see or follow or care, and Ella would shove him down, and—

"Is there anything I can do, to help?" she said, biting off that thought, but it was still there, whispering behind her eyes. And behind Natt's eyes, too, as he blinked tired and half-lidded toward her in the lantern's faint light. As his tongue came out brief, tantalizing, to wet his lips.

But he didn't speak, and maybe that was because—Ella took a breath—she was the one who needed to prove this to him. To prove that she was here, by his side, no matter what. And what had he said, in the cave that day, what felt like an age ago? *Pleasure is always good, for edging away pain.*

So without thinking, without taking her eyes off his, Ella slithered herself downwards, until she was kneeling on the fur-covered floor at his feet. And when her audacious hands reached to shove up at his kilt, the bemusement in his eyes flicked toward astonishment, and then, oddly, toward the door.

"My guard shall return soon," he said, soft, but a challenge. "Are you sure of this, lass?"

But Ella didn't care about anything, in this moment, beyond that look in Natt's eyes, the slight tremble in his fingers as they went for the waist of his kilt, and loosened it. Not all the way, but more than enough to release—*that.*

And suddenly it did feel like an age had passed since Ella had seen this, so strong and hungry and swollen. Jutting up and out toward her, impossibly large, with that smooth tapered head, that deep tantalizing slit, already glimmering with a bead of thick, growing white.

Ella's mouth betrayed a low, heated gasp, her eyes fluttering as she watched, drank in the sight, waited for more—but Natt hadn't moved in the slightest, because he was waiting for her. And she'd done this before, surely she could do it again, she could—

Even so, it took nearly the whole of Ella's willpower to raise her hand, and brush her trembly finger into that slit, to feel that delectable white liquid pooling onto her finger. But then she was doing it, and it was touching her back, twitching and vibrating and clenching against her. *Kissing* her.

Ella's groan was guttural, humiliating, and so was the way her finger slipped deeper, feeling the reward of his kiss on her skin, the bubbling splutter of that white nectar against her touch. He wanted to kiss her, he wanted her to kiss him, her mouth was watering as she stared, she was leaning up closer, she could—

And then, oh gods above, she was. Her lips brushing brief, soft, tentative, against that slick smooth head—and in reply Natt's entire body flailed up in his chair, that delectable thick wetness spurting hard against her tongue. And oh, that was good, tasted good, felt so good—enough that Ella could thrust all thought away, and do it again, lingering longer this time. Taking him deeper, carefully nudging her tongue further into him, as her traitorous throat greedily swallowed his bubbling sweetness, and her hungry tongue searched for more.

Natt's groans were already harsh, steady, thoroughly thrilling, and one of his hands carded into her hair, his claws sinking deep. His eyes hazy, warm, breathtaking on hers, fluttering hard whenever she sucked, and even more when she delved her tongue deeper against that filthy kissing slit, with its beautiful sputtering sweetness—

And it was then, curse Natt, curse the entire world—that Thrak, Thrain, Dammarr, and Varinn walked into the room. Their voices chattering, legs striding, swords clanking—and then it all skidded to a halt at once. The room frozen, the world frozen, and catching Ella on her knees, with Natt deep in her mouth, and her tongue sunk almost *inside* him.

The mortification was like an eruption of flame, burning Ella alive in its wake, but there was nowhere to go, nowhere to hide—and Natt,

Natt's eyes were glittering, pleased, *eager*, as his hand came to pat her scarlet cheek, and his eyes gave a brief, easy glance up toward the four watching, staring orcs.

"Ach, I am busy with my lass," he said, with astonishing coolness. "But you may yet stay, if you wish."

They could stay. Because Natt wanted them to stay, he wanted them to see this, Ella bent over him, with her mouth stretched around his thick, veined grey cock. And curse these damned orcs, because they wanted to see it too, Thrak and Thrain looking with frank curiosity, Varinn with a kind of wide-eyed awe, and Dammarr with a staring, open-mouthed disbelief.

It was that look on Dammarr's face, oddly enough, that somehow kept Ella there, trapped with Natt's huge heft in her mouth, trapped in her complete and utter humiliation. Because Dammarr's frowning disbelief wasn't even focused on her, but instead on Natt's admittedly dazed, hooded eyes. Dammarr was surprised, and he was—*jealous*.

And Natt was saying something with this, with the brief challenge of his eyes on Dammarr's, before dropping his heated gaze back to Ella's face. Saying, perhaps, *Will you show him you're worth it, will you show me*—and Ella was lost in this, lain waste in it, because she actually gave a shaky little nod, and then sucked him deep.

Natt's replying groan was raw heat, shuddering hard down Ella's back, but it was enough, just enough, to make her keep going. To thrust away the awareness of all those watching eyes, and just to do, to taste, to be. To let her tongue seek as it willed, delving furtive and ashamed into that deep slit, almost as if to hide—but it only kissed her back with startling force, pulsing out more of that sweet seed, drinking her up, as she drank him.

But now *that*, dear gods, was the sound of one of the orcs, finally moving—and it was Thrak, coming to sprawl his tall form beside Natt on the bench, so he could *watch*.

The mortification burned again, screeching wide across Ella's thoughts—but Natt only gave Thrak a smug, satisfied glance as he settled his hand deeper into Ella's hair. As if to say, *Yes, come, look at what she does to me*—and it was perverse, it was pure depravity, but Ella's traitorous mouth only seemed to suck harder, her tongue plunging further into his secret depths, into the reward of his kiss, the splutter of surging sweetness.

"She knows how to kiss an orc, at least," cut in Thrak—and he was *commenting* on Ella, and that was *amusement* in his watching eyes, oh *gods*. "She is not afraid to seek for her seed."

And Natt *liked* this, Natt was revelling in this, in shamelessly kissing her, feeding her, his hooded eyes alight with wickedness. "Ach, this is truth," he said, with an unmistakable, heated pride. "I did not even need to teach her this. She is a clever, filthy little lass, who has always closely watched me, and then quickly learnt to meet me, and please me."

The praise was warmth all its own, thrusting back at the still-lingering shame—at least, until Thrak spoke again, now nudging his elbow into Natt's side. "Has she learnt yet, then," he said, with a diabolical smile, "of the other secret places her little pink tongue might seek?"

Oh gods in heaven, he could *not* possibly mean what Ella thought he meant—but Natt actually laughed between his groans, husky and low. "Not yet," he breathed, "but soon she shall, I ken."

This was not happening, it wasn't, because something in Ella's throat had groaned, all on its own, with a base, mortifying hunger, while her tongue thrust slick, powerful, starving, into his depths—and it was then, oh, that he opened wide, sucked her deep. "Ach, lass," he choked, "my seed, I—"

But he was already shouting, and spraying out against her like a geyser. His hot liquid surging into her with so much force that the whole room seemed to shake with it, exploding alive with the sheer power of her mate's pleasure, drawn pure and holy from his wounded ravenous soul—

It was beyond ecstasy, beyond warmth and light, and Ella somehow even managed to swallow most of the flooding sweetness, gulping it desperately and fervently down her throat. And the responding touch of Natt's hands was so warm, so tender, so approving, all the reward that a mate might wish. Tilting her face up so he could look at her, smile at her, open his mouth to whisper, *Good lass, this pleased me, I love you—*

But instead, from across the room, Ella heard a hard little laugh, cutting through the surreal, melting pleasure like a claw on stone. Dammarr. His eyes snapping with rage, his teeth bared, his hand clenched to his sword-hilt.

"At least we'll finally get *some* reward out of this whole *farce*, then," he hissed, cold, vicious. "Watching her kiss your arse will surely be a treat for us all, *Speaker*."

There was an instant's awful stillness, shuddering down to Ella's bones—and then a deep growl from Natt's throat, and a furious jerk of his hand toward the door. And thank the gods Dammarr spun around and left, his sword loudly clanking, while Thrak leapt to his feet, and strode out close behind him.

But the shame had finally gotten the best of Ella, leaving her shaken and cold and hurt, trembling on her knees. Drawing her away from Natt entirely, her body empty, exposed, prickling, untouched. What in the gods' names was she doing, what had come over her, she was supposed to become a *lady*—

And before Ella could stop it, or see it, or even know it, she leapt to her staggering feet, clutched for the lantern, and ran.

24

Ella ran fast and deep into the mountain, pelting her way down the twisty black corridors, while her lantern's light bounced and flashed against the endless stone walls.

The orcs she encountered in the corridor only looked at her, some nodding in greeting, some even stepping to the side to let her pass. And when she very nearly charged straight into two shirtless orcs against a wall, a pair of capable hands immediately shot out to catch her, steadying her on her trembly feet.

"Woman?" asked a vaguely familiar voice, and when Ella glanced up, gasping for breath, she realized it was the kind Grisk orc, Baldr. And the orc with him was the other one, Drafli, tall and deadly-looking, with the frank, unnerving eyes.

"Are you well?" Baldr asked, with genuine concern in his voice. "Is there aught we can help you with?"

Ella blinked at him, unsettled, because surely this strange orc wouldn't actually help her with anything? But the earnestness in his eyes said that perhaps he would, and that perhaps he'd even drag this terrifying Drafli into it, too—but then Baldr's gaze flicked up behind her, settling on something Ella couldn't see. "Ah, here comes Nattfarr," he said, quiet. "Do you wish to see him now?"

Again, his words and his eyes spoke of true concern, hinting that he might whisk Ella away somewhere else, should she not wish to see Natt at this moment. And in the mess currently swirling Ella's thoughts, there was also a deep, powerful gratefulness, and she managed a wan smile at his scarred, worried face.

"Oh, that's quite all right, Baldr," she said, still rather breathless, giving an instinctive little curtsey. "But I'm very grateful for your kindness."

He nodded back, his eyes again flicking up behind her—and here, indeed, was Natt. Striding toward them with sure, prowling steps, his eyes glinting in the flickering lamplight.

"Hands off, brother," he said, with a lightness that wasn't light at all. "Lest you want both your Speaker and your Skai at your throat."

"He's not my—" Baldr began, glancing up behind him, to where the Drafli orc was indeed looking even more murderous than usual—and he hurriedly let go of Ella's shoulders over her cape. After which Natt, oddly enough, briefly brought his own hands to the exact same place on Ella's cape, and *rubbed* it, almost as if to scrub off the remnants of Baldr's touch.

"Now come, lass," Natt said, drawing Ella away, and then slipping a warm arm around her waist. "Should you like to run further? Or mayhap only walk? Or"—his unreadable eyes angled down toward her—"mayhap I could take you to a sparring-room, where you may punch at me for a spell? I ken this shall please you."

And curse her, because Ella gave a choked laugh, even as she felt herself turn away from him, her head shaking. She was supposed to be a lady, ladies couldn't punch orcs in sparring-rooms, they didn't run alone through mountains, they weren't absurdly grateful to abominable orcs for doing basic things like asking her if she was all right, or—or explicitly giving permission to run, or fight, or just *be*, as she wished.

But Natt was still here, he was still touching her, his big warm hands still spreading wide over her bare skin. Still wanting her, even after the shameful things she'd just done, after one of his oldest friends had openly mocked her, after she'd run away—

"Why did Dammarr say that," Ella said, her voice cracking. "Why did he want to humiliate me. Why did he call this a *farce*."

Natt's eyes fluttered closed, an unmistakable grimace tightening on his mouth. "I am sorry he spoke thus toward you," he replied, quiet. "He only—envies you, lass."

"Why," Ella said, frowning at Natt's closed eyes, and when they opened again they were tired, resigned. Perhaps even guilty.

"Dammarr and I have oft taken pleasure together," he said, with a sigh. "Before this."

The misery surged all at once, boiling deep in Ella's belly, and she twisted away from Natt, and pressed her hands against her hot, sweaty face. She'd known, of course she'd known, so why the hell did it still feel like this, she was an heiress, she was to become a *lady*—

"It was only pleasure," Natt's voice cut in, quickly now. "Naught more, on my part, and Dammarr knew this. I ought to have stopped this, when I knew it was more for him—but I am Speaker, lass, I cannot play with this as other orcs do, I can only do such things with those I trust. And Thrak and Thrain are too close to my blood, and Varinn cares only for women, so—"

Ella's head was shaking, her whole body almost shaking, and she thrust her trembly hand flat against Natt's chest. "But you did it," she said, her voice wavering. "You willingly took pleasure with Dammarr, and however many others"—she forcibly shoved back the memory of Skaap speaking, earlier today—"that you chose, while I was left alone, and untouched, and *waiting for you*. For *nine years*."

The words came out sounding plaintive, and perhaps entirely unfair. Because Ella knew what Natt had gone through, being hunted, trying to keep her safe, thirty, *thirty*—and his replying laugh confirmed it, coming out cold and disbelieving.

"Ach, and you truly think I would have chosen all this, over you?" he said bitterly. "And you yet pretend as if you were truly waiting for me, keeping your pledge, all this time? When you yourself have said that your maidenhood had value, and you meant to use it to buy this man? *This man*, lass?"

His voice broke at the last, his head shaking. Betraying the truth, suddenly almost staggering, that *this* was why Natt had never recognized that Ella had kept her pledge. Because he honestly didn't believe she had. He still thought she'd been saving herself for *Alfred*. Waiting to use her maidenhood as a transaction, as an ultimate reward, handed carelessly over to Natt's greatest enemy, along with enough wealth to start a war.

And of course Natt believed that, because Ella had told him that, hadn't she? And had she ever corrected it? Had she ever spoken the truth of it?

Natt's angry eyes had moved away from her, glittering toward the wall behind her head, while his arms crossed tight over his chest. Shutting Ella out, leaving her standing there searching for words, for truth, without the escape of his magic, or even the touch of his hands.

And looking at him, feeling the rage and the misery crackling all over him, suddenly there was only—resignation. Defeat. She'd run so long, for so many years, and perhaps finally she just needed to be, to face it, to speak. Truth.

So Ella swallowed hard, and blinked hard, and again faced her own mortification, her own shame. She'd come to Orc Mountain, she was wearing an orc's clothes, she'd sucked off an orc in front of his friends. Surely she could do this. Speak.

"I would have done it, with Alfred, if it had come to that," she said, almost a whisper. "But I truly was waiting for you all that time, Natt. I never forgot you. I never stopped missing you, or hoping you'd come back."

"Why," came Natt's reply, immediate, relentless, so Ella took a bracing breath, and kept ploughing on. Speak.

"Because we were—*friends*, Natt," she said, with a sigh. "And I know you hate that word, but that's what it was, for me. You were a friend, a real one. You knew me, and you wanted to know me. *This* me."

She gave a shaky, frantic wave at her clothes, her unkempt hair, herself. And though she could feel Natt's eyes now, she couldn't make herself look at him, and instead kept her gaze on the floor, her breath coming out far too loud. Speak.

"I'm not really a good lady, Natt," she whispered. "I'm not a good heiress. I'm not—*real*, like that. I dress up and smile and pretend, and I do it all quite well, so no one ever notices. But with you—"

Ella's breaths were catching, tripping on her too-thick throat, and she had to scrub again at her face, make herself keep going. "It was just so—*easy*, with you. And it never was again, after that, especially after

Papa died. And once you were both gone, there was no one left who'd ever seen this part of me at all. And even Papa didn't want me to be this, he wanted me to be a *lady*—so I thought, well, maybe if I really was a lady, maybe at least *that* part of me would finally be real, after all. Maybe I would finally forget the rest—forget *you*—and find a way to be happy again."

The words echoed against the silence, against the solid truth of Natt's form before her, and suddenly they sounded so petty and foolish and shameful. The whining of a rich, privileged woman who hadn't gotten her way in life, and who couldn't accept the choices she'd herself freely made.

But Natt, the Speaker of the Grisk, the twelfth in his line to speak for his brothers, had lifted Ella's wet face toward him, and wiped at her cheeks with his clawed thumbs. And his eyes were here, his own truth was here, easy, mercifully easy, between them.

"You finally speak truth to me, lass," he whispered. "This honours me."

But Ella wasn't honourable, she was selfish and foolish and utterly shameful—but Natt's eyes didn't falter. "You are not a real lady, lass," he said, so quiet. "But you are yet quick and curious and clever and kind. It pleases you to run and laugh and play and fuck. You are hungry and filthy and wicked. You are *you*, lass, and you bring me joy like none else. And most of all when you speak such sweet truths, and proudly flaunt them before me."

Oh. Ella couldn't move, suddenly, could only blink at the bright, furious purpose in Natt's beautiful eyes. And when he abruptly sank to his knees on the cold stone before her, there was no humiliation, no shame—only wonder, and longing, and then sheer, pulsating pleasure as he yanked her skirt up, and thrust his tongue deep between her thighs.

Gods, it was glorious, that slick slippery tongue licking and slurping with eager abandon, his mouth opening to drink more, to taste more, to suckle and kiss and swallow. While those dark powerful eyes held steady to hers, brazen, outrageous, unrepentant. Truth.

Ella's fluttery hands dropped to grip in his hair, and perhaps they even drew him closer, deeper. Earning a rumbling laugh from his mouth, vibrating straight into the very core of her, while her own mouth desperately cried out, the sound carrying down the black corridor.

But Natt liked that too, both rewarding her and taunting her with another shockingly deep thrust of that possessive tongue—and it was so good, so gods-damned intoxicating, that Ella finally just opened her mouth, and let the truth spill out with every gasping breath.

"Oh gods," she choked. "Oh gods, Natt, you're so good, you feel so good, I *dreamed* of this for *years*, deeper, harder, suck me, kiss me, kiss *me*—"

Natt did, he kissed *her*, his eyes on fire, his lips desperately sucking, his throat compulsively swallowing, his tongue thrust so deep it might have reached her very heart. Truth, truth, that was this, it was real—

Ella's scream seemed to shake the corridor, but she didn't care, she couldn't, not with her whole body screaming too, shouting its pulsing, flaring release all over Natt's tongue. Exploding again and again in a shower of light, of sparks, of colour and wonder and—peace.

And the peace remained, even as the pleasure faded, flickering away into the shadows. Even as Natt finally pulled back to look up at her, his eyes glimmering with warmth and danger, his tongue licking at his lips with a slow, forceful satisfaction.

"Ach, this was a good lesson, was it not?" he breathed, perhaps a caress, or a challenge. "What do you say, my lass?"

Ella drew in a shaky, rattling breath—and then, for some inexplicable, beautiful reason, she *laughed*, the sound carrying light and joyful down the dark corridor. "I say," she murmured, her hands sliding into the mess she'd somehow made of his hair, "that you are a heartless outrageous *scoundrel*, Nattfarr of Clan Grisk."

He laughed too, deep and warm and utterly glorious, and in a surge of movement he leapt to his feet, and caught Ella bodily up in his arms. "And *you*," he murmured into her hair as he hitched her closer to his chest, "are all my lifelong hungers thrust into one lovely, filthy, screaming little beast, that the gods have dropped upon my head. Or, in truth"—he nuzzled at her hair—"upon my prick. And now that you have spoken these truths, I fear that you shall not so easily escape their will, my fair, foolish one."

His voice lowered at the end, and surely there was a warning in it, perhaps more truths yet to be spoken. More truths, perhaps, of

Alfred—but in this lovely, peaceful moment, Ella was quiet, content, at ease. At peace with her truths, and what she was, in this instant, curled safe and close in Natt's arms.

"Well, maybe I don't want to escape," she murmured at him, with a twitch of a smile up at his face. "Maybe I'd rather stay trapped here on your prick, and your tongue, until the end of my days."

Natt's replying grin was so stunning it ached, and he was already licking his lips, drawing her even closer against him.

"Why do we not begin with this night, my filthy little lass," he whispered. "And then, mayhap, we shall see."

25

Ella scarcely slept that night.

Instead, she spent the night sprawled and naked and writhing on Natt's bed, lost in wave after wave of fierce, furious pleasure. Finally, *finally* letting herself sink into the truth of her hunger, drowning into it, shamelessly embracing all that she wished.

And if she wished to tackle Natt's huge body flat to the bed, and climb atop him, and ride his smooth bucking hips as if he were a horse, why should she not? And then, if she then wished to scooch herself upwards, and seat herself full upon his mouth, and teach him what it was like to drink such a flood, why should she not do that too, and laugh out loud as he flailed and sucked and choked?

And if Natt then threw her to her knees, and knelt deadly and aggressive behind her, with his slick hardness delving into her most secret depths, why should Ella not arch her back for him, and curse him and beg him all at once? While he sweetly, powerfully pierced the last of her maidenhead, and then fucked it with raging abandon while she screamed?

Afterwards he tried to murmur apologies, whispering nonsense about blood and pain, but it only hurt a little, and Ella kissed his words away, and nibbled at his delicious-smelling neck, and asked what depraved, outrageous thing he would do to her next. A challenge which Natt met with full force, his body wild and fluid and furious as he took her again, and again, and again.

They slept for a while, with Natt still hidden deep inside her, and then they awoke, and did it all again. And Ella was truly disappointed when there was finally a furtive knock at the doorframe, and then the sight of Varinn setting a candle on the shelf, and politely murmuring that it was morning, and that the captain wished to see Nattfarr at his earliest convenience.

"Really?" Ella heard her languid voice ask, lower and smoother than she'd ever heard it. "He needs to see him *now*? Are you *sure*?"

She'd snaked her hand toward Natt's still-half-hard heft as she spoke, feeling it give a sustained, satisfying twitch against her fingers. "Just once more," she purred into his neck, audacious and impossibly brazen, but she didn't care, because Natt gave a low, gasping laugh, a rewarding thrust of that slick hardness into her hand.

"Only if you suck me," he breathed, and perhaps it was utterly shameful, but Ella immediately obeyed. Sliding her sticky, naked, sore body down his, and taking him deep into her mouth while he moaned—and then, the bastard, while he also actually beckoned Varinn further inside the room, and began talking to him in the tangled, rumbling black-tongue.

Varinn replied in kind, only sparing the briefest of glances toward Ella's ongoing ministrations, and despite the still-present shameful-ness of this—of doing this, to an orc, while another orc watched—Ella soon discovered that there was a whispering, fundamental power in it, too. Giving Natt a moment to speak, waiting for his voice to come smoothly—and then sucking him hard and deep, and smiling to herself as he choked mid-sentence, and fought to find his place again.

Finally Natt sent Varinn away with a shaky wave of his hand, and then turned his full attention to Ella, sending heat skittering down her spine. "Greedy little lass," he murmured, his eyes hazy with warmth, approval, undeniable affection. "Look at you, suckling my prick down your hungry little throat. Suck harder, my sweet, and I shall give you a good breakfast."

The filthy words had the desired effect, setting Ella immediately and desperately dragging the seed from him, while he laughed and bucked and moaned. And when he came in the usual flood, and Ella couldn't possibly keep it all in, she didn't even care when he laughed again at her humiliation, and smeared the mess wide across her cheek.

"Ach, my filthy, lovely lass," he breathed, with a sigh. "You shall be my ruin, I ken."

There was only warmth, only grinning back at him and wiping at her cheek, and then licking her finger while he watched with fluttering eyes. Earning another slow, sultry stroke of his hand over her bare breast—but Varinn coughed from outside the door, and Natt dropped back onto the bed, digging his palms into his eyes.

"You shall now stop taunting me and dress, lass," he said, in his best Speaker voice. "And you shall save up all your hunger, and give it to me after this meeting. If you can wait this long, my filthy beast."

Ella slowly smiled at him, her hand reaching toward the nearest part of him—his knee—and giving it a slight squeeze. "I shall make my best attempt, Nattfarr," she said lightly. "Though surely I shall pine away while I wait for you. You have"—she drew in breath, felt her eyes blinking—"brought me unspeakable joy this night, my wise and generous Speaker."

There was a moment where Natt only looked at her, for perhaps an instant too long—but then he leapt bodily to his feet, and began rummaging through the mess of clothes on the floor. Not quite looking at her as he found his kilt, and yanked it on, hiding himself away from her.

"I wish you to dress, lass," he said, lightly, but it was an order this time, and they both knew it. "The way I like this."

He'd torn off her various clothes and adornments the night before, leaving only the earrings to bite and snap at, and Ella obediently ducked her head, and went to dress. Fighting to ignore the odd twist in her belly as Natt began pacing across the room, offering her no help this time, and surely he was just tired, or perhaps preoccupied with this meeting?

"Good," he said, once she was done, but that felt preoccupied too, and he'd already gone for the door, barking something in black-tongue toward Varinn. And when Ella strode out after him, with the candle in hand, it was to the realization that all four of his guard were there—that they'd all probably witnessed all that, *again*—and that Dammarr still looked mutinous, glaring between Natt and Ella with bare, unconcealed contempt.

Natt was walking through the midst of them, and knocked Dammarr on the side of his head with his hand as he passed—an action which Dammarr immediately returned with a swat to Natt's passing arse. Bringing a chuckle to Natt's mouth, and he reached back behind him, and actually rustled his big hand in Dammarr's *hair*, before reaching to grasp one of the apples on the table between them.

The jealousy was so sudden, and so bizarrely powerful, that Ella's entire body felt frozen in place—even when Natt turned and beckoned her toward him, his forehead creasing. "Come and eat, lass," he said, tilting his head. "You cannot only have my seed for your breakfast, as much as we both might wish for this. You must keep rebuilding your strength."

It was an offering, Ella realized, from this orc who always just knew when she needed such things, and she twitched him a grateful smile, and lurched over toward him. Realizing, in the process, that she was very sticky, and very sore, and not only in the places where Natt had made himself so at home.

"Ach, I have used you roughly this night, lass," Natt said, with a familiar pat to her face, and a not-quite-regretful smile. "You shall go see Efterar again today. I have asked the captain's mate to take you there, and spend this morning with you, whilst I work with my brothers."

Oh. Natt was leaving, for the whole morning? But of course Ella couldn't argue that, especially if he'd arranged for her entertainment while they were parted. And especially—Ella tried to smile—if the entertainment was already here, striding through the doorway with her overlarge exposed belly, and her broad, contagious grin, lit by the swinging lantern in her hand.

"Good morning, all," she said, beaming first toward the orcs, and then at Ella, and then toward the apples on the table. "Have you all heard"—she quickly reached for an apple, and bit into it with a loud crunch—"of that big brawl over in the Skai common-room last night?

Sounds like Simon nearly murdered Skaap, he's been with Efterar ever since."

She spoke with surprising gusto for someone who was supposed to be a lady—and when Dammarr muttered some kind of response in black-tongue, she actually chuckled, and replied something about Efterar indeed being about to spit rocks at this point. To which Thrak asked for a play-by-play of the fight's known details, sparking an immediate and animated discussion among them, culminating in a mock punching-match between Thrak and Dammarr, while the rest of the orcs—and Jule—laughed.

Their discussion was admittedly entertaining, and Ella gave the occasional chuckle as she ate her own apple—but she also couldn't seem to stop glancing toward Natt, who had remained notably silent beside her, his clawed hands clenched on his knees. Because that fight between Simon and Skaap would have been because of him, what he'd done in that room yesterday—but he didn't speak of it now, or even hint at it. And here, suddenly, was the sobering understanding that Natt's work as Speaker even separated him from his brothers, those he trusted most.

"Ach, we must go, brothers," Natt said at the first break in the conversation, rising to his feet. "There is much we must address today."

The other orcs accordingly stood, and Natt bent to press a kiss to Ella's hair, and then strode to the door, with Dammarr close by his side. While Ella watched him go, and fought to ignore yet another twist of bitter jealousy in her gut. Natt wanted *her*. She'd honoured him by embracing her truth. They'd taken a whole night's pleasure together. Surely he was still pleased with her. Right?

"Ready to go too, Ella?" Jule asked brightly. "I've been told I'm to take you to Efterar. Let's go see if he's decided to kill Skaap himself yet. Or perhaps Simon. Or both."

Efterar was indeed in a black humour when they found him, this time in what appeared to be a small sickroom, with a smattering of beds and sleeping orcs scattered about. "Nattfarr again?!" he said, with a single glance toward Ella, and then a roll of his eyes heavenward. "It doesn't look serious, at least. Over there, I'll be a moment."

With that, he stalked over to bark at another orc—Skaap, Ella noticed with a wince, who was lying in a bed, and indeed looking like death, with cuts and mottled bruises all over his huge ugly form. But he at least seemed well enough to argue with Efterar, snapping at him in black-tongue—to which Efterar growled something back, his clawed hand making a jabbing gesture toward Skaap's bruised chest.

"Oh good, here's Kesst," Jule said, as another orc strolled into the room. Ella hadn't met this orc yet, and he was lanky and graceful, his long black hair hanging unbound against his bare back. And as Jule and Ella watched, this Kesst orc strode over to Skaap and Efterar, grasping for a water-basin on the way. And then he casually dumped out the water-basin onto Skaap's sputtering face, and then threw a nearby large fur on top of him, hiding his now-flailing form entirely from view.

"There, now he's gone, Eft," Kesst said, as he turned toward Efterar, and then drew his taut body close, rubbing his hands smoothly up and down his back. "No more looking at him, or speaking to him, unless he's actually about to die. Now, how about a quick suck? Or a fuck? Whatever you like."

Efterar had visibly relaxed under this orc's ministrations, sagging into his touch, and the telling rumble in his throat suggested that he might very much like whatever was on offer—but then he gave a brief, meaningful glance over toward Jule and Ella. To which Jule only waved a hand, and took another large bite of the apple she'd still been eating.

"Oh, don't mind us," she said cheerfully. "We'll wait, right Ella?"

Ella's mouth had fallen open, her eyes goggling at this so-called *lady* beside her, who was currently giving her a conspiratorial wink. As if watching these two orcs—do *that*—was something she would quite thoroughly enjoy.

But the new orc—Kesst, his name had been—was looking at them first with surprise in his dark eyes, and then a slow, sparkling amusement. And then, after giving an audacious pat at the rather shocking bulge in front of Efterar's trousers, he turned to stride over toward them, his gaze sliding frank and appreciative up and down Ella's form.

"I truly thought you were Nattfarr," he said, with a chuckle. "Gods above, you smell exactly like him. What's he been doing, licking you all over, and bathing you in his spunk?"

Ella's face was furiously heating, because that wasn't a terrible summary of the previous night's activities—but Kesst only kept grinning at her, stepping back to survey her scantily clad, rather scratched-up body. "And just look at you," he said, with a genuine-seeming admiration. "It's even better than I imagined. Nattfarr is one devious, obnoxious Grisk, isn't he, Jules? This is *marvellous*."

He'd reached a clawed hand to flick at the emerald dangling in Ella's ear, and shot a swift, amused look toward Jule beside her. "Ol' Grim must have been furious that he didn't think of it," he said to her. "I'm surprised he didn't immediately bust out some jewels to deck you out in, and claim they were from his great-great-grandfather's long-lost Ash-Kai hoard."

Jule laughed, and gave a wry shake of her head, and another bite of her apple. "Oh, I'm quite sure he wanted to," she said as she chewed, in a blatant repudiation of all genteel table-manners. "But he also couldn't bear to give Nattfarr the satisfaction."

Ella's confusion had been rapidly increasing throughout this little exchange, finally enough that she just took a breath, and spoke. "What are you talking about? What do my clothes have to do with anything?"

Jule flashed her an apologetic smile around her mouthful of apple, and nodded toward Kesst, whose head had tilted, his lips pursed. "In truth, more than you might think," he said. "The Grisk have good noses, and long memories. They care more than the rest of us about the past, about fidelity, about family. About stability—and about the rules and laws to support that stability."

That made sense, based on what Ella had seen so far, and she nodded, and waited for him to continue. "And when the Grisk's favoured son openly starts in on all that against the captain," he said, slower now, "and then shows up arm in arm with a woman who's scent-bound to him, and dressed like the loyal mothers in the old tales, and wearing the ancient Grisk jewels—*and*, oh so coincidentally, she's rich, and betrothed to one of the men the captain's currently desperate to quash"—Kesst shrugged, his smile gone rather wry—"well, Nattfarr might as well have pissed on Grim in public. And then laughed. And did it again."

Oh. Ohhhh. Ella's thoughts were suddenly clambering over each other all at once, rising shouting screaming, because Natt—Natt had brought her here on *purpose*? To make some kind of—*statement* to his brothers, to his captain?

But no, no, Ella had wanted to escort Natt here, she'd been the one who'd wanted to stay—but then, Natt had been the one to put all those terms on it. *You shall reek all over of my scent. You shall please me, and obey me, and seek to honour me before my brothers.*

It shall be pure joy to walk my home by your side, and flaunt such a rare prize...

And dear gods, Natt had even told her, hadn't he? He'd wanted to use Ella to make a statement, and she had known that, and agreed to it. So why did she feel so ill, suddenly, like this whole room had gone dark and close and cold?

Both Kesst and Jule were watching her closely, Jule with a crease between her eyes, and Kesst with a new grimness on his mouth. As if the words he'd just said, seemingly with such careless ease, hadn't been careless at all.

"Well," Ella made herself say, with a valiant attempt to hold herself still, to keep the calmness in her eyes. "It's rather ridiculous that Natt needs to go to such lengths at all, isn't it? It's entirely unfair that your captain has refused to help him, or recognize him as Speaker, only because it is more convenient for him to have Natt out of the way!"

Her voice was loud and angry, her indignation far too clear—and too late she caught the meaningful glance between Jule and Kesst. And wait, Jule was *mated* to that awful captain, and had she ever said what clan this Kesst was from, and would they go tell this to Grimarr, who would then just make all of this worse?

But Jule's gaze had darted meaningfully toward Skaap, who'd thrust off the fur Kesst had thrown on him, and was glaring at the ceiling while Efterar hovered a hand over his belly. And with a sigh, Kesst spun on his heel and went over to Efterar, murmuring something in his ear as he slid a wandering hand around his front—and then he strode for the door, giving a meaningful jerk of his head toward Jule and Ella.

Jule promptly grasped for the lamp and followed, tugging Ella along behind her. "This way," she said, as she led Ella down a narrow, unfamiliar corridor. "We can talk more freely in John's library."

John's *library*? Ella blinked at that, but after following Jule and

Kesst through a tricky little set of connecting passages, she indeed found herself tumbling into—a library. A tall, cavernous, rounded room, lined with smooth circular shelves that appeared to be carved straight from the stone—but strangely enough, most of the shelves were empty, with only a smattering of books and scrolls neatly placed within them.

But this library also had a handful of tables and chairs, and at one of these tables sat the handsome, elf-like orc. John. Sitting in the light of a single candle, with his arms folded over his tunic, his grey face frowning down toward the open scroll in front of him.

"Morning, John," Jule said, as she went to drop herself into a chair across the table from him. "You don't mind if we have a chat here where it's private, do you?"

John only shrugged, so Ella accordingly went to sit beside Jule, glancing around the room, and at the open scroll, with genuine curiosity. Wishing, irrationally, that Natt were here to tell her about it, to put his hand to her waist, to say, *I care naught for your hoard, I only love you…*

"So Ella's been asking about this whole Speaker business," Jule said to John. "And I thought she should have some context. When I first came here, I didn't know half of what was going on around me, and—"

Her voice broke off, her mouth grimacing, and on the other side of Ella Kesst gave a heavy sigh. "And it made liars out of us all," he said, "and very nearly killed you, Jules. So, this time—Ella knows what we know. The truth."

The truth? Surely that was foolishness, surely Ella had heard all she needed to know from Natt, and from when Natt had demanded the truth from Grimarr, her first day here—but already Kesst had leaned forward toward her, while a flat, curious heaviness settled across his eyes. And then, with his voice carrying a careful, unfamiliar inflection, he spoke.

He spoke first of Kaugir the Iron-Claw, and the cruelties he wreaked against his own brothers. He told of Kaugir's son Grimarr, who grieved his father's ways, and finally killed him with his own sword, and took his place as captain. He spoke of how Grimarr had then solemnly sworn to restore peace between all five clans, and then between orcs and men.

But to gain the clans' fealty, Kesst's oddly hypnotic voice continued, Grimarr also vowed to honour each clan's own ways, and uphold their beliefs and traditions, with all the power at his hand. But this soon proved to be tenuous, for the five clans' ways were not the same—and most of all when it came to their women and sons, who were not always treated as they ought, or as they wished. This provoked the Grisk most of all, for they have long sought to protect their own.

"And thus, the Grisk's favoured son has risen up to right this wrong," Kesst's slow, mesmerizing voice continued. "He sets himself against the captain, and begins to call for laws and rules and power. He begins to Speak for his weaker brothers. He brings a woman to the mountain, and honours her with care and pleasure and healing and fine clothes and jewels.

"But in this, he also sets himself against his own brothers. He sets himself against our fragile peace, and the promises our captain has made to achieve it. He sets the clans to choose sides, and revolt against one another. He opens the door to death from within, when it already knocks again and again from without."

Kesst's voice stopped there, breaking off into a hushed, heavy silence, and for a moment Ella couldn't seem to speak, or lift her eyes from the table between them. Natt was setting up a revolt? Natt was opening the door to death? With Ella's *clothes*?

But then, startling and vivid, was the memory of Stella, moaning and writhing naked upon her mate's lap—and sitting here, right before Ella's eyes, was the high-ranking captain's own mate, a true *lady*, wearing ill-fitting, chopped-off clothes that had clearly been made for men. And while neither woman had seemed unhappy with their current lot, Ella knew very well that many women would be. That the women she'd counted as friends, back home, would never tolerate being exposed or disrespected thus, especially before a mass of strange and highly terrifying orcs.

"Well, I'm sorry, but if you orcs truly want to survive," Ella heard herself say, "you need to change, and learn to respect women's wishes. And surely you need to follow human laws as well. Don't you?"

"We do follow human laws, in public," replied another voice, and when Ella blinked up it was John speaking, his black claw tracing against his open scroll. "As per the peace-treaty we signed, any human law or regulation currently in effect within this continent's four signing provinces may have the word 'orc' freely exchanged with the word 'man'. We orcs have sworn ourselves to this, across all five clans. But—only *outside* the mountain."

"And inside the mountain?" Ella asked, glancing around the table, to which Jule made a face, Kesst laughed, and John's eyebrows furrowed, his claw tapping on his scroll.

"In the mountain, each clan enforces its own rules, in its own way," said John, his voice crisp. "These rules do not always align with those of the humans. One thinks most of human laws against sodomy, bigamy, and public obscenity, none of which are forbidden here—but there are many other laws which are thorny for orcs as well. Trespassing is one—we do not all share this view of owned land—and also our bent toward public maiming, rather than banishment or imprisonment, to redress wrongdoers."

Ella winced, thinking again of that scene in the Skai commonroom the night before, which had likely broken a half-dozen human laws alone, Natt's activities included. "All right, so maybe you can't implement *all* the humans' laws here," she said, "but surely that's not what Natt wants. He wants to"—she cast her thoughts backwards—"create age laws. And put in lamps. And work on science and medicine to help women."

"Yes, and we need those things," Jule said beside Ella, her voice flat. "Very much so. The thing is, they won't happen just because Nattfarr and the Grisk decide they should. When it comes to the clans—especially to Skai and Bautul—we need to negotiate openly and fairly, with concessions on all sides. We can't risk alienating each other, and driving them off again. The Skai are already halfway out the door, and if they leave here now—especially under these new human laws we've bound them to—it'll be a week before we're at war again. And Grimarr will do *anything* to prevent that."

Oh. Ella scrubbed at her eyes, fighting to follow all this. "So you're just going to let your most, um, *unpalatable* orcs hold your whole people hostage, over things like age laws, and medical care?" she demanded. "At the expense of your own women and sons? How many women die each year trying to give birth to your children?"

Ella's voice had gone rather shrill, and it was answered by a moment's silence, another tap of John's claws against his scroll. "Four and ten," he said finally, quiet. "This past twelvemonth. That we know of."

Dear gods. Ella's head was shaking back and forth, her arms crossed tight over her chest, her fingers gripping against the soft comfort of Natt's fur cape. "That is *abominable*," she snapped. "How are those women's lives worth less than those of orcs. That alone is worth *everything* Natt is trying to do!"

No one argued, thankfully, and the heavy silence was finally broken by a short laugh from Kesst, a wry wave of his hand toward her. "Nattfarr clearly knew what he was doing with you, sweetheart," he said, in a voice that sounded almost amused, but not quite. "Grisk through and through. Stubborn, idealistic, loyal to a fault. You'll make him a good mate. And, help spark war for us all."

Ella didn't know how to answer that—was he insulting her?—and beside them, Jule gave a heavy sigh. "Grimarr won't let it come to that," she said firmly. "Under all his bluster, he does care for Nattfarr, and agrees with much that he's trying to implement. And they're finally talking to each other today like rational adults, rather than just sniping and baiting each other, and that's a promising sign. Although"—her gaze flicked up to Ella's, her head tilting—"if you do actually care about all this so much, Ella, why didn't you want to be involved today?"

Involved? Ella blinked at her, and then at the orcs, all three of whom were staring at her with watchful eyes. "What do you mean? Involved in what?"

"In their negotiations this morning," Jule said, slowly now, her eyes not leaving Ella's face. "Grimarr and Nattfarr are meeting, along with Simon and Olarr and Sken, to hammer some of this out. To settle some terms, at least for now, given the current circumstances."

Terms. For now. Circumstances? Ella blinked at Jule, not at all following, and Jule muttered a short curse, her eyes briefly closing, almost as if she were in pain. "These damned orcs," she said, with a sigh. "Nattfarr didn't tell you. You don't know, Ella, do you?"

Ella did not know, whatever the hell Jule was talking about, and

Jule opened her eyes, and sighed. And took a breath, and another, while the dread began to rise, thrumming shrill under Ella's skin—

"Lord Tovey, your betrothed, has publicly refused our offer of hospitality," Jule said, her voice quiet, but sure. "He has called his new allies together for an urgent council. And he now rides at full speed toward us, and has demanded you be returned to him at once. Or else, he will launch a *war*."

26

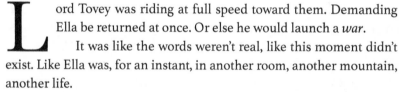

Lord Tovey was riding at full speed toward them. Demanding Ella be returned at once. Or else he would launch a *war*.

It was like the words weren't real, like this moment didn't exist. Like Ella was, for an instant, in another room, another mountain, another life.

"How long?" she asked, her voice sounding flimsy, far away. "Have you known this?"

She was leaning toward Jule, almost as if begging her to say, *I only learned it just today, perhaps an hour past*—but Jule grimaced again, and gave a slow shake of her head. "Yesterday morning," she said. "Alfred's men caught up with him the night before that, and he sent out the call for the war council at once, and turned around within the hour. He should be here by sunrise."

Good gods. They'd known Alfred was coming, *yesterday*, and he would be here *tomorrow*, this had to be a dream, it had to be...

"And Alfred's—his men?" Ella heard herself ask. "They're still here?"

Jule grimaced, and nodded. "Two of them are still camped in the forest, two of them are riding back with him, and the other one's gone north to Khandor, where Alfred's called for his war-council to meet—

in my cousin Otto's jurisdiction. It even sounds like Otto's planning to attend, the slimy bastard. Playing both sides at once, as usual."

Genuine anger was flashing in her eyes, and Ella's stilted brain fought to follow, to pull that together. If Alfred and his father had new allies in Preia and Dunburg, and then gained Otto back to their side, with all Otto's forces in Sakkin and Salven and Yarwood—that was nearly half the realm's provinces. Ready to wage a new *war* against the orcs.

"And what will you *do*?" Ella's wavering voice asked. "What happens next?"

Jule made a face, and frowned down at the table. "That's the question, isn't it?" she said. "But we know Tlaxca's very short on funds right now—and already deeply in debt to Preia—so Alfred needs to get either Otto or a few of the realm's northern provinces on side before he can actually afford to start fighting again. And believe me, Grimarr's doing everything he can to prevent that—and Grimarr almost *always* gets what he wants."

She flashed Ella a wry smile that was probably meant to be comforting, but it abjectly failed, and Ella gripped her sweaty hands tight together. Alfred would be here *tomorrow*. And had Natt known that, he *couldn't* have...

"And you're saying Natt *knew* about all this?" Ella heard herself ask, her voice even fainter than before. "Because there must be some mistake. He would"—she gulped for air—"he would have *told* me. I spoke truth to him, just last night, he'd have spoken it to me. He *believes* in truth."

But it wasn't working, the room was still here, still wrong. Still with Jule looking at Ella like this, with unease and perhaps even sympathy rising in her eyes—and there was a distinctive sound from Kesst, rather like a snort.

"Oh, Nattfarr believes in truth, all right," he said dryly. "And the more convenient it is to his cause, the better. A good match for Grim, really, Jules."

Jule gave Kesst an unmistakable kick under the table, and then lurched to her feet, and grasped for her lamp. "You're probably right, and there's just some mistake," she said firmly. "Come on, Ella. Let's go find Nattfarr, and he can straighten this out with you himself."

Ella numbly went, casting an uneasy look behind her, toward John and Kesst still sitting at the table. John with a considering expression, and Kesst with something that might have been pity.

Ella's heart was beating erratically, and she could scarcely seem to walk, suddenly, tripping over even the slightest indentations in the smooth stone below her feet. Yes, she'd known Alfred might be returning, but not *tomorrow*, not already calling for *war*. If that were true, Natt would have told her. *Surely* Natt would have told her. They'd been together all this time, they'd taken that impossible pleasure together. They'd spoken truth.

But the whispering nagging misery only grew deeper, stronger, as Jule led Ella up and up, back into the Ash-Kai wing. Where they found Grimarr and Baldr and Drafli huddled together, conferring in blacktongue, with no one else to be seen.

"Looking for Nattfarr?" Baldr asked, raising his head, and giving a careful sniff. "He's gone to the Grisk training-room, I believe."

Ella's scattered thoughts could barely skirt at the impressiveness of that as Jule said a sincere thank-you, and then drew her away again. Taking her toward the Grisk wing, and then into the training-room— where, indeed, the light of Jule's lamp revealed the sudden, oddly painful sight of Natt's familiar muscled body, grappling with another orc on the floor. With *Dammarr*.

Natt and Dammarr were growling and grabbing and swinging at each other, while Thrak and Thrain circled around above them, casually pointing out when various hits were made, and kicking at an arm or leg that had perhaps gone awry. It was clearly only practice of some kind, but Ella's heart was still clanging in her chest—and then plummeting at the sight of Natt pinning Dammarr's muscled body to the floor, their hips thrust together. While Dammarr purposely glanced sideways at Ella, his eyes narrowing—and then he deliberately bucked his hips up under Natt, and gave a slow, provocative lick of his lips with his long black tongue.

"Un-*necessary*," Jule hissed beside Ella, but thank the gods Natt had already leapt up and away, snapping a harsh word toward Dammarr before whirling around to face them. And something in Ella's chest was wrenching too tight, so tight it was difficult to breathe, while the compulsion to move, to leave, kept rising and shouting in her thoughts. She should go, run, run—

But Jule's hand was gripped to hers, and Natt was still standing there looking at them, and he was—Ella took an unconscious step backwards—*wrong*. His jaw tight, his eyes dark and narrow, his lip curling as he snapped something else at Dammarr, and then stalked toward her.

The urge to run was shouting again, loud enough that Ella yanked away from Jule, and backed into the hallway—but Natt was here, suddenly, striding straight into her, plunging her into his scent and his warmth. And then—despite everything, Ella's eyes had closed, her breath heaving out her chest—he ducked his face into her neck, and *smelled* her.

His deep, dragging inhale was its own kind of truth, a solid strength in the madness, and Ella clung to it, to him. Even as he finally raised his head, and those eyes—wrong, *wrong*—fixed on Jule beside them. And then on Grimarr, who'd somehow appeared out of nowhere to stand behind Jule, his huge clawed hand spreading wide against her swollen belly.

"I leave my lass for *one morning*," Natt hissed, his voice low, danger-ous, "with the Ash-Kai, and"—he ducked his head, inhaled again—"the Ka-esh, who both claim to be Grisk's *allies*—and you bring her back to me *reeking* of such fear and despair? What have you done to her?!"

He looked surprisingly furious, his claws out, his eyes flashing with rage—but Jule crossed her arms over her chest, and glared back at Natt with deep disapproval. "If you don't want your m—your *friend* to be upset," she snapped, "perhaps you could begin by not allowing your *brother* to taunt her like that. And, perhaps you could also tell her crucial information that directly affects her, before she hears it elsewhere!"

Natt's replying growl sounded almost feral, his teeth bared, his clawed hands thrusting Ella behind him. "You have told her this?!" he nearly shouted. "You said you should not speak to her of this, until I had done so!"

He was glaring at Grimarr, Ella realized, rather than at Jule, and though Grimarr's claws were out too, his body behind Jule's was very still, his eyes steady on Natt's face. "Ach, and I did not," he said, his deep voice even. "But I cannot speak for my mate. She speaks for herself."

Natt's growl turned toward Jule, rising and rising, while she took an uneasy step closer into Grimarr behind her. And without thinking, Ella darted around, thrusting herself between Natt and Jule, and glaring up at Natt's wrong, wrong eyes.

"Jule didn't do anything," she said flatly. "She was only looking out for me. And surely, Natt, if you truly have known about this for *days*, you could have found a moment to tell me before now?!"

The wrongness on Natt's face didn't change, his big body almost vibrating as he looked at Ella with those blank, unreadable black eyes. And again, the fear lurched up, so powerful she was going to choke on it, what was wrong, *why*—

Without warning Natt's strong hand grasped at hers, pulling hard toward the corridor. And Ella willingly went, lurching along after his long striding steps, blinking in the sudden blackness. He was angry, he was furious, what had happened today, why hadn't he told her about Alfred, why why why—

Natt drew her to an abrupt halt in the dark, still in what felt like the corridor—but after a purposeful-feeling shove of his body, there was the telltale sound of shifting rock. And suddenly, there was—fresh air, and light so bright it hurt Ella's eyes. Natt was taking her *outside*?!

The fear screamed again all at once, so strong it was dizzying, and Natt whirled around to face her in the light, his hand snapping to his side, closing on his scimitar-hilt. "What is it, lass," he demanded, or perhaps pleaded. "*Why* do you keep shouting at me thus. Is it truly Dammarr who has alarmed you so? I told you, I shall never care for him as I do for you. I shall *never* touch him thus again, after you."

Ella's sudden, swirling relief at that statement was almost visceral—but it was still warring wildly against confusion, and disbelief, as her blinking eyes darted between Natt's face, and the opening in the rock before them. He was taking her outside, *outside*, to the world beyond, to where *Alfred* was coming, *tomorrow*—

"Ach," Natt said, giving a hard shake of his head, and he abruptly leaned in, plucking Ella's trembly body close against his solid, reassuring heat. "I take you not—*there*, my lass. This is only so you may have some air, and sun, to help calm you. You are human, you need these things."

Ella couldn't seem to speak, but when Natt again drew her out toward the light, this time she went, following on shaky legs. Out into sun, and warmth, and air that smelled cool and fresh and astonishingly sweet.

And despite everything shouting in her head at this moment, Ella was suddenly starving for this, and her body seemed to stumble out further on its own, drinking it up. They were still high up on the mountain, but perched on a grassy little bluff with soaring stone walls on three sides—but the last side was wide open to the sky. Beautiful, deep blue sky, scattered with bright white clouds, on a level with Ella's staring, blinking eyes.

She could feel Natt coming to stand close behind her, his arms circling around her bare waist, his chin resting on top of her head. And Ella didn't know whether to laugh, or weep, or shout at him, or whirl around and tackle him to the earth.

But she did none of those things, only stood there blinking and breathing, while she felt Natt's chest rise and fall against her. Alfred was coming. Alfred *wanted her back*. Alfred, who wanted to use her money to destroy the orcs, forever.

Alfred wanted to start a *war*.

"I am sorry I did not speak to you, of this," Natt said, finally, quiet, into her hair. "I am sorry I forbade you to speak of this. I only did not wish for this foul man to again come between us, and cut off our joy. I was selfish."

Ella should have called him to account, and said, *Yes, you are abominable, how dare you hide such important truths from me*—but she could only seem to stand there, and blink, and fight to breathe.

"And I was cruel," Natt continued, even quieter. "To seek your truth, whilst hiding mine. You ought to spurn me, lass. You ought to shout at me, and send me away."

But his arms had squeezed even tighter around her, saying, *Please, don't*, and Ella swallowed hard, her eyes held to the breathtaking blue before them. This was it. One more day, before Alfred ruined everything, once again.

And gods, it hurt that Natt would keep such a secret from her. But even the thought of sending him away, now, and wasting what might be her last day here alone and in anger, was so much worse, so painful she wanted to weep.

"So when Alfred comes tomorrow," Ella said instead, almost a whisper, "what happens then?"

"What do you wish to happen?" came Natt's voice, immediate, and Ella swallowed again, and blinked out at the sky. What did she want to happen? Truly?

And here, between Natt's warmth behind her, and the sky's brightness before her, and the air's sweetness inside her—the answer came, quiet and simple, as though it had been there all along.

She wanted to *stay*. She wanted to be Ella, of Clan Grisk. She wanted to be Natt's—*mate*. Not just for a visit. But—*forever*.

But suddenly the chaos was swirling again, because what did that mean, how did that even happen, what would then happen to everything else? What would happen to Ella's lands, her home? The money, the inheritance, all her father had done to ensure she would have it, to provide for her? What would it mean, if she threw all that away, to live in a mountain, with an orc?!

And worst of all, what happened with the war? What would Alfred do next, if she refused to go back to him, and told him she was jilting him for an *orc*? The orc he'd been trying to *kill*, all these years?

Ella's breath was coming shallow, her body shivering against Natt's behind her, and she could feel his breaths too, heavy and hoarse and harsh. Thinking, perhaps, that she didn't want to stay, and she shoved around to face him, to look up at those eyes. Still dark, still... wrong.

"I don't want to leave you, Natt," Ella said, and she meant it. "I've loved being here with you. And I don't want Alfred to use a *copper* of my father's money on waging more war against you. And of course even the idea of another war is *abominable*. I just..."

She couldn't finish, because she just—what? She wanted Natt to ask her to stay, and be his mate? She wanted him to say he loved her? She wanted him to find some neat solution to fix everything? She wanted everything, her home and Natt too, and no war or death. And that was impossible, it was all impossible, it was all ruined, once again Alfred had ruined *everything*...

"You must not," Natt said, his voice hitching, "needs speak of this now, should you not wish. This man shall not come here until daybreak. Until this, mayhap"—his mouth twitched up, in a pathetic farce of a smile—"we shall take joy in this day together. And in my first Truth Revel tonight."

His Truth Revel. "What's that?" Ella asked, confused again, and Natt quickly explained, his voice still strangely stilted, how on the first night of every full moon, his father had held a Truth Revel. An opportunity for him to share his gift of truth with his brothers, to allow them to partake of it however they wished.

"And today," Natt continued, "I have finally gained the right to do this, from our captain. I shall host my first Revel, for all my brothers, as a true Speaker would."

As a true speaker would. And that was enough to jar Ella's brain out of the mess currently drowning it, and she drew in a bracing breath, and attempted a smile up toward him. "Well, that sounds like a big concession, right?" she asked, as brightly as she could. "You must be delighted, Natt. You'll be a full Speaker sooner than you think."

She could see the warmth finally whispering in his eyes, his exhale coming out slow. "Ach, I am pleased, lass," he said. "But I have not yet gained this, and there is much that must needs be done. Much weight, that I did not ken should be mine to bear, so soon."

Oh. And Ella could almost feel that weight, suddenly, hanging about him, dragging down on his shoulders—and maybe that was why he'd felt so wrong today. He was supposed to be lighthearted Natt, running and laughing and playing, and now he had to be a leader, he had to carry on his father's traditions, he had to draw truth from his brothers, and speak it for all to hear.

"So what do you have to do tonight, exactly?" Ella asked. "Your brothers just—talk to you? And do you talk to them too?"

"Ach," Natt replied, with a nod. "As we have, these past days. It is not always an easy thing, to face one's truth, without some help."

Ella felt herself nodding back at him, her hands reaching instinctively to his bare chest, spreading wide against his warmth. "How wise and generous you are, Nattfarr of Clan Grisk," she said, soft. "You'll be a spectacular Speaker, I know it. You'll make this mountain a better place for *everyone*."

There was wetness welling behind her eyes, and she blinked as

Natt's hands came up, and gently cradled her face between them. "You honour me, my fair lass," he murmured. "Now may we leave all this behind, and only have our joy, for today?"

His voice sounded almost pleading, his eyes just the same, and Ella swallowed hard, and nodded. Joy, for today. And then...

"Right," she said, too quickly. "Right. Um. Well"—her eyes were casting about, and had thankfully caught on the sheer wall of the mountain behind them—"are those *steps* in that stone, Natt?"

Natt blinked, his eyes darting up toward it, and then flicking back to her face. And this time, thank the gods, they finally, truly looked like him again. Warm, amused, alive.

"Ach, they are," he replied, his voice light. "But I ken such a pretty, pampered lass like you should never be able to climb this wall with me."

Ella was smiling at him again, blinking back the last of the wetness behind her eyes as she jabbed her finger into his chest. "And I *ken*," she said, "you're wrong, you arrogant Grisk. Not only shall I climb it, but I shall do it so quickly, you shan't be able to keep up, and will need to concede defeat, on your knees."

"On my knees?" Natt echoed, with his old familiar grin, sharp-toothed and wicked. "Mayhap I shall allow you to defeat me, to gain this."

Ella made a face at him, but he was still grinning at her, the warmth and affection bared and true in his sparkling eyes.

And that was enough, in this moment, so Ella kicked off, and ran.

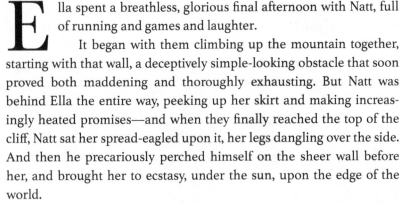

27

Ella spent a breathless, glorious final afternoon with Natt, full of running and games and laughter.

It began with them climbing up the mountain together, starting with that wall, a deceptively simple-looking obstacle that soon proved both maddening and thoroughly exhausting. But Natt was behind Ella the entire way, peeking up her skirt and making increasingly heated promises—and when they finally reached the top of the cliff, Natt sat her spread-eagled upon it, her legs dangling over the side. And then he precariously perched himself on the sheer wall before her, and brought her to ecstasy, under the sun, upon the edge of the world.

"You utter *hellion*," Ella breathed afterwards, once she'd dragged him up, and was frantically kissing his wet, tangy-tasting mouth. "What if you'd fallen?!"

But he only grinned at her, curling his long, slick tongue against hers with saucy lewdness. "Then you should have forever grieved me," he said smugly, "and never found such joy again."

Ella elbowed at him, and also at the nagging, dragging thoughts that had arisen with the words, and thankfully Natt shoved her back onto the earth, his body heavy and sweaty over hers. "And now," he said, "I must be repaid, for this grave danger I have faced, upon your behalf."

Ella laughed and protested and kicked at him, but of course he was far too strong. And when he sat on her chest, and drew out his dripping, sticky hardness, her only recourse was to grasp for it with her trembly fingers, and draw it close between her hungry lips.

It led to Natt hovering low on his elbows and knees over her, blatantly driving himself down into her slobbering sucking mouth, and howling at the sky. And oh, it was good, it was the rightful Speaker of the Grisk taking his base, unfettered pleasure with his woman, and then flooding her with seed until she choked.

"This pleased me," Natt murmured, afterwards, as he pulled Ella to her feet, and wiped her face clean again. "Who should have thought that a pretty lass like you should take such joy in having her throat plundered by an orc's prick? No foul man shall ever please you again, after this."

He smiled as he spoke, but there was again that odd whispering darkness in it—and Ella pushed it away, and then dragged him close into her arms. "No, he shan't," she said firmly. "Now, can we go up further, from here?"

Natt immediately nodded, guiding her in the direction he wanted to go, toward a rocky but manageable-looking ascent. "There is a pool, this way," he said. "We ought to bathe you there. You are always such a filthy lass."

Ella loudly protested, but willingly went along anyway, until Natt drew her to a halt before the breathtaking sight of a tall, rushing waterfall, tumbling into a misty pool beneath. And as she watched, the world hitching all around, Natt's gentle hands carefully undressed her of everything but her earrings, and then drew her in.

The water was shockingly cold, setting Ella's teeth immediately chattering, but Natt was here, as warm as always, tucking her close against him, rubbing her all over with his big heated hands. But not quite meeting her eyes as he did it, and the nagging heaviness seemed to drag ever deeper in Ella's stomach. Whispering of Alfred, of wars, of money and her father and her home. Of *something* being ruined, gone forever, no matter what path she took.

When Natt drew her out of the water again, the cold was all that remained, so strong Ella's shivering body could scarcely stand. And in a single movement he swept her up, along with her clothes, and tucked her close and safe against his hot chest.

"Next, I must dress you again," he murmured, into her ear, as he easily leapt up onto a bank of rock, nimbly leaping from one boulder to the next. "For my Revel. This shall begin at nightfall."

The sun was indeed sinking lower in the sky, and Ella nodded as Natt eased her toward what appeared to be a solid wall of stone. But it turned out that there was a tiny crevice just above it, entirely invisible from below, and soon they were back in the Grisk wing, and Natt was carrying Ella into the Grisk storage-room. Where he again stood her between the rows of shelves, while he rummaged around her, holding up item after item against her still-shivery skin.

"These must stay," he said decisively, flicking a claw at the earring still in her ear. "And these must also."

These were those two gold chains, which he'd carefully tucked beneath her breasts again, taking a moment to kiss at each of her cold, rock-hard nipples with his blessedly warm mouth. And then he drew back, frowning, as he absently tapped at her nipple with his claw.

"You are sure you do not wish me to pierce these?" he asked, tilting his head. "Or mayhap only one? You are yet so cold, you shall scarcely feel this."

Ella's heart leapt at the thought, hammering wild against his touch—and curse her, but in this moment, she was somehow actually *considering* it. Actually looking down, and then back at Natt's face, at the odd glittering intensity in his watchful black eyes.

"Um," she heard herself say, her tongue suddenly thick in her mouth. "Do you really know what to do? Have you done it before?"

"Ach, with Dammarr," he replied, his eyes challenging on Ella's now, because he knew exactly what kind of statement that was, the bastard. "And should I truly cause you pain, I shall take you to Efterar at once."

Well. Ella's breath was dragging in deep, her body again shivering, for reasons now entirely unrelated to the cold. And somehow, unbelievably, her head was actually—nodding. Saying—*yes.*

"Fine," she whispered. "One. You pick."

The astonishment flared wide in Natt's eyes—he truly hadn't

expected her to agree, Ella realized, too late—but next was the hunger, warm and powerful and utterly thrilling. Curving into a true smile on his mouth, a wicked snap of his sharp white teeth.

"Brave lass," he purred, as both his hands cupped both her breasts at once, squeezing tight. "This honours me."

Ella felt herself smile back, breathless and still shivery all over. And then she watched, with increasing bemusement, as Natt stepped slightly backwards, frowning down at her bare breasts, and then began alternately weighing and plucking at each one. Pinching at one side, and then the other, before snapping off one of his own gold earrings, and holding it against each nipple as he did it again, and again.

Finally he'd seemed to settle on her left side, giving it a final little tweak before turning his attention to the earring in his hand. First scraping at the post with his sharp claws, drawing it to a finer point— and then tearing a bit of fabric off something nearby, and setting it aflame with a quick snap of his claws. And then he was burning the earring in the flame, turning it over and over, scraping again, turning more—and then dropping the fabric to the floor, and stomping out the fire with a grind of his bare heel.

"You shall look at my face," Natt said firmly, as both hands finally came back to Ella's breast, one holding the earring, the other pinching at her hard, chilly nipple. "And be a brave Grisk, for your orc."

A brave Grisk, for your orc. The heat unfurled again, and Ella desperately nodded, fixing her eyes to his face. Even as his glinting gaze dropped, looking intent at his hands, his fingers tight—

The pain was surprisingly sharp, drawing a choked cry from Ella's mouth—but then it faded just as quickly, slipping into a raw, pulsing ache. And then warmth, nudging slick and careful against the ache, because Natt had ducked his head down, and taken her nipple fully into his mouth.

He held her gaze as he suckled it, his wet tongue brushing gentle against the wound again and again, until the pain had almost entirely faded, in favour of the rising, thudding pleasure. And when he slowly drew back, revealing the impossible sight of her own familiar peaked nipple, but with his gold ring embedded deep into it, Ella could only seem to blink, and gasp, and stare.

Natt was looking too, bringing a careful finger to brush against it, and it occurred to Ella that his breath was rasping too. And a swift, belated glance downwards showed a telltale bulge under his kilt, visibly twitching, seeking its escape.

"Not yet," Natt whispered, as he caught her hand that had been snaking down toward it, all on its own. "Once I have finished dressing you, then I shall fuck you, my filthy little lass."

The promise was dark and delicious in his glittering eyes, in the slow lick of his tongue against his lips. And then, while Ella watched, heat sparking in her groin—and in her still-aching nipple—Natt intently, purposefully kept dressing her. First slinging another gold chain around her waist, and then dangling more chains from that one, both in front and in back, so that the rippling gold teased and tickled whenever she moved. And then there were polished gold cuffs, too, which Natt slid over her hands, and up to her upper arms—and then he knelt to snap on another cuff, clamping it close around her ankle.

Ella had never worn so much jewelry before—in her old life, such a display of wealth would have been considered pathetically gauche—but as Natt stepped backwards, again eyeing her with that hungry warmth in his eyes, there was only pleasure, perhaps even pride. He'd called her a Grisk. He'd called himself her orc. And maybe even if he didn't love her, maybe he did truly want her to stay, maybe he would ask—

The question was very nearly on Ella's tongue—*if I stay, will you make me your mate?*—but Natt had abruptly drawn her away, further down the aisle, toward the plentiful piles of clothing, which had clearly been neatened since the last time they'd done this. A fact which Natt didn't seem to notice in the least, frowning as he once again yanked out an item from the bottom of the stack, and then another, holding each one up against Ella's skin.

He finally seemed to decide on another cape-like garment, this one made of a thin, floating fabric that clearly showed the hard jut of Ella's new nipple-ring beneath it. And on her hips, this time he hung another skirt, this one longer but lighter, flowing easily against her thighs.

He stepped back from her then, his critical eyes sweeping up and down her form. Looking more and more approving with every breath, his hand reaching out to tilt up her chin—and his slow, heavy sigh was another jolt of pleasure, flaring and tickling deep.

But then he whirled around, and stalked toward yet another shelf. And there he shucked his own kilt, leaving it abandoned on the floor, before yanking on a new one. One that was made of fur, but with strips of leather around the waist and down the sides, with beads of gold studded into it.

Next he threw on a cape of his own, this one also made of fur, and then he snapped on more earrings, two into each pointed ear this time. And then there were thick gold cuffs for each of his arms, and finally he tugged out his braid, which had admittedly become a frayed mess during the day's activities, and impatiently combed out his hair with his claws until it fell over his shoulders in a silken black sheet.

And when Natt finally turned toward Ella again, his hair loose, his claws extending sharp from his fingertips, his big body bedecked in fur and leather and gold, her heart seemed to stutter, and leap into her throat. He looked *massive*, tall and broad-shouldered and breathtakingly dangerous. And shameless, and monstrous, and *delicious*, and Ella nearly moaned aloud when he beckoned her closer, with a single flick of his claw.

"There is one more trinket I ought to wear," he said, so smooth, "if you should wish to place this upon me?"

This, it turned out, was something that looked like a large gold bangle, thick and seamless and perfectly rounded, with no sharp edges to be seen. Ella had willingly taken it into her hands, tracing her fingers against it, and she could feel her heartbeat thumping, her throat swallowing, as she glanced up at those dangerous dark eyes.

"Of course," she said, her mouth dry. "Where does it go? Your arm?"

Natt's replying slow grin was tolerant, affectionate, with a telltale flare of wickedness. "Foolish lass," he said. "This is for my prick."

His—what? Ella was struck entirely, speechlessly shocked—for perhaps the first time in a full day, really, and that had to be some kind of improvement, didn't it?—and she gave a hard, flustered shake of her head. "Your—your *prick*," she heard herself echo, her voice faint. "Truly, Natt?"

But he only laughed, the sound husky, warm, teasing—and then his hand dropped beneath his kilt, and brought out—that. His huge, tapered grey hardness, jutting straight toward her, and already pooling white at the tip.

"Ach, truly," he said, stroking up the full length of it, milking out more of that delectable white. "Come, lass."

Ella took a twitchy, uneasy step closer, gripping the gold ring with both hands, her eyes darting between it, and *that*. "But," she whispered, "it's so—large. Not that you're not, but—"

Natt only laughed again, guiding her hands downwards—and Ella watched, her eyes caught, trapped, upon the unnervingly arousing sight of her fingers carefully sliding the ring over the head of him, and all the way down. Until it hung on the hard base of him, loose, like the most obscene necklace she'd ever seen in her life.

"More," Natt murmured, earning another shocked, darting look from Ella, up toward his still-amused eyes. "All the way."

All the way. He meant—Ella swallowed—he had to mean those swollen bollocks, hanging heavy and full below his cock. And that was impossible, the ring was far too small for all of—of *that*—but Natt's steady hand only guided hers down further, saying yes, this was exactly what he meant.

So Ella's trembly hands did it, or tried to, and managed to ease one of those bollocks through, confronting her eyes with a sight absurd enough to make her laugh out loud. And thankfully Natt laughed again too, and finally he finished the job for her, letting out a low, heated hiss as he settled the ring tight against his groin.

But then it was done, it was there, and Ella's laughter had sliced into absolute silence, her eyes staring, her mouth gone entirely dry. Because here was Natt, her Natt, the rightful Speaker of the Grisk, proud and brazen, his magnificent cock and balls encircled in gold, utterly on display, looking fuller than they ever had before. And they even felt fuller, too, when Ella reached for a tentative touch. Her hungry fingers gently stroking down the silky length of him, while her other hand came to cup at the thick, bulging weights below, too large to even fit in her hand.

"This pleases you," Natt murmured, soft, and Ella didn't care if that was smugness, or even triumph, in his watching, glittering eyes. "You wish me to fuck you with this, do you not?"

There was no countering it, not a single word, and Ella could only bite her lip, and look him in the eyes, and nod. And his replying growl was everything, all her nagging doubts hurled away in this moment, as Natt grasped her arm and strode down the aisle, the obscene sight at his groin swinging with every step.

But then—Ella's breath choked, again—they'd halted before the looking-glass. And when Natt thrust her close in front of it, there was another blaring screeching shock, because the woman who was supposed to be her—supposed to be a *lady*—was an unknown, unimaginable stranger.

Her eyes were large and dark, her face freckled and flushed, her lips swollen a deep red. Her hair was a chaotic reddish mess, tumbling down over her shoulders, contrasting against the green and gold glinting in her ears, and around her neck. Her midriff was almost entirely bare, but for more gold chains, and a diaphanous scrap of fluttery fabric over her shoulders and breasts, one side looking markedly more peaked than the other. And when her trembly hand came to lift the fabric up, there was her breast, cupped beneath with gold, and boldly displaying a gold ring, embedded deep into its jutting nipple.

The woman's breath was heaving, and even more so when the huge, fur-covered orc behind her reached a sharp claw to nudge, very gently, at that gleaming gold ring. To which the woman gasped and choked, her body writhing against the orc, because gods, the pain and the pleasure, she hadn't even imagined, it was beyond anything, *everything*—

But this audacious orc wasn't done, not even close, because with another flick of a claw, he'd caught the flowing fabric at her hips, and tucked it up, into the gold belt around her waist. Exposing her naked groin to his eyes, and then sliding his thigh between, spreading her legs apart.

She could hear her wetness clenching, greedy and desperate, but the orc in the glass only gave a sly, devilish grin—and then, in a swift, easy movement, he reached down, and yanked her up. So that she was fully off the ground, propped on his powerful bare thigh, with her legs spread, her shamefully clenching heat exposed wide and humiliating to the glass, to their joined watching eyes.

"Touch it," came the orc's voice, close and insolent in her ear. "Show me what is mine."

The woman in the glass whimpered and trembled, but the orc's long, slithering black tongue snaked out to swirl blatantly against her ear, her reddened neck, even trailing its stunning length over to tickle at her lips. And the woman's pink tongue darted out to meet it, tangling with it, craving it, needing it.

"Touch yourself," he said, ordered. "Show me you can learn this lesson. Show me you are a Grisk. You are not afraid to seek joy with your own."

A Grisk. Seeking joy, with her own. His. *Hers.* And it was enough, somehow, to finally bring her trembling fingers downward. To stroke them lightly, tentatively, against the spread-apart, dripping-wet heat between her parted legs.

Her answering moan was harsh, humiliating, but her entire body had arched with pleasure, her wetness clenching in response, pleading for more. Seeking joy, with its own, so she stroked it again, harder this time, slipping her finger deeper between, drawing the moans louder from her throat.

"Good," the orc's voice hissed, close in her ear. "More. Open it for my kiss."

He'd shifted his body behind her as he spoke, pulling away his knee, and instead revealing—*that.* The shadowy, but unmistakable, sight of his huge, hungry heft, encircled tightly in gold, bulging out bold and brazen toward her slick pink wetness. Wanting this, craving this, just as much as she did. *Open it. My kiss.*

So she did, using her shaky hands to open herself wide, clenching, waiting. While that swollen, dripping, gold-bound vision in the glass slowly moved up, breath by breath, nearly close enough to touch.

And as the sight of this, the longing of this, the sheer fevered aching of this pounded white and wild—suddenly it was like the world screeched still, juddering its truths into place all at once. The orc was Natt, the woman was her, Ella Riddell, Ella of Clan Grisk, just Ella. With her bared body sprawled back against an orc, her legs spread wide, her most secret parts desperately clenching, craving his taking—

It was shocking, outrageous, scandalous, salacious, all the most shameful, miserable parts of Ella lain bare and foul and vulgar—

Until somehow, it—wasn't.

It was only Ella. Here, true, seeking joy with her own. Speaking truth, with every movement, every breath.

And when that gorgeous, gold-bound cock finally came close enough, Ella arched her back against Natt, baring her newly pierced nipple, and—kissed him. Kissed him, *there*, with astonishing lewdness, her greedy pink lips searching and clenching for him, drowning in the glorious hardness of him, seeking to take him inside.

It should have been a shock—but perhaps wasn't at all—when she saw, and actually *felt*, that smooth, swollen slit *kissing back*. That grey cock vibrating erratically as its dripping head sought and delved, almost seeming to meet her kiss with its own. As it slowly, surely, began to sink its way between her kissing lips, disappearing steady and deep into her slick wet heat.

It didn't stop once it started, it couldn't, and Ella's fluttering eyes feasted on the sight. That huge, invading hardness yielding to her kiss, sliding breath by breath into it, deeper and deeper and deeper—until it had entirely vanished up between. Leaving Ella's frantic, greedy, swollen lips to kiss at those bulging bollocks now pressed tight against her, thanks to that hard, uncompromising ring of gold glinting close beneath.

It was without question the most wanton thing Ella had ever seen in her *life*, and nothing else had ever looked so good, or felt so good, and it was like the pleasure was bubbling inside her, churning and boiling, threatening to escape. And she couldn't escape, she never wanted to escape, she was being taken by an orc before a looking-glass, kissing him with screaming abandon, and she never, ever wanted it to stop—

"Fuck me," she was gasping, her entire body shuddering, yearning, on fire. "Fuck me, Natt, fill me, make me a Grisk, yours, please!"

A hard, heated growl burned through his chest, so deep it seemed to vibrate Ella's whole soul—and then he shoved her up close to the glass, pressing her hands flat against it. His strong hands gripping on her waist, holding her there between him and the glass—and at his first full thrust Ella actually screamed, her body pierced, filled to furious bursting—

But even as her own pleasure crashed over her, sending her face in the glass pained and howling, Natt's hunger was still rising, driving into her again and again, holding her there against the glass as if she weighed nothing. And there was only seeing this, taking this, being this, as Ella was viciously, brutally fucked by a huge, fur-and-gold-covered orc, his sharp teeth scraping hard against her neck, his entire muscled body arching, the gold glinting pure and bright between their joined bodies. It was a gift, a ring, a pledge that could never be ripped asunder—

Natt's joy came with an almost deafening roar, howling against Ella's ear, while that invading truth inside her opened wide, and fired. Blasting her in pulse after heated pulse, filling her with his will and his might and his hope and his faith, her Nattfarr of Clan Grisk, her pledge, her own.

Ella's.

She seemed to drift there for a moment, lost in that, in the truth the glass had shown, in the truth of his kiss. And when those hard hands on her skin finally loosened, setting her on her numb, trembly feet, she could only turn, and slide her arms close around his waist, and bury her face into the swift, beautiful thud of his heartbeat.

"I love you, Natt," she breathed. "And I want to stay."

28

She wanted to stay.

Ella's whole body was trembling in his arms, the words echoing relentless through her thoughts—but even as part of her rebelled against them, another part knew they were true. She would give up everything, her inheritance, her reputation, her home— if it meant she could have this. If she could have Natt.

And this time—Ella drew away, enough to blink up at his frozen face—Natt was the one who was shocked. He was the one who couldn't seem to speak, his mouth opening and closing, his eyes gone entirely still with a truth Ella couldn't at all identify.

"I want to stay," she said again, to those eyes. "I'll give up everything. If you'll have me, Natt."

But he was still staring, his eyes so caught, so still—and there was a sound that might have been a laugh, curdling hoarse from his throat. "I fuck you with a cock-ring this one time," he said, "and now you shall give all for me? I ought to have done this many years past, lass."

It was a joke, Natt was making a *joke*, about what that had just been—and it felt like a kick, suddenly, choked and forceful against Ella's chest. Enough that she wrenched away from him, her heart wildly pounding, because what did that mean, what had he just said—

"Wait," Natt breathed, his voice thick, his hands gripping tight on

Ella's arms, drawing her back toward him. "Lass. I ought not—this only"—he squeezed his eyes shut, gave a bracing shake of his head— "you have near felled me, with this. I thought you only wished"—he shook his head again, almost as though it hurt this time—"to play at being my mate. I thought this was—a game, for you. Only pleasure. Before you return to your *real* life."

A game. *Pleasure.* Ella blinked at him, uncomprehending, because surely he must have seen it was more than that, surely she'd said something, surely—but as she frantically cast her thoughts backwards, there was the comprehension, hurtling and astonishingly cruel, that perhaps she hadn't. At least not openly, but Natt had always been so intuitive, so understanding, all the things he'd said, *Show me what is mine, show me you are a Grisk...*

"I have," Ella began, but then gathered her courage, looked him in the eye. She could speak truth. She could.

"I have—struggled, with this," she said, slowly. "With weighing the rest of my life, and everything I thought I wanted, against you. And I still"—she took another breath—"I still want my home. I still want to honour my father's last wishes, and to grant our family's lands to his grandchildren. And I'm scared of what happens next with Alfred, and this war. But—"

Natt was staring at her, his eyes drawing out her truth, and Ella drew in another breath, and kept speaking. "But beyond all that, Natt—I want *you*. I love you. And I will give up everything else, to keep loving you, and being with you, like this."

The look in Natt's eyes was so distant, and again so wrong, that it almost hurt to see—but Ella held her gaze there anyway, waiting, while her heart beat faster, wilder, desperate. What was he thinking. What was wrong.

"But a life here with me, *Ella*," Natt said, and that was wrong too, he never called her that, ever, "is not only playing and fucking, as we have these past days. It is hard choices. It is risking all for truth, and justice. It is being alone, being hunted, and facing *death*. It is you"—he stepped forward, his eyes suddenly glittering, almost angry—"risking all to bear my sons. To carry on my gift for the years and wars to come."

But Ella swallowed, nodded, kept her eyes to his. "Yes," she said. "I know, Natt. I will."

The wrongness was still there, still glittering, still so breathtakingly alarming—but without warning Natt clutched for Ella, and roughly yanked her into his arms. His grip against her so tight it was painful, his body rocking back and forth, his face pressed to the top of her head.

"You honour me, lass," he whispered. "I have never *dreamed* that you should one day speak these truths to me."

Ella could feel herself slowly relaxing, the jagged tension unspooling deep under her skin, and even more when Natt's oddly shaky hands drew her face up, and he gave her one of his sweet, succulent, filthy kisses. And then went back to holding her again, so tight she thought she might break, but there was only relief, only sinking into it, into him. He did want her, after all. It would be *fine*.

"We must needs speak more of this tonight," Natt said firmly. "But I am now late for my first Revel. Shall you"—he drew back, his eyes blinking—"come join me there, and stand bravely by my side, and greet my brothers with kindness and with truth? As a sworn Speaker's mate would?"

Ella nodded, and even tried for a smile, and Natt slowly smiled back, sharp-toothed, true. And then grasped for his lamp and led her toward the door, leaving yet another unholy mess in the storage-room behind them.

"So what's the reason for the ring, anyway?" Ella made herself ask, as they walked. "To impress all your subjects with your alarmingly large genitalia?"

She'd cast a furtive, appreciative glance down toward Natt's kilt, which was still noticeably tented in front, but he only laughed, and shook his head. "Did you not see, my filthy lass," he said, "what the reason for this was? Did you not see yourself squealing in the glass for me?"

Ella elbowed him in the side, and he elbowed back, and it was enough to drain away almost the rest of the tension, almost. "But if it's for me," she said, "or your mate, or whoever—why wear it before your kin, to your Revel, like this?"

It was a moment before Natt replied, their matching steps silent on the stone floor. "It is, in our tales," he said slowly, "a way to honour one's mate, and to enforce one's pledge, and one's fealty. A Grisk's mate places this ring upon him, marking him as her own, and in return he only bestows his gifts upon her. Their scent is untainted by any other, their sons and their joy only their own."

Oh. So that moment, in that room, before that looking-glass, *had* been more than just pleasure. It had been to enforce their pledge, and their fealty. And if Natt had known that, and perhaps even felt that too, why had he dismissed it afterwards, in a way that had felt so uncommonly cruel, from him?

But there was no time to question it, because they'd reached what Ella now knew to be the Grisk common-room, which seemed to be spilling orcs and noise out into the corridor. And when Natt ushered Ella through the door, it was like the party suddenly exploded to life around them, swarming with sound and colour and laughter.

The large, firelit room was filled with dozens of Grisk orcs, all seeming to be talking and moving at once. Many of the orcs were eating—there was a table piled with food to one side—and some were playing games, or wrestling and sparring together. And in the far corner, there was even music, as two orcs pounded out elaborate rhythms on a set of huge, hide-covered drums, while a group of listening orcs nodded and stomped along.

But most interesting of all, perhaps—and when had Ella begun to find this *interesting*, rather than shocking?—were the orcs who were taking their pleasure together, without secrecy or shame. There was the massive Simon orc, sprawled upon a bench, with an unfamiliar orc kneeling between his legs. There was Baldr, with his eyes squeezed shut and his back against a wall, while the tall Drafli orc pinned him there, his dark head bent deep into his neck. And there, across the room, were even Stella and Silfast, Stella facing Silfast on his lap, her flimsy robe already falling down her back as she ground and arched against him.

It meant there were at least a few orcs from every clan here, beyond just the Grisk—and a sidelong glance at Natt showed him looking almost stunned by that fact, his eyes darting from Baldr and Drafli, to Simon, to Silfast. And then to even John, who was leaning against a nearby wall with his arms crossed, and an unmistakably pained look in his dark eyes—but as Ella watched, his gaze flicked to meet Natt's, his head giving a curt little nod.

Suddenly a shrill whistle rent the air—it was Thrak, standing across the room, with both fingers in his mouth—and in response, the room's blaring noise juddered to a halt. As the mass of partying orcs seemed to turn toward Natt and Ella, all at once.

There was silence, for an instant—and then a shout, and then another. And then a slowly rising chorus of cheers, along with clapping hands and stomping feet. The orcs were applauding, for *Natt*. For the orc who would soon be their Speaker, after he'd suffered so many years of hunting, and hiding, and misery.

Ella's eyes were prickling, and she willingly went as Natt drew her deeper into the room. He was nodding and smiling, speaking thanks to his well-wishers in black-tongue, while also guiding Ella steadily toward an empty couch, set slightly apart from the rest of the revelling. And as they approached, Ella realized that Natt's guard was already standing around behind it, waiting.

"Thank you, my brothers," Natt said to them, earning a nod from Dammarr, and genuine grins from the other three. And when Varinn waved at the empty couch before them, Ella could see Natt's shoulders rise and fall, his throat convulsing. And again there was the appreciation, sudden and fervent, of how important this was to him. How weighty this moment was.

So Ella watched, her smile slowly broadening, as Natt strode for the couch, and turned, and sat. Looking, for a jarring, twitching instant, like a wild warlord, a fierce devastating king—and behind her multiple orcs were cheering again, shouting in black-tongue, while the drumbeat shuddered loud and celebratory through the room.

Natt again nodded, and smiled, and raised his arms in thanks—and when his gaze sweeping the room finally settled on Ella's grinning face, it was like those eyes crackled, fusing with warmth and approval. And that slight jerk of his head meant *come*, so Ella did, moving as gracefully as she could to sit at his side, leaning close into his powerful bright safety.

"I thank you, my Grisk brothers, and our guests," Natt's voice said, deep and carrying, once the cheers had faded. "It shall honour me to Speak with you this night. In the way of my father, and his fathers before him, I shall meet all you ask, and ask you all you wish. You only must approach me, and Speak."

There was another round of stomps and cheers, and then the odd sense of the room stilling, as if waiting for someone to approach him. But no one did, not yet, and again Ella could almost taste the unease, the whispering fear. The dual-edged weight of this strange role of Natt's, commanding all this respect and honour, and so much mistrust and loneliness.

And before she quite knew what she'd done, Ella had leapt to her feet, and stood tall before Natt's seated form. He was blinking at her, betraying an unmistakable surprise, but she was doing this now, and she swallowed, and gave her best curtsey.

"You honour us all, wise Nattfarr, rightful Speaker of Clan Grisk," she said, as loudly as she dared. "My question for you is"—she took a breath, was she really going to say this, she was—"do you love me?"

The room had fallen almost entirely silent, and Ella was suddenly, deeply aware of all the eyes on her, on him. Of the fact that perhaps she'd just put herself, or Natt, into a potentially disastrous situation, because what if this wasn't what one was supposed to do, what if he said no, what if he refused to answer—

Natt's eyes hadn't betrayed anything, not approval or disapproval, but his hand beckoned toward Ella, saying, *come closer*. So she did, and here was the sheer relief of Natt's fingers cupping her face, his eyes holding steady to hers. Speaking truth.

"Ach, my lass," he said, quiet, but still enough to carry. "I have loved you for half my life."

Oh. *Oh.* The relief and the pleasure were alive, swarming through Ella all at once, and when she hurled itself at him, her arms clinging around his fur-covered back, thankfully there were only chuckles behind them, and a rising murmur of voices. And Natt, Natt was holding her tight and close, his face bent into her neck, and that meant he approved, he was glad she'd done it. Even if she'd asked—*that.*

"Sorry if I should have waited," Ella murmured as she pulled away, sliding back into her seat beside him. "Or if I put you in an uncomfortable position."

But Natt only shot her a rueful smile, twitching with a tolerant, affectionate warmth. "You have done just what you are meant to," he said. "You asked me a heavy question, a tricky question, that I was now bound to answer, before all my kin."

Ella smiled back at him, and fought to ignore the whispering unease—why was that such a tricky question, if what he'd given was his true answer?—as another orc broke from the crowd to stride toward them. It was Baldr, Ella realized, and she could almost feel Natt's surprise beside her. And then his appreciation, that the captain's powerful Left Hand would so openly show his support of Natt's rightful place as Speaker, before all these watching eyes.

"Brother," Baldr said with a nod toward Natt, as he stepped close, to the same place Ella had been. "I wish to know where your loyalty shall lie, once you gain the title of Speaker. Shall it be only to the Grisk?"

The room had hushed again, listening, for this surely was a tricky question, perhaps planted by Grimarr himself—but Natt only raised his hand up to Baldr's face. And when their gazes locked, Ella could feel the strength of Natt's magic this time, stuttering into the air between them.

"When I am Speaker," Natt said, his voice low, smooth, utterly compelling, "my fealty shall be to all who call this mountain home. I shall always care for my Grisk kin, but a Speaker must strive most of all for justice and for truth, no matter who speaks this, or needs this."

Baldr gave a slow nod, clearly approving of Natt's answer, but then his head tilted, his eyes still held to Natt's. "And what, Nattfarr," he said, "do you most long for, when you are Speaker?"

It was another tricky question, one that set Ella's heartbeat rising, every eye in the room watching, waiting—but Natt's gaze didn't falter. "I long most of all for a son," he said, quieter than before. "I long to carry on my father's name, and his gifts, after my death."

Oh. None of the watching orcs seemed surprised by that—sons were surely a common theme among them—but Ella felt almost struck by that confession, that truth. Natt wanted a *son* most of all? More than anything else? He had never told her that, had he?

But there was no time to ask, because once Baldr had turned away, there were more orcs standing behind him, waiting. The first of these was the huge Bautul orc Olarr, surveying Natt with skeptical eyes—but came a step closer, squared his shoulders, and met Natt's gaze.

"Before all my clan," he said, his voice deep and gravelly, "I wish to speak of my grief for the price our young Speaker paid, to gain safety among my kin. I offer you my pledge to help right this wrong."

Ella could feel Natt's disbelief beside her, his eyes blinking, his body gone very still. "I accept your pledge, Olarr the Fearsome, of Clan Bautul," he said finally. "And I thank you, for speaking this truth."

Olarr bowed his shaggy head, and then stepped away, ceding his place to the next orc in the line. And this one, to Ella's vague surprise, was John. His handsome head tilting, his mouth pursed, and Ella gained the distinct impression that this was a fulfillment of his intellectual curiosity, more than anything else.

"Nattfarr," he said, meeting his eyes, and again Ella could feel Natt's magic lock and hold between them. "I wish you to ask a question of me. For what do I wish most?"

This was also a trick question, without doubt, but Natt nodded, and brought a hand to John's face, drawing him closer. "John of Clan Ka-esh, Last of the Ka, and rightful Priest of Orc Mountain," he said, his voice slow and deliberate. "What do you most wish for?"

"I wish also," came John's reply, immediate, "for a son. And a clever mate, to help me raise him in the way of the Ka."

His eyes blinked, several times, as though he'd been surprised by his own answer—but Natt only nodded, holding his gaze. "Ach, a wise wish," he said gravely. "To gain this, mayhap you shall also finally hear my wish to place lamps in our mountain, to make our mates at home."

John's throat visibly swallowed, his clawed hands clenching at his sides, but his eyes were still fixed to Natt's, caught. "But what if I spend this time, and these resources, on lamps," he said, "and the women do not come. Or what if I spend this and the women come, and die"—his mouth spasmed—"because I did not spend enough on our learning, to keep them safe."

His fists were visibly trembling, now, his eyes alarmingly wide on Natt's face, and Natt gave a slow, watchful nod. "I know this fear also, my brother," he said. "But we must be brave enough to yet seek a better way for our kin, and face our own pain and loss, when it comes."

With that, Natt looked away, squeezing his eyes shut, breaking the spell. Leaving John standing there, blinking hard—and without another word, he spun around, and strode straight toward the door.

While Natt watched him go, his eyes hinting at darkness, at something Ella couldn't follow.

But there again wasn't time to ask, because Natt's attention had already shifted to the next group of orcs before him. His guard, all four of them, clustered close, waiting.

"What do you believe is our greatest threat," was Varinn's question, his earnest eyes trapped to Natt's without the slightest hesitation. "What do you fear will be our downfall."

Natt hesitated, and Ella fully expected him to say the men, the war, Alfred, coming here *tomorrow*—but he didn't. "I fear we will fall to our lies," he said finally. "I fear we will smile and laugh and play"—his hand waved broad to the room—"and pay no heed to our true grief and pain and loss, and to the ways these must be met, and learnt from. I fear we will not learn to face our truths, and that they shall then rise to devour us, unawares."

Varinn nodded, drawing back in silence, and Ella felt herself nodding too. Thinking, disjointed, of how brilliant Natt had always been, how considering and thoughtful, even as he'd also been wild and carefree and laughing. And even this moment seemed to reflect that, as Thrak came up, and coolly demanded that Natt tell him the dirtiest joke he knew, to which Natt snapped something back in black-tongue, and all five orcs laughed.

"Ask me about the best fuck of my life," was Thrain's grinning question, to which Natt easily nodded, and gamely repeated the question toward him. But rather than freely answering, Thrain twitched and choked, his face suddenly drained of colour. And Ella could see his eyes straining and bulging, as if he sought to look away from Natt, but couldn't.

"The best fuck of my life," Thrain said, his voice a monotone, "was when Varinn and I drank too much old berry-juice, and got lost in the catacombs, and he ploughed me until I screamed on the graves of our forefathers."

Natt had abruptly broken the eye contact, leaving Thrain shaking his head and grimacing toward Varinn, whose face had gone deathly pale. While Thrak looked back and forth between them, the disbelief rising in his eyes. "You're serious?" he demanded. "When? Why'd you never say?"

But the distinctly ill look on Varinn's face was clearly why he hadn't said, and Thrain's eyes were on Varinn too, his mouth still grimacing. "Sorry, brother," he said, and Ella couldn't tell which one he spoke to, or perhaps it was both. "I swore I wouldn't tell. And then did all I could to hide the scent."

But Varinn had already turned and stalked off, leaving Thrain to blink, and then rush off after him, with Thrak close behind. While beside Ella, Natt looked both pained and amused—at least until Dammarr walked up, his eyes glinting with a chilly, watching danger.

"Shall I have you ask me this same question, brother?" he asked coolly. "I ken you shall know my answer before I do."

Natt's whole form had gone hard and guarded, his eyes settling angry on Dammarr's. "You must ask what you wish," he said flatly. "But then, I must ask whether I wish to keep an orc such as this on my guard—or even keep calling him my brother—when he seeks to further harm a blameless, foolish woman who has done *naught* but seek to please me, and honour me!"

Ella blinked, and there was suddenly an odd, prickling ice up her back. A blameless, foolish woman? *Further* harm?

But neither orc was looking at her, their eyes locked together, something Ella couldn't at all follow passing between them. And when Dammarr spoke again, this time it was in black-tongue, and Natt hissed back in kind, before Dammarr abruptly turned, and strode away.

"What did you mean, Natt?" Ella heard herself ask, very quiet, to where he was still frowning at Dammarr's retreating back. "About further harming me? And do you"—she drew in a shaky breath—"do you truly still think I'm foolish? Even after I've told you all my truth, and offered to *stay*?"

Natt turned to blink at her, almost as though he'd forgotten she was there—and he belatedly smiled, and gave a rapid shake of his head. "You ought to pay no heed to my angry words, lass," he said. "I am the fool, when it comes to my brother, to allow him to stir my ire thus."

He turned away then, smiling at the next orc before him, a Grisk whose name Ella knew, but couldn't quite recall, in this moment.

Because instead, her shouting brain was trapped on the memory, only seconds ago, of Natt holding Dammarr's eyes, and saying those words.

He'd been speaking truth, to Dammarr, of her. And he'd called Ella foolish. He'd spoken of further harm. *Further.*

And as orc after orc walked up, asking Natt questions both banal and weighty, personal and impersonal, Ella made every effort to smile, and welcome each orc by name, and hear their truths with respect and kindness. But that memory kept swirling, screaming at her, and joining it now were other ones, ones she'd perhaps forgotten, until this moment.

I betray my own soul. He too often robs himself. At least we'll finally get some *reward out of this whole farce.*

And then, swirling stronger still, were all the truths that had gone unsaid. Why Natt hadn't told her about Alfred's coming, why he hadn't even wanted her to *speak* about Alfred. Why he hadn't said he loved her. Why he hadn't asked her to be his mate.

Why he hadn't asked her to stay.

But this was Natt's first Revel, this was his moment, so Ella waited, and smiled, and greeted the orcs, and waited. While she could feel the weariness creeping into Natt's form, the slowly rising tension—but instead of touching him, or seeking to set him at ease, or make him smile, she only sat there, pretending, waiting, lying.

And when the final orc finally walked away, and the party all around had risen into an almost-deafening hubbub of carousing orcs, Ella made herself turn, and smile up into Natt's tired eyes.

"Could I have one more question?" she asked, her breath only slightly hitching. "Please?"

Natt's eyes had gone suddenly wary, but he gave a slow, careful nod. And Ella nodded too, and this time climbed up into his lap, straddling him, stroking her shaky hands against the soft fur covering his arms. Looking into his beautiful eyes, into the orc she loved, her oldest, best, dearest friend. As she dragged for courage, bravery, she had to face her truth, before it rose to devour her, unawares...

"I beg you to speak truth, Nattfarr of Clan Grisk," she said, very quiet. "Of how you have betrayed me."

29

Even now, Ella hoped she was wrong. Prayed she was wrong, begged all the gods for it, silently desperately pleading, while she held Natt's staring, blinking eyes.

But he wasn't denying it. He wasn't denying it, he wasn't saying anything, and his face, his face looked suddenly ashen, deathlike, wrong.

"Why," he said finally, his voice a croak, "do you ask this."

The hurt and the misery swirled up with sickening force, and Ella fought her way through them, fought for air, for words. "You said," she whispered, "if we hid the truth, it will rise up, and—and *devour* us, Natt."

Her breath was gulping, her eyes searching his face, and all he had to do was say, *No, I would never harm you*, like he had before, that time—

Or had he? *I should never* wish *to harm you*, he'd said. *Foolish lass. You know not what you ask for. You know not what I shall want from you. What vengeance we shall take.*

Ella's head was shaking, her hands fluttering up to cover her open mouth, because dear gods, he'd already told her. He'd already said it, again and again. She was foolish. He'd only been in this for vengeance, all along.

It was a *farce*, Dammarr had said.

The room seemed to be slowly spinning around them, the voices and drums far too loud in Ella's ringing ears, and her body was badly trembling, her stomach churning. And she should get up, she should run, but where was there to go, why couldn't she move—

"Lass," said Natt's voice, hoarse and deep, and she realized that she was still staring at him, still caught on his lap, still ensnared in his truth-spell. "Listen to this. These days with you have been a great joy. A bright gift to me. You have shown yourself kind and loyal and hungry and sweet and true. You have honoured me again and again. But—"

His chest was heaving, his eyes squeezing shut, but Ella was still held, still lost, waiting. "But this is not enough," he said, every word a choking, dizzying thud. "I do not"—his chest heaved again—"I do not wish you to stay."

What? Ella felt herself flinch all over, the partying room juddering sharply, wildly sideways. "You don't?" she heard her wavering voice ask. "But *why*, Natt?"

His eyes were still closed, and she could see his jaw clenching, his entire body gone rigid beneath her. "I do not," he said, "believe that you are the right match for the Speaker of the Grisk. You are a good woman, but you are not the woman who ought to carry on our gift to our sons."

The disbelief was shouting, suddenly, warring with the hurt and the misery. And somehow Ella was clinging to him, gripping her hands in his furs, fighting and failing to shake his huge, unmoving body.

"*Why*," she heard her voice say. "Why aren't I, Natt. I learned to speak truth to you, I've eagerly welcomed you and learned from you, I shared your bed, I gave you my *maidenhead*, I'm wearing your *clothes*, I let you—I even let you *pierce* me, I told you I'd give up everything. I *kept* my *pledge*, Natt!"

Her shrill, rising voice was drowned out by the party all around, but Natt had to have heard, even with his face gone so still, his eyes now intently blinking past her. "I am sorry, lass," he said, choked. "It is not yet enough. I wish you to leave here, and go back to your home, with your betrothed, come morning."

He wanted her to go? Tomorrow? With—with *Alfred*? It was like Ella was falling, sinking into an ever-deepening hole, a curse, a nightmare, and she felt the fear wildly lurching, her head shaking, her hands shaking, everything shaking, why couldn't she wake up, why—

"You are yet dear to me, lass," Natt's hitching voice said. "I shall never forget the joy you have brought me. Mayhap we shall yet be—friends, after this."

Friends. And it was that one word, suddenly, that set the nightmare stark against the truth, and Ella's trembly hands grasped for his face, and fought to turn it toward her. "No," she choked at him. "You're—you're *lying* to me, Natt. Look me in the eye, and say all that again."

But his face was a mask, his eyes so wrong, he was lying, *why* was he lying. "I am weary," he said, his voice thick. "My Speaking is worn, from all this use. I can do no more tonight."

Lying, lying, and Ella's head was frantically shaking, her twitchy hands coming to press over Natt's mouth. The mouth that had kissed her, tasted her, drunk her, demanded her truth, the rightful Speaker of the Grisk, her oldest dearest friend, *lying*—

"Stop," she choked, and dear gods she was weeping now, the wetness streaking down her cheeks. "Stop, Natt. Don't do this to me. Please."

But he was, and the look in his eyes said he was going to keep doing it, and why had he done this, what was happening, why, why, *why*—

Ella stumbled off him, backwards, staggering so badly she nearly fell—but then, somehow, she was running. Ducking her head as she weaved for the door, dodging the masses of huge, partying orcs. And then almost barrelling straight into one, into *Dammarr*, and even as she physically recoiled, he was still a Grisk, he was still Natt's guard, his *real* friend, maybe—

"Would you please," she gulped at him, "take me to Jule? And the captain? *Please*?"

Dammarr gave a dark glance over Ella's shoulder, and for an instant she was sure he would refuse, mock her, laugh—but finally he jerked a nod, and strode out of the room. Leaving Ella to follow blindly behind him into the pitch-black corridor, straining to hear his footsteps in the utter emptiness. And here was the dull realization that Natt had so rarely taken her anywhere without a lamp, she had never before had to do this, stumbling first this way and that, her hands and shoulders scraping painfully against unyielding stone.

"Ach, women," Dammarr's voice muttered beside her, as a warm hand clamped around her arm, and guided her down the corridor. "If my brother rails at me for placing my scent upon you, you must tell him it was your doing."

Ella could only gulp for air, shake her head, dash at the constant surge of wetness pooling from her eyes. "He won't care," she gasped. "He said I wasn't good enough. He wants to send me—*away*. Tomorrow. With *Alfred*."

There was a distinctive snort from Dammarr, a tightening of that hand on her arm. "You are a foolish woman," he said flatly. "He ought to send you away, if you believe this as truth."

"I *don't* believe him," Ella's wavering voice countered. "But what else am I supposed to do, I'm not a Speaker, I can't make him tell me the truth, why has he been *lying* to me!"

Her voice was far too high-pitched, echoing in the blackness all around, and she could hear Dammarr give a harsh, impatient sigh. "You are a foolish, fickle, cosseted, selfish human," he said. "And you are betrothed to the man who has destroyed my brother's *life*."

"I am *not* betrothed to that man," Ella hissed back, without thinking. "No matter what happens now, I will *never* marry that man. I made a pledge to *Natt*!"

Dammarr's steps seemed to falter, at perhaps the same time Ella's had, and she blinked her unseeing eyes into the darkness. Did she mean that? Truly? She would never marry Alfred, ever, no matter what?

But yes, yes, that was true, and Ella bit her lip and waited until Dammarr started walking again, drawing her along behind him. Not speaking, not even acknowledging that she'd said anything, and she blinked at the floor, again and again, until he finally pulled her around a corner, into—light.

The light was from a little fire, in a cozy little stone room, which featured Jule lying long on a couch, her legs and lips parted, her cheeks flushed a deep pink. While her huge, hideous captain mate knelt beside her, his head bent to her rounded belly, his hand spread wide over it.

It had clearly been leading to something, but they were both still dressed, and they both rose up at once, Grimarr's eyes wary, Jule's full of sudden concern. "Ella!" she said. "What's wrong?"

The genuine worry in her face and her voice had Ella very close to bawling again, and she gulped for air. "Natt's been l-lying to me," she said. "I—I think he's betrayed me. I c-can't trust him. I can't trust *anyone*."

Jule's eyes had closed, in something looking like pain, and Ella felt her own eyes settle on Grimarr beside her. The Captain of the Orcs, of all five clans, who Natt had struggled against all these years, who had left him to *die*. *You seek to force me to do your bidding*, Natt had told him, *and betray my own soul.*

And maybe, Ella realized, with another blinding flare of truth, Natt's vengeance hadn't just been upon Alfred. My *enemies*, he'd called them, more than once, and maybe that had been these enemies too. His own *kin*, who fought to keep truth hidden and safe, until it rose up to devour them all.

"You know the truth," Ella hissed, to Grimarr's wary, watching eyes. "You know what Natt's not telling me. And unless you want me to run out there, and urge my former betrothed to launch this new war against you, *you will speak truth to me.*"

30

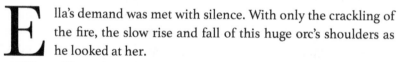

Ella's demand was met with silence. With only the crackling of the fire, the slow rise and fall of this huge orc's shoulders as he looked at her.

"You will speak truth to me," Ella said again, into the silence, her voice cracking. "Unless you want me to start this war. *Tell me.*"

Beside him Jule had leaned up, quickly murmuring something in his pointed ear. And when Grimarr still didn't move, Jule turned back to Ella, and gave her a sharp nod. "He *will* tell you," she said, clipped. "And whatever it is, he ought to have told you from the start. Don't you agree, Grimarr?"

Grimarr sighed again, but he nodded too, his big arms crossing over his chest as he met Ella's eyes. "Here is truth, woman," he said. "I sent Nattfarr to you, on this night of your party. His quest was to rebuild a mating-bond with you, and seek to sire a son upon you."

Ella's feet felt rooted to the floor, and there was a distant pounding in her skull, constant, throbbing, terrifying. "Natt came to me on *your* orders?" her faint voice echoed. "To do—*that*? But *why*?"

But she knew, curse this awful orc, she knew before he even spoke. "Lord Tovey seeks to use your hoard to fire a new war against us," Grimarr said slowly. "We thus sought to forestall this, and remove your wealth from his hands."

We. *Natt.* Natt had come to Ella that night on Grimarr's orders. Natt had wanted to build a *mating-bond* with her. Sire a *son* upon her. Natt had done all this, all his laughter and affection and soft filthy kisses, because of—Ella's *money.*

Just like Alfred.

And here were the images, hurling across Ella's thoughts in a cruel, constant, dizzying stream. All Natt's smiles, his sweet words, his warm hands, his beautiful fluid body, his truth. *We shall have this now, you belong with me, you shall speak truth to me, my sweet pretty lass...*

"I—I don't understand," Ella heard her shaky voice whisper, sounding very far away. "Why would Natt do that to me. For *you.*"

Her churning, screeching thoughts were suddenly stuck on that, tripping on it over and over again, because surely Natt wouldn't have done such a thing for Grimarr, for the orc who'd been so callous to him, surely it was all some kind of horrible mistake—

But Grimarr's slow, heavy sigh was like a blow, struck straight against Ella's heart. "I swore to make Nattfarr Speaker of the Grisk," Grimarr said, "once he proved to me that he had done this."

Oh. *Oh.* And in a breath everything crumpled all at once, Ella's heart Ella's hopes, even the world behind her eyes, under her feet—

But before her staggering body could sink to the floor, there was warmth, strength, familiar hands spreading wide. *Natt.* He was *here.* And for a jolting, hurtling instant Ella let herself sag into him, he was here, she was safe—

But no, no, he'd *betrayed* her, and Ella's flailing arms suddenly thrust at him, clawed at him, away, away—and somehow she'd been set down onto the couch, her entire body wildly trembling, her eyes blinking again and again up at Natt's pale, staring face. Wrong. *Guilty.*

"You came back to me," a voice gasped, someone else's voice, choking from Ella's mouth. "You made love to me, made me believe you cared about me—so you could get a *promotion?!*"

Something flared across Natt's eyes, and there was a hoarse noise in his throat, rattling, wrong. "It is not a *promotion,*" his voice said, so distant, so strange. "It is my rightful place among my kin. It is what I have been owed, since my father's death."

The world was stuttering again, so badly Ella couldn't speak, couldn't keep her eyes on his face, and beyond them there was another noise, this one more like a snarl. "You were not owed this, Nattfarr," came a deep voice, Grimarr's voice. "You are not just granted this, because of your father. We are not like the men, with power and titles thrown at foolish weak sons. You needed to *earn* this."

Ella could hear Natt snarling back, but Grimarr's growl was louder, and he stalked across the room, his body huge and coiled and deadly. "Leading our brothers in a time such as this means we must make hard choices, Nattfarr," his deep voice hissed. "We must choose our brothers over our own wishes again and again. You had not yet shown me that you could do this, so I set you a hard choice."

A hard choice. Doing this had been a *hard choice*, for Natt. And Natt hadn't spoken, wasn't denying or affirming that, and somehow Ella raised her wet face toward Grimarr, and desperately sought for truth.

"So this was about more than just the war?!" she heard her incredulous voice say. "This was some kind of *test* for him? Your own brother, who you already allowed to be hunted, for *years*?!"

There was another harsh growl from Grimarr, a furious shake of his black head. "You have not dealt with my *brother* all these years," he snapped at her. "Nattfarr has shown himself oft petty, selfish, ungrateful, and short-sighted. He scorns those above him, wields his magic as a weapon, and assumes power he has not been granted. And most foolish of all, he drives deep wedges between his own brothers. He smears the Skai and Bautul, and holds up Grisk above all else."

But Ella's head was shaking, the unfairness of that still curdling, even now. "If you had had the bravery to come to his Revel tonight, you would have heard that he does not," she shot back. "And even if he did, could he truly be blamed for feeling that way? Or have you forgotten how the Bautul abused him, after *you* sent him there?! And the Skai seem to be fine with that sort of thing, too!"

She was thinking of Timo, of his pale quivering face in the corridor, but Grimarr only growled again, deep and angry. "They are not," he snapped. "And Nattfarr knows this, which is why he spoke as he did in the Skai common-room, this day past. And"—he turned sharply toward Natt—"I shall always regret what befell you in the south. But I did not know of this then, and my aim was only ever to help you. To keep you alive. And not once have you thanked me, or come alongside me as a brother. You have only fought me at every turn!"

And Ella was not looking at Natt, she was *not*—but suddenly his form seemed small, cowed, alone. And he still wasn't speaking, wasn't defending himself against any of this *rubbish*, so Ella again shook her head, hugged herself close. "Of course he's fought you," she countered. "Because you let him be hunted all these years, and apparently even forbade him to lift a weapon to defend himself!"

"Ach, I did," Grimarr hissed back, "because this was what had to be done, to keep our brothers safe, and keep away more war and death. I should be a weak, shameful captain to allow the Grisk to be led by an angry, untested, unthinking fool. I needed to know that he would not lead them to ruin, to gain his own ends. I needed to know that he would put the wishes and needs of his brothers over his own!"

His voice had risen to a roar, almost seeming to shudder the room, and there was only a choked, deafening silence in its wake. But then, in the silence, Natt slowly seemed to draw himself tall, his head lifting, his eyes steady on Grimarr's, unafraid.

"And I did this," he said, very quiet. "I betrayed my own soul, and I did this. I faced the scent of the man I most hate, upon the woman I most love. I kept my true aims secret from her, and earned her maidenhood for my own. And when I saw I could not yet fill her with my son, I then took her in the night, against her will, in hopes of gaining this. I wreaked all these wrongs upon her, Captain, just as you wished."

He spoke the last words with an emptiness Ella had never before heard on his voice, and it was wrong, so wrong, so ugly Ella felt sick. But Grimarr still wasn't satisfied, he was still looming and angry and cruel, his head still whipping back and forth.

"Ach," he growled, "you *kidnapped* her. Without leave, without my blessing. You went well beyond my orders, and broke the human laws, and risked our treaty, and wished another *war* upon our mountain! And then you strode in here as though you had won a shiny new prize, and dressed her up like a make-believe, scent-bound Grisk mother who lived only to worship you! You again sought to provoke me, and flaunt your power before your brothers, and show that you are petty and foolish and care only for your own!"

But Natt's stiff form still hadn't moved, his hands in tight fists at his sides. "No," he said, chilly, brittle, *wrong*, his gaze unflinching on Grimarr's face. "I show you that I know these games you play,

Grimarr of Clan Ash-Kai, Captain of Five Clans. I show you that I am your match, and I shall always be a thorn to you, and you shall never find a better Speaker than I to check you. I show you"—he took a slow, steady step toward Grimarr—"that I can survive this darkness, I can make these choices, I can earn both the fear and trust of our brothers. I can earn the eager fealty of a good woman of high standing, even after I have betrayed her, and thus wreak my vengeance upon a man I hate more than any upon this earth. Just—like—*you, Captain.*"

And as Ella stared at Natt, her entire being caught on his body and his face and his words, there was the dull, bitter understanding that he *was* this. Natt, her oldest and dearest friend, had somehow become this, speaking these horrifying truths. A stranger.

And why had Ella ever trusted him. Why had she so blindly believed what he'd shown her. Why had she given him her—*eager fealty*, he'd said. She was a woman of *high standing*—good gods, in another world, she might have laughed at that odious phrase—and she was vengeance. And that was all.

She was a fool.

"That is *more* than enough, you two," a distant voice said, Jule's voice, almost vibrating with rage. "We are going to *talk*, Grimarr. And Nattfarr, you need to fucking *beg* for Ella to have mercy upon us all, and then stay the hell away from her, before you traumatize her even more than you already have. You unfeeling *pricks*."

No one spoke, or moved, and Jule dragged both hands through her hair, and turned back toward Grimarr. "So what happens now," she snapped. "What orc-induced *bullshit* does Ella get to deal with next."

There was another instant's silence, and finally another sigh from Grimarr's huge form. "The woman must go," he said, his eyes fixed to the wall behind Ella's head. "This man is yet her betrothed, for now. And as she pledged, she shall defend us to him, and deny that Nattfarr has kidnapped her."

Ella's body flinched all over, her eyes blinking down at her visibly trembling hands, gripping sweaty against her bare knees. "And if I don't?" she whispered. "Go to Alfred? Or defend you to him?"

"Then you shall give him all the cause he needs to spark his war at once," came Grimarr's immediate reply. "You shall wear a mountain full of blood on your hands. *Nattfarr's* blood."

Ella's gasp of misery was reflexive, desperate. "But by going away with Alfred," she choked out, "won't I start a war then, too?"

There was an awful, hanging silence, during which no one spoke, not even Jule—but finally Grimarr sighed. "War may yet come," he said. "But it shall have naught to do with you. And it shall have none of your hoard behind it."

Ella's eyes squeezed shut, while the comprehension finally blared with sickening, staggering force. The orcs had gotten their way, in this, after all. *Natt* had gotten his way.

Because Ella didn't *want* to marry Alfred anymore. And more importantly, once she told Alfred she'd come here of her own volition—one she insisted, again and again, to everyone who asked, that she hadn't been kidnapped after all—Alfred certainly wouldn't want *her*. Alfred would never touch her again, let alone publicly *marry* her, after she'd spent all this time in Orc Mountain, making love to an orc. Allowing an orc to take her maidenhead, to pierce her *nipple*, even— her shaky hand came up to her neck, felt at where Natt's teeth had gently scraped again and again—to *mark* her.

No. No man of standing would dare to touch Ella ever again, after this. Not even to gain a fortune.

And had Ella *known* that, all this time? Had *Natt* known that?

There was a sudden flare of movement, flashing before Ella's blinking eyes—and oh dear gods, Natt was here. Here, filling her eyes and her breath, kneeling on the floor before her, his hands fumbling to grasp at hers, clutching her shaky fingers tight and still.

"Please, lass," his low voice choked. "Please. I beg you this. I know I do not deserve this, but please"—his shoulders heaved, his eyes snapping, holding onto hers—"please, grant me this one more gift. Please do not betray us to these men. Do not say I have kidnapped you, or forced you. Say again and again that you came here of your own will. Do all that you can to save my brothers from more war, and more death."

And looking at him like this, begging her like this, her oldest friend with such earnest miserable eyes—it was only more pain, more breaking. He'd built a—*mating-bond*, Grimarr had called it. He was pleading for her mercy, like Jule had said. He was again seeking to use her, to bend her to serve his whims. He'd wreaked these wrongs. He could never be trusted. He was a stranger.

And here in the gaping miserable emptiness, there was only— truth. Only Ella's own soul, cut open, laid bare, true.

So she held herself still, looked at the stranger's familiar beloved eyes, drew a breath. "I did come here of my own will," she whispered. "And I will speak this truth, as many times as I'm asked."

Natt was fervently nodding, his eyes very bright, and there was a sudden, unnerving trickle of blood, from where his sharp tooth was biting his lip. "And you shall go," he whispered. "Even when this foul man no longer wishes for you. Even when you lose your home and your hoard, and all you have longed for."

It was a promise, a cruel merciless pledge, but it was truth, and maybe it was all that was left, in the waste Ella had made of her life. She was a fool. He was a stranger. She should never have trusted him. She was alone, with her truth.

"Yes, Nattfarr of Clan Grisk," she said, quiet, wretched, empty. "I will."

31

Ella walked back to the Grisk wing in silent, echoing darkness. Dammarr again led her there—he'd clearly been waiting outside the room, and had again grasped her wrist as soon as he'd seen her, and began towing her down the black corridor. And in the mess currently clogging Ella's thoughts, there was the dull, sickening realization that he'd known all along. Maybe they all had.

"Why didn't you tell me?" she asked, pathetically, once Dammarr had drawn her into what felt like Natt's rooms, thankfully well away from the noise of the ongoing Revel down the corridor. "You really disliked me that much? Enough to stand back and watch me ruin my whole *life*, and still"—she had to gulp for breath—"taunt me, and belittle me, as you have?"

Dammarr had snapped his claws over a candle, finally flaring light through the constant blackness, and when Ella blinked around, she was in Natt's bedroom, with those lovely carvings of his ancestors all over the walls. But she couldn't bear to look at them, suddenly, and instead she sank her trembly body down to the floor by the bed, and stared blankly at the cool flat stone beneath her.

"I—misjudged you," came Dammarr's voice above her, making her twitch. "I thought this was all a game to you. A whim of a silly, bored, rich woman. I did not know you held such loyalty to my brother."

Ella heard herself sniff, and she wiped at her eyes with her forearm. Truth. She could speak truth, even to this orc. "I *loved* Natt," she whispered. "I missed him so much, all those years he was gone. He's so wise, and generous, and free, and—*alive*. He makes the world around him so bright. He's—"

She couldn't seem to finish, the sobs bubbling dangerously in her throat, and she could hear Dammarr's sigh above her. "Ach," he said slowly. "He is a good orc. He is among the best of us. He does not deserve such cruelty from our captain."

Ella still couldn't speak, and Dammarr sighed again, his clawed foot kicking at the floor before her. "I know it is of no help now," he continued, "but I fought him in this from the start. I knew it should break him, to rebuild this bond with you, and then betray you thus. He was not raised to harm and lie and cheat. He was raised to laugh and love, and lead us with truth and kindness."

Ella was nodding, even as she was still sniffing, wiping again at her eyes. "Well," she croaked, "I hope he might find that again, after this. With whoever he decides to—someone who's good enough to—"

And why was she even thinking these things, why was she saying them to this orc, of all orcs, and she dug her palms into her eyes, so deep it hurt. "With you, maybe," she gritted out. "He truly cares, for you."

There was an instant's pained silence, a shift of Dammarr's body above her. "He cares for you also," he said, voice low. "You ought to have seen his rage when he heard you were betrothed to this man. He did not speak for three days."

But that almost made it worse, somehow, the thought that maybe Natt *had* really cared—dear gods, he'd said he loved her, hadn't he?— and had still done this. That he'd take someone he loved, and gain their love in return, and then turn around and purposely, systematically destroy all they had.

"But he *seduced* me," Ella said, and though she knew it was pitiable, she couldn't seem to stop. "He would have gotten me with *child*, for this horrible test. And if I had even survived the birth, what would have happened then? Would he have taken the child from me? Or would he have abandoned me altogether, and disowned my son, because"—she gave a frantic wave at the wall all around—"we would never be *real* Grisk? Not good enough for him?"

The words were choking out of her, in a humiliating series of rising lurching sobs, but there was no reply from above her. Only a slight shuffle of feet, an odd telltale scent—and when Ella's tear-streaked face snapped up, it was to the bitter, unsurprising sight of—him. Natt. Standing there entirely bared to the room, stripped clean of his furs and his gold. Not the Speaker of the Grisk. Just—him.

"Ach, my lass," he said, his voice a hoarse, broken whisper. "Had I ever been blessed enough to bear a son upon you, I should never have left your side. I should have taken you both, and run, and run, and *run*."

There was a sound like a laugh, ripping out Ella's throat, because of course he would say that now, now that it would never happen. He would lie. He was a stranger. He couldn't be trusted. He valued his brothers, his *promotion*, over her.

"And you *were* good enough, lass," he continued, almost fierce this time. "You *are*. Before I did this, I told myself again and again that you would have changed, you would be an enemy to me, you had chosen to wed this man—but then I found my sweet, laughing, trusting lass still there, just the same, only hiding hurt and afraid beneath. And you came out for me, because I told you this was safe, I pledged this to you. And then I—"

His voice broke off, and he sank to kneel before her, his claws gripping deep into his bare knees. "I ensnared you, and I stole you from your home," he said, very quiet. "And in return, you saved me from my enemies. You tended to me when I was wounded. You vowed to see me safe back to my mountain, even when you knew this risked all your own dreams. And once you were here, when I again pushed you, you only met me in this, and showed me what a true prize you are. You bore my scent and my seed and my jewels without shame. You honoured me and played with me and freely took joy with me. You spoke kindness and bravery to me. You granted me peace like none I have ever tasted, since the day my father died."

Ella's wet eyes were blinking at him, her head shaking, saying no, no, *no*—but Natt's hands snaked out to grasp hers, and they were hot, clammy, sharp. "You showed yourself a true Grisk," he said firmly.

"The best Speaker's mate I could have dreamt of. Not once did you shame me. Not once did you falter. Ach, just tonight, at my Revel, you spoke the name of almost every orc you met, and welcomed them to my side. You are a true gift from the gods, my sweet lass. And I"—he hauled in a breath—"I have harmed you. I have *betrayed* you."

There was only stillness, only emptiness, only those beautiful painful eyes, holding her with desperate truth. "I ought never to have done this," he whispered. "But you must believe, my lass, that I did not wish to do this. I sought to send you away from me, again and again. I sought to warn you, I told you this was goodbye. I told you that you knew not what you wished for. I *told* you the gods should make us pay."

His voice sounded pleading, his eyes glittering bright and broken, but Ella could only keep shaking her head, gulping for air. "Are you—*blaming* me, Natt?" her distant voice choked. "For not—catching your cryptic hints? For wanting to believe that what we had was real?"

And here, looking at those exquisitely agonizing eyes, was more truth, more shame. Ella had *wanted* to believe it. She'd *wanted* to trust him. She'd overlooked so many things, ignored so many questions. She'd been such a fool.

"No," Natt said, his voice flat and fervent, his eyes still intent on hers. "No. I do not blame you. I only wish you to know that it was not only falsehood in my heart. I wish you to know that I longed to warn you, and speak truth to you, and keep you safe. I wish you to know that my love for you is true. I wish you to know"—there was a single line of wetness, streaking from the corner of his eye—"that were this a fairer world, I should have long ago claimed you as my mate, and you should even now be standing tall and bright and brave at my side."

Ella still couldn't speak, could only look, and shake her head, but Natt was nodding, again, again. "But even without this," he whispered, "you yet bear the name Ella, of Clan Grisk. You have always held this, since the day you spoke this pledge to me."

But the words were only more pain, more misery, because it couldn't be true. Ella couldn't trust him, she wasn't, she couldn't.

"But it was vengeance, for you," she gasped. "You said. You *said*, Natt."

Natt was still nodding, and there was another streak of wetness, escaping from his eye. "Ach, I did," he said. "And I shall speak no more falsehoods to you, lass, and thus I shall tell you that this was the sweetest vengeance I have ever tasted. It was joy, to take you from this man, who had taken so much from me. It was joy to make you my own. It was joy to see you bloom and smile and grow hungry under my touch. It was joy to know that no matter how this man hunts me, even if he yet kills me and takes you for his own, he can never, *ever* take this from me."

That was true, that was there in his eyes, and there was a strange rising heat in it, a compulsive wild longing, surging deep and hidden within. Ella was Grisk. She was *his*. That was truth. Wasn't it?

And like always Natt *knew*, his eyes shifting, his hands gripping hers harder, so tight it was pain. "I know I ought not to ask this," he breathed, "but after this is done, will you yet see me, upon your terms? Even if you yet wed this man? May we yet be—friends?"

Friends. That single word, so loaded and cruel and miserable, seemed to set the heat shattering into ice all at once. And even as a distant part of Ella marvelled at it—Natt would still want to be friends, even if she still married *Alfred*?—she couldn't dare face it, couldn't trust him, please—

"You—you said we couldn't be friends," she whispered, her voice wooden, a monotone. "You said you would never be a pet again."

"Ach," Natt said thickly, his too-bright eyes still held to hers. "But for you, lass, I would bear this."

He would bear it. Being her *friend*. And suddenly Ella just felt sick, and broken, and chilled all over, and she drew her hands away from him, and shook her head. No. No.

"You can't, Natt," she whispered. "And I can't. I can't do that to you. I can't trust you. I can't trust anyone, ever again. I just"—she dragged in breath—"we just *can't*, Natt."

She was searching his face, silently pleading for him to understand, to know. Like he always did, and was it relief, or something else, when it was there, flaring familiar and pained and broken across those eyes. He knew.

"Ach, my lass," he said, his eyes finally closing, his body smoothly rising to his feet. "I shall hear your truth, and go."

32

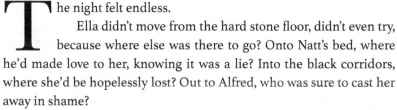

The night felt endless.

Ella didn't move from the hard stone floor, didn't even try, because where else was there to go? Onto Natt's bed, where he'd made love to her, knowing it was a lie? Into the black corridors, where she'd be hopelessly lost? Out to Alfred, who was sure to cast her away in shame?

Her dull thoughts kept circling back to Alfred, again and again, and each time the dread seemed to rise higher, stronger, laced with fear and unease. She had to go with Alfred, Grimarr had said, to prevent this war. She had to swear to Alfred that she'd come here of her own volition. She had to look him in the eye, and say—what?

I've fallen in love with an orc? I've betrayed you, as you've betrayed me? I know why you want to marry me? I know the horrible, unforgivable things you've done? I will never support your war?

Or perhaps it would be best to pretend? To lie, apologize, and smile? And if Alfred didn't immediately cast her away, perhaps she could wait until he'd escorted her back home again, and then quietly break off their betrothal at some later date?

But no matter what—Ella's eyes darted up to where her engagement-ring was still sitting innocuously on Natt's shelf—it was sure to be hellish. It would be the chagrin and judgement and fury of her mother. It would be gossip and mockery from everyone Ella knew. It would be firing her servants, packing up everything she owned, saying goodbye to her family's home, forever. And then what?

Perhaps her father's heir would allow her to rent one of the estate's smaller outbuildings, she thought, disjointed. And then, maybe, once she broke it off with Alfred, Natt could still come visit her, and—

She squeezed her eyes shut, and gave a wild shake of her head. No. *No.* Natt had lied to her. Betrayed her. He was sending her back to *Alfred.* She could never trust him *again.*

And even if Ella managed to stay on at her lands somehow, that would never be the same, either. Her father's house, her beloved forest, taken over by strangers, and the forest was likely to be sold for timber, or rented for game hunting, or gods knew what else. It would never be home again. It would never be *hers.*

Ella was weeping again, the water dripping steadily from her eyes, and she rubbed at them, dragged in air. She was being selfish. Entitled. She would survive this. She was fortunate enough to have some money squirrelled away apart from the estate, so she wasn't likely to starve. And if she were careful, and lived very frugally, she might not even need to find work. She could sit around all day, and do—what? She had no practical skills, no training, she'd always been terrible at proper lady-work like needlepoint, so what the hell was she supposed to *be,* after all this?

Who *was* Ella, without her father, without Alfred, without Natt? Who *was* she, when she was so alone, with no one left to trust?

She lifted her head to wipe again at her eyes—and found herself blinking at one of the carvings in the wall. The first in the line, the orc with the huge pickaxe, and with the smiling, naked woman on his arm. Akva, Natt had called her. The mother of all five clans. The goddess who, Natt had said, would bless Ella. *She sees you,* he'd said. *She knows you.*

And without at all knowing why, Ella lurched to her feet, and over to the carving. Looking at the woman's smiling face, at the knowing, whispering warmth in her eyes. The mother of all five clans. The mother of the Grisk.

And when Ella reached out a hand, tracing her fingers against the woman's bared belly, it was almost like the woman's eyes had fixed on hers, seeing deep inside. *She sees you. She knows you.*

"But I don't know me," Ella said, barely audible. "I'm not sure I ever have."

But Akva only kept smiling, kept knowing, and Ella drew in a gasping breath, let it out. "I was supposed to be a lady," she whispered. "It was my parents' deepest wish. I wasn't to be poor like my father, raised among sheep, weaving until my fingers bled. I was to be wealthy, comfortable, safe."

Akva kept listening, and Ella nodded, swallowed again. "But there was a price, for this," she continued. "I had to be all that they wanted. I had to"—she thought of Natt's words, his truth—"I had to hide. I had to be quiet, to pretend, to learn to become all that they wished. The only time I was truly myself was with Natt, and then he disappeared, and—"

Ella's breath was heaving again, and she impatiently wiped at her eyes, and jabbed at Akva's bare belly with her wet finger. "Your son betrayed me," she hissed. "He *knew* me, he wanted that part of me, he told me it was safe—and then he threw it away. He didn't throw away Ella the heiress, Ella the rich proper lady, like Alfred did. He did it to—*me*."

The sobs were choking from Ella's throat again, echoing against the stone walls. Because maybe that truly was why it hurt so much, why she felt so broken. Not only had she lost Natt, again—but it was like he'd taken her with him. Like he'd locked her away again, forever.

But Akva's eyes kept watching, kept knowing. And beneath Ella's sobs, beneath her hands scraping against the stone—there was the realization that there were marks, carved into Akva's lovely form. Not flaws or cracks in the carving—it was too perfect for that—but intentional, almost imperceptible cuts. Gouged into her breasts, her arms, her thighs. One deep one spraying wide across her belly, where a son might have been cut free. One telltale cluster at her neck, that could have been teeth-marks. One over her heart.

They were *scars*. Not visible at first glance, but still there.

And when Ella's eyes darted to the huge orc beside Akva—Edom, the father of the orcs—there was the realization that he had them, too.

And some of them were even the same, matched together, earned together.

Even so, Akva's body was still tucked up against Edom's, her hand still gripped hungry and brazen around his massive orc-prick. She'd been hurt, by him, because of him, with him, and she would forever wear his scars—but she had endured. She was still there. Still true. Still herself. Still taking her joy as she wished.

I see you. I know you.

And before she quite knew what she was doing, Ella's trembling legs walked away from the wall, and toward the door. Toward where she somehow knew she'd find—Natt. Sitting there alone on a bench, just outside the room, with his elbows on his knees, his head bowed, his braid falling over his shoulder.

His head snapped up, his bleak wet eyes searching Ella's, swarming with something that might have been hope—but Ella drew in breath, shook her head. "I still—can't," she whispered. "But I should like"—she took another shaky breath—"a proper farewell from you this time, Nattfarr of Clan Grisk."

Natt's nod was immediate, his eyes glimmering, and he smoothly rose to his feet, looking down at her. And in a breath, a flash of heat, he grasped Ella up whole into his strong arms, and strode to the bed.

He laid her carefully down upon it, and then climbed up, and knelt close over her. Gently unfastening her cape, and then her skirt, with reverent, whispering fingers. And then tossing the clothes away, exposing her naked, bejewelled body to his watching, blinking eyes.

But he didn't take off any of the gold, only trailed his clawed fingers against each piece, one by one. The earrings, the necklaces, the cuffs on her wrists. The new gold ring, still glinting in her peaked, reddened, swollen nipple.

"Ach, my lovely lass," he whispered, his voice choked. "You are so bright. So kind and fair and sweet. You are all a Grisk could wish for."

It was true, it was glittering there in his eyes upon hers, and Ella felt her shivery hand reach to cup against his dear, familiar face. Natt, her oldest friend, a stranger, who twice now had hurt her, and abandoned her.

But he had still *known* her, at least that was truth, and he turned his head to gently kiss against her palm, his tongue swirling soft against her skin. And then moving to her fingers, suckling the tips of each one, and then to her wrist, her forearm. Kissing licking biting, while Ella's eyes fluttered, her breath hissing out between parted lips.

He did it all again on the other side, nibbling even on her elbow, licking and kissing up and up. Skating his hot breath over the gold cuff she still wore, until he'd buried his face into the dark hair hidden beneath her arm, licking and teasing, tickling enough to draw a choked, twisted noise from Ella's mouth. A sound that made Natt jerk up over her, looking down into her eyes with first concern, and then relief.

"Ticklish little lass," he whispered, his voice wavering. "The scent of your laughter is so sweet, my love."

With that he dropped again, his hands skirting warm as he moved down her leg, all the way to her bare foot. And then he *licked* it, the sight and the feel of that almost shockingly unimaginable, but of course it was, it was Natt—and Ella felt herself give another choked laugh as he sucked on her toes one by one, holding her eyes, speaking this truth.

He kissed and caressed her foot all over, and then her ankle, her calf, her knee. And then all again on the other side, setting gooseflesh flaring, hunger rising steady and smooth—and lancing into light as he finally, finally came up, kneeling close and purposeful between her thighs, lowering his head deep—

His first long, deliberate lick against her sent a loud, betraying moan to Ella's mouth, her legs eagerly spreading wide. And gods bless him, curse him, because he only moaned too, his clever fingers so easily finding her swollen wet heat, and sinking deep inside. While his brilliant mouth licked and suckled and tasted, his tongue swirling, kissing, delving, drinking. His fingers slipping out, while his tongue slid in, taking their place—

And then those slick fingers trailed backwards, deeper along Ella's crease, finding another secret place to delve into. And here was the howling, screeching, impossible sensation of slowly, purposely being pierced in both places at once. Those fingers seeking and thrusting in back, while his filthy tongue twisted and flicked and licked in front, his eager lips suckling and slurping and kissing. And oh, that was his other hand, claws out, stroking up Ella's bare front to find her mouth, scraping sharp against her gasping lips, easing inside—

It meant Ella was filled with orc, filled with Natt, in every possible place all at once, and it was like she was firing with it, flaring bright and wide, her body desperately writhing and squeezing and suckling against him. Needing him, needing so much more of him, even trailing her tongue intent against his claw, sparking pain and blood and impossible ramping hunger—

Natt tasted the hunger, he *knew*, and in a swift jolt he was gone, every part of him snatched away from inside her, leaving her gaping and quivering and empty. And protesting, silently pleading, grasping with frantic scraping fingers at his hot sweaty skin as he loomed up over her, his entire body heaving with his stuttering breaths.

"Ach," he gasped, and Ella realized that his hungry, flaring eyes were fixed on her mouth. On where—she held his gaze, her eyes hooded—she was licking her lips, taunting him, trailing her fresh red blood against her skin.

Natt's moan sounded like pain, his black eyelashes madly fluttering, and when he made to jerk away Ella held him there, clasping her arms and legs around his beautiful weight, dragging him close. Trapping him, in what he'd done, and he knew, his dark head slowly lowering to hers, caught, compelled—

He sucked her bloody tongue slow, steady into his mouth, his eyes held to hers with a quiet stilted reverence. And then he was swallowing her, drinking her, so gently at first, but then harder, hungrier with every breath—

It was abominable, it was utterly shameful, it was the orc who'd betrayed her desperately sucking her own lifeblood out of her tongue. It was filthy and it was pleasure and pain and longing, it was, she was, *I see you*—

And when Ella spread her legs wider around him, wriggling her hungry emptiness to search for him, he was already there. His swollen smooth hardness already kissing, already demanding, pressing, seeking to split her apart upon its delving head—

Ella yanked her mouth away from his, earning a growl of protest from his throat—but she needed to see this, know their truth. And as they were held, seized in the life and the magic, she took a shaking, shuddering breath—and opened. Opened to him, against him, around him, and he cried out, loud and guttural, as he sank slow, smooth, slick inside. With no resistance whatsoever, just his hot swollen skin sliding home into Ella's wet dripping heat.

Gods, it was glorious, and their moans had risen at once, together, true. And Ella's fingers were fluttering over his face, the red of his mouth, the wetness of his eyes. "Speak to me, Natt," she whispered. "Speak all the filthy truth you can. Please."

He nodded, blinked, nodded again. And then rose up onto his elbows, looked deep into her eyes. "Look at you, my sweet pretty lass," he whispered, his voice hitching, as he pressed himself in tighter, harder, his hips circling, setting off sparks behind Ella's eyelids. "Look at you, with your pretty bloody mouth, and your pure maiden womb spread wide open and easy for me, dripping with my scent and my seed. Look how you have bloomed for me."

He dragged himself out as he spoke, those eyes hard and arresting on hers—and then sank himself back in, in one deep, devastating stroke. Bringing a sound very like a scream to Ella's mouth, her arms and legs desperately gripping at him, and suddenly he was smiling at her, his teeth brilliantly sharp, black eyes blazing, hungry, bittersweet.

"You should have made me a wondrous mate, lass," he breathed. "You should have made me so proud to claim you and flaunt you as my own. I should have been the envy of all my mountain. I should"—he dragged back out, and drove back in, wringing another scream from Ella's mouth—"have boasted of my fair mate, who eagerly bares her lovely form, and thrusts open her womb, and drinks up my seed. I should have shown, again and again"—he drew out again, sank back in, oh *hell*—"how she screams, how she wriggles and writhes upon my prick, how she bestows her many riches upon me *alone*."

Oh gods, oh fuck, he was truly fucking Ella now, carving into her again and again, rocking her entire body with it, wringing raw, gasping noises from her mouth. Her arms and legs clinging to him, her eyes staring into his, gods he was appalling and gods this was good and there had never been pleasure like this in her *life*—

"I shall show them," Natt gasped, those eyes briefly slipping away, dazed and fluttering, as he slammed in again, again, "my fair mate with her belly rounded, filled with my son, reeking of my scent alone. I shall show them her pierced, dripping teats, her open dripping womb, ach"—he drove harder, higher—"her dripping *neck*, scarred by my teeth, all of her marked and filled and *mine*—"

The world was spinning wildly, the only truth Natt's glittering eyes, Natt's huge body, Natt's impossible words, slamming into her, making her beautiful and bright and whole. Making her into his mate, his true orc's mate, marked and stretched and screaming, oh gods—

And in the chaos the hunger, the wicked heat of an orc's sweaty driving body over her, Ella reached for his head, and drew it down. Pressing him close into the curve of her neck, and she could feel his inhale, deep and swarming and desperate, filling up his lungs his cock his heart.

His lips and tongue were already there, suckling painfully on her skin, and when Ella groaned he yanked himself up, the world rocking sideways, his eyes dark and staring. "You must," he gasped, between heaving breaths, "speak this, should you wish me to stop, I know not what I speak, I ought not—"

But there was only this, only the frantic shouting craving, and Ella grasped tighter, dragged his head back down. Feeling his muffled shout, his body arching, his lungs filling, his tongue hot and dragging as his teeth scraped soft, sharp, deadly—

He bit down, hard, as that hardness inside her soared up, gouging deep. And Ella screamed again even as she clung to him, clawed at him, bared herself whole to this invading violent orc, his teeth in her neck his cock between her legs his throat greedily swallowing, oh gods oh gods have *mercy*—

The ecstasy surged like a living thing, like a hammering trammelling beast, laying waste to all in its path. Flaying Ella bare beneath it, stretched and swollen and screaming—and then hurling it even higher when he plunged inside her one last time, and sprayed out his seed in a flood. Filling her, drinking her, her orc her mate her own, her love, her *truth*.

The world was still spinning when Natt's body finally slowed above her, his driving thrusts replaced by thick, gulping breaths. His head was bowed, his big shoulders heaving, and when Ella's trembly hands went to tilt his face up, he didn't resist.

And the *sight* of him, he looked dazed and debauched and utterly *terrifying*. His eyes stunned and gleaming, his mouth smeared with blood, his slick, sinuous tongue coming out slow to lick his lips, his sharp white teeth now rimmed with red.

Ella felt her body give a strange little shudder, with something that was alarmingly close to triumph—but it seemed to shake Natt awake, somehow, his eyes refocusing, blinking at her, and then squeezing shut. And she could see his throat convulsing, could feel the sudden rising tension as he dragged in a hard, bracing breath.

"Ach," he choked, his voice harsh. "Curse me, lass. I did not—I ought not—I should have first spoken to you of this, you shall think me a *monster*—"

But his tongue had slipped out again, licking yet more of that red off his lips, and Ella twitched at the sight—and then, somehow, impossibly—she *laughed*. The sound bubbling on its own out her throat, warm and almost giddy, her whole body shaking beneath him.

"Sorry to say, Natt, but I'm not in the least surprised," she said, her voice a smooth, easy caress. "Didn't I always tell you? Orcs are the most shocking creatures *imaginable*."

Natt was blinking, his weight gone still, and Ella slid her hand into his silken hair, brought him down for a slow, succulent, metallic-tasting kiss. His tongue careful, hesitant at first, but Ella teased hers against it until he was properly kissing her in return, deep and slick and filthy, just the way it should be.

But when he pulled back, his eyes were dark again, distant, bleak. His throat swallowing, his head shaking, and Ella almost sobbed as she felt the pleasure ebbing away, vanishing into emptiness. He'd betrayed her. He wasn't her mate, and she wasn't his. She had to go back, or else she would start a war.

"I am sorry, lass," came his low whisper, hitching from his still-bloody lips. "I am so sorry for these many wrongs I have wreaked upon you. I ought to have been a better orc. A better—friend, to one who has given me such gifts."

It was truth, spoken from his eyes to hers, and Ella nodded, drank it up, held it close. He saw her. She saw him.

"And yet, Nattfarr of Clan Grisk," she heard herself say, her voice only slightly wavering, "you have continued to prove yourself devious, and obnoxious, and utterly *indecorous*. As usual."

He smiled at her, slow, miserable. "You ought to have better, my lass," he said. "You ought to betray me in turn, and thus spark this war against me. It is what I deserve, after what I have done to you."

But Ella couldn't, never, and he saw it, he knew. And his kiss on her lips was so soft, so sweet, it made her very soul ache.

"I shall never forget you," he whispered, hoarse, as the wetness dripped from his eyes, onto her face. "I shall never forget my sweet, laughing, blooming lass, who so bravely kept her pledge toward me. You shall always be my Ella, of Clan Grisk."

And Ella was smiling again, and weeping, and nodding, all at once. "Ach, my Nattfarr," she whispered. "Farewell."

33

Ella somehow slept the entire night through, curled close into Natt's arms. Held in the warm whispering safety of him, while she dreamed dreams of full mountains, full bellies, her form and her sons carved forever into stone, with her mate standing tall and strong and dangerous by her side.

But when Ella finally blinked awake, into the light of a guttering candle, she was alone, and cold, despite the heavy fur covering her naked body. And the wall where their likenesses should have been was still flat and empty, her belly still flat and empty, the room flat and empty. Alone.

But someone had put something new on the end of the bed, and when Ella sat up to peer down at it, there was the dull recognition that it was—clothes. Proper women's clothes, lady's clothes. A shift, a high-necked day-dress, even her old boots.

It almost hurt to look at them, to think about what they said, lying there so innocuously—but this was where she was. This was what had to be done, to prevent a *war*.

So Ella numbly, methodically pulled off the gold cuffs, and then the chains at her waist, before she grasped for the clothes, and yanked them on. Fighting to ignore the odd close fit of them, the unnecessary swathes of fabric, covering her nearly from chin to foot. Even the heavy-feeling boots were still the garb of a lady, hiding Ella's true self away, concealing everything.

But then again—Ella blinked, and brought a shaky hand to her chest—she'd forgotten to take off the rest of Natt's jewelry. It had begun to feel so—right, somehow, those chains tucked beneath her breasts, the mismatched earrings in her ears, and even—Ella swallowed, and then carefully hovered her fingers over it—her new nipple-ring, its jutting gold only barely visible through the layers of thick fabric hiding it.

But the truth of that, suddenly, was an odd, inexplicable comfort, embedded in her very skin. True Grisk gold, hidden from other eyes, perhaps, but still known to her. *I see you. I know you.* Ella Riddell, of Clan Grisk.

Ella's gaze had flicked to Akva's carved likeness upon the wall, still scarred, still smiling. And at this angle, the long thin scar on her belly looked almost astonishingly deep, almost as though one could slide a knifepoint into it, and the knife would then stay there, sunk deep into her stone womb.

It was a horrible image, a hint of terrible past wrongs, of the awful suffering these orcs and their mates had faced—and of the suffering they still faced. Fourteen women dead, just last year, bearing orc sons. The look on Timo's face, in the corridor. One hundred Grisk, killed by their own captain's betrayal. The cruelties Natt had had to accept, and conquer. His father's death, the abuse he'd endured, the way he'd been hunted.

The way he'd been forced to betray someone he truly loved, to gain the leverage he needed to finally bring real change.

And even if Ella's part in this tale was finished, there was suddenly a quiet, shuddering stillness, deep inside. She was Ella, of Clan Grisk. She hadn't added to the suffering. She'd treated her hosts with kindness, and acceptance, and thankfulness. She'd faced her deepest fears, conquered her deepest shame, and conducted herself bravely, honourably, with truth. *I see you.*

She felt her booted feet walk over to Natt's messy shelf, her gaze settling on Alfred's glittering diamond ring, still sitting so innocently upon it. A real lord's ring, meant to make her a real lady.

Ella slowly reached for the ring, and tilted it to the candlelight. It was a beautiful ring, and she had so naively accepted it, and then proudly worn it, even here, into Natt's own home. She'd been foolish, false, unthinking—but she'd learned to do better, to think. She would. She *was*.

She closed the ring into her fingers, and walked back to Akva and her scars, her smiling, seeing eyes. And then, Ella carefully turned the ring, and slipped its gold band into the deep line of Akva's scar.

It fit perfectly, leaving only a glittering diamond on Akva's belly, where the scar had been. A gift, a Grisk jewel, given in gratitude from her own Grisk daughter.

"Thank you," Ella whispered, trailing her fingers against the stone. "I see you too, Mother of Five Clans."

The stillness seemed to settle again, spreading wide, and Ella drew in breath, courage, truth. She could do this. She was.

So she abruptly turned, and strode for the door. Out before the waiting eyes of five orcs, all dressed and armed, and rising at once to look at her. And at the centre of them was Natt, his bleak dark eyes sheer misery to look upon, as they swept up and down her fully covered form, again and again and again.

"I should have asked," Ella heard her voice say, distant, oddly formal. "Do you wish me to return all your jewels to you?"

Because at least some of them had belonged to Natt's mother, and to the other Grisk women on that wall, Ella knew that now—but Natt shook his head, hard enough that his thick braid, plaited new and perfect, swept out behind him.

"No," he replied, in a voice that wasn't his. "I gave them to you. They are yours now."

Ella nodded, twisting her hands together, her eyes dropping to the floor. It was time. She couldn't trust him. She had to do this. She was.

"Thank you for such generous gifts, Natt," she said, quiet. "I am ready, then."

There was an instant's aching stillness, in which no one moved or spoke—but finally Natt gave a jerky nod, and clutched for his lamp. And then reached his slightly trembly hand toward her, waiting.

Ella blinked at it, for long enough that Natt's bleak eyes dropped, and he began to draw his hand away—but then she belatedly grasped for it, gripping tight. Closing her eyes at the familiar warm safety of it, those claws brushing against her skin.

Natt led her into the dark corridor without speaking, his four brothers following close behind, their scimitars slightly clanking. And as they walked, Ella felt herself reach out her other hand, tentative, to trail against the cool stone wall. She could do this. She was.

"I have a few last questions, Natt," she said, her voice catching. "If you'll speak truth to me?"

She wasn't looking at him, she couldn't, but she could hear his breath, coming out heavy and slow. "Ach," he replied. "From henceforth, always."

Ella nodded, and blinked at the darkness up ahead. "Will you face any consequences from your brothers," she said, "for so publicly—positioning me, as you have, only for me to leave you, after? Will this call any question upon you, as Speaker?"

Natt's fingers clenched tighter on hers, and it was a moment before he spoke. "Only a few of my brothers know why you must leave me, this day," he said. "And it has been a boon to me, that you did not smell of this man. Many Grisk have mates that do not live in the mountain, and if you truly do not mean to wed this man, as you have said to Dammarr—"

There was shock, suddenly, sparking up Ella's spine, because she'd said that to Dammarr, yes—but had she ever said it to *Natt*? Had she ever actually told him that she wouldn't marry the man who'd sought to kill him, all these years?

Her feet halted abruptly in the corridor, making the four orcs reel back behind them, but Ella only had eyes for Natt, waiting for his gaze to catch hers, and hold. Even if she couldn't trust him, she would speak truth to him. She was.

"I will *never* marry Alfred, after this," she said, quiet, fierce. "And you must tell the rest of your kin anything you wish about me. Anything that helps you gain your rightful place as Speaker, and prevents any doubt from falling upon you. You may tell them that I have not left you, that I shall always be faithful to you, that I shall forever wear your jewels, and await your return to me. You may even tell them I have died, perhaps in childbirth, if at any point that is—convenient, to you."

There was a sudden stillness on Natt's face, but also relief, flaring in his eyes. And that was the confirmation, thank the gods, that this should be enough. That under the truth-spell's thrall, Natt should now be able to say these things about her. He should keep his position safe, after he'd sacrificed so much to attain it. The Speaker of the Grisk would again lie, to help his brothers—and as wrong as that was, in this moment, Ella truly didn't care. Natt had given too much, for this to be his downfall.

"I thank you, my lass," he said, in a whisper. "I shall never forget your kindness toward me."

His eyes were shifting, betraying a meaning Ella couldn't bear to see, and she made herself turn away, and keep moving in the direction he'd been taking her. "Is there any chance," she began, to the corridor, "that I might be pregnant?"

There was silence from Natt beside her, more silence from the listening orcs behind them. "You are not now thus," Natt said, finally, "else I should smell this upon you. And there ought yet to be time enough, that this ought not to befall you. But if, by some whim of the gods, it does"—he audibly swallowed—"mayhap you shall find a way to come here again, for another visit, so that Efterar shall free you of this."

Oh. The urge to weep surged again, almost breathtakingly powerful, and Natt's hand twitched on hers, his throat making a sound that might have been a cough. "And should you ever wish to visit again," he said, "you must. You shall always be welcome here."

Ella gulped for breath, and tried to nod. "I will keep that in mind, thank you," she managed. "But I should think you would rather claim me as dead, once you have taken another mate, and fathered your sons upon her."

There was only more silence, stretching out too wide between them, because that should have been where Natt might have said, *I would never take another mate, lass, after you.* But of course he would. He was the Speaker. He needed these sons.

And even as Ella wiped irritably at her traitorous leaky eyes, she knew she wanted him to have his sons, his greatest wish, even if it was another woman who granted them to him. A woman who he wouldn't even *think* of betraying, perhaps, and their sons together would be beautiful, wild, laughing little beasts. And Natt would surely raise them only with kindness, and protect them from the kinds of cruelties he'd had to face.

But Natt still wasn't speaking, and Ella took another hitching breath. "Though I shall very much regret not meeting your sons," she whispered. "You'll be such a good father, Natt."

He still didn't reply, but his hand on hers had clamped painfully tight, and why in the gods' names was Ella saying such things, when she was already so near to weeping? "And also," she made herself go on, fighting desperately to make her voice light, "I shall regret not seeing your lamps, and exploring your mountain with proper illumination for once. You should ask Dammarr, yesterday I nearly became quite grievously injured from merely attempting to walk down the corridor."

There was more heavy stillness, Natt still saying nothing—but then, thank the gods, there was a snort from Dammarr behind them. "Ach, woman, you were useless," he said, but his voice was kind, an offering. "I have never seen anything so laughable in my life."

"Not even when Thrain drank all that berry-juice, and fell off the mountain?" came Thrak's voice behind him. "Come to think of this, brother, you ought to scotch the berry-juice. It only seems to bring you grief and woe."

"Ach, and the best fuck of his life," came Dammarr's dry reply. "Right, Varinn?"

Varinn snapped something back in black-tongue, earning a hoot of laughter from Thrak. While beside her, Ella could feel Natt slightly relaxing, and her own relief seemed to swarm deep and fervent inside. At least Natt would still have his brothers, after all this. There would still be someone by his side, someone he could trust. Even if it was Dammarr.

"The captain and his mate are here, in the muster-room," Natt said finally, his voice stiff, as he waved at a nearby opening in the corridor. "They wait here to escort you out to the eastern side of the mountain, where this man and his band now await you."

Ella blinked at him—and was struck by a sudden, irrepressible flare of true, blaring fear, pelting through her thoughts. "I'm going to

Alfred with *them*?" she heard her voice say, unaccountably shrill. "Why can't *you* take me?"

Natt's eyes had oddly shuttered, and again, it was Dammarr who spoke. "If the idea here is to avoid a war," he said, "Nattfarr cannot walk even within *scent-range* of this foul man. Most of all if it is to give *you* into his hands. This would not be safe, for either him, or you."

Right. Of course. And Ella was being foolish, and she was doing this, she *was*. So she gave a shaky nod, and turned, and strode into the muster-room.

She'd only expected to see Grimarr and Jule, and they were indeed there, both fully dressed in surprising human-looking finery—but milling all around them were more orcs. There were Baldr and Drafli, and Kesst and Efterar. There were a variety of Grisk, including Ymir, and then also Olarr and Silfast and Stella, and Simon. There was even John, standing apart from the others with his arms crossed over his chest, and intently ignoring Timo, who was hovering about and eyeing him with unmistakable fascination.

"W-what's going on?" Ella asked Jule, who had strode over to greet them, her long blue dress billowing out behind her. "Why are they all here?"

Jule flashed Ella her typical smile, though her eyes looked more tired than usual, her mouth rather grim. "Oh, you know orcs," she said. "They can't do anything without making a fuss. They wished to say farewell to you, of course."

That seemed difficult to believe, but the assembled orcs did seem to be hovering closer, eyeing Ella with unmistakable intent. And this truly was goodbye, perhaps forever, so Ella nodded, and smiled at the orc nearest. It was Efterar, thankfully, but he wasn't smiling back, and was instead frowning at Ella's neck through the high collar of her dress, and then, oddly enough, toward her mouth.

"I honestly cannot fathom," he said toward Natt, his voice clipped, "why my presumably intelligent brothers feel this compulsion to taunt the men they seek to avoid warring with. Did you really need to *bite* her, Grisk? In multiple places? And stab an *earring* into her? And what did you do, *bathe* her in your saliva?"

Beside Ella Natt felt very rigid, but his head was raised, his eyes flinty on Efterar's. "Ach, I did," he said. "I covered her with my scent and my jewels, and gave her the farewell she was due. I took great joy in this."

Efterar huffed a heavy, irritable sigh, and behind him Kesst sidled up, and brazenly snaked his long fingers around to Efterar's front, grasping at his already-swelling groin. "Deep breaths, Eft," he purred, though his eyes on Ella were just as disapproving. "Perhaps you'd like to be cleaned up a bit for your man, sweetheart? Keep him from losing his shit—and deciding to start a war after all—when he takes you to bed tonight?"

But even the thought was making Ella feel suddenly, powerfully ill, and she gave a hard shake of her head. "No, thank you," she said firmly. "I'm fine, just as I am. Alfred will not be taking me to bed, ever. And I would appreciate"—she darted a glance around at the milling-about orcs—"if you are quite clear, when you so publicly speak, of my full intention to remain faithful to Natt."

There was unmistakable surprise, flaring across both Kesst and Efterar's eyes, but Ella didn't elaborate, and thankfully they didn't push further. And when Baldr came up, speaking a sincere-sounding farewell, with Drafli standing close behind him, it was easier to smile at him, and to thank him, for all his help and kindness.

After him the orcs kept coming, first the group of Grisk—Ella, fortunately, remembered all their names, and was gratified to note that none of them seemed to know her real reason for leaving—and next was John, giving her a curt, watchful nod that suggested he knew rather more than the others.

"This will, your father made," he said to her, out of nowhere. "How was it filed? Privately, or publicly, with the Sakkin magistrate?"

Ella blinked at him, but obediently cast her memories backwards. "Publicly, with the magistrate," she replied. "There's a copy at the library in Dusbury. He sought to protect me with it, and he was quite proud of how he'd managed it, so he wanted to make it as official as possible."

John gave a thoughtful little nod, but backed away, leaving Ella to consider that, her thoughts suddenly, incongruously, filling with images of her father. Her father, who'd cursed her with this horrible marriage deadline. But who'd also sought to protect her, in any way he could. Who'd worked so hard to keep her home, and safe.

The warmth of that truth was almost overpowering, and Ella put a hand to her chest, feeling the gold chains hidden beneath her layers of clothing. Her father had been misguided, selfish, perhaps even cruel, Ella knew that now—he had still known her, and loved her. She had been given so many gifts. She was grateful.

"Are you ready to go?" a voice asked, and when Ella blinked up, it was Jule. Smiling, but still with that tiredness in her eyes. "We'll be with you."

But Ella hesitated, and her gaze slid past Jule, toward the huge orc standing behind her. Grimarr, with his scarred face and wary watching eyes. The orc who'd given Natt this hard choice. The orc who'd let Natt be hunted, for all these years. Natt's enemy, who he hadn't been able to defeat. Not yet.

"Thank you," Ella said, with an attempt at a smile toward Jule. "But I have one last request."

The room was growing quiet all around, the assembled orcs' attention slowly settling upon them, and Ella lifted her chin, found Grimarr's eyes, and spoke truth.

"Before I go," she said, "I want to see my—Nattfarr, of Clan Grisk, made full Speaker. Not only of the Grisk, but of all five clans. *Now.*"

34

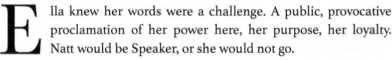

Ella knew her words were a challenge. A public, provocative proclamation of her power here, her purpose, her loyalty. Natt would be Speaker, or she would not go.

The threat didn't need to be said, especially before all these uninformed orcs, but Ella almost enjoyed watching the discomfort in Grimarr's eyes, his brief, telltale glance around the room. At his mate, his two Hands, his loyal brothers, the Grisk. At Ella.

"Natt deserves to be made Speaker," Ella said, into the too-tense silence. "He has proven his fealty beyond doubt. He has proven that he can make hard choices, on his brothers' behalf. He has proven that he can host a Revel, and only speak of brotherhood, and call for truth. He has proven that he is a match for the men. He is a match for *you*."

She held Grimarr's gaze with all the force she could muster, glaring deep and strong and true. And the look in those eyes upon hers might have been angry, or perhaps appreciative, or perhaps—Ella blinked—even *approving*?

And when Grimarr's mouth finally, slowly twitched up, Ella almost thought she might faint, right here in this room full of orcs. "You have proven yourself a fierce and loyal mate, Ella of Clan Grisk," he said, with a careful incline of his shaggy head. "And for this, most of all, I shall grant your request to your orc. Come, brother, and have your due."

Ella was still holding Natt's hand, and her sudden, relieved grin back toward him found him looking utterly, entirely shocked. His mouth hanging open, his eyes gaping between Ella and Grimarr, his huge body almost radiating his astonishment and disbelief. But Ella tugged at him, and abruptly he came, his steps uncharacteristically jerky, his fingers suddenly trembling in hers.

But then, Natt was there. Here. Standing tall before his captain, looking straight into his craggy face, while Grimarr brought a heavy hand to each of Natt's shoulders, and looked him in the eyes.

"Nattfarr, of Clan Grisk," he said, his deep voice rumbling through the room. "I grant you today the place of Speaker of the Grisk, and of all five clans. I call you to Speak for your brothers, and thus earn their truth, and their fealty. I call you to set aside your own wants, your own vengeance, and serve us all with kindness, fairness, and justice. And, I also call your guard"—Grimarr's eyes flicked up toward them— "Varinn, Thrak, Thrain, and Dammarr, to uphold you as you serve."

The words seemed to unfurl throughout the room, sinking into Natt's shoulders with the strength of Grimarr's hands, the deep power of his voice. And Ella could almost taste the truth filling Natt, settling him, brightening him with its light.

"I answer your call, Grimarr the Fierce-Heart, of Clan Ash-Kai, Captain of Five Clans," Natt said, his gaze steady, alive, speaking its own truth. "I shall be the twelfth orc of my line to Speak for my brothers. Should you not grant me your truth, I shall draw it from you, and speak it for all to hear. I shall set aside my own wants, my own vengeance, and serve all my kin with kindness, fairness, and justice."

There was a wry smile on Grimarr's mouth, a slight nod from his head—and Natt nodded too. And then, to Ella's distant surprise, Natt gently dropped her hand, and then reached up both his arms, to rest on Grimarr's huge shoulders.

"And I thank you, my brother," Natt said, "for saving my life, when your own father sought my death. I thank you for the shelter you have given me. I thank you for the wisdom and bravery you have shown in Speaking with me as you have, and seeking most of all for the safety of all Grisk, and the future of our clan. I do not agree with all your ways, and I shall always be a thorn to you—but I am honoured to call you our captain."

There was a hurtling silence, a look in Grimarr's eyes that surely hinted at astonishment—but then, in a swift, lurching movement, the two orcs were locked together, their arms tight around one another, Grimarr's messy head buried deep into Natt's neck.

Suddenly there were stomps and shouts all around, hoots and clamours and claps, and Jule was rubbing at her eyes, and sidling up to Grimarr, and tucking herself into his side. And he immediately maneuvered the hug to include her, dragging her close, while Ella watched from a distance, and wiped at her own liberally leaking eyes.

Natt was Speaker. Finally. They'd done it, and she'd seen it, and it was right. *Natt* was right again, after so long.

He even looked right, too, the bright sparkling warmth back in his eyes, as Grimarr finally released him. As Natt gave a quick bow toward Grimarr, back to his usual lovely smoothness, and then spun himself around, and immediately launched himself toward his brothers. Toward Dammarr, first of all, clasping him close into his chest, while the rest of them piled on, and Ella swallowed hard as she watched, and fought to keep the smile on her face.

Her part here was done. Natt had gained his dreams, all that he'd longed for. He would help other women, he would help their sons, he would be a marvellous Speaker. But he'd still betrayed her, and she still couldn't trust him, and they were still on the verge of war. She still had to go.

The urge to run was almost unbearable, suddenly, shouting in Ella's entire being, but she clasped her hands tightly together, and made herself wait. She would do this. She was.

Natt had finally disentangled himself from his brothers—Thrak had somehow gotten him into a headlock, and only let go after Dammarr did the same to him—and his familiar face had lifted toward Ella, his eyes blinking hard. And then, oh gods, he took the two steps toward her, his body smooth, purposeful, *right*. And then—Ella's eyes fluttered closed—he buried his face deep into her neck, and inhaled.

It was like time stuttered, or skipped backwards. Caught in the warmth of Natt's breath, the brush of his lips, the slight, reverent slip of his long tongue down the neck of her dress, trailing against where he'd bitten her the night before.

And as Natt's chest slowly filled with the scent of her, there was the jolting, overpowering need to grasp at him, draw him away with her, escape back to their forest. Where they would play and run and laugh, and Ella would chase him and tackle him to the earth under the sun, and she would—

The sudden feel of him reeling back, away, was almost painful, and so was that shuttered look in his blinking eyes. He was shaking his head, biting his lip, looking like he was bracing himself, holding himself still. And Dammarr had quickly stepped toward him, grasping a clawed hand around his arm, yanking him away, away, away.

And Natt didn't fight it. He went. Stumbling away from Ella, forever, and somehow she could read his truth, flashing straight from his eyes to hers. *I wish to run away with you, my lass. I wish to hide with you and mate and laugh with you until all else is gone.*

But he couldn't. He'd betrayed her, he'd lied to her, she could never trust him again. Her part here was done. She had to go.

So Ella bowed her head, and took a breath, and went.

35

It was only a moment before Ella found herself outside Orc Mountain again. Walking in the bright sun and clear air, with Grimarr and Jule and Baldr and Drafli flanked close around her.

But within that moment, Ella had begun badly trembling, the unease and the fear and the regret clawing and shouting all at once. She had to face Alfred. She had to face the misery to come, the end of all she'd known. She had to face her mother, her servants, the loss of her home.

"Thank you for doing this, Ella," said Jule's voice, quiet, beside her. "You truly honour us all. It's been such a pleasure getting to know you."

Ella nodded, but she couldn't speak back, or even raise her eyes. Just walked, every shaky step slower and slower, until—her breath hitched, choked—they'd turned around a wall of rock, and come out onto a grassy plain.

And there, on the plain before them, was—*Alfred*. Tall, regal, handsome Lord Tovey, standing here, and *smiling*.

He was surrounded by a small band of perhaps fifteen horses and men, including—Ella's unease clutched tighter—the awful Byrne. The men were all fully armed, and dressed in travelling-clothes, and they even had the three familiar hunting-dogs, leashed to one of the horses.

But it wasn't an army, their weapons weren't drawn, and Alfred, *Alfred*, was *smiling*.

It felt wrong, suddenly, a jarring clash of fear, of danger—but Alfred was walking blithely toward Ella, appearing entirely unconcerned by the three huge orcs surrounding her.

"Ella, darling!" he said brightly. "I can't tell you what a relief it is to finally see you safe and sound. Are you well? Have you been harmed by these vicious kidnapping beasts?"

Ella twitched—it took some nerve, to walk up to Orc Mountain, with only fifteen men at one's back, and call the orcs vicious kidnapping beasts—but here, too late, was the dull reminder that thanks to the new peace-treaty, the orcs couldn't dare attack Alfred, or even speak a word of threat to him. He was an earl's son, he was extremely influential, he was immune, proud, safe—and he damn well knew it.

He is a lord, Natt had said that day in the cave, a lifetime ago. *He shall do all that he wishes.*

"I'm very well, thank you," Ella said, as steadily as she could. "I haven't been harmed in any way, and I haven't been kidnapped, either. I had a severely injured employee upon my hands, and decided to see him home to safety, and stay until he was well."

Alfred's eyes had been sweeping up and down Ella's form, lingering with meaning upon her mismatched earrings, and her empty hand, conspicuously lacking its engagement-ring. And then—Ella fought not to cover herself—those eyes held to her slightly peaked nipple, still visible even through the thick layers of her clothing.

"You'll forgive me if I choose not to believe you, darling," came Alfred's voice, smooth, through his still-smiling mouth. "These foul orcs have devious means of manipulation beyond what we can even imagine. They wield dark, dangerous magic to gain innocent women to their side. I'm afraid that coming here was a *very* foolish decision on your part, darling, and sure to breed only scandal and shame."

Ella's teeth were gritting together, and she lifted her chin, and held his glinting blue eyes. "And I'm sure you'll forgive me if I choose to disagree with you," she said coldly. "I faced no danger whatsoever during my stay here. I was welcomed with only kindness, and generously hosted and supervised by a woman who was"—she nodded toward Jule—"once a lady, and who also invited you and your parents and allies to join us. There is no scandal, and no shame."

Alfred's eyes had gone oddly still, but the smile was still there, still spread wide across his handsome face. "Well, I am indeed eager to hear all about it, darling," he said, without inflection. "Now, if you please, we must leave at once. Your household is surely frantic at your prolonged disappearance, and I'd like to return you to safety by nightfall."

The unease flared up again, and with it the rising urge to run, run, run—but Ella swallowed hard, and forced her legs to stay still. She had to do this. She would. She was.

"Very well," she heard her wooden voice say, her eyes casting an unseeing glance toward Jule and the three orcs beside her. "I thank you for your generosity, and your hospitality."

They made some kind of collective response, Jule's full of heartfelt encouragement and exhortations to return, but Ella couldn't hear it through the rushing in her ears, the hammering beat of her heart. And once they'd finished speaking, Ella stepped away, and put her trembly hand to Alfred's arm. She would go.

Alfred played the part of the perfect gentleman as he walked Ella toward the horses, and then pulled down a cloak to tie around her shoulders. Dressing her, *Alfred* was *dressing her,* and she couldn't meet his eyes, couldn't breathe, could only taste the bile rising in her throat—

"Why don't we walk for a few moments together," Alfred said, his voice thin, not a suggestion. "I'm sure there are a few items we must discuss."

Ella numbly nodded, and allowed Alfred to lead her away, toward what seemed to be a road, leading away from the east of the mountain. She hadn't even known it had existed, but Alfred's men surely did, half of them riding ahead on horseback, half behind. They'd also let the dogs go, and suddenly all three of them were here, circling and running and barking fiercely at Ella's heels.

Ella froze mid-step—they were doing this because they smelled *Natt*—and beside her, Alfred shoved his foot at one of the dogs, sending it yelping away. "They seem to smell something upon you, darling," he said, not pleasantly. "I wonder what that might be?"

Ella's heart was wildly racing, and she drew in breath, let it out. "They smell the orc who your men attacked, without provocation, upon my lands," she replied. "He was the orc I escorted back to the mountain. He was grievously injured and bloody, and needed much assistance, so I'm sure his scent has lingered."

She held her gaze straight ahead as she spoke, but she could feel the twitch in Alfred's arm, the bore of his eyes into her skin. "Yes, the orc my men tell me you claimed to know. You claimed he was working for you."

"Yes," Ella said firmly, "he was. I hired him to patrol my forest. I have been seeking to support the peace-treaty, especially since we live so close to the mountain, and thought this would be a good means of accomplishing it."

But beside her, Alfred gave a light, tinkling laugh, sending a hard chill up Ella's spine. "I'm afraid you're lying to me, darling," he said coolly. "You see, I *know* this orc. I have known this orc for a very long time. And he is not an orc that would agree to be hired by a human as a petty forest-warden. He is a kind of—prince, among his people. He bears a rare, powerful dark magic, that the orcs seek to use against us."

Damn. Ella's eyes briefly closed, and she sought for a reply, a rebuttal, something—but nothing was there, and beside her Alfred laughed again, harder this time. "I *know* you're lying, darling," he said. "And it's a waste of your breath and my time, and quite frankly, an unmerited insult to my intelligence, and my generosity in coming here to rescue you, and being made to cool my heels outside *Orc Mountain* for half this morning. So"—he drew her to a halt, his voice deepening—"why don't you try telling me the truth."

The truth. The word dragged at Ella, plucking deep inside, and it was enough to bring her eyes darting up, finally, to Alfred's face. His handsome, oddly pinched-looking face, so smooth and unmarked. He hadn't suffered, like Natt had. He hadn't given his soul for his people, like Natt had. But he *had* come for her, he hadn't yelled or shamed or called for war, yet. And maybe—Ella swallowed hard—she could, at least, give him truth.

"The truth is, that orc and I are friends," Ella heard herself say, to those watching blue eyes. "More than friends. I care for him very much. And therefore, Alfred"—she took a breath, drew herself tall—

"I'm sorry, but I'm afraid I must call off our engagement. I no longer wish to marry you."

Something seemed to slip in those blue eyes, sudden and alarming, but then they blinked and it was gone again, only the smile remaining. "I rather expected you were going there, judging by your missing engagement-ring," he said, with astonishing coolness. "I must say, it is rather brazen of you, trying to jilt a *lord* for an *orc*."

The unease pounded higher and higher in Ella's chest, but she gave a hard shake of her head. "That's not the only reason," she said. "In truth, Alfred, I should never have agreed to marry you in the first place. I barely knew you, you barely knew me, and our entire engagement was only a—a transaction. I mean, you only want my inheritance, your attempts to bring me pleasure were positively laughable, and you betrayed me with another woman at our *engagement-party*."

Those eyes seemed to change again, flaring into something bare and frightening, and this time it reached Alfred's smile, cold, brittle, vicious. "And you think an *orc* would do better?" he hissed. "You really think an orc would stay faithful to you, once he got what he wanted from you?"

Ella kept her chin lifted, her gaze fixed on his face. "Yes," she said, "he would. If he swore a pledge to me now, he would keep it. He *loves* me."

The certainty was there, thankfully, the conviction true in her voice, but Alfred's blue eyes were only blinking at her, again, again. "Does he, now," he said, slowly, sending ice down Ella's spine. "Well, darling, at least you've made *some* use of yourself, in all this foolishness."

He grasped at Ella's arm again, propelling her forward with surprising strength, but her feet were dragging on the earth, her eyes searching his smooth, pinched face. "What do you mean," she said. "*What*, Alfred."

But Alfred only shoved her harder, setting her stumbling, and he glanced darkly over her shoulder, up to one of the riders behind her. "Change of plans," he snapped. "You're taking her home to Tlaxca, Byrne, while I go on to the war-council. She's too deluded to be anything but a rubbish witness anyway, and also, I can't stand the smell of her."

Ella couldn't move, couldn't think, and when Alfred shoved at her again, she dug her heels in, and glared up at his face. "I do *not* want to go to Tlaxca, Alfred," she hissed. "I want to go *home*."

Alfred gave an exasperated sigh, and then another rough, impatient shove toward Byrne's horse. "Too bad, darling, because we are getting married, as planned," he drawled. "As soon as my allies properly sanction this war, in retaliation for your kidnapping. This ordeal has made you quite mentally unsound, I'm afraid, and in need of much care—and likely even confinement, once you arrive in Tlaxca. You truly ought to be grateful for my *excessive* generosity in keeping my *pledge* to you."

It felt like a slap, like a sharp punch deep into Ella's undefended stomach, and she had to gasp for air, gaping into Alfred's eyes. They were getting married. Mentally unsound. Confinement. His *pledge*.

"I will *not* marry you, Alfred," she breathed, through her suddenly chattering teeth. "*Ever.*"

But Alfred only snorted, and grasped for something Byrne had thrown at him—and then there was pain, jolting and screaming, as Alfred wrenched Ella around, and shoved her wrists against her back. Lashing something around them, binding them together, good gods, what was *happening*—

Ella desperately squirmed and kicked and flailed at him, but it was too late, and Alfred was still far too strong, yanking the knot tight. And when he thrust her away from him, he was breathing hard, and—Ella pulled and twisted—her hands were firmly bound behind her, with what felt like a length of thick leather.

"Let me go!" she shouted at Alfred, but he only grasped for her again, dragging her over the dirt toward Byrne. And here was the understanding, thoroughly, brutally horrifying, that Alfred was truly going to *kidnap* her, and take her back east, and force her to *marry* him?!

"You utter swine," Ella spat at him, aiming a hard kick straight toward his leg. "I will *never* marry you. I will see you *dead* first."

Alfred's face spasmed, but his grip on Ella's arm only went tighter, lancing pain wide in its wake. "Lovely," he muttered, still breathless. "I always knew there was something seriously wrong with you, *darling*. I *knew* there was a reason that bastard's scent was all over your lands. And I *knew*"—he shoved her bodily upwards, into the hard clutch of Byrne's gripping hands—"if I proposed to you, that slippery fucker would finally show himself, and get what he fucking *deserves*."

The words streaked through Ella like a shot, like burning ice from her head to her feet, and she whipped around to stare at Alfred, while the disbelief—and then the sickening comprehension—screamed white in her thoughts. Alfred had only proposed to Ella because of Natt?! Alfred was kidnapping her, now, to get at *Natt*?!

"You truly mean that?" she gasped, her voice not hers. "You proposed to me as part of your *hunt*?"

But Alfred only gave that cold, terrifying smile, and reached to grip at Ella's chin, giving it a hard little shake. "Yes, you fool peasant," he said smoothly. "Well, for that, and your coin, which we plan to make *very* good use of, after today. Now, unless you want to find yourself dead on this road, reeking of orc, wearing ugly orc gold, with orc-spunk leaking between your legs"—his smile tightened, his hand roughly releasing her chin—"you'll do as you're told, and be the bait you were always meant to be."

With that, Alfred turned and stalked away, while Byrne's rough hands dragged Ella bodily up over his horse, and pinned her like a sack of potatoes over its back. Her head hanging down one side, her feet desperately kicking against the other—until Byrne gave her arse a hard shove, and then an actual *slap* of his hand against it, squeezing tight.

"Stay still, wench," Byrne's awful voice snapped over her. "Else I'll pull up your skirts, and we'll have a bit of fun while we ride."

This couldn't be happening, it couldn't be happening, not before fifteen watching men—but the horse beneath Ella was moving, suddenly, kicking up to a trot, and then a canter. Taking her away from the mountain, away from Natt, and Alfred was using her to try to kill Natt, and start his war anyway, he couldn't, this was not why Ella had done this, truth, love, Natt, run, run, *RUN*—

Ella gulped in breath, squeezed her eyes shut, said a fervent prayer to Akva—and then she wrenched herself to the side, and dropped. Landing with shattering force on the ground below, her body rolling painful and uncontrolled beneath the horse's hooves—but somehow she'd avoided being kicked, and though Byrne's horse was already rearing up, Ella was here. On the earth. In the forest, on her feet.

She kicked off, and ran. Sprinting with surging, breathless force, not down the road, but straight into the trees. Leaping over rocks and roots, ducking and dodging under branches, spraying up dirt under her booted feet. Running up and down and sideways, jumping over a rushing brook, clambering up a rocky hill, *go go GO*—

Her heart was screaming, her legs screaming, and she was wearing a cursed useless *dress*, which kept catching on rocks and brambles. But she'd already grown stronger and faster, these past days, and she was still making good distance and good time, and had even somehow managed to yank her hands free of the leather binding them. And though there was noise behind her, crunching feet and snapping branches, it was far enough that she might just escape them, if she could just keep running, keep going, please, please—

But then, sharp and clear, a bark. More barks. The *dogs*. The dogs, who were trained to follow Natt's scent—the dogs were following *her*.

Fuck, *fuck*, and though Ella only sprinted faster, her fool dress kept catching, brush and branches scraping, her legs bloody and aching. And already there was a dog, here, racing close behind her, nipping at her heels—and even when Ella tried climbing a steep, rocky wall the dog only ran around, and was waiting for her at the top. Barking so loud it hurt her ears, while the crashing noises of the men came closer, from both the south, and the west.

Ella abruptly changed course again, hurtling down and to the east, her feet sliding in muck and water, rapidly becoming deeper—and here was the horrible, miserable realization that they'd chased her into a gods-damned *swamp*.

Another one of the dogs had caught up to her, madly barking with the first, and when Ella made to double back, she reeled up before one of the men, blocking her path. And then more men, one of them *Alfred*, panting heavily, stalking straight toward her, with his unsheathed sword in his hand.

Ella was trapped. And these men were going to *kill* her, and leave her body out to find, with the proof of Natt's taking all over her. They would use her to break the treaty, and launch another *war*.

They couldn't, they *couldn't*, and Ella frantically backed deeper into the cold slippery muck. Gulping for air and courage, quaking all over with every screaming beat of her heart.

"Please, Akva," she choked, between her ragged, hitching breaths. "Please, see me. Help me. You were supposed to bless me."

Alfred had reached the edge of the swamp, eyeing both it and Ella with clear distaste, and he jerked a hand over his shoulder, at Byrne. Clearly about to make him brave the muck instead, and Byrne immediately ran over, wading toward Ella, while she backed away, deeper, deeper.

No. She would drown herself in this swamp before she let them kill her. And at least then her body would never be found, there would be no more war, she was Ella of Clan Grisk and she would *not allow it*—

When suddenly, in the treetops behind the men, there was a quiver, and a crack. And then a huge, grey-green shadow, soaring through the air toward them, and landing in a smooth, graceful roll before rising to its clawed feet.

And with one swift, breathtaking movement, the shadow lunged straight for Alfred's staring, struck-still form—and hurled him with furious force to the ground below.

It was—*Natt*.

36

Natt. Was *here*.

Ella couldn't follow, suddenly, could only gulp and stare, while the truth flashed and shuddered before her eyes. Natt was here, his huge body pinning Alfred flat to the muddy ground, his knee dug deep into his chest. And Natt's sword was gripped in his fist, the steel blade flashing in the light—and then the blade snapped down, and thrust hard against Alfred's exposed neck.

"You foul piddling *warmonger*," Natt growled, his deep voice carrying through the trees. "Who seeks to kidnap and *kill* my blameless, brave mate. Should you now beg her forgiveness, I shall have mercy upon you, and only cut your throat. Should you not"—the flash of Natt's blade streaked downwards, the sharpened tip suddenly digging hard into Alfred's belly—"we shall start here, and I shall *laugh* whilst you *scream*."

Alfred was kicking and flailing and cursing under Natt, shouting wildly for the rest of his men, for help—but Natt's head jerked up toward the men, his eyes blazing, a bloodcurdling growl roaring from his throat. "One more step," he snarled, "and he forever loses this choice. And *you* forever lose your *heads*!"

His sword-point was digging harder into Alfred's gut, already pooling a spot of bright blood onto Alfred's tunic, while Alfred writhed and shouted—but the band of men weren't moving, their wide eyes darting between Natt's face, and that growing spot of blood.

"You shall *beg*," Natt growled at Alfred, deep and threatening. "*Now*."

Alfred's body under Natt was visibly trembling, and his mouth opened, almost as if to speak, to agree—but wait, he still had his own *sword* in his hand, and suddenly he flailed up, swinging the sword straight for Natt's head—

But the movement of Natt's huge body was impossibly fast, ducking and twisting—and somehow he'd caught Alfred's sword-blade with his bare hand. And with another blurry flare of movement, the sword spun in mid-air and came back again, the hilt now grasped tight in Natt's clawed grip, the shining blade-edge flashing down to press powerful and deadly against Alfred's throat.

It left Alfred unarmed and shivering, with a massive, snarling, bloodthirsty orc kneeling over him, pressing two blades against his skin at once. And every muscle in Natt's body was coiled and rigid and ready to strike, his tongue coming out to lick his lips—and then he *laughed*, the sound hard and cruel and devastating. And his sword at Alfred's waist was making a smooth, eager circle, taunting, seeking, about to drive deep—

No. *No.* And suddenly, somehow, Ella was running. Not away, not to safety—but pelting straight toward this. Toward *Natt*.

"NO!" a voice screamed, Ella's voice, and thank the gods Natt heard it, his head rearing up, his eyes flashing with rage. But the blade hadn't sunk home yet, even as it kept drawing circles on Alfred's waist, eager, mocking, hungry for blood.

"*No*, Natt!" Ella choked again, and suddenly she was upon him, her hands grasping desperate for his face, pulling it toward her. Finding the truth in his glittering eyes, truth and rage and death—

"You can't," she gasped, over the thunder of her shouting heartbeat. "You *can't*."

"You shall *not* protect him, woman," Natt barked back at her, all roaring shaking fury. "You are *mine*. And you shall take *joy* in his death with me!"

There was a pathetic-sounding whimper from Alfred beneath

them, but Ella ignored it, and held her wildly trembling hands to Natt's face, held her eyes to his—and nodded. Again, again, again.

"Yes," she choked. "Yes, I should take great joy in this with you. But you *can't*, Natt. You're finally the Speaker. You *need* to be the Speaker. You've given so much for this. You can't just throw that away, and give these horrible men all the grounds they need to start a war. You *can't*."

The rage stuttered in Natt's eyes, but there was a hard shake of his head, a choked noise from his mouth. "This foul man sought to steal you, and force you, and *confine* you," he hissed back. "You are owed vengeance. You are owed his suffering, and his *head*. You are owed a *feast* of his fresh blood!"

They were shocking, vicious words, from this shocking vicious orc. Not only for their violence, but also because—Ella's breath choked—they were Natt throwing away *everything*. His brothers, his place as Speaker, everything he'd worked for all these years—for Ella's vengeance.

Giving up everything, for *her*.

But Ella's hands were still firm on Natt's face, her eyes still true on his soul. "Yes," she breathed, "I know, Natt, and it's so lovely of you to offer me such generous gifts—but you're the Speaker. You're *my* Speaker. I need you. I can't lose you to a war, for this foul *scum* who pretends at being a lord. *Please*, Natt."

It was truth, bare and pure and powerful—and Ella could see it finally sinking home, striking behind those eyes. *You're the Speaker. You're* my *Speaker.*

"I need you, Natt," she choked. "Your brothers need you. Your *sons* need you. *Please*."

Natt blinked, once, and again—and suddenly, Ella knew he was here. He'd heard her. He saw her. He knew.

He *understood*.

His answering nod was pained, bitter, reluctant—but it was *there*. Here, and the relief was alive, catching and sparking and flaring with light. So powerful that Ella nearly staggered with it, and she flung her arms around Natt's stiff neck, and dragged him close.

"Thank you," she breathed, into the delicious warm scent of him. "My wise, generous Speaker. I *love* you."

She could feel his rigid form finally beginning to soften against her, his head bending to her neck—when all around them, suddenly, there was noise and movement and shouting. And when Ella blinked up to look, there was—Natt's *guard*. Yes, Dammarr and Varinn and Thrak and Thrain, all charging out of the trees at once. Coming to circle close around Natt and Ella and Alfred on the muddy earth, swords drawn, throats growling, eyes glaring toward Alfred below them.

And behind them, somehow, there was also—Grimarr. Looking huge and deadly and terrifying, with Baldr and Drafli at each side of him, claws and teeth bared. And then, unbelievably, there was Jule, popping up from behind Grimarr's shoulder—from where she'd been riding on his *back*?—and giving Ella a friendly, cheerful wave.

Beneath Natt, Alfred had begun kicking and flailing and cursing again, but the rest of his men had been backed together by a band of even more orcs. Including Simon and Silfast, both massive and deadly-looking, with Stella close behind Silfast, and John, though he appeared to be entirely unarmed. And there was even Timo, who was still nearly as tall as the men, and brandishing a scimitar toward Byrne with surprising fierceness.

But there had been no actual bloodshed, yet, and every eye seemed suddenly focused on Natt, and Ella, and Alfred. On where Alfred was still writhing and shouting beneath Natt, as if all the commotion had returned his courage again. As if he knew, now that all these witnesses were here, that the danger was past, and he was safe again. A lord. Untouchable.

"How dare you try to murder me, you disgusting *brute*," Alfred spat at Natt's face. "You are going to *regret* this. Now"—he frantically waved toward the cluster of his cornered men—"get over here, Byrne! Help me! And get *her*!"

But Alfred's men didn't move—they were outnumbered by the orcs at least two to one—and John had casually stepped away from the group of orcs, his eyes steady on Natt. "In section two of our Treaty, article four," he said, with astonishing calmness, "reasonable force may be applied to prevent a woman being kidnapped. If that helps."

Alfred was shouting again, but Natt's growl had been steadily rising too, and he swiftly thrust aside both the swords he'd still been holding. And then he also placed Ella away from him, up onto her feet in the mud, with a sharp look that meant, *stay*.

And then, in one smooth, blindingly quick movement, Natt's huge bare fist snapped back—and then slammed down again, straight into Alfred's face.

The punch landed with a sickening crunch, and Alfred's replying howl seemed to shake the air—but his flailing body beneath Natt had sagged limp against the earth, and then, suddenly, there was silence. Blessed, twirling, hurtling silence, broken only by the sudden movement of one of the dogs, who had belatedly rushed over to Natt, and started wildly barking.

The other two dogs eagerly joined in, jumping and dancing around him, and to Ella's vague surprise, Natt reached a tired-looking hand to pet one of them on the head. And then the other ones shoved in, clearly needing to be petted too, and Natt actually obliged, running a familiar, gentle hand over their furry wriggling bodies, using his claws to scratch behind their floppy ears.

But then he smoothly rose to his feet, and turned. And it was like his eyes were again locked to Ella's, and hers to his, and he was being drawn to her, and her to him. And suddenly Natt was here again, *himself* again, his strong arms clamping close and powerful around Ella, his face buried deep into her neck.

Ella was clinging to him too, her muddy legs and feet wrapped around his waist, her arms tight to his back. And she was finally weeping, the tears streaking freely down her cheeks, while Natt's body under hers shuddered too, his harsh breaths lurching thick and desperate against her neck.

"Ach, my lass," he choked. "I am sorry I frightened you. I am sorry I harmed you and failed you. You shall never smell so vexed and afraid again, I swear this to you with my whole soul—"

He abruptly drew back, his huge clawed hands cupping her face, tilting it up with a twitchy reverence. Pleading with her wet eyes to meet his bright ones, to find his truth.

"I ought never to have used you as I did," he said to her, with another shuddery shake of his hands. "I ought never to have hurt you, or harmed you, or put you in such danger, for my own gain. I ought *never* to have kept my truth from you, most of all after you so freely granted yours to me. I was cruel, lass. I was *wrong*."

Ella gave a jerky nod—he *had* been wrong, in too many ways—and he nodded too, strong, fervent. "I shall understand," he continued, his voice hitching, "should you wish to never forgive me, or again see me, or even speak to me. But I shall never stop missing you, or dreaming of you, or longing for you in the night. I shall *never* stop loving you, my sweet lass."

It was truth, stark and bare in his eyes, and he gulped for breath, blinking hard. "And I shall never fail you thus again," he gasped. "I shall never again hurt you or harm you or betray you. I made a pledge to you, and I shall keep it, as you kept yours to me. I shall keep you *safe*. I swear this to you, with my whole soul. From henceforth, *always*."

Ella couldn't speak, but it was still truth, shouting from his eyes to hers, streaming power in its wake. Natt meant this, with his whole soul.

"You shall be mine," he continued, hoarse, vehement. "You shall always be mine, and I shall be yours. And we shall laugh and run and play together, and I shall speak only truth to you. I shall show this to you, I shall please you, I shall teach you I can learn this lesson. If you should grant me trust once more, I shall guard it always. I pledge this to you. As your Speaker, and your friend, and your mate."

He was fully weeping now, the wetness streaking down his scarred face, but his glittering eyes were still here, still bright, still true. Ella's Speaker, her friend, her *mate*. Speaking a new pledge, before all these watching eyes.

And Ella believed him.

She felt herself nodding, nodding, saying yes, *yes*—and there was a guttural, growling sob from Natt's throat. And then a sudden, jolting burst of movement, of heat, as his powerful arms clutched Ella close again, wrapping around her, squeezing so tight she thought she might break.

"Ach," he whispered, thick into her ear. "My brave, lovely lass. Who sees me, and speaks truth to me—and has *saved* me, this day. I love you more than aught else upon this earth. My own Ella, of Clan Grisk."

Ella was gulping into his neck, her entire body clinging to him, dragging in the warm powerful safety of him—when behind them there was a telltale sound. A voice. Alfred's voice.

"How *dare* you beasts do this to a *lord*," it was insisting, and when Ella finally angled her blinking eyes to look, Alfred was sitting up, rubbing at his head, and then spitting out one of his *teeth*. "This is utterly *unconscionable*. Do you fools not realize you've just broken your treaty, and brought *extinction* upon your doorstep? Do you not realize that at this very moment, half this realm's provinces are coming together to prepare for *war* against you?!"

He spoke with a cruel, malicious satisfaction, sending a sudden tension flaring through Natt's body against Ella—but across the way Grimarr had raised a meaningful hand toward Natt, and gave a hard shake of his shaggy head.

"We have broken naught," Grimarr said, his deep voice radiating power. "As my brother says, we have used reasonable force to prevent a woman's being taken against her will. This is all."

"Reasonable force my arse," Alfred hissed back. "You will pay for this, you great lout. You've just given me so much cause for war that even your fool ally Otto won't be able to deny it. Which means, after today, I'll have the combined armies of six whole *provinces* at my back. Thousands upon *thousands* of men. Ready to slaughter you *all*."

A hard jolt of fear chased down Ella's back, but behind Grimarr Jule had rolled her eyes, and stalked out from behind him. "Oh, don't be a fool, Alfred," she snapped. "No one's going to war over this—most of all Otto, when you haven't given him any actual reason to risk his hide, or his coin. You haven't been seriously hurt, and you're the one who's blatantly breaking your own laws, before dozens of witnesses. We've been trailing you ever since you left the mountain, and we heard *everything*."

"Ooooh, *orc witnesses*," Alfred snapped back. "And the word of a few compromised women, against the sworn statements of all these well-born, well-spoken men. Who do you think gets heard in this scenario?"

Jule briefly closed her eyes, looking visibly pained, and turned to Grimarr. "Can we just kill him? Please? I really think Nattfarr could make quite a show of it for us."

Alfred shot a rather gratifying look of sheer terror toward Natt, who was already baring his teeth, his growl vibrating through his chest—but Grimarr slowly shook his head, entirely unmoved. "We have one more witness, whose word ought to weigh well against yours," he said. "Olarr?"

Everyone seemed to look around at once—and there, indeed, back near the trees, stood the massive Bautul battle-captain Olarr. And standing beside him, his handsome face wholly unreadable, was a *man*.

The man only came up to perhaps Olarr's chin, but that meant he was very large for a man, and his broad, muscular form wore well-fitted riding-clothes, his dark head bared to the sun above. And he was someone Alfred clearly knew at a glance, judging by the way his body twitched, his hands clenching tight into the mud beneath him.

"I am Aulis Gerrard, Right Hand to Duke Warmisham of Preia," the new man said, his deep voice carrying. "I have answered Lord Tovey's summons to this council at Khandor on the Duke's behalf, and I wished to, ah"—his eyes betrayed a brief, telling glance toward Olarr's bulk beside him—"review how matters here stood for myself. And I can confirm, Lord Tovey"—he shot a sharp, disapproving frown toward Alfred's muddy form—"all that you have said and done here today."

Alfred was looking even more aggrieved than before, while Jule glanced back and forth between the newcomer and Alfred with an expression of pure glee lighting her face. "Oh, Duke *Warmisham*," she drawled toward Alfred. "I'm sure he'll be delighted to hear all about this from his most *deeply* trusted general. Especially when the Duke has been so generous to your lord father these past months, given your straitened financial situation? Though I did hear some talk of excessive debts owed, and expectations of imminent repayment, but"—Jule thoughtfully tapped her chin with a finger—"surely that's all past now?"

Alfred gave a visible grimace, his slim shoulders rising and falling—and without warning, he lurched up onto his unsteady feet, staggering sideways. And then weaving around to limp toward Natt and Ella—which immediately prompted Natt to set Ella to her feet, and ease his big form in front of her.

"Indeed," Alfred said, the word sounding thick and slurred, and

Ella was unnerved to see that it was because he now seemed to be missing both his front teeth. "In truth, this is all just a foolish misunderstanding, isn't it, Ella darling? I was only trying to rescue you from these vicious orcs. I was trying to keep you *safe*."

Ella huffed an unladylike snort, and glared at Alfred over Natt's shoulder. "You wanted no such thing," she shot back. "You were trying to force me to marry you. And failing that, you were trying to *kill* me, and use my body as a justification for *war*."

Alfred gave her an alarming, toothless smile, and lurched a step closer. "Again, a misunderstanding, darling," he said. "I was only looking out for your future. If you don't marry a man of standing within the next three weeks, you're about to lose *everything*."

He kept giving that awful smile, and there was a vicious, vindictive satisfaction in his blazing eyes. "You'll lose your inheritance," he hissed. "Your father's house. Your precious ancestral *home*."

Ella winced, but Alfred only came a step closer, still giving that horrible smile. "And without all that," he said, "I guarantee you that *they*"—he gave a clumsy wave at the orcs all around—"disappear too. *He* disappears."

He meant Natt, eyeing him now with a pure, triumphant hatred—and Ella quashed down the surge of whispering doubt, and raised her chin. "Natt," she said, "do you care about my inheritance? The truth, if you please."

Because this was a truth they'd never spoken of before, something that had never seemed to come up—and in this moment, Ella realized that she hadn't wanted to bring it up. That she'd been afraid of what Natt's answer might be.

But Natt's hard, purposeful eyes had immediately snapped back to hers, without the slightest hint of hesitation or unease. "Your hoard means naught to me," he said flatly, "beyond what it means to you. It belongs to you, by rights. No one else."

The last of the tension in Ella's body seemed to swirl away at once, and she gave him a wry, relieved grin. "You're sure? You wouldn't even want it to help purchase your lamps?"

But Natt only shook his head, sparing not even a glance to where Alfred was sputtering again beyond them. "It is yours," he said.

"Should you wish to trade for lamps with it, I shall be glad—but should you not, I shall also be content."

Well. And looking at Natt's eyes, so bare and beautiful on hers, it was like the last, missing truth between them had finally settled into place. And without moving her gaze from his, Ella tilted her head toward John, still standing only a short distance away.

"John, when you asked about the filing of my father's will," she began, "you meant to ask whether it had properly become law. Didn't you?"

"I did," replied John's even voice. "And as you confirmed, it has."

"And you also said, previously," Ella continued, her eyes still held to Natt's increasingly uncertain gaze, "that under the terms of our new Treaty, any laws currently in existence that referred to men now refer to orcs, also."

"I did," John said again, with perhaps the faintest trace of impatience. "And as Nattfarr is now an orc of standing—our filing tomorrow with the humans shall call him a duke—you are thus free to proceed as you wish."

Natt was fully frowning, now, his eyebrows furrowed close together, but Ella only nodded, gathering her courage. Her heartbeat was galloping in her chest, her body shivery and trembling, but her eyes were steady, true on Natt's. She was Ella, of Clan Grisk, and she would choose to trust, one more time. She would speak her heart.

"Nattfarr, of Clan Grisk, Speaker of Five Clans," she said, each word a thudding, echoing truth. "Will you marry me?"

37

T he stillness descended with powerful, deafening force. Radiating out from Ella to swallow the world in its strength, in the truths playing one by one across Natt's staring eyes.

Shock. Astonishment. Disbelief. Slowly giving way to understanding, and then appreciation, and then to a rising, deepening awe.

To *joy*.

And in a jolting, forceful movement, Natt's clawed hands grasped for both of Ella's, holding them tight. While those black orc eyes searched her, found her, looked deep into her soul.

"Ach, my Ella, of Clan Grisk," he said, the words sure and fierce. "I will."

The stillness seemed to unfurl for one last instant, almost like approval, like a blessing, and Ella felt herself give him a slow, true smile—and then the quiet around them snapped away all at once. Replaced with shouts and cheers, calls of luck and congratulations, and a bitter curse from Alfred that Ella didn't even blink at.

And when she hurled herself into Natt's strong arms, they were waiting. Grasping her painfully close as he spun with her, his head again buried deep into her neck, his eyes dripping unmistakable wetness against her skin.

"Ach, my sweet, lovely lass," he choked. "You honour me. I have never dreamed of such a gift."

Ella was weeping too, and perhaps laughing at the same time, her face bent into his neck, too. And gods he smelled so good, he was about to be her *husband*, and did that truly mean she could keep everything, the house, the money, his jewels, their forest—

Ella wanted to run, suddenly, or dance, or tackle Natt straight into the swamp and take her filthy pleasure with him—but she was in his arms, warm, safe, it was perfect, perfect. Inhaling that damned intoxicating smell of him, nuzzling her face deeper into his skin, her tongue tasting, his head tilting, her teeth ready, bared, desperately hungry—

And then, to Ella's pure and utter shock, she bit down, hard, sinking her sharp teeth deep into Natt's perfect silken skin. Flooding her mouth with his delicious salty sweetness, the very essence of him, her orc, her mate, soon to be her *husband*, and she should stop and why couldn't she stop and what in Akva's name was she doing, what the hell was Natt thinking, what would he *say*—

She finally shoved herself away, her breaths desperately heaving, her face prickling and flustered and hot. Her eyes wildly, shamefully seeking Natt's, even as she felt her traitorous tongue brazenly come out to lick, slow, at her bloody lips.

But Natt, Natt was only looking at Ella with a rising, trampling warmth, the hunger and the appreciation flashing deep and forceful across his half-lidded eyes. "Look at you, my hungry lass," he said, his voice all liquid melting heat. "With my blood all over your sweet maiden mouth. Such a filthy, clever little beast, who learns all my wishes without even a word from my tongue."

Oh. So he'd—*wanted* that. Ella was gulping for air, the relief feeling like a physical force, while Natt gave a low, rolling laugh, his shameless hand come down to brush at her nipple-ring through her dress. "But should you do this again," he murmured, promised, "I shall tear off these fool clothes at once, and fuck you where we stand."

A shiver of delicious heat swirled down Ella's back at the too-tempting thought, but when she shot a belated glance around, they still had quite a sizeable audience. Olarr and the Duke of Preia's man had seemed to vanish, as well as John, but the rest of Alfred's men were all still here, lurking uneasily about.

And, of course, there was still Alfred himself. Who was standing only a few steps away, and gaping at Ella and Natt with a shocked, glittering rage in his eyes.

Natt growled again, the sound rumbling deep in his chest—and in reply, without warning, Alfred hurled himself toward them. His toothless mouth shouting, his fists swinging—and this time, Natt's swift, powerful punch landed Alfred straight in the chest. Sending him wheezing and staggering backwards, his arms flailing, until he finally collapsed back onto the earth, and lay still.

"Somebody get this fool out of here before he gets himself killed," said a voice, Jule's voice, clipped and annoyed. "Byrne, is it? Why don't you toddle off and get a horse to strap him to, and we'll have a band escort you all back to Tlaxca. And if this titled arse ever expresses a wish to return—either to here or Ella's lands—please do us all a favour, and remind him that he'll lose more than a few teeth next time."

Byrne gave a pathetic-looking nod and obediently shuffled off, and after a jerk of Grimarr's head, Baldr and Drafli went prowling close behind him. And Natt began leading Ella away too, his arm heavy and warm around her shoulder—but Ella had stopped, briefly, to look down at Alfred's sprawled form beneath them. Alfred, her former betrothed, the man who'd betrayed her, and given them such grief.

He was still conscious, if seemingly deprived of breath, his eyes glaring balefully between Ella and Natt—but suddenly Ella felt only contempt, and maybe even a distant, detached pity. She could do this. She was.

"Why don't we make a deal, Alfred," she said, voice flat. "I won't bring any kidnapping accusations publicly against you, if you stop hunting my betrothed, *forever*. I mean, you finally got him"—she waved at Natt beside her—"and see how well that worked for you."

Alfred's rapidly bruising mouth did something that might have been a grimace, but Ella was taking it as a yes. "And as surety for your pledge to cease all orc-hunting at once," she continued, "I'll be keeping these dogs for my own, thank you very much."

The dogs were indeed still sniffing and jumping at Natt's legs, one giving what seemed like an approving little bark—and when Alfred groaned, Ella ignored it, and gave him a decisive nod. "Oh, and a word of advice," she said. "Next time you become betrothed to a woman, I would suggest keeping your hands to yourself at your engagement-party."

Natt gave an appreciative grunt beside Ella, and then ushered her away, with the dogs following close at their heels. "My bright, clever lass," he murmured—and then hesitated, mid-step, to frown down at where Ella was slightly limping on her soaked boots. "Ach, are you *hurt*?"

She tried protesting—it was only a few cuts and scrapes—but Natt cut her off with a disapproving growl, and snatched her up bodily into his powerful arms.

"I shall carry you back to the mountain," he said firmly. "You have faced much today, my lass. You must needs be tended, and petted, and fed, and healed. And bathed, also, for you are filthy, yet again."

Ella attempted a snort, and an elbow in his gut, but Natt only chuckled and cuddled her closer as he walked, bending his face to nuzzle into her hair. "You have brought me such pride this day, my lass," he said. "Even as I raged against this man, it was such joy to see you run from him as you did, so free and swift. You should have easily escaped them, if not for my scent upon you."

Ella pulled back a little to blink up at him, her head tilting against his shoulder. "Um, how did you see?" she asked carefully. "You weren't—there. Were you?"

"Was I not?" Natt replied, his lip twitching up, enough to show a sharp white tooth. "I could follow your scent to the end of the realm and back again. You think I should not follow when you are taken away from me, by my greatest enemy?"

Ella kept blinking at him, slowly putting that together. Natt, his guard, all the orcs, even John, and Olarr, and the Right Hand to Preia's *duke*...

"You planned it all?" Ella asked, her voice faint. "You *planned* to follow me, and rescue me from Alfred?"

Natt gave a twitchy shrug, a wry smile. "I only meant to come with you, and be sure you were safe," he said. "But the captain had this plan instead. He claimed he only did this because I should be a better Speaker with you by my side, and his mate wishes you to stay, but"—Natt's mouth grimaced—"I ken this was what he meant to do all this time. To test my fealty, and foil this man's plans for war—and also to halt my being hunted, and push me to reclaim my bonded mate, all at once."

Ella had been nodding along, considering that—until those odd, unexpected words *bonded mate*. And she didn't even have to ask, because Natt was already grimacing again, and letting out a long, heavy sigh.

"And here is the one last truth I ought to have spoken of, my lass," he said. "And it is one you ought to have known long ago, but I did not wish to frighten you, or give you cause to think you could not yet leave, or break it. Or that I had tricked you into it before you knew what it meant. But I—"

He'd been speaking very quickly, the words tumbling from his mouth, and Ella brought up her trembly hand to spread against his chest, feeling the rapid thuds of his heartbeat. But then feeling his heart slow, too, at her touch, his breath coming out thick and deep.

"You and I are mated, lass," he said, quiet. "We have been mated since we spoke that pledge, all those summers past. Do you remember what I spoke to you that day, after you spoke your pledge to me, and granted me your blessing?"

Ella's thoughts hurtled backwards, back to that peaceful, magical day deep in the forest, when Natt's hands had held both of hers, and his eyes had looked into her soul. When she'd said *Yes, Nattfarr of Clan Grisk. I will.*

And then, after that. When Natt's gangly body had seemed to shiver all over, his black eyes flaring with purpose, determination, relief. With truth.

"I pledge you my troth, my Ella," his voice said, so soft, matching the words he'd said so long ago. "I grant you my favour, and my sword, and my fealty. I shall keep you safe. So long as I am able, and so long as you shall wish."

There was a pure, powerful prickling under Ella's skin, a warmth unfurling bright and wide, understanding finally settling deep. Natt had been her *mate*. All this time.

"I swore, before all my fathers and mothers, and all the gods, to keep you safe," he whispered. "It was why I could not return to you, for all these years. I sought to keep my pledge to you."

Oh. Ella's eyes briefly closed, her thoughts reorienting themselves, settling around this new truth—but then she was blinking at him again, shifting in his arms.

"But you," she said, oddly breathless, "you didn't keep it. Did you? You said you took pleasure with others, you—"

Her hand had given a fluttery wave toward where all four of his guard were striding a short distance behind them, Dammarr included—but Natt only gave a hard, jerky shake of his head. "Pleasure, mayhap," he said, "but never fealty, lass. Not the same as what I held toward you. And I ken I have not told you this either, but I have never done this with another woman. You are the only woman I have ever touched. The only one whose scent is upon me."

His voice had gone low and fierce at the end, his head bowing to hers, his breath inhaling deep. "And when I first was taken by another," he said, "it was not of my choosing. And I had thus lost all hope of becoming scent-bound to you, and after this, it seemed better to claim this for myself. Better to take what peace I could find, in a world that had stolen my true mate, and my true calling, away from me."

Ella's throat felt very thick, suddenly, too much to speak, and instead she nodded, quick and fervent, her hand clenching against his bare chest. And Natt nodded too, and squeezed her even closer, rocking her against him.

"It—shocked me," he breathed, "when we met again, and you had kept your pledge. We were so young when we spoke this, I ought to have waited, it was not right for me to speak such a vow without first teaching you the full weight it carried for me, and among my kin. I was short-sighted in this, and selfish, just as the captain has said. You could have broken this pledge. You *ought* to have broken it."

Ella grimaced, and tried to clear her throat, to find words again. "Well, I kind of did break it," she said. "With Alfred."

But Natt only gave a derisive snort, a hard shake of his head. "This broke naught, it was so pitiful," he snapped. "I washed away his foul scent from you our first night. And all the rest"—his voice went lower, assured, triumphant—"you kept for *me*."

Ella nodded, without hesitation, and Natt shot her another wry, breathtaking smile. "I have never been so felled in all my days," he murmured, "or so hunger-drunk, as I was that night. It is a gift of the gods that I did not frighten you away from me for all time. Or that you did not have me killed, when I sought to kidnap you."

Ella's laugh was choked, but warm. "Compared to Alfred's kidnapping," she said, "yours was a pleasant diversion, Natt. I mean, apart from those *clothes.*"

Her shudder at the thought was still real, even now, and Natt laughed aloud, and again bent his head to inhale at her hair. "Ach," he said. "I did not yet ken that you only longed to be dressed as the orc's mate you truly were."

Ella couldn't even argue that, giving a disapproving frown down at her current ensemble, earning another peal of laughter from Natt's mouth. "Soon, lass," he said. "Once I have brought you home."

Home. There was something in that, suddenly, charging to life between them, and Natt's head had already tilted thoughtfully, his eyes studying hers. "To your second home, mayhap," he said. "You wish to keep your own also, do you not?"

The possibility of that was still too new, too tenuous, to really feel real—but Ella made herself consider it, drawing in a deep breath. Seeking truth.

"I do want to keep my home," she said. "But I also want a home with you, Natt."

His answering nod was firm, quick, decisive. "Thus, you shall have both," he replied. "It is a gift of the gods that these two homes are so near to one another. You shall live upon your lands, and come to our mountain as oft as you should wish. And thus"—his eyes twinkled—"we shall have ample time to run and play between them, also."

The thought was suddenly almost too delightful to be true—Ella could run the forest with Natt again, with no fear, and no shame. She could be Ella of Clan Grisk, and perhaps even still Ella Riddell, when she wished.

She was grinning up at Natt, her audacious fingers coming up to gently brush at her teeth-marks against his neck, and his broad replying grin was so viciously wicked, it took her breath away.

"There is much you must yet learn, my lass," he said, his voice heated and smooth. "You cannot *fathom* all the lessons your hungry mate shall teach you. First, I ken, shall be how to best bring an attacker to his knees, when next you are so rudely kidnapped."

The words sent a marvellous surge of heat straight to Ella's groin, and she gave a choked, breathless laugh. "*Next time?*" she asked, husky. "You orcs are the most devious creatures *imaginable*, Nattfarr."

But he only kept grinning, holding her, warm and rich and wonderful. "Ach," he said. "Just as my filthy beast has always wished."

And in a breath, in that truth, Natt clasped her closer against him, and ran.

38

Ella and Natt's triumphant return to the mountain was met with more hoots and hollers and congratulations, and with Ella being bodily brandished again and again over Natt's head.

"My mate has defeated the man hunting me!" he said to every orc who approached, no matter the clan, no matter how warily they greeted him. "My mate has asked me to *wed* her!"

Even the wary-eyed orcs—even those from Skai and Bautul—smiled and nodded at that, and gave Natt careful claps on the back, which he returned with force, and an almost maniacal grin. "You ought to have seen this man mewling through his missing teeth," he gleefully told a huge, bewildered-looking Skai orc. "We even stole his hunting-dogs!"

The three dogs had refused to enter the mountain, and had halted outside it, whining—but Jule, who'd caught up to them with surprising speed, had promised to take care of the dogs for the time being, and had accordingly taken them off toward a nearby timber-framed building that appeared to be an actual *stable*.

"This is good," the Skai orc said, in a heavily accented voice. "Shall we thus make merry tonight?"

"Yes, we shall," replied a familiar voice behind them, and when

Ella whipped around, it was again Jule, giving a grin that looked almost as maniacal as Natt's. "In the muster-room. I'm having a fresh supply-cart delivered. We're so glad you're safe, Ella. And that everything's all worked out."

"I'm glad too," Ella said, with a true, genuine smile toward her. "I'm so grateful to you and Grimarr for coming up with that plan, and rescuing me. Thank you."

But Jule only waved it away, and beamed at them again before taking off back down the pitch-black corridor. And Natt hoisted Ella up again, and then jogged off in the opposite direction, still speaking delightedly to every orc that passed.

They spent a short stint with Efterar, during which Efterar became so annoyed with Natt's bounding about that he sent him out of the room altogether. And next was a trip to the baths, where Natt carefully, reverently removed all Ella's jewels but the piercings, and drew her into the water—but their heated embrace was almost immediately interrupted by Thrak and Thrain and Dammarr and Varinn, who had also been sunk half to the knees in swamp-muck.

"This is *your* fault," Thrak informed Ella, as he shucked off his muddy trousers, revealing a tall, scarred, muscled grey body, and an alarmingly large orc-prick. "Why you thought it was a good idea to run us all into the bog, I can't fathom."

Ella belatedly dragged her eyes away, from both him and the other undressing orcs, and fixed her gaze on Natt's amused face. "Well," she said, with a wince, "if those awful men were going to kill me, they at least weren't getting my body to frame Natt with."

Natt's face briefly stilled, a darkness passing across his eyes, and he clutched Ella closer against him in the water, his clawed fingers sinking almost painfully into her skin. "Brave lass," he murmured, against her neck. "I love you, my sweet mate. I thank you for such kindness toward me."

There was a snorting noise from above them, and a massive splash from what had clearly been Dammarr, who was now shaking the water out of his long, loose black hair. "If you want to thank anyone," he snapped, "thank the captain. Or Olarr. I know he swore to help you, but I ken the captain had *something* on him, to make him trot out his pretty man on command like that."

"Ach, surely it was something good," said Thrain, with gusto, as he also leapt into the pool, with Varinn close behind. "That man looked ready to faint."

"Or, mayhap Olarr had just ploughed him, straight before this," Thrak cheerfully pointed out. "I ken I should be ready to faint from this also."

They all laughed, even Ella—but across from them Varinn was looking thoughtful, stretching his muscular arms out wide along the pool's stone edge. "Olarr has seemed in good spirits these past weeks, though, has he not?" he asked. "Timo said he has even offered to help Simon train with him. That is not like him."

"Ach, mayhap it is the power of a good mate," Natt replied, with a wink toward Ella, as he maneuvered himself behind her in the water, his familiar glorious hardness teasing at just where she most wanted it. "Or a good prick, wielded hard and often. There is great joy in this, ach, my lass?"

He grinned at Ella, waggling his black eyebrows, his hungry hand already sliding with purpose down her front—but Dammarr snorted again, and with a sharp slice of his hand, sent a stream of hot water straight in Natt's face. "Ach, you prick, there is," he snapped. "Rub it in, why don't you. Again. Why don't you remind us again that she's scent-bound to you, too?"

"Ach, just wait until she blooms with his son," interjected Thrak, with a wink toward Ella. "You may find yourself without a mate, woman, if his raving becomes too much for his guard to bear."

His son. The thought sent an odd, thrilling surge of heat through Ella, and perhaps through Natt too, judging by the sudden press of his hardness between her legs—but Natt's gaze was still on Dammarr, a speaking, sparking glint in his narrow eyes.

"Let us speak further upon this, Dammarr," he said coolly. "Now that I have found my mate again, no, you shall no longer have my ploughing whenever you wish. But there is naught stopping you from seeking this elsewhere. I ken, like Olarr, it shall do you much good."

Thrak hooted, rather loudly, while the other two grinned—and it was to Thrak that Natt turned next, his eyebrows raised. "And I ken, Dammarr," he said, "that Thrak should take much joy in this. I ken he shall make you scream, just as I did."

The room had fallen instantly, utterly silent, every eye darting between Thrak and Dammarr. Both of whom had also gone very still, Thrak with a telltale glitter in his dark eyes, Dammarr with a creeping pink beneath his grey cheeks. And it occurred to Ella, suddenly, that Dammarr was probably quite a nice-looking orc, what with his straight nose and long thick hair, and that Thrak clearly thought so too.

"*He*," Dammarr said, into the silence, "is a smug, prideful fool, who thinks he is funny, when he is not."

"Ach, and Nattfarr is better?" Thrak shot back, with surprising defensiveness. "All you need for a good ploughing is a good prick, and this I have. Bigger than his, too."

There was more stillness, during which Natt slowly grinned, and across the pool Thrain gave a hard shake of his head, as if seeking to rid something out of it. "Och, time to go, I ken," he said. "Varinn?"

His voice at the last was tentative, his eyes uneasy on Varinn—but Varinn fervently nodded, his big dripping body already leaping up out of the pool. "Ach, I have no need to witness this," he said. "Though I am sure we shall, sooner or later."

With that, he grabbed a towel and strode off, with Thrain close behind. Leaving only Natt and Ella, and Thrak and Dammarr, both of whom now seemed to be intently avoiding one another's gaze.

"Do you wish to go also, lass?" Natt murmured in her ear. "Or do you wish to see Thrak make Dammarr scream?"

The proper thing to do would be to leave, of course, but Ella's brazen, betraying body seemed entirely caught still, her fingers clenching at Natt's thigh behind her. And in reply Natt chuckled, nuzzling brief at her neck, before turning back to Dammarr again, with a decided smugness on his mouth.

"Ach, Dammarr, this settles it," he said cheerfully. "My mate wishes to see this, filthy lass that she is. And after how vexed you have made her these past days, you truly ought to offer her some relief."

Dammarr muttered something in black-tongue, but Natt only laughed, and drew Ella's back closer against his chest. "Now watch and learn, my filthy little lass," he murmured. "I ken they shall make this a good show, for you."

Thrak's eyes angled toward Ella, and he actually *winked*, along with a cocky jerk of his head—but then his gaze settled back onto Dammarr again, a feral, hungry heat kindling beneath his half-lidded eyes.

Dammarr was looking back, his face gone rather startled, the whites of his eyes visible all around. And when Thrak strode through the water toward him, slow and purposeful, Ella could see Dammarr's lips actually parting, his broad shoulders rising and falling. "No biting," he murmured. "You're not scarring me, you prick."

"Not yet," came Thrak's reply, smooth, arrogant, as his clawed hand slid up, and gently hooked a finger into Dammarr's nipple-ring—and then yanked him forward, closing the space between them. "When I do mark you, you shall beg me for it."

His other hand had come up to stroke at Dammarr's long hair, petting it almost sweetly, drawing it together into his fist. Leaning closer, closer as he wrapped it around his hand, thick and black and shining, until his hand was up at Dammarr's neck, tilting his head back. So close their mouths were nearly brushing, even as Dammarr bared his sharp teeth, and Thrak slowly, wickedly smiled back—

And in a swift, dizzying movement, Thrak whirled Dammarr bodily around, bending him double, his fist still caught deep in Dammarr's hair. And though what was happening below their waists was mostly concealed by the water, Ella could hear Dammarr's gasp, could see the sudden tension shivering across his grey skin.

"Stubborn, pretty orc," Thrak purred, his eyelashes fluttering, as his other hand disappeared under the water, stroking along the hard curve of Dammarr's bent-over arse. "Feel how tight you are for me. Shall I make this easy for you? Or not?"

Dammarr's chest was already heaving, his eyes squeezed shut, his head shaking. "Not," he gasped. "Bastard."

Thrak's growl was deep, choked, shuddering, as he shifted his hips, seeking his place. His eyes closing, his head bowing, almost as if in supplication, or worship, the moment caught and still all around—

And then, in a swift thrash of movement, he drove forward. Hard enough that Dammarr's whole body arched up, a guttural howl rippling from his throat.

"Fucker," he hissed, between choking breaths, but when Thrak circled his hips, Dammarr moved too, their bodies now locked, joined as one. And Thrak murmured something in soft, heated black-tongue as he drew out, smooth, sweet, almost gentle—

Until he slammed inside again, deep and brutally powerful, while Dammarr shouted and flailed, his clawed hands grasping at nothing. And when Thrak dragged out again, slower this time, there was a sound much like a whimper from Dammarr's throat, his body taut and jerking, waiting, waiting—and then flaring up as Thrak drove inside and stayed there, circling, taunting, demanding.

"Tell me you like it," Thrak breathed, tugging back on Dammarr's hair, bringing his face close. "Tell me I please you."

Dammarr only bit his lip and gasped for breath, his clawed hands scrabbling for the side of the pool. Earning another hard yank from Thrak on his hair, another slow, torturous drag out—and then a punch inside that made Dammarr's whole body arch and thrash against him, another guttural howl tearing from his throat.

"Tell me," Thrak hissed, as he thrust forward again, again, again, Dammarr's shouts rising with every stroke. "Speak this, you stubborn wench, I can feel you, I can *smell* you—"

But Dammarr was baring his teeth, and furiously shaking his head against Thrak's grip. And when Thrak growled back, Dammarr somehow shoved away from him entirely, whirling around to face him, and—Ella gasped—he swung his fist straight at Thrak's *face*.

Thrak ducked, just in time, but one of his hands was still caught in Dammarr's hair, and Dammarr's other fist shot up, clipping Thrak on the cheekbone. Hard enough that Thrak's head snapped sideways, his mouth hissing—and then he lunged for Dammarr, shoving him bodily to the opposite side of the pool.

Dammarr swung for Thrak again, making impact in the hard muscle of his torso this time—but then, with astonishing speed, Thrak leapt out of the water entirely. Dragging Dammarr after him by the hair, and slamming him on his back to the stone floor beneath.

"Too slow," Thrak growled, as Dammarr sucked in desperate breaths, and Thrak shoved his legs up and apart, deftly maneuvering his hips between. "Fuck-drunk. Weak and foolish for me. Wishing for more. Ach?"

Thrak held himself there, poised, his tall, dripping-wet body hovering over Dammarr's heaving, trembling one—and Ella realized he was truly waiting this time. Searching Dammarr's blinking eyes, as his big hand slowly unwound from Dammarr's hair, letting it fall to the stone beneath them.

"Ach?" he said again, quiet, almost a caress, and Ella could see Dammarr swallowing, gasping, and—nodding.

And then Thrak's hips sank deep, Dammarr crying out and arching up—and this time it was like their smooth, muscled, dripping-wet grey bodies were moving together, writhing swift and graceful with each other, rather than against. Thrak gasping in black-tongue, Dammarr's moans once again rising, his claws scraping hard on Thrak's back, faster and wilder and so desperate Ella could almost taste it—until Dammarr's whole body jerked still, and he shouted, so loud it echoed across the room, while thick white suddenly sprayed wide from between them, splattering on the floor, on their joined bodies, even toward Natt and Ella.

Natt swiftly yanked Ella out of the way, hissing toward them—but neither one noticed, because now it was Thrak shouting, his hips rammed deep and quivering against Dammarr, every muscle in his grey body taut and corded and sharp as his dark head arched back, his face contorted with sheer, violent pleasure.

And then the tension seemed to leave Thrak's body at once, as he sagged down onto Dammarr. As Dammarr's hand on his back splayed wide, now bearing no claws, while his own body sagged beneath.

"This pleased you," Thrak murmured, almost too quiet for Ella to hear. "I wish you to speak this to me."

"I shall not," Dammarr replied, though his voice wavered. "You have only shown yourself even more of a rude and selfish prick than I knew you to be."

"Ach, and I drew your seed without one touch to your prick," Thrak shot back. "*He* has never done such for you."

"And you were watching each time for this, were you?" Dammarr retorted. "Pathetic."

Thrak bared his teeth at Dammarr, but Dammarr only gave a chilly smile in return—at least, until Thrak lowered his face into his neck, inhaling deep. "I smell you," he murmured. "This pleased you."

Dammarr huffed some kind of protest, but didn't move, and behind Ella Natt chuckled, his clever hand slipping between her parted legs, tracing light and teasing against her shamefully swollen heat.

"Ach, and this pleased you too, did it not?" he purred. "My hungry, filthy little mate. Taking such joy in your enemy's utter defeat."

Dammarr had turned his head to growl at Natt, but Natt only grinned back, and then twisted and jumped up out of the pool, reaching a hand to pull up Ella after him. "We must dress," he said, "and ready ourselves for this party."

Ella's mouth was watering, suddenly, her eyes darting up and down Natt's naked, dripping-wet body, with his huge cock standing fully at attention. And when her hands reached for it, seemingly on their own, Natt gave her a jaunty, approving smile, a meaningful pat at her arse.

"Ach, you shall have this, lass," he said. "Soon."

With that, he grabbed for Ella's jewels, and then strode toward the door, still dripping and entirely naked, leaving Ella to blink at his gorgeous rounded arse. And once she'd belatedly grasped for a towel and chased after him, wrapping the towel around the essential parts, he immediately tugged down the top of it, enough to expose her bare breast, with the jutting nipple-ring.

"Better," he said, with a smug grin. "You shall learn, lass."

That became all too evident as Natt once again dressed her in the Grisk storage-room. Tying on her usual leather kilt, and then adding the gold cuffs back on her arms and her ankle, and slinging the gold belt around her waist. But other than the chains cupping beneath her breasts, Ella was still bare from the belly up, and Natt stepped backwards, his assessing eyes sweeping up and down her form.

"Good," he said, as he brought up a finger and gently nudged at Ella's nipple-ring, sending a series of jolting shivers deep into her breast. "You are ready."

Ready, like this, with nothing covering her top half whatsoever—but there wasn't even space to protest, suddenly, what with the heated hunger buzzing through Ella's skin. "Are you?" she murmured, stepping forward, reaching a hand to his groin, to curve around that too-tempting hardness. "Just like this?"

Natt raised an eyebrow at her, glancing downwards, but his mouth twitched up, his shoulder giving a rolling shrug. "If this is what you wish, my fair one," he purred, "I shall wear naught at all."

Of course he would, the bastard, but Ella's eyes had angled toward the shelf opposite, where a familiar-looking fur was neatly stacked on top. And she *had* liked how he'd looked in those, so with a twitch of a grin she reached for it, and shook it out. It was indeed the kilt, so she carefully tied it around his waist, briefly lamenting the loss of her previous view, but—she slipped her hand under, gave a little squeeze—rather enjoying the massive tent he made in front.

His cock flared in reply, but the rest of him only stood there, watching with approving eyes, waiting. So next Ella pulled out the fur cape, and tied it around his shoulders, once again giving him the sudden look of a huge, dangerous warrior prince.

"Ach," Ella said, with another teasing grin, and another pat at the front of his kilt, before going for the box with the jewelry, and rummaging through it. There wasn't much left—between the two of them, they would clearly be wearing most of the Grisk hoard—but maybe that was just how Natt wanted it, his eyebrows still arched, waiting.

She began with a thick, plain gold cuff, slowly sliding it over his clawed hand, and up into place on his muscled forearm. And then the same on the other side, and then—she had to hold up the next piece, frowning at its intricate, flexible braided ropes—one for his upper arm, over his bicep, the gold weaving made stretchy enough to allow the muscle to flex beneath it.

Next she slid another gold hoop into his left ear, and a long, sharp-looking earring for the other side, almost resembling a curved tooth. And last, one more thick gold chain, with a huge emerald hanging off the end, and when Ella lifted it up, Natt willingly ducked his head, and let her settle it around his neck.

When he looked back at her, his eyes were heated, glinting with meaning, but Ella made herself ignore it, in favour of sidling behind him, and tugging out his wet, messy braid with her fingers. And then combing through his thick black hair again and again, while he tilted his head back, and the past and the present suddenly jolted together, all at once. He was Ella's mate, her best and oldest friend, and her hands slightly shook as she braided his beautiful hair, and tied it off with a black ribbon, and stepped around to look at him.

And for an instant, it was like she was seeing him with entirely new eyes. A hulking, heavy-featured orc, with a badly crooked nose, and scarred grey-green skin. With huge shoulders and arms, a hard, muscled torso, a twitching tented kilt. With flashes of gold studded all over him, blatantly flaunting not only his wealth and his position among his kin, but also his strong, rippled body, his smooth burnished skin.

He was hideous, frightening, shocking, shameless—and also fierce, powerful, rugged, with a deadly, defiant beauty that seemed to choke at Ella's soul. And he was *hers*. He was Ella's bonded mate, soon to be her husband, the father of her *children*...

Her shaky hand had reached up to brush against his scarred cheek, earning an immediate, snaky lick of his tongue against her fingers. Making Ella gasp, even as she blinked back the rising wetness behind her eyes, and slipped a finger between those parted lips.

"Gorgeous orc," she murmured, her gaze holding his, speaking her truth, as Natt brazenly sucked on her finger, twirling his tongue around it. "You are the most thrilling creature *alive*, Nattfarr of Clan Grisk. Gods, I just want to pin you down and *fuck* you."

The shocking words rolled off her tongue without the slightest hesitation, sparking a sudden, wolfish grin on Natt's mouth. And then a swift reach of his arm toward the box, his clawed hand grasping, and finding—

That. The thick, gold, rounded ring, for down *there*. And when Natt held it up to Ella, eyebrows raised, she willingly took it, and then reached down beneath his kilt, and drew him out.

And as she eased the ring down his length, their eyes stayed locked, silently speaking, held on this truth. *It enforces the vow of a mate*, Natt had said, and there'd been meaning in that Ella hadn't known at the time—but she knew now, and somehow it did feel like another truth, another pledge, as she slid it flush to the base of him, and then drew those heavy bollocks through, pressing her gold close against his groin. Her orc, proudly wearing her ring, on the part of him that from now on would always, only, be hers.

And it felt right, suddenly, that Natt not take her here, in secret, where no one could see—but that he should instead grasp his lamp, and guide Ella's topless form out of the room. Out into the corridor, where he slung his warm arm over her shoulder, his warm hand reaching down to cup at her breast. Leaving the other—the pierced one—fully exposed, peaked, hungry.

At the sight of the first orc, striding up the corridor toward them, Ella felt her steps falter, the old familiar shame surging—but Natt's hand was firm, his body solid and close, his eyes flaring with unmistakable pride as he nodded at the orc and murmured a greeting, his voice husky, warm, triumphant.

And that was enough, suddenly, to keep Ella's head held high, her stride steady, as more staring orcs passed. As she and Natt approached what had to be the muster-room, what with the considerable noise emanating from within, and many more orcs spilling out of the door, all seeming to talk and laugh at once.

The orcs easily parted for Ella and Natt, though many of them fell silent, their eyes sliding to Ella's bare chest—but Ella only looked at Natt, at the flashing pride in his eyes, and shoved down the whispers of unease and shame. She was Ella, of Clan Grisk, and why should she not dress to please her beautiful hungry mate? Why should she not dress to please *herself*?

That was a new thought, but one that suddenly felt surprisingly true, as Ella turned her attention, perhaps for the first time, to the current ease of her movements, the freedom of her arms and legs. The lack of constriction anywhere, the beautifully forged gold all over her, teasing and whispering when she moved. The expanses of her bare skin ready to be touched, stroked, at any moment.

The truth of that seemed to brush the shame further away, perhaps just in time, as they stepped into the crowded, bustling room—and then Ella's mouth dropped open, and all other thoughts vanished into nothing, because even after Natt's Revel, she had never seen a party like this.

There were drumbeats and dancing, games and competitions, sparring and wrestling. There was what appeared to be a mountain of food in one corner, including several entire *boars*, and multiple barrels of wine and ale. And there had to be *hundreds* of orcs, all laughing and shouting and celebrating at once, and the noise was almost deafening, fighting against the drums to create a pounding, heart-jolting chaos.

And amidst it all, there were orcs taking their pleasure. Not only against the walls and in dark corners, but in the centre of the room a cluster of benches had been pushed together, and upon them was a sight that rivalled what Ella had seen in the Skai common-room. Orcs writhing and gasping together, some taking some giving, with mouths and hands and bare exposed arses.

And—Ella very nearly choked—there was even Grimarr, and *Jule*. With Jule's tall, heavily pregnant, entirely naked form straddled close upon Grimarr's lap, her hips slowly rising up to reveal the massive, glistening-wet orc-prick embedded deep between her legs.

Good gods. Ella couldn't move, suddenly, but beside her Natt only laughed, his claw gently teasing at her peaked nipple. "This is one more lesson for you, lass," he murmured, close in her ear. "How to honour your mate by taking him before all his mountain. Should you wish to try this, with me?"

Should she. And as Ella watched Jule sink down, her back arching while that invading thickness disappeared deep inside, there was the shuddering, heated realization that perhaps she should wish to try this. Or, rather, she *did*.

Ella's mouth was dry, her body prickling, her face heating—but looking at Natt, at her rugged shameless mate, she only felt a raw, compelling craving, pounding louder with every deafening beat of the drum. She was Ella, of Clan Grisk. And she wanted her mate, longed for him, needed to flaunt his beauty and power for all to see.

So she grasped her shaky hand to his, squeezing tight—and then led him through the gathering of orcs, and straight toward the nearest empty bench. Only turning to look at Natt once they'd reached it, and drinking up the surprise, the warmth, the blazing hunger in his watching black eyes.

But Natt wasn't moving, he was waiting, the audacious beast, and slowly licking his lips with his long black tongue. And Ella was suddenly, forcibly reminded of their first night together, of his teasing words and sweet, patient kisses. *We shall have this, now. Kiss me. Feel how I long to fill you.*

Ella's own tongue had come out to lick her lips, her eyes running up and down Natt's beautiful form, drinking him up. And when her hands finally reached up for his broad, fur-covered shoulders, shoving him downwards, he didn't resist, just sank his body heavily onto the bench, blinking up at her with greedy, crackling eyes.

It was easy to straddle him, to find her way into the safety of his warmth. Her hands sliding around the back of his neck, her head ducking to drink in the familiar, delicious scent of him. While he did the same to her, his breath inhaling thick, hard, deep, as though he too were drowning, lost in the power of this, mated, together, at last.

His thighs beneath her had sprawled wider, drawing hers further apart over him, but there were still two layers of clothing separating them—at least, until Ella felt Natt's hand tugging on her kilt. And suddenly the leather had fallen away entirely—and Ella was straddled fully naked over an orc at a *party*. Her legs spread wide apart, her bare arse exposed, her swollen wet heat visibly, desperately clenching for relief.

The shock and the shame were back again, swarming Ella with furious force, and it was all she could do to keep herself from leaping up and running away—but suddenly Natt's warm hands were here, on her hot face, making her meet his dazed black eyes.

"You honour me, my brave lass," he breathed. "You honour your mate when you show your hunger for all to see. You honour me when you are bared, scent-bound, dripping wet for me. You honour me when"—he dropped one of those hands, and slid his finger between her legs, setting her wetness madly clenching against it—"you flaunt your sweet fat womb for me, and show that the only scent upon it, the only seed within it, is *mine*."

The last came out a growl, his wet finger slowly rising to his lips, his tongue curling long and tantalizing against it. "Honour me," he breathed, the words a deep, thudding heat in Ella's exposed, clenching groin. "Show me."

The hunger was striking with the drums, with every choked breath from Ella's mouth, and somehow her head nodded, her tooth biting her lip, her eyelashes fluttering. "Ach, Nattfarr of Clan Grisk," she whispered. "I will."

She could almost taste the replying surge of his desire, locking close and breathless between them—and when she felt the hard flare of his groin, pressing up against her through his tickling-soft furs, it was, somehow, enough. Enough to send Ella's fingers skittering down-wards, yanking at the tie on his waist, dropping the fur away, and showing—*that*.

It bobbed up before her, huge, swollen, already liberally dripping from the slit. And bound at the base with gold, so tightly that she could almost see him pulsing, could feel how urgently he wanted this, how he needed to split her apart—

So Ella held those eyes, and fought to ignore the ever-increasing silence behind them, the feel of curious watching eyes on her bare skin. While her shaky hands reached downwards, found that thick hardness—and then guided its slick, smooth head up against her, settling it deep against her exposed, humiliating, dripping-wet heat.

Natt gave a rough, rumbling growl at the touch, one hand sliding against Ella's hip, the other rising to gently tug at her nipple-ring. Earning a choked gasp from her mouth, a convulsive grip of her wetness around the hard, shuddering tip of him, jutting just slightly inside her.

But when Ella went to sink down, to take him deep—perhaps to hide this unthinkable sight from the watching eyes behind her—Natt only gave a sharp-toothed hiss, another gentle tug at her nipple-ring with his claw. Drawing her upper body closer against him, angling out her bare arse even more. Keeping her trapped in this shocking moment, with her clenching greedy wetness perched on the hungry head of him, the obscene sight clear to every eye behind—

"Kiss me," Natt ordered, soft, his tongue licking slow and delicious against his lips. "Taste my seed. Feel how I long to fill you."

They were the same words he'd spoken that very first night together—but this time Ella knew all his truths, knew she was safe. And that was *everything*, suddenly, and she felt herself nodding, holding those eyes—and then—she obeyed. Her exposed body eagerly, openly kissing her bonded mate's driving orc-prick, blatantly clenching and flaring against it, while an entire mountain watched.

And Natt longed for this, he was swelling and vibrating back against her, whispering his pleasure, his approval, his pride. And he was actually dripping, or perhaps that was her, the slippery wetness streaking down her bare thigh—and Ella cried out as Natt's hand snapped down to catch it, spreading it wide against her skin.

"Filthy lass," he breathed. "Already leaking your mate's strong seed."

But he liked it, he wanted more of it, and Ella arched her back, felt her body suckle and push against his driving hardness, drinking him up, spitting him out—and there was more, oozing out of her, slipping down the thick length of him this time. Actually bringing a sharp moan to his mouth, his teeth snapping, and Ella was desperate, craving, on fire—

"I need more," she gasped at him, and she didn't care who knew, who heard, who saw her frantically gripping, dripping wetness, kissing at her mate's ramrod cock. "Please, Natt. Give it to me. *Fuck* me."

The words came out too loud, too choked, filling the trembling silence around them—but Natt was still only gasping, gazing at her through his lashes, waiting, waiting. And through the slamming chaos, Ella recognized that look, knew it, held it close and safe for her own. He wanted her to speak truth, before all his kin.

"Please," she gasped, to those eyes. "Kiss me, Natt. Taste me. Fill me. Feel how wet I am for you. How easy it is for you."

He was, he could, his huge heat so slick and smooth and tapered, made to fill her, to seek its way inside. And he was doing it, sinking just slightly deeper, the head of him finally, slowly opening her up, oh gods—

"Feel me, Natt," Ella breathed. "Feel yourself inside me. Feel how I long to drink up your seed. Learn what it is"—her chest heaved, her eyes fluttering—"to fill your bonded mate, who has only ever tasted you, and who has kept her pledge to you, and given you her ring. Learn what it is to do this before all your kin, and to fill her with your seed, while they witness this truth."

It was working, gods in heaven it was working, Natt's body sinking deeper inside her, hot and close, while his gaze held hers with a fierce, glittering force. Tighter, deeper, harder, his body shuddering, his breath gasping, every muscle corded and clenched, he had to, he had to give this to her, please—

"Yes, Natt," Ella gasped, husky and breathless. "You will take me, you will pierce me, you will feed me and fill me and fuck me until I scream, you will flood me with your seed and give me your *son*—"

And that was it, fuck that was it, Ella's filthy words meeting his filthy driving kiss—and with one guttural, heart-stopping moan, he sank all the way home. Ella's groin pressed flat and flush against his, clenching against the hard whispering gold of his ring. Enforcing their vow, sealing it tight and powerful between them.

"Fuck," Ella groaned, arching and grinding against him, because damn he felt good, flaring like that inside her. Needing this just as much as she did, needing to kiss her drink her consume her alive, needing to give her his *son*—

His hips drove up, as hers drove down, and fuck, fuck, fuck, Ella was writhing, jolting, shouting. Being driven into again and again, bouncing and bobbing and clinging to him, the driving wailing truth that was her mate, her Natt, taking her giving her kissing her—and with a flick of his tongue he'd caught the curve of her neck, and the room went white and blinding as his sharp teeth bit down, tearing into her skin, her soul. Drinking her up, drinking her alive, kissing her and fucking her and worshipping her, gouging so deep that the entire world slammed still—

His explosion felt like it rocked the room, spraying inside Ella with so much force it sent pain screaming in its wake. Spurting out in wave after wave, filling her marking her drenching her, while her howling body sparked and drove and drank. Still fervently kissing his driving spraying cock, even as it kissed her back, firing her all through with the strength of his promise.

It was—joy. It was beauty, power, it was a pledge brought to life, it was a blessing. It was Ella of Clan Grisk, bared full upon her mate's cock and his teeth, drunk on his bounty, on the sweet, soft kiss of his lips to her neck. On the wild, powerful truth in his blinking, leaking eyes.

"Ach," Natt whispered, wiping an impatient palm against his wet cheek—and then he dragged Ella close, strong, safe into the heat of his arms. And Ella clutched him back, gripping with all the strength she could hold, burying her own dripping-wet face deep into his neck.

"Ach, my lass," he breathed, and suddenly he was rocking with her, his hands skating against her shoulders, her hair. "I have again drawn your blood. And your shame, I ken, or your anger, are you vexed, are you afraid—"

He'd yanked back from her, his clawed fingers now stroking against her face, tilting it up. Wiping frantically at her wet cheeks, as though to shove away her misery with the force of his hands, and Ella grasped for those hands, held them tight. And then smiled, slow and true, into her mate's eyes.

"It's good, Natt," she heard herself say, warm, earnest. "It's so good. You're so good. I am"—her breath came out, deep and shuddery—"so happy. So blessed, to have finally found my mate again."

Natt gave a twitchy nod, his eyes still almost painfully bright. "Akva has blessed us," he whispered. "She has received your offering, and your jewel, and blessed you."

Her jewel. The engagement-ring Ella had left in his wall. And when Natt had seen that, she couldn't fathom, at the moment—but his hands had come to Ella's bare belly, spreading wide. "Akva has blessed you," he said again, quieter this time, his gaze dropping to follow his hands. "You asked for my son, before all five clans."

Wait. Natt truly meant this, his eyes again streaking wetness down his cheeks, and Ella twitched as she looked at him, her breath lost, her thoughts suddenly, rapidly thudding. "I haven't even had my courses," she whispered. "You said—you said I shouldn't—there shouldn't be a seed yet—"

But Natt was blinking at her, his eyes still dripping, true. "There ought not," he whispered back. "I did not speak false to you. But now, as you gave me this great gift"—his eyes squeezed shut, opened again—"I could smell it blossom within you. Seeking to meet mine."

Oh. And Ella was currently flooded full of Natt's seed, and any softness that had previously come upon him had entirely vanished again, replaced only by the huge heft of him, filling her, blocking his seed's escape. Wanting this, wanting it so much he was still weeping with it, his eyes pleading, saying, *Don't reject it, don't reject me, please*—

But there was only love, warmth, affection, peace. And even a surprising, whispering eagerness, at what was next to come. And as Ella held Natt's eyes, she leaned in, and wiped at his wet cheeks, and kissed him. Kissed his mouth, gentle and sweet, as her still-impaled womb kissed his hard, twitching heft inside her.

His moan was deep, broken, lost, but he was kissing back, both inside and out, above and below. Already spluttering more seed up into her, Ella could feel it, so full she surely couldn't keep it all inside— but then that hardness seemed to swell even fuller, blocking it within her, while she reflexively clenched back, locked, trapped upon its strength.

Don't move, Natt's kisses silently whispered, *please, don't take this from me,* and Ella didn't, couldn't. Could only meet his kisses, meet his breaths, give him this, while he emptied himself out inside her, again and again, and the party raged around them, the drumbeat keeping steady time with her heart.

When Natt finally leaned back he looked dazed and almost dizzy, his eyes stunned and blinking, his big body sweaty and sticky. His hands still trembling against Ella's flat waist, spreading wide beneath the gold of her belt.

"Ach," he whispered to her eyes, with a shaky, quiet reverence. "We have made him, I ken."

Made him. *Him.* The word sent a deep, visceral shudder all down Ella's back—*him*—and then, for reasons she couldn't at all comprehend, she *laughed.* Laughed, her hands clutching at her mate's astonished face, while her shoulders shook, and the world unfurled with joy.

"We did?!" she gasped, grinning—and then she dragged Natt close, hugging him as tightly as she could, before drawing back again. "You"—she jabbed him in the chest—"are the most appalling, devious orc *imaginable,* Nattfarr of Clan Grisk. I told you about your shocking virility. I *told* you."

Natt was eyeing her warily, his head tilting, his lips twitching. "I do not ken you should laugh, lass," he said, quiet. "Carrying an orc's son is no small thing, for a woman."

Ella's hands seemed to move to her belly on their own, spreading wide and wondering, even as she kept smiling at him, perhaps even warmer than before. "Yes," she said, with a roll of her eyes. "I know that, Natt."

He replied with a low, not-quite-angry growl, and Ella again dragged him close, and kissed him. Feeling the heat spin and swarm as he kissed back, willingly, gently, his hand sliding into her hair, his tongue twining slow and tender against hers.

"We'll figure it out, Natt," Ella said, once he'd pulled back again, his eyes still intent on hers. "We'll fund your science, and your research.

We'll hire good physicians and midwives. I *am* the wealthiest heiress in the land, you know."

She gave him her best mock-haughty look, tossing her hair over her shoulder, and finally there was his smile, slow, sharp-toothed, tugging up the corner of his still-quivering mouth. "Ach, this is true," he said. "But in all my dreams of this, never did I dare to think you would *laugh*, after I have filled you with my son. You ought not to spur your mate thus, lass. You know not what I might do to you next."

Ella couldn't suppress the moan rising out her throat, and in reply Natt laughed too, deep and delicious and warm. But then he sobered as his eyes came back to hers, his clawed hands again spreading against her belly. "I have also made you miss this party," he said, and when Ella belatedly glanced around, she discovered that the party had indeed quieted significantly, and only held several dozen orcs, most of them caught in similar poses to her and Natt's, many of them sleeping.

"Oh," she said, and here was the odd, twirling realization that they must have been there for *hours* like that, and that she felt very stiff, and also—she yawned—very tired.

"Ah, well," she said lightly. "I certainly had a spectacular time. Did everyone else? Did you notice? Did Thrain get into the berry-juice again?"

Natt only blinked at her, incredulous, and gave a slow, disbelieving shake of his head. "I seed the first of my brood within you this night," he murmured, "and here you are pondering Thrain and berry-juice. Ach"—his head tilted, a sudden amusement flaring across his eyes— "you only wished to see if Varinn should take him again, did you not? Has seeing Dammarr get his due whet your hunger for such sights? My filthy, leering little lass."

He gave another grave shake of his head, all mock disapproval, and with a flail of shoving limbs Ella thrust him downwards, onto his back on the bench. But he easily sprawled upon it, dragging her close on top of him, even as his hardness stayed strong and hidden inside. And it was a glorious feeling, suddenly, Ella's tired body stretching out over his warm silken one, and she yawned again, and nuzzled her face into his neck.

"My filthy, devious orc," she murmured. "It's all your doing, you know. Without your shocking influence, I might have grown up to be a proper fine lady."

Natt's laugh was husky and unfeigned, shaking his chest beneath her. "You, a lady? This was always laughable, lass. If you had in truth wed this foul man, he should have pushed you to breaking, and you should have then eaten him in his sleep."

Ella laughed too, and wriggled herself more comfortably atop him. "And you should have come and watched, and cheered."

"Ach," he said, chuckling too. "Though I should have rather carved out his guts, or cut off his head. Had you granted me this, that first night, as I asked, I should not have needed to kidnap you at all."

"Oh, it's the *kidnapping* you'd regret, in that scenario?" Ella demanded, lifting her head to roll her eyes at him. "Devious, wicked orc. You *liked* that part."

"Ach, so did you," Natt shot back. "For all your fine protests, you did all that I asked. With that, and all else. You *wished* to escape this man, and this empty life as a lady, and return to me."

The words seemed to strike at something, settling deep, unfolding themselves as truth. A truth Ella hadn't quite considered, until this moment. Natt had smelled her. He'd *known*.

"I did want to escape that life, and return to you," she said, quiet. "Thank you for making it possible, Natt. Thank you for showing me another way. Thank you for coming back to me, and—*seeing* me."

Natt knew what she meant, as always, his head giving a solemn nod, his warm arms circling close around her back. Holding her naked, sticky body trapped against him, in a huge room studded with equally naked orcs, and in this moment it was contentment unlike anything Ella had ever tasted.

"I thank you for seeing me also," Natt said, his voice so soft. "Thank you for learning my truth, and speaking yours to me. Thank you for helping me to gain my place as Speaker, and then helping me to keep it. I needed this. More than you know."

But Ella did know him, too, and she nodded, quick and fervent, her eyes held to his. Watching them whisper of peace, hope, love. Of joy.

"Now sleep, my lass," Natt said, blinking those shining eyes, and they were back to warmth again, and a twitch of disapproval. "You have a whole orcling to grow. You know not how wearying this shall be, foolish woman."

Ella rolled her eyes again, but accordingly dropped her head back to his neck, giving it a sharp nip of protest. Revelling at the answering flare of his hard body still inside her, and—she twitched up to look— at how her previous bite hadn't quite healed, the little tooth-marks just barely visible in the fading firelight.

"Ach, you have marked me, lass," Natt murmured. "As you surely shall again, inside as well as out. Now sleep, my pretty, filthy beast. I shall keep you safe."

Safe. And with the sheer, sparkling comfort of that truth radiating bright through her soul, Ella finally closed her eyes, and slept.

EPILOGUE

Ella Riddell's housewarming party was supposed to be perfect. It *was* perfect, she told herself firmly, as she cast an assessing gaze over the crush of people currently filling Ashford Manor's ballroom. She had incorporated some ideas from the orcs on holding proper festivities, and had arranged for games and dancing and music, and multiple tables piled with astonishing amounts of food and drink. There were even a pair of orc drummers in one corner, Bjorr and Othan from Clan Ash-Kai, beating out a steady, cheerful rhythm.

"You're looking well, Little Miss," said a familiar voice, and Ella easily turned toward the interruption. It was their elderly neighbour Mr. Kemp, and he was eyeing her with clear curiosity, his gaze lingering on her freckled face, her mismatched earrings, the unmistakable swell of her belly under her clingy, stylish frock. "I was sorry to hear the news about Lord Tovey, but it was great luck that your lawyers found a way to keep you here at the old place, after all."

"Yes, they were very clever," Ella said, with a quick smile. "I'm so glad to be staying on here for good. Though Lord Tovey and I remain on cordial terms, the prospect of permanently leaving my home was just too difficult to contemplate."

Mr. Kemp nodded, fixing Ella with a knowing, keen-eyed look that had again, briefly, flicked down to her swollen waist. "Well, I'm sure you'll move on," he said pointedly. "Or perhaps you've done so already?"

Even the thought brought a flare of warmth to Ella's belly, and a flush to her cheeks. She had more than moved on—she and Natt had in fact been married at once, many weeks ago now, in a small, joyous ceremony beneath the trees, with a human priest officiating, and the exchange of new, matching, proper rings. A solid gold band for Natt that set smoothly against his father's ring, and a beautiful, gold-and-emerald ring for Ella, made clean and bright from the Grisk forge.

And afterwards, within the mountain, they'd performed a traditional Grisk ceremony, and exchanged far more intimate jewels. Ella sliding a new, even thicker gold band flush against Natt's groin, while he'd slipped a smooth, heavy gold ring up deep and hidden inside.

Ella was wearing that ring tonight—she could feel its weight there, a constant whispering teasing—and her hand dropped reflexively to her waist, again drawing Mr. Kemp's eye. "Yes, in fact, I have been seeing someone," she said belatedly. "Though I'm keeping it rather quiet for now, just until everything's settled."

It was all part of the master plan—a plan Ella and Natt had willingly embarked upon these past months, under Grimarr and Jule's clever guidance. Taking their time introducing Natt into Ella's old life, especially to avoid any unwanted questions about Alfred, or the inheritance, or the rumbling whispers of war—which had thankfully only remained whispers, so far. And in the meantime, their goal was to consistently use Ella's plentiful resources and considerable influence not to shock, or demand, or push—but to carefully, methodically support this peace, easing the orcs and humans together.

And tonight's party was another cautious step forward. Showing Ella's pregnancy to her neighbours and acquaintances, and introducing orcs to her home in a benign, non-threatening way. While also serving as a true housewarming, a celebration of the legalities all finally being finished, and the proper transfer of Ella's home to her and Natt's command, for good.

"And your mother?" Mr. Kemp asked Ella, with another sharp-eyed look. "Is she pleased with all these new developments?"

Ella didn't try to hide her wince, because her mother had quite possibly been the most difficult part of all this. There'd been no way to keep Natt secret from everyone, and Ella's mother had of course needed to be told, as well as her staff. And while her staff had kept it reasonably quiet so far—Ella had accompanied that staggering information with equally staggering wage increases—her mother had immediately launched into no fewer than three fits of hysterics, and multiple threats of exposure and ruination.

But Ella had managed to stay firm through it all, and had offered to grant her mother a generous allowance, and relocate her permanently to the new residence of her choice. An offer that her mother had finally, disdainfully accepted, choosing to move halfway across the continent to the realm's capital, in an arrangement that was far preferable to all.

"Yes, Mother seems quite content in Wolfen," Ella replied. "She's much happier in town, I think, hobnobbing with like-minded folks, enjoying fashion and parties. Rather than stuck out here with me next to Orc Mountain."

Mr. Kemp grimaced, darting a meaningful glance toward Bjorr and Othan in the corner. "Well, she does have a point about that damned mountain," he countered. "And I must say, it's an odd choice, on your part, bringing *them* to a party."

But Ella only smiled again, and gave an unladylike shrug of her shoulders. "I am committed to supporting this new peace between men and orcs," she said. "And Bjorr and Othan are excellent musicians, and very kind as well. Should you like me to introduce you?"

Mr. Kemp's eyes bugged alarmingly in their sockets, but his curiosity prevailed, and he finally gave a tentative nod. To which Ella promptly led him over to where Bjorr and Othan were currently taking a break, Othan already giving a sharp-toothed smile toward a pretty young woman, whose face was rapidly turning a deep, flustered red.

Ella quickly made the introductions, easing the three of them into a creditable conversation about the state of the hunting nearby—until she was rudely interrupted by the sudden arrival of Teppo, Tommi, and Trot. All rushing their furry, wriggling little bodies around her skirts, and joyously barking at once, bearing the unmistakable excitement of dogs with important news to share.

"You'll have to excuse me," Ella said to Mr. Kemp, as she scooped Tommi up into her arms. "I'll be back shortly."

With that, she followed Teppo and Trot across the bustling ballroom, toward the small side door. It led to the servants' back hallway, and Ella felt her heartbeat rising as she trailed the dogs down the quiet, dim corridor. Toward the side drawing-room, which currently had its sliding door closed—but the first two dogs had already scratched it open a crack, shoving their wriggly bodies in between, and Tommi leapt out of Ella's arms to chase after them.

Ella quietly followed, edging through the door, and sliding it almost shut behind her. The room was dark, settled deep in shadow, but the dogs had rushed straight across it. Toward where a large, muscular silhouette was leaning casually against the wall opposite, next to an open window. Natt.

The dogs were already barking and wriggling around him, demanding at once to be rewarded for their efforts, and Ella smiled as Natt complied and knelt, taking time to rub and scratch each of their heads before quietly ordering them back out the door. To which they reluctantly obeyed, squeezing their little bodies out past Ella again, while Natt slowly stood tall, and met her eyes.

It had been nearly two days apart, with all these damned party-preparations, and the scent of him was unfurling through the air, the sight of him weakening Ella's knees. And with a choked, hitching breath, she hurled herself across the room, and straight into his warm, waiting arms.

He grasped her close, swaying her back and forth, and his head was already nuzzling at her neck, his breath drawing in reverent and deep. "Ach," he murmured, with a heavy sigh, and a light nip of his sharp teeth against her skin. "It has been too long, my lass."

Ella desperately nodded, her hands finding his face, and dragging him down for a heated, hungry kiss. Soft, sweet, succulent, his long tongue tangling into hers, sending furious sparks of hunger scattering wide beneath her skin.

He was only wearing his kilt, and Ella's starving hands were already grasping at it, feeling his bulging hardness behind it—but Natt gave a husky laugh, and gripped for both her wrists. Raising them up over her head, and drawing her back so he could look at her, the assessing sweep of his eyes barely visible in the dark.

"Look at this," he murmured, his voice low, appreciative. "My fair, filthy lass plays a fine lady tonight. This is a new frock, ach? Made just to flaunt my son?"

One of his hands had come to her waist, spreading wide and quietly worshipful against it, and Ella gave a shaky little nod. Earning a flash of an approving smile, and then a slide of his hand upward, cupping at her already-fuller breast. "And made to hide my jewels also," he murmured, plucking at the ridge of the hard ring beneath the multiple layers of fabric. "Such an upright, pretty fine lady tonight, who play-acts as though she should never wear orc-rings in her teats."

Ella could only seem to nod, and arch deeper into the delicious heat of his touch, the warmth of his smooth voice. Into the truth of his other hand, coming up to curve against the other side, teasing against the new gold ring there. Which he'd placed under Efterar's watchful supervision this time, making sure there'd been no pain, and that Ella could still nurse their son without any difficulty.

"Ach, but I know better," Natt's thrilling voice continued, and in a quick, fluid movement, his hands snapped up to the low neckline of Ella's dress, slipping down inside—and before she'd quite caught what had happened, her breasts were spilling out over the top of the dress, looking full and peaked and obscene, their gold rings glinting in the dark.

"*Natt*," Ella whispered, with a scandalized glance toward the not-quite-closed door, but he only replied with a low growl, a warning tug at her nipple-ring. And as Ella watched, dry-mouthed, he reached up to trail a claw against the necklace she was wearing—a long, thin gold chain, looped about several times—and then he snatched it off, with the uncaring ease of one who'd given it to her. And then he carefully threaded it through first one nipple-ring, and then the second, stringing them together, and then stepping back to admire his handiwork.

"Mark this," he murmured, reaching an insolent hand to tug on one end of the dangling chain, sending hard jolts of pleasure into both breasts at once. "Such a pretty fine lady should never wear trussed-up teats with her fancy frock. Should she?"

Ella swallowed, shook her head, and Natt came a smooth step closer again, the mouthwatering smell of him whirling through the air. "And a fine lady," he breathed, as he grasped for a generous handful of her heavy skirts, "should never wish to have an orc up her skirts at such a fine party."

Ella had to bite back a moan, but shook her head again, and in return Natt flashed her another broad, sharp-toothed smile. "Speak, my pretty lady," he purred. "What should one such as you *never* take joy in, at a fine party such as this?"

His hand was already sliding up her thigh, purposeful and possessive, and Ella's eyelashes fluttered, her gaze still bound to his. "A lady like me," she gasped, breathless, "should *never* agree to be impaled upon an orc's long tongue, at a party like this."

Natt's grin was broad and wolfish, utterly spine-melting—and within a breath, he was on his knees before her, and shoving her skirts up toward her hands. Silently saying, *Hold these, I want you to see what I do to you*—and Ella eagerly yanked them up, and feasted her starving eyes on the sight. The sight of a rugged, vicious orc, kneeling before her, leaning in to press a soft, sweet kiss to her bared rounded belly, while his careful hands slid down between her legs, spreading her apart—

There was no warning, only the sudden, shocking thrust of his slick, massive tongue, sinking up deep inside. Dragging a sound much like a scream from Ella's mouth, and she belatedly clasped a hand over it, staring down at Natt's watching, glittering eyes. At the fierce kiss of his lips, the faint brush of his teeth, the curving writhing torture of his long tongue, already plunging and twisting and slurping inside her.

"Fuck," Ella choked, into her hand, as she fought to spread her legs further, take him deeper—and in a quick, effortless movement, Natt thrust her left leg up to rest on his shoulder, while his strong hands held her steady, trapped, opened wide. His tongue and his kisses already pressing harder, stronger, his hot slick mouth fully open against her now, consuming her whole, lurid and lascivious—and Ella choked back another cry as she felt his tongue catch on something. Her secret gold ring, hidden deep inside.

Natt moaned against her, his eyes briefly closing, the room suddenly seized, hung still all around. With an orc kneeling in supplication before her, his lethal, sharp-toothed mouth opened wide and gentle over all her most secret places, his tongue caught on his gold, on his promise.

And as Ella gulped for air, she could feel that clever tongue clasping at his gold, sliding it onto its length. Drawing it down and away, and then out of her entirely, leaving her pulsing wetness open, empty, bereft—but instead here was the sight of him, her wicked mate with his wicked tongue ringed in her gold, licking his lips with dazzling, deadly intent.

He rose to his feet without warning, swiftly dropping Ella's leg back to the floor, his strong hands finding her face, claws spread wide. And then that beautiful, slick tongue delved between her lips, opening her mouth for him, slipping that gold ring deep inside.

It tasted of her, he tasted of her, and his crackling eyes on hers spoke, without speaking at all. *It pleases me to find my gold inside you*, they whispered. *It pleases me to know that you are always mine, even when you play-act as a fine lady.*

He drew away from her, leaving only the ring behind, and Ella slid it onto her own tongue, and brushed it against her parted lips. Saying in return, *Yes, Natt. Yours. Always.*

His throat convulsed, his eyes fluttering, his hand spreading on her cheek. "My fine, lovely lady," he murmured, so smooth, so delicious. "Who first has her fat teats trussed, and then begs for an orc's tongue up her womb. And who now"—the danger caught, flared in his eyes— "shall beg for an orc's prick, to fuck her tight little ass."

Ella nearly choked on her ring, her face flushing, and for an instant she was held still, gaping at him, while that image—and those words—rang through her thoughts. Natt's filthy vocabulary had only expanded these past months, as he'd plumbed the depths of her truth for the most shameful words she knew, but he couldn't truly mean— she was wearing a new *dress*, she had to go back to a *party*—

But Natt had brought a single claw to the chain connecting her bared nipples, giving a brazen, purposeful tug upon it. "A fine, proper lady," he breathed, ordered, "who shall beg an orc for a hard, rough ass-fucking, at her fine fancy party, whilst she holds her orc's womb-ring in her mouth. Ach?"

The hunger was rising, pounding, shoving away all Ella's protests

at once, and she gave a red-faced nod, and dragged up her courage—
and then obediently turned away from him, bending slightly, putting
her hands flat to the wall behind her. "Yes, my lord," she whispered,
around the ring still in her mouth. "I wish you to—"

Natt was already yanking up her skirts again, revealing her bare
arse, drawing her hips toward him. Spreading her apart for him,
exposing everything with an easy, efficient familiarity, and Ella was
quivering, trembling, the words stuttering, caught—

There was a light, purposeful slap at her arse, a warning squeeze of
a clawed hand on her skin. And then the feel, thrilling and terrifying,
of a single sharp finger tracing down her parted crease, slow, gentle,
deadly.

"A fine lady," Natt purred, "who wishes for what, lass. *Truth*."

Oh gods, but Ella frantically nodded, drew up truth. She wasn't a
lady. She was pretending. And in truth she was Ella, of Clan Grisk, and
always had been. And she wished for this, so desperate it was
consuming her alive—

"Please, my lord," she gasped, thrusting her bare arse back, into the
touch of his claw. "Please. Take me."

Natt's heated, answering growl was truth itself, and so was the
sudden, jolting feel of that hard, slick, tapered cockhead, pressing just
there. Kissing her there, with sweet, lurid approval, while Ella kissed
back, helpless, wriggling, shameless. Knowing what he wanted,
without him even saying it. Her voice. Her truth.

"Please," she choked. "Please, my lord. My husband. My Speaker.
Fuck me, with your huge, gorgeous orc-prick."

But Natt only held her there, trapped and writhing on just the tip
of him, silently demanding yet more, while his mouth let out a sound
that was half-laugh, half-groan. And too late it occurred to Ella what
she must look like, fully done up, dressed in her costly new frock, but
bent over double in her side drawing-room, with her bare arse jutting
out, kissing at an orc's bare cock, seeking to take him deeper.

But in this moment, in this truth, there was no shame. Only
arching back more, bringing down her own shaky hand to pluck at her
exposed nipple-ring, and then to curve over the swell of her waist,
feeling the heat of Natt's approving eyes following her every movement. Truth. She could speak truth.

"Please, my lord," she breathed, her voice husky, hungry, sweet. "Please, take me. Fuck me. Fill your lady's tight little ass with your huge orc-prick, and your hot dripping orc-seed, at this fine, fancy party."

There was another instant's stillness, a catch of Natt's breath in the dark—and then, in one powerful, heart-stopping stroke, he sank inside. Filling her with him, pain and pleasure crashing keen and bright—and then staying there, holding her tight, taut, trapped on the huge, invading heft of him. Rewarding her, for her truth. *I liked that*, it said. *More.*

"Fuck, oh gods, *fuck*," Ella was already babbling, her entire body squirming and sparking, her hands scraping at the wall. "Fuck, Natt, oh gods, please—"

He knew, he always knew, drawing out slow, smooth, almost tender, until they were just kissing again, tasting, teasing—and then driving back inside, all the way, so hard Ella staggered against the wall, her cheek pressing flat against it. "Please," she choked, "please, please—"

But he was already doing it, easing out, giving her one more sweet, filthy, sensual kiss. A whisper, a caress, a promise of his patient gentleness toward her, always—and then it was blown apart, shot and ravaged, as he pounded into her, again and again and again. Their bodies slapping together, his hands dragging painfully on her hips, his heated invasion firing harder and brighter with every thrust, with every silent shouted word, *mine mine mine MINE*—

He flared out with a raw, guttural groan, his body wildly pulsing, flooding Ella full with his slick, succulent heat, while she shivered and writhed and moaned, drinking him up. Still craving him, longing for more, even now—and he knew, of course he knew, the flat of his hand coming around easily, almost casually, to rub at her front once, twice. And then she was truly screaming, still impaled on a massive orc-prick while the pleasure ran rampant under her skin, and Natt's other huge clawed hand had snapped up to clamp hard against her mouth, muffling the sound within it.

"Foolish lass," he whispered, shaky, but his other hand circled around her waist, drawing her close against his warmth. And in a shifting blur of movement, he dragged them both back onto the nearest couch, him sitting with Ella sprawled on top, still impaled deep into his lap.

Ella's shock was still circling, still not quite settled yet, but Natt was everywhere, behind her and inside her, his strong arms slung tight around her. "Ach, this was good," he whispered, his mouth kissing soft into her neck, his breath inhaling deep. "I have not harmed you, lass, have I?"

He was smelling her, Ella knew, searching for it, but he would find nothing, because she was all liquid lazy languor, full of contentment and lingering pleasure. "*Gods*, no," she breathed, wriggling herself closer into his solid safe warmth. "I've been dreaming of you showing up and doing that all damned *day*, Nattfarr."

He gave a low, appreciative chuckle, and his hand came back to her mouth, his finger delving between her lips. Finding the ring—she'd somehow kept it there, that whole time—and drawing it out. And then he brought that hand down, against her slick wetness, and slid the ring back up where it belonged, deep inside.

"This pleased me," he murmured. "That you wore this, tonight."

"I knew it would," Ella whispered back, with another contented little wriggle against him. "And you liked the dress, too?"

He gave an approving, careful glide of his hands against the delicate fabric, drawing it up to bare the fullness of her rounded belly. "Ach, I did," he said. "If you must wear these foolish lady-clothes, they ought to yet give me leave to have you, whenever I wish. And"—those hands spread wider, protective, claws gently slipping against skin— "they ought to show my son thus, also."

Ella nodded, and moved her own hands to cover his, feeling the warm strength of his fingers, the quiet reverence hidden beneath. "Have you thought of a name yet?"

She'd tasked him with that when last they'd parted, and she could feel the odd tension in him now, just the same as she'd felt then. But she only waited, curling her hands tighter on his, while he breathed in the scent of her neck, let it out.

"I thought," he said, a little stilted, "mayhap—if it did not displease you—that I should like to name him after my father. Rakfarr. Mayhap Rakfi, when he is small."

Rakfi. Ella felt it settle, warm and whispering, like a pledge all its own—and she nodded, her hands squeezing on Natt's still-tense fingers. "Rakfi, of Clan Grisk," she said firmly. "It's perfect, Natt. I love it."

Natt gave a choked laugh behind her, his tension seeming to snake away all at once. "You are sure of this?" he asked, low. "Mayhap you should rather name him after your father, instead?"

But Ella shook her head, still squeezing her fingers tight on his. "One orc named John in the mountain is quite enough for all of us, I think," she said. "I'm happy to honour my father in other ways. Did you see my shrine?"

She'd built it just this week, in the little back room of the hunting-cottage, where her father had often slept. She'd cleaned it out by hand, scrubbing until every surface was spotless, and then she'd furnished it with furs and candles. And upon a table, she'd set one of her father's portraits, alongside a small, distinctive carved statue with a swollen belly, and knowing eyes.

"Ach, I did," Natt said, his voice soft. "With your father, and Akva. This suits you, my lass. I hope you shall teach Rakfi of this, also."

Rakfi. As though he were already real, here under their hands, and Ella snuggled back into the truth of that, into him. Her Natt, her mate, her husband, her best friend. The father of her son. Rakfi.

"I don't want to go back to the party," Ella murmured. "But I probably should. Shouldn't I?"

"Ach, no," came Natt's decisive reply, and with it, a telltale clamp of his teeth to the gold ring in her ear. "As much as I should like to see you try to preen about this party with your sore dripping arse. I have come"—another light nip at her ear—"to kidnap you from this. There is no escaping my thrall, my pretty lass."

Ella's answering shiver was heated, already breathless, and Natt carefully lifted her off him, standing her on shaky feet. And then he pulled down her skirts, and tugged up the top of her dress over her bared breasts, hiding them—and the chain—inside.

"I mean to take much more joy with my trussed-up lady tonight," he said as he stood, giving a purposeful pat at her now-clothed breasts. "But first, we must needs give you a bath. You are filthy, yet *again*."

His grin was wry, teasing, thoroughly delicious, and Ella tried for a glare, even as she leaned up to kiss his scarred cheek. "And you are the most provoking creature *alive*, Nattfarr of Clan Grisk, Speaker of Five Clans," she replied. "I'll meet you in the usual spot?"

He nodded, giving one last purposeful, proprietary pat at her breast—and in an instant, he'd gone for the nearby open window, and gracefully leapt out of it. While Ella propelled her still-shaky feet out toward the front door, where she traded her slippers for her hardy leather boots, and informed her butler, Hani, that she was taking a lengthy constitutional, and would he please fetch her sturdy wool coat, and manage the party from here?

He would, of course—Ella had in fact tripled Hani's salary, particularly for these kinds of moments—and then she finally stepped outside. Dragging in deep breaths of the cool night air as she strode away from the busy drive, across the lawn, over the grounds, and into the edge of the dark, dense forest.

And there was Natt, leaning tall and silent against a tree. Waiting for her, as he'd so often done all those years ago, a monster lurking in the moonlight.

And just like then, Ella walked straight up to him, and held out a hand. And without a word he took it, grasping tight—and together, they turned to the darkness, and ran.

BONUS EPILOGUE

Installing lamps in Orc Mountain had sounded so simple, when Ella Riddell had first heard of it. An easy, negligible task that could quickly be managed, especially if one threw enough of one's money toward it, and shoved off the work onto someone else.

How wrong she had been.

It was more than two years later, and here she was. *Still.* Sitting at a table surrounded by tiny parts, and desperately fighting the urge to hurl the lamp in her hands toward the nearest wall.

"Gods-damned tiny fucking pieces," she groaned, as she squinted toward what felt like the hundredth lamp today, and again sought to carefully place the burner deep inside. "This is *your* fault, John. Couldn't you Ka-esh have designed something bigger?"

"No, we could not," replied John's cool, maddening voice, from where he was sitting at the table across from her. "We shall not permanently install cheap, shoddy work into our home. You were the one who wished for these, and paid for these. You even volunteered to use your tiny hands to assemble these for us. Or have you forgotten all this?"

Ella groaned again, but of course she hadn't forgotten, the cold merciless bastard. And she finally managed to place the burner where it belonged, before sliding the carefully cut glass into the intricate iron frame surrounding it, and then placing the peaked iron cap on top. "There," she snapped. "Ready to be sealed. Are you happy now? Lamp four hundred and twelve, done."

"And nine hundred and eighty-eight remaining," replied John's infuriating voice, to which Ella shot him a baleful glare—but then, thank the gods, an interruption burst into the room, in the form of a small, running, messy-haired orcling.

It was Rakfi.

"Ma-ma!" he crowed, with visible delight, as he hurled his little body across the room. Leaving Ella scarcely enough time to leap up from the table, away from all the tiny parts that were sure to be scattered everywhere, and open her arms wide, so Rakfi could charge straight into them.

Ella was already laughing, whisking his wee grey body up into her arms, and hugging him close. "You little hellion," she informed him, pulling back to grin at his bright black eyes. "Aren't you supposed to be off in the Ash-Kai wing, *behaving*?"

"Ma-ma," he said again, with satisfaction, as he promptly lifted up Ella's cape, nuzzled his face against her breast, squeezed his eyes shut, and began enthusiastically nursing. Leaving Ella to shake her head at him, and smile, and curl his little body up so she could rock him in her arms. Caught in the quiet, precious magic of him, still so strangely, deeply powerful it sometimes made her want to weep.

"There he is!" came another voice from the door, this one sounding decidedly exasperated, and Ella looked up to find Jule's heavily pregnant form, running into the room. "Dear gods, how can he move so fast on such tiny legs?!"

She was breathing hard, and glowering fiercely down toward where Rakfi was currently still the picture of pure innocence, nursing sweetly at Ella's breast—and Ella laughed, and gave a rueful shake of her head. "Oh, I know," she said wryly. "Thank you for trying, Jule. I finished twenty lamps! Did they get along all right?"

She was eyeing the little orc who'd come into the room with Jule, his small clawed hand clasped tightly into hers. It was Tengil, Jule and Grimarr's son, and though he was only six months older than Rakfi, sometimes it seemed like there were years between them. Tengil was already large for his two years, showing every sign of growing into a massive orc, and while he often laughed and smiled, he was at heart a quiet, watchful, well-behaved orcling, who slept on a schedule, and did as he was told. The utter opposite of Rakfi, who never seemed to sleep or stop moving, and did his utmost to provoke Tengil's infrequent but explosive temper.

"They mostly got along," Jule said, glancing down at where Tengil had tugged on her trousers, and then awkwardly bending to catch him up into her arms. "Well, until they started fighting with those little wooden scimitars, and Tengil tried to cut Rakfi's throat. Why Grimarr thought those were a good idea, I can't imagine. I really ought to hide them away for a while."

She gave Ella an apologetic smile, but Ella easily waved it away—such things were a constant hazard, raising orcs—and then she watched with amusement as Tengil frowned up at his mother, his little face very grave. "I need this sword, Mama," he said, the words slow and careful. "For my enemy."

He turned to frown mightily toward Rakfi, who was still innocently nursing at Ella's breast—and both Ella and Jule burst out laughing, Jule giving an affectionate rub at Tengil's little black braid. "Yes, my love, I know," she said. "But even if he is your enemy, he is still your brother, and you can't run about trying to cut his head off. Ask your father, there are cleverer ways to deal with one's enemies."

Tengil seemed to carefully consider that, and gave a thoughtful nod. "I shall ask Papa," he said. "Now, Mama?"

Jule laughed again, but nodded, and waved goodbye as she took off out the door. To which Rakfi immediately popped up again, ceasing his innocent act in favour of squirming wildly in Ella's arms. "*My* Papa," he said firmly. "Ma-ma, *my* Pa-pa!"

His eyes had stayed fixed on Ella's as he spoke, and Ella could feel the tiny snap of compulsion in his gaze, tugging at her truth. A skill that Rakfi had seemed to develop and apply almost instinctively, using it liberally to obtain his obstinate, devious little ends. And while Ella could still resist it—for now—it was far easier to just hold his adorable black eyes, and speak truth.

"Papa *was* here," she said, "trying to help with these lamps, but he couldn't stand it any longer, and went off to spar with his brothers. Can you smell? Papa?"

Rakfi accordingly gave a series of careful little sniffs at the air, and then squirmed to the floor, and dashed for the door. Leaving Ella to call a farewell to a bemused-looking John, and chase off after Rakfi down the corridor.

The lamps were thankfully installed here, lending a cozy glow to the surrounding stone, and Ella ran after Rakfi's scampering body down the length of the corridor, and then around one corner, and another. Very nearly colliding straight into Olarr and Aulis—Olarr had had Aulis' gasping form pressed flat to the wall, but they were both following one of the mountain's newer rules, and thus remained clothed below the waist in the corridor—and Ella called out a laughing apology as she chased Rakfi up into the Grisk wing.

"Pa-pa!" Rakfi shouted delightedly over his shoulder toward Ella, as he made a hard pivot, and dashed into Natt's quarters. Into the training-room, where Natt's flailing, muscled body was currently being pinned to the floor, with Dammarr's heaving, long-haired form kneeling close over him.

"Finally got you, you squirmy bastard," Dammarr was gasping—but then his head snapped around, because Rakfi had given a fierce, high-pitched growl. And before Ella could stop him, Rakfi charged forward into the room, rushing past a blinking, amused-looking Thrak to launch his little form onto Dammarr's shoulders, punching at his back with his tiny fists.

"*Bad* Dammarr," he said. "Bad! Pa-pa!"

Dammarr's body had briefly stilled over Natt—but then he laughed, and reached up to carefully detach Rakfi from his shoulders, holding out his frantically swinging form at arm's length. "Even your son knows I have bested you this time, brother," he said smugly. "And I've bested you too, you wee beast."

He gave a sharp-toothed smile at Rakfi, his grip visibly loosening on his wriggling form—to which Rakfi took full advantage, and crawled straight up Dammarr's muscled arm, and swung his tiny fist at his face. Making Dammarr blink, the grin twitching on his mouth—and then he made a show of rolling his eyes back in his head, and then collapsing down onto the floor beneath, splaying his limbs out wide.

"Ach, I have been felled after all!" he said to Rakfi, with a mock sigh of defeat. "You have protected your father with all strength, little brother."

Rakfi only crowed his delight, scampering up onto Dammarr's chest, to pat a tiny clawed hand at his face—and then he ran back down his prone body, to hurl himself at Natt.

Natt swiftly sat up to catch him, and grinned broadly as he yanked Rakfi's squirming body into his bare chest. "You are indeed brave, my son," he said, with a kiss to Rakfi's forehead. "Ach, this pleases me."

He was squeezing him close, and Rakfi's small body relaxed against him, his arms clinging around Natt's neck. "Pa-pa," he said, with a happy little sigh. "Pa-pa."

Natt pulled him even tighter, his eyes closing, his head ducking into Rakfi's neck, inhaling deep. Filling his lungs with the scent of his son, before finally raising his eyes, and settling them warm on Ella. And giving a jerk of his head that said, *come*, and Ella eagerly obeyed, dropping herself down against his heated, sweaty form.

"He escaped Jule, again," she said, muffled, into Natt's delicious-smelling neck, into the set of familiar tooth-marks upon it. "And almost succeeded in provoking Tengil to *kill* him. Our offspring is a *menace*, Nattfarr."

Natt gave a wry, knowing chuckle into her hair, even as he hauled her up closer, holding Rakfi's pliant body with one arm, and hers with the other. "Ach," he said, through his deep inhale, his chest filling with her scent. "I ken I was also, when I was small. I am sorry, lass."

He did sound sorry, for an instant, and when Ella glanced up he looked it, too. Thinking, maybe, of how they hadn't been alone at nights for months, whether here or at the house, what with Rakfi's little form sprawled all over them. And how their regular attempts at compensating for that, throughout the day, were interrupted with almost comedic regularity.

And how—Natt's hand had slid lower around Ella's waist, spreading wide against the very slight swell in her belly—she was so often exhausted and sickly these days, and had felt particularly ill this morning. And she'd begun to have nightmares about giving birth again, because despite all her resources and careful planning, Rakfi's sudden, violent entry into the world had proven to be the most excruciating, terrifying thing she'd ever done.

But Natt had been there through all of it, fierce and unwavering, her best friend, speaking truth again and again. *You honour me. You please me. Tell me what you wish for. Tell me what should help you. I wish to bring you joy. I love you.*

And he was saying it now, silently kissing her hair, rocking her slightly against him. A movement which snapped Rakfi's head up, his dark eyes sparkling, his little body suddenly wriggling with excitement. "Play," he said firmly. "Play, Pa-pa?"

Ella could feel Natt's hesitation, the slight clench of his hand against her—but she flashed him a rueful grin, and nudged him away. And though he went, he still looked regretful, his mouth lingering on her hair, his breath inhaling deep.

But Rakfi was already climbing up his chest, and swinging a tiny fist at Natt's face with impressive ferocity. Natt narrowly avoided it, but he grinned, quick and genuine, his dark eyes brimming with affection as he grasped Rakfi's little form, and pinned him to the furs beneath with a strong clawed hand.

Rakfi squirmed and squealed, finally escaping once Natt eased the pressure, and then launched himself again at Natt's face. An action that quickly devolved into their usual combination of wrestling and tackling and tickling and biting and hugging all at once, full of mock growls from Natt, and exuberant shrieks and giggles from Rakfi.

It was pure joy to watch them together, Ella's mate and her son taking such delight in each other, and beside her Dammarr had leaned back on his haunches to watch too, a small smile playing on his mouth. "He's getting better, ach?" he said, with a brief glance up toward Thrak, who was still standing behind them. "That was a good straight punch, little brother."

Rakfi paused to beam beatifically at Dammarr before launching himself at Natt again, making both Ella and Dammarr laugh—but behind them Thrak had clucked at Rakfi in black-tongue, something about watching his elbows, and not forgetting his claws. And since Thrak was perhaps Rakfi's favourite person, beyond Natt and Ella, Rakfi actually seemed to listen, snapping out his little claws as he launched toward Natt again.

Thrak gave a grunt of approval and stepped closer to watch, sliding a casual hand into Dammarr's hair. To which Dammarr leaned back, his eyelashes fluttering, and Ella didn't miss his brief, lingering glance toward Thrak's groin, on a level with his eyes.

"Want to go, after this?" he asked Thrak, voice low, and in return Thrak gave a wicked smile, and slid his hand down to curve around Dammarr's neck. Murmuring a soft reply in black-tongue, something filthy about kisses and holes, earning a heated, unmistakable gasp from Dammarr's throat.

But they were abruptly interrupted by Rakfi, who had apparently decided to include Dammarr in their play-fighting again, and thus threw his wildly swinging little body toward Dammarr's crouching form. And in the process—Ella hissed through her teeth—he'd scraped her bare arm with his claws, leaving four deep cuts in her skin, already pooling bright with blood.

"Ach," Natt snapped, with sudden hard disapproval, as he grasped for Rakfi's form, and placed him aside, away. And then he was here, grimacing as he caught Ella's arm, surveying the damage—and then he swiftly lowered his mouth to it, cleaning the blood away. His long tongue sweet and careful on Ella's skin, his eyes furrowed and apologetic. *I am sorry, lass,* they said. *Is it pain.*

Ella gave a twitchy shake of her head—it was really just a scratch, and she knew by now that orc saliva had some impressive healing powers—and Natt nodded, and gave it one more soft kiss, and then pulled away. And then turned his gaze toward Rakfi, who had gone unusually still and silent, his eyes fixed on Ella's arm.

"Rakfi," Natt said to him, his voice grave. "You know you must be careful with your mother, and with all humans. You must be gentle, and in control. They do not heal as we do, and they feel pain very strongly. You could cause great harm, if you are careless."

Rakfi's eyes were stubborn, perhaps even rebellious, still fixed to Ella's arm. "Then Ma-ma go," he said, pointing his little claw toward the room's exit. "Safe."

Ella flinched, her heart oddly plummeting—but Natt gave a deep, guttural growl, his hand coming to clasp hers. "No," he hissed back. "Mama belongs here, with me. With us. Women and humans belong here. We must never push them away, even if this seems to help them. We must be the ones to learn, and make them safe among us."

Rakfi was still pouting, obviously not appeased by this, and Natt growled again, deeper this time. "If you cannot keep humans safe, my son," he said firmly, "then you shall never be Speaker of Five Clans, after me. You must earn this place, with truth and justice and kindness. You must seek to make right your wrongs, without anger or blame. And"—his eyes angled, brief, toward Ella—"you must know the great gifts our women grant to us. You must learn that we could not be, without them. *You* could not be, without your mother. Without her kindness to me."

The room had gone oddly silent, Ella's heartbeat still jangling uneasily in her chest, but Rakfi finally gave a subdued nod, and slowly trotted over toward Ella, his dark head bowed. And then he lifted her arm with his tiny hands—without claws—and then carefully began licking at it, with his little black tongue.

"I sorry, Ma-ma," he said, once he'd pulled back, his eyes brimming with wetness. "I love, Ma-ma."

Ella couldn't speak, suddenly, through the choke in her throat, but she grasped for Rakfi's trembly little body, and held him tight and close. "Thank you, Rakfi," she managed, into his tiny pointed ear. "I love you too. So much."

The room was still uncommonly silent, the only sound the quiet sniffles from Ella's nose, and abruptly Natt was here, lifting Rakfi off Ella, and giving his dark head a brief kiss before unceremoniously handing him off to Dammarr. "I must tend to my mate," he said, perhaps to Rakfi, or Dammarr, or both. "I wish for some time. Please."

The word made Ella blink—Natt was still so rarely polite, especially to his brothers—but perhaps it had the desired effect, because Dammarr only nodded, and rose to his feet. "Come, little brother," he said. "Thrak and I wish to play a game with you. Hide and seek, mayhap? Who hides first? My swift, strong mate?"

His eyes had angled meaningfully toward Thrak, whose ear-tips had gone a slight, telling shade of pink. "Ach, I shall go first," he said. "You shall never catch me, little brother."

With that, they were off, Rakfi already squealing with glee as he chased Thrak out the door. Leaving Natt and Ella finally alone, with no lamps or brothers or children between them, for the first time in days—and Natt gave a heavy, shuddery sigh as he dragged Ella close into his strong arms.

"Ach, my sweet lass," he breathed. "You are vexed. First these cruel dreams, and then this sickness that has come upon you, and how oft we have been kept apart these past weeks. And now these endless lamps of mine, and my careless son."

But Ella shook her head, even as she gave another unwilling sniff. "It's fine," she said. "It's good. It is, Natt, and I mean that. I just—"

And she didn't even know, couldn't even explain it, but thank the gods, like always, Natt understood. And he gathered Ella close, and drew her face into his hands, and bent his head, and kissed her.

It was warmth and peace and craving, surging smooth and exquisite under Ella's prickling skin. Twirling bright flares of heat with every soft, reverent sweep of Natt's tongue, tasting her, knowing her, from the inside out.

And suddenly this was all Ella needed, everything she needed, and her body seemed to sink into him, slipping over to straddle him, seeking her place. His clever hand already thrusting away both their kilts, baring them to the room, and Ella shuddered and moaned as Natt's thick hungry hardness found her open dripping heat, and slowly sank its way deep and powerful inside.

It was easy, beautiful, right, and Natt kissed Ella again and again as she they locked and flared together. As she ground close against him, and his body rocked back up against hers, rolling fluid and smooth. Filling her with his tongue and his cock and his warmth, with all his silent truths, etched deep upon her soul. *I love you, my fair mate. You please me. You honour me.*

The pleasure rose like water, filling all the cracked hidden places, and Ella arched over him, drinking up his truth, his kiss. His strength and light and kindness, holding her safe upon him, while their bodies meshed and spoke and caught, rising rising rising—

Ella's release crashed with dizzying force, blaring white behind her eyes, and then hurling even higher as Natt's body answered her call, and flashed out its own joy within her. Swelling and spraying deep within, flooding her with the truth of him, while he moaned broken and guttural and powerful into her mouth, her very heart.

But Natt didn't draw away, after. Just kept kissing her, soft and almost unbearably sweet, while his hardness inside her did the same. Twitching and caressing, gently brushing against the womb he'd once again filled, speaking of his joy and pride and reverence. Two whole sons, for Ella's own bonded mate. And while Efterar and the midwives and the Ka-esh had all said this would likely need to be the last of their sons, if Ella wanted to survive it, Natt had sworn it was perfect, and Ella knew it was truth.

"Ach," Natt said, soft, when he finally pulled away, and rested his forehead against hers. His hands were still on her face, still brushing away the inexplicable streaks of wetness there, and he was shuddering too, his breath inhaling thick and heavy against her skin. "This is better, my lass."

He meant her smell, Ella knew, and she nodded against him, her arms circling tighter around his neck. "Much better," she murmured. "I missed you."

"Ach, and I missed you," he breathed back, leaning in for another soft, succulent kiss. "I cannot tell you how you taunt me, striding around my mountain in my clothes and jewels, smelling thus. Looking thus. Tasting thus. Bearing my *sons*. You shall break me, I ken."

He kissed her again, so gentle and lovely and right, and then pulled back again, with a wry chuckle. "Or mayhap you have broken me already. How long since you have had a good strong fucking, lass? I ken you shall think I have forgotten how to make you scream."

Ella gave a choked laugh, a shake of her head. Not having to say that she'd needed it like this lately, these moments of stolen quiet sweetness, of finding each other again in the chaos. Because Natt knew, of course, and that's why he'd kept doing it this way, with only warmth and reverence and kindness.

But Ella did miss the wickedness too, suddenly, and she felt her mouth twitching up, her fingers curling into his black braid. "Oh, I know how devious you are, Nattfarr," she murmured. "You're just waiting for me to let my guard down, and then you'll pounce with something so appalling, I'll never recover from the shock."

The grin was tugging up his mouth too, slow and dangerous. "Ach," he said. "Have you been thinking of this these long weeks, my pretty, hungry beast? Waiting for a new lesson from your orc?"

Ella gave a shameless, eager nod, flaring more warmth in his eyes—and with a swift, head-swarming flail of movement, she was on her back, with her knees thrust up, and Natt looming close and deadly between her legs. His eyes flashing with hunger, his claws spread wide on her bare thighs, his long black tongue brazenly licking at his lips.

He was here. He was hers. Her best friend, her lover and mate, the father of her sons. Delicious and rugged and hideous and beautiful and terrifying. All that an heiress could ever wish, kneeling close and deadly between her spread legs.

"Ach, you shall scream, my lass," he whispered to her eyes, a tease, a promise, a pledge. "Watch, and learn."

~

THE END

~

THANKS FOR READING
AND GET A FREE BONUS STORY!

Thank you SO much for joining me for Ella and Natt's tale!

If you're not quite ready to leave Orc Mountain yet, join my mailing list at www.finleyfenn.com for some fun extra content, including some awesome artwork from *The Heiress and the Orc*, and a free Orc Sworn story. I'd love to stay in touch with you!

FREE STORY: OFFERED BY THE ORC

The monster needs a sacrifice. And she's naked on the altar...

When Stella wanders the forest alone one fateful night, she only seeks peace, relief, escape. A few stolen moments on a secret, ancient altar, at one with the moon above.

Until she's accosted by a hulking, hideous, bloodthirsty *orc*. An orc who demands a sacrifice—not by his sword, but by Stella's complete surrender. To his claws, his sharp teeth, his huge muscled body. His every humiliating, thrilling command...

But Stella would never offer herself up to be used and sacrificed by a monster—would she? Even if her surrender just might grant her the moon's favour—and open her heart to a whole new fate?

www.finleyfenn.com

ACKNOWLEDGMENTS

My deepest thanks to my readers, and my wonderfully generous beta readers and advance reviewers. I'm especially grateful for the support, insight, and encouragement of Jesse, Jennifer N., Marcia de Souza, and my spirit guide Amy, who always makes everything better. Special thanks also to Ann for all the wisdom and laughs (and your great patience!).

I'm also SO grateful to my lovely Facebook group members at Finley Fenn Readers' Den (come join us, they're awesome!), and to my many fellow authors who have been so kind, warm, and encouraging. I had no idea such an incredible community existed, and I'm so honoured to be part of it.

I also need to thank (and highly recommend!) Toni Weschler's life-changing book *Taking Charge of Your Fertility*, for giving Natt and Ella a week of worry-free fun (well, at least until the orc magic inevitably kicked in). ;)

Finally, my utmost gratitude and devotion to my own brilliant mate, without whom none of my writing would be possible. I love you, my filthy lad.

ABOUT THE AUTHOR

Finley Fenn is "the queen of dark orc romance" (Virgo Reader), and her ongoing Orc Sworn series has been praised as "sexy, romantic, angsty, and captivating ... utter brilliance" (Romantically Inclined Reviews).

When she's not obsessing over her stories, Finley loves reading, drooling over delicious orc artwork, and spending time with her incredible readers on Patreon, Discord, and Facebook. She lives in Canada with her beloved family, including her very own grumpy, gorgeous orc husband.

For free bonus stories and epilogues, special offers, and exclusive Orc Sworn artwork, sign up at www.finleyfenn.com.